WHAT DOES
LOVE
SOUND LIKE?

ALSO BY PADGETT GERLER

Getting the Important Things Right

Lessons I Learned from Nick Nack

The Gifts of Pelican Isle

WHAT DOES

LOVE

SOUND LIKE?

For my dear friend, Alice. With love, Muffin

PADGETT GERLER

DISCLAIMER

DEDICATED TO

Equality

ACKNOWLEDGMENTS

Thank you, Amanda Nordin, for showing me the sheer joy of creativity. Your commitment to your art has awed me, inspired me, and encouraged me to dig deep to find my passion.

I am so grateful to my beta reader, Janine Nicholson. Thank you for your enthusiasm and honesty. You have helped me make *What Does Love Sound Like?* the best it can be.

Thank you to my family for loving me, encouraging me, and for giving me five-star reviews.

Thank you, Ed, for starting me on this journey and for walking with me every step of the way.

WHAT DOES
LOVE
SOUND LIKE?

Family isn't what you're given.
Family is what you make.

--Polly Ann Bondurant

TYBEE ISLAND

Prologue

"Charlie, wake up! You're going to be late."

Jinx had stopped caring if Charlie got up.

Each morning, though, she said, "Charlie, wake up! You're going to be late," out of habit.

Not only didn't Jinx care if Charlie got out of bed, it really didn't matter if Charlie went to his office at all. How much money did they need? Charlie was the senior partner at Robinette and Robinette, the law firm founded by Jinx's great-grandfather, Archibald Robinette, Sr. and, in time, partnered by Jinx and Charlie's fathers, Arch Robinette III and Vernon Collier. Charlie had made more money from the firm than he and Jinx could spend in several lifetimes. He had a client list that included practically every resident of Savannah, Tybee Island, and neighboring communities, many of whom were on retainer. What's more, his partner, Horace, and their three associates could easily run the office in his absence.

So when Charlie didn't budge, Jinx got out of bed and headed for the shower, leaving her husband to fend for himself. She had built such a wall of resentment between the two of them that she could hardly carry on a civil conversation with him anymore. She was so angry with him for shunning Knox, damned his convictions. But more than being mad at Charlie, she was furious with herself for failing to stand up to her husband in defense of their only child.

Even worse, she hadn't gotten in touch with their son since Charlie's ultimatum. Now she felt it was too late. Knox would be angry with her for siding with his father and for her refusal to support him. He would hate her for her weakness. She was so ashamed of herself. But she was still Charlie's wife; and as a good southern wife, she had been programmed to stand by her husband and keep the peace, regardless of the cost.

And as a good southern wife, she did her resenting in silence.

So when Jinx finished showering and found Charlie still in bed, she sniffed in disgust and headed downstairs to start the coffee. If she couldn't rouse Charlie, she figured the smell of coffee would.

She used her mom's old electric percolator, not one of those new-fangled, one-cup-at-a-time Keurigs. She filled the pot with water and pulled out the bag of coffee she had just ground the afternoon before at the Piggy Wiggly. She untwisted the top and clamped the open bag around her nose, inhaling. She loved the smell of freshly ground coffee, and she buried her face in each new bag, unwilling to let that aroma go to waste. She measured the coffee into the strainer, plugged in the pot, and sat at the kitchen table to wait.

As the coffee brewed, she thrummed her fingers on the table and played the what-if game. What if I'd stood up to Charlie? What if our friends had given me some support? What if Knox hadn't moved to New York? It was a game she played with herself often that threw her into a never-ending, painful loop. It only deepened her resentment and despair.

When the coffee finished perking and the fragrance wafted through the house, Charlie still didn't appear. Jinx gritted her teeth, poured herself a mug, and carried it to the porch just off the kitchen.

She eased herself into her Adirondack chair, careful not to slosh, and, with her free hand, shielded her eyes against the already-scorching early morning sun. She looked out past the crashing waves at the commercial fishing boats headed for the horizon and their day's catch. The beach was deserted, the way she liked it, except for the ever-present screeching gulls and a few pelicans fishing for breakfast just off shore.

Jinx loved this old place. It was the site of everything and everyone she held dear, all the memories she cherished. It was the only home she'd ever known, save for the small Savannah fixer-upper she and Charlie had bought when they first married. Her daddy, Archibald, had bought this place right on front beach at Tybee Island shortly before Jinx was born, and her mama, Emma Frances, had brought her baby girl home to the small pink and white nursery perched high in the eaves, overlooking the dunes.

Arch had taught his daughter to surf fish right out in front of this house, and her mama had held Jinx's hands as she'd shown her little girl how to jump waves so they wouldn't swallow her up, tumble her end over end, and spit her out onto the sand. On Sunday afternoons the family would churn peach ice cream in the crank freezer out on this very porch overlooking the Atlantic; and on those warm, semi-tropical nights, her mama would teach her to sew on her grandmother Mimi's old Singer treadle sewing machine, as the sea breeze lifted the white, organdy curtains at the living room windows and made them wave and ripple like flags.

And Jinx recalled those wonderful week-long house parties her mama helped her host each summer while she and her friends were students at Savannah High. Caroline would be the first to arrive at the Robinettes' wonderful, weathered home facing the Atlantic where she and Jinx would work feverishly to prepare for the arrival of the rest of the girls: Constance, Beth Ellen, twins Maitland and Taylor, Sarah June, Tweezle, Blue, and Harper Ann. They'd make beds and lay pallets for the overflow on the weathered-to-a-fine-patina pine floor, bake Toll House cookies, and stock the big, rusting fridge beneath the house with Coca-Colas. They'd buy a copy of every teen magazine at the Rexall drug store and several new bottles of Revlon nail polish for group pedicures. They'd dust off the Ouija board and drag out all the inner tubes and pump them up with the old bicycle pump and then hose off all the dust and cobwebs that had collected on them in the shed over the winter. By day the girls would bake in the sun on the beach and giggle about boys; by night they'd tend their sunburns with Noxzema and giggle about boys.

And it was on that wonderful, creaky porch under a full moon that the fifteen-year-olds, Charlie and Jinx, first professed their love for each other.

But all that had changed. Every bit of it. Jinx felt that everything was gone, including her friends. They had shown whose friends they were when they'd all sided with Charlie and left her to suffer her guilt and remorse alone.

And then there was Charlie, the only man she had ever loved, the man she'd once adored with her whole heart and now didn't care if he even got out of bed.

And Knox. Knox was her only child. And she had lost him.

The hot tears had just filled Jinx's eyes and spilled over her cheeks when Polly Ann came trudging up the back stairs and lowered herself with a thud into the other Adirondack chair. Letting out a groan, she pulled a large man's handkerchief out of her bosom and mopped her dark dewy face.

"Whooee, gonna be a scawcher out there t'day."

When Jinx didn't respond, Polly Ann glanced in her direction and noticed the tears streaming down her cheeks.

"What's the matter, Sugah Pie?"

Polly Ann had called Jinx Sugah Pie since the day she was born. The beloved family maid had been in the waiting room, wringing her hands in her apron and praying audibly to Jesus for an easy birth, when Emma Frances brought the Robinettes' precious only child into the world. The young mother had been unable to nurse her baby, so Polly Ann had swooped in, gathered her Sugah Pie in her loving, ample arms, becoming Jinx's mammy and wet nurse. The two had had a special bond ever since.

When Jinx's silent tears became a torrent and she began to sob, Polly Ann reached over, took her Sugah Pie's hand, and pulled her into her sturdy lap, just as she had done when Jinx was a child and needed comforting.

Jinx buried her face is Polly Ann's neck and, through muffled sobs, cried, "Oh, Polly Ann, I'm a terrible mother."

"Now, I won't be hearin' such a thing. You stop that nonsense right this minute!" Polly Ann snapped.

"But, Polly Ann, I've let Charlie and our friends make me believe that they're right, and I hate them all for it. Just hate them! I'm Knox's mother, for heaven's sake. I knew better. But I didn't have the strength to fight them all, and it was easier to keep my mouth shut and keep the peace. Now it's too late."

"No, Sugah Pie, it's never too late for nothin'. Now, my heart has broke for you and Knox. And, yes, it has broke something awful for me, 'cause I miss my precious boy more than life itself. But it weren't my place to speak my mind. But now that you done opened that can 'o beans, I'm gonna say it right out. You dry them tears, and you give that man of yours what for. You are going to call your son and tell him that you love him and that you sure sorry for hurting him that way. What Mr. Charlie does is his business, but it ain't right he tell you what to do."

Jinx sniffed and wiped her tears on the sleeve of her pink terry cloth robe.

She wrapped her arms around Polly Ann's neck, kissed her cheek, and said, "I love you, Polly Ann."

Polly Ann swatted Jinx's thigh and said, "I know that. But one more thing, Sugah Pie. I agree that them so-called friends of yours are holier-than-thou, stuck-up you-know-whats, but you ought not be saying you hate. You better than that."

"Okay, Polly Ann, I promise I won't say that anymore."

But she didn't say she wouldn't think it.

Giving Jinx one more swat, Polly Ann told her, "Now, you get a move on and go tell that Mr. Charlie what's what."

Jinx stood up from Polly Ann's lap and walked over to the porch rail. She stared out to sea and found that the fishing boats had disappeared for the day and the pelicans were nowhere in sight. Breakfast was over. She stood for a long while, taking in the beauty, feeling the rhythm of the crashing waves. She didn't know if she were stalling for time or gathering strength from her surroundings to steel herself for what she knew she had to do. It wasn't until she heard Polly Ann clear her throat with a loud "Ahem," that Jinx returned her attention to her confrontation with Charlie. She felt as if she were wearing lead boots as she crossed the porch and looked back at Polly Ann.

"No, ma'am. This is one thing your Polly Ann can't do for you. Now, I know it ain't pleasant, but this just has to be. Now, you go on and get it done. I'll be right here praying to the Lord to guide your tongue. You'll be fine, 'cause he'll be looking over you. Now, go."

With that, Jinx opened the creaky screen door to the kitchen and, once inside, let it slam shut behind her, knowing this time Polly Ann wouldn't bellow, "How many times do I have to tell you not to slam that door? You know it gives me a headache!"

She trudged down the hall and up the stairs to confront Charlie. She hadn't heard the shower, so she assumed that he was still languishing in bed.

And he was.

"Charlie, wake up. I have to talk to you," Jinx said through gritted teeth.

Charlie didn't budge.

"Charlie, I mean it. I don't care if you go to work or not, but I want you to wake up so I can talk with you. It's very important."

Still Charlie didn't move.

Jinx propped one knee on the bed, leaned over, and nudged her husband—hard.

"Stop it, Charlie! I know you don't want to talk about it anymore, but I'm going to talk, whether you like it or not."

One more swift nudge and Jinx knew.

When Polly Ann heard the ear-splitting scream, she sprang from her chair, ignoring her arthritic hip. Forgetting her own no-slam rule, she threw open the screen door on the run and didn't care if it slammed off its hinges.

She took the stairs three at a time, reaching the bedroom just in time to hear Jinx bellow, "Damn you, Charlie! How dare you die without telling Knox that you love him?"

One

Virginia Claire Robinette, better known as Jinx, had known Charlie Collier forever. Their fathers, Archibald Robinette, III and Virgil Collier, had been childhood friends, had played football together at Savannah High, and had shared a room as undergrads at the University of Georgia. After college graduation, they rented an apartment in Atlanta, where they had both been accepted to Emory University's School of Law. Upon earning their law degrees and passing the bar, the two returned to Savannah, married their high school sweethearts, and joined Robinette and Robinette, the law firm established by Arch's grandfather. Arch, Sr. was long deceased and Arch, Jr. was anxious to hand the reins to his son and Virgil so he could commence with his life of fly fishing and yachting. So the young lawyers stepped into a law partnership that was firmly established, with a client list that included every Who's Who in Savannah and Tybee.

Jinx and Charlie were born just two months apart and would be the only children of the Robinettes and the Colliers. Because of their circumstances, they couldn't have been closer had they been brother and sister. When they were babies, their mothers, Emma Frances and Molly, would rock them on Arch and Emma Frances's porch overlooking the ocean on Tybee Island. When the children nodded off, the mothers would bed them down side-by-side in the big rope hammock, where the sea breeze would sway them through their afternoon naps. As toddlers, Jinx and Charlie tumbled in the sand in front of the Robinettes' home and squealed with glee as they held hands and padded in the tidal pools at the edge of the sea, built sand castles, and dug with their pudgy toes for fiddler crabs.

As they grew, they found delight in tearing through the halls of their daddies' staid, prestigious law offices, annoying the secretaries and the other attorneys with their antics. But the employees at Robinette and Robinette knew better than to complain about their senior partners' kids. Arch and Virgil's children were their daddies' joys and could do no wrong.

Charlie and Jinx especially loved playing in their daddies' big conference room with the long cherry table and the big leather chairs that spun round and round. They'd take turns twirling each other until dizziness took over; then the twirlee would hop down to wobble and stagger all over the room. Then both would collapse onto the soft, carpeted floor and giggle until they were breathless. They also loved making a fort beneath the huge conference table, Charlie telling Jinx ghost stories and Jinx telling Charlie princess love stories.

It was while they were playing in Arch and Virgil's conference room that they'd held hands and, for the first time, said, "I'll pick you up, you'll pick me up, and we'll go up together."

After several dozen attempts before discovering that they could not levitate by picking each other up at the same time, Jinx had cried, "Oh, Charlie, it isn't working."

Charlie put his arm around six-year-old Jinx's shoulders and said, "Don't cry, Jinxie." Charlie was the only person Jinx allowed to call her Jinxie. "Please don't cry. I will pick you up."

And that's all Jinxie needed to hear. They might not levitate, but she knew that she could always depend on her Charlie to pick her up.

Jinx raked her sleeve across her eyes, drying her tears. She wrapped her arms around Charlie's neck and said, "I'll pick you up, too, Charlie."

"I know that, Jinxie," Charlie said before grabbing her hand and galloping around and around the massive conference table.

Over the years *I'll pick you up, you'll pick me up, and we'll go up together* came to mean so many things to Charlie and Jinx. It meant I'll protect you; I've got your back; we'll always be best friends; you can count on me; I love you; we're family, even if we can't take flight.

Jinx Robinette had always loved Charlie, but she couldn't put her finger on the exact moment she had realized she was in love with Charlie Collier. But as soon as she could comprehend the meaning of love and marriage and family, she just knew. She was confident that she would one day be Mrs. Charlie Collier. And, unlike her friends who dreamed of the perfect wedding and the perfect gown and the perfect reception, Jinx dreamed of planning the perfect life with Charlie. She didn't care about the dress, the bridesmaids, the bridal luncheons and showers, the tea cakes, the formal room at the yacht club. She wanted the home, the family, the future.

And although everyone viewed Charlie and Jinx as siblings, as much as he pretended, Charlie didn't see Jinxie as his sister. For as long as Charlie could remember, he had been in love with her—as much as a child could be in love. He thought she was the most beautiful creature imaginable and was mesmerized by her ice blue eyes, her dark auburn hair, her infectious laugh. So smitten was he that he would do anything just to be around her. He'd play dress-up with her and thought nothing of lying on her bedroom floor reading movie magazines, if doing so would please his darling Jinxie.

When Jinx would accompany her and Charlie's mothers to the tea room at Needham's Department Store for tea and watercress sandwiches and fashion shows, Jinx would beg Charlie to go along. Though he would much rather have been kicking a ball, washing his daddy's car, or even mowing the lawn, he'd give in to Jinxie, put on a shirt and tie, and be the only male at the Needham Department Store fashion show. By the time Charlie was eleven years old, he knew far more about manners and women's fashion than he cared to admit. But he did it all for his Jinxie.

As they grew, they opened their circle of two to welcome others. There were the house parties at the Robinette home on Tybee Island, which culminated in Saturday night parties with the Savannah High boys, the object of the girls' giggling. Jinx's mom and dad would open their home for hot dogs on the grill, dancing on the wide porch overlooking the Atlantic, and some moonlight beach strolling.

"It's just not fair," Blue had whined one Saturday night as they primped in preparation for the boys' arrival. "None of us even had a fair chance with Charlie. You laid claim to him when y'all were babies."

"Guess you're right, Blue," Jinx had said, laughing at her friend's honesty and giving her a consolation hug.

Everyone knew that Charlie was the catch of Savannah. Tall, a little over six-three, he was stunningly handsome with his shock of strawberry blond hair, dazzling green eyes, and a dimple in his chin. Taking after his father, he was a natural athlete who excelled on the football field. But Charlie was also a natural in the classroom, ranking number one academically in his class and holding the office of student council president. It was no wonder all the girls would have given anything to be Charlie's girl, but, like Blue, they knew that Jinx had his heart. Yet it wasn't as though Jinx had hatched some devious plot to trap Charlie. It was simple: Jinx had always loved Charlie; Charlie had always loved Jinx. Case closed.

It was a given that Charlie would follow his father and Arch to the University of Georgia. Offered both academic and athletic scholarships, Charlie looked no further. And just like Virgil and Arch, Charlie hoped to study at Emory School of Law and return home to practice at Robinette and Robinette.

Jinx, on the other hand, though smart and a reasonably good student, was bored to tears with traditional school. Her interests leaned toward the arts, in particular, interior design. Neat little school desks all in a row and institutional green walls punished her senses, and quadratic equations and frog dissections gave her a headache and made her skin crawl. As her geometry teacher lectured, Jinx used her ruler, compass, and protractor to sketch rooms and draw small furniture to scale. When her history teacher lectured on Europe, Jinx daydreamed about the décor of castles, country estates, and cathedrals. And she'd have much preferred designing a hat for a frog to cutting it open and examining its innards.

She couldn't remember a time when she hadn't wanted to decorate something. When she showed creative promise, her daddy set up accounts at the local hardware store and the fabric shop so that Jinx could have access to all the supplies she'd need for her decorating. He bought her her very own electric Singer sewing machine for her ninth birthday, graduating from her grandmother's old treadle machine; and she taught herself how to make café curtains and bedspreads for her and her parents' bedrooms. Over time she upholstered furniture, wallpapered walls, and stenciled borders. When she'd decorate her room, she'd make matching outfits for her dolls. By the time Jinx was a teenager, she had a trunk full of fabrics, had redecorated her bedroom a half-dozen times, and was working her way through her girlfriends' bedrooms.

When it came time for college, Jinx applied only to Marywoods, a small, private Georgia girls' school specializing in home economics and interior design. Despite her lack of interest in anything academic, her extensive portfolio wowed the admissions committee, and the school eagerly accepted her into their design program. Jinx shone at Marywoods, even though she still drew rooms in math class and dreamed of castles in history class. Despite her dismissive attitude toward her actual schoolwork, her professors and the administration overlooked her boredom and cultivated her extraordinary eye for design.

For four years Charlie and Jinx alternated weekend visits. Jinx would drive the two hours to football games and fraternity parties at the University, and Charlie would drive the two hours to sorority dances and teas at Marywoods. The set-up wasn't ideal. The young couple was apart for the first time in their lives, and the absence was painful for both of them.

"Oh, Charlie, my heart hurts," Jinx would cry into the phone.

"I know, Jinxie. I need you here to pick me up."

But they knew the separation was temporary. They simply had to endure as they prepared for their future together.

When they graduated, Jinx returned home, laden with letters of praise and recommendation from her design professors. Within a week she was employed by Solange Lebeau, premier interior designer to Savannah and Tybee aristocracy. Solange's given name was Sadie Ledbetter; but after a stint at a fancy New York design school, Savannah society overlooked the name change, embraced Solange's credentials, and welcomed her into their homes. Jinx was in a glee and the envy of all her friends who struggled to land jobs but, in actuality, only wanted to land husbands. And it was a major coup for Solange Lebeau, as well. Not only was Jinx the most talented designer she had seen south of New York City, her family was also part of Savannah-Tybee society. Jinx knew everybody who was anybody. Jinx's hiring was a win-win for all concerned.

Charlie was admitted into Emory Law School, the alma mater of his and Jinx's daddies. The young couple loathed the continued separation, but they both knew that law school wouldn't last forever and that they would soon be together. What's more, Solange graciously gave Jinx many of her Atlanta clients, so that Jinx and Charlie could spend their coveted times between clients and classes in each other's company.

By the time Charlie graduated from law school, sat for and passed the bar exam, and returned home to join his and Jinx's daddies at Robinette and Robinette, Jinx's design services were in bigger demand than her mentor, Solange.

To no one's surprise, his first Christmas back in Savannah Charlie slipped his great grandmother's emerald-cut diamond engagement ring onto Jinx's finger and made it official. Still not interested in the trappings of a wedding, Jinx knew she'd never get away with eloping, going to the Justice of the Peace, or standing on her family's porch at Tybee, pledging her undying love for Charlie before a small group of family and friends. No, Jinx was aware that her family was expecting a lavish affair at the Episcopal Church, followed by the customary reception at the Savannah Yacht Club. And if her parents weren't reason enough for a blow-out, Solange reminded her that her clients were expecting the biggest and the best from their designer. Anything less would be an utter disappointment and would just never fly in Savannah-Tybee society.

So Jinx threw herself into the challenge and didn't disappoint.

Not surprisingly, Jinx designed her nine attendants' dresses. Though she'd have loved decking them out in miniskirts, Constance and Harper Ann's thighs begged for a little length. Ignoring the glitz-and-glamour fashion trends of the early '80's—Jinx knew they were tacky even then—she chose a yellow raw silk for the dresses. Fashioned with simple lines and scooped necks, the skirts belled just above the knee, her compromise to miniskirts. The girls would wear dyed-to-match ballet flats, in lieu of high-heeled, strappy shoes that most brides favored. Jinx also despised the currently fashionable big hair with bangs that she called hair claws, so she asked all of her attendants to wear their hair in sleek, neat ponytails, anchored with simple pearl clasps.

Her only hold-out was Blue.

"You know I could never wear a ponytail," she whined. "My right ear sticks out."

"Blue, do you really think your right ear is going to be the star of my wedding?" Jinx said through gritted teeth and a glued-on smile.

"Well, I just don't like ponytails," she huffed.

"Blue, I did not complain when you asked all of your bridesmaids to wear those powder-blue Cinderella dresses with the puffed sleeves and sequins. And I didn't hear Roderick's groomsmen belly-aching about the baby-blue tuxes and ruffled shirts."

Blue took her colorful name to heart.

"And, believe me, there was a lot to complain about," added Jinx.

But no one had ever told Blue no. She'd always gotten her way, had everything handed to her on a silver platter.

She and Roderick had dropped out of college after two years because, as Roderick said, "What do I need that for? My daddy's gonna leave me his Ford dealership anyhow. Don't need no degree for that."

Nothing trumps ambition like the promise of an inheritance.

Blue and Roderick had set up housekeeping down by the river in a charming cottage their adoring grands had bought for them, and the two of them commenced to spending Daddy's money and making babies. And life continued to go Blue's way, everyone telling her, "Yes, yes, yes."

But Jinx was about to be the first person to tell her friend that she couldn't have her way all the time—at least not at Jinx's wedding.

So Jinx said, "Blue, I don't give a flip about this wedding and would be going across the border to a justice of the peace, if it were left up to me."

Blue gasped and cried, "Oh, Jinx, you shut your mouth right this minute. Miss Emma Frances would faint dead away. You know very well you would never do such a tacky thing."

"Oh, yes I would, Blue. But, apparently, my means of gettin' hitched isn't up to me. So if you don't want to wear a ponytail, then don't."

"Oh, Jinx, I just knew you'd understand. You're just so accommodating."

"Yes, Blue, if you don't want to wear a ponytail, please feel free to sit in the congregation with your mama and your daddy and your young'uns."

"But, Jinx…"

"Zip it, Blue. If I have to do this, and apparently I do, I'm going to do it my way. My attendants are going to wear ponytails."

And Blue scowled and huffed, trying to decide if she'd rather expose her ear or be excluded from the festivities.

Jinx ignored her theatrics.

The bride's gown, also her own design, was fashioned of snow-white silk overlaid with delicate French lace. It had capped sleeves, a high neck, and a silhouette that made a very gradual, graceful A-line from waist to floor. Jinx wore her shiny, auburn hair soft and flowing to her shoulders. Her only adornment was her grandmother Mimi's diamond drop earrings, earrings that both her mother and grandmother had worn on their wedding days.

The society page of the Savannah Times called the bride a vision of taste and understatement and the wedding the must-be-seen-at event of the season, even outshining the debutante ball over in Atlanta. Every bride-to-be wanted a wedding just like Jinx Robinette's. Sequin and glitter sales plummeted, and there was a run on tasteful ponytail clips and faux diamond drop earrings, as well as chaste, high-neck bridal gowns. And to this day ballet flats are a favorite for all occasions, from casual to formal. Many in the fashion world say we have Jinx Robinette to thank for that.

Jinx laughed at the accolades and thought to herself, *All you have to do to have the society wedding of the century is not want a wedding at all.*

As Jinx had promised, Blue's prominent right ear was barely noticeable—though her third pregnancy was beginning to strain the seams on her oh-so-fashionable yellow raw silk, bell-skirted attendant's dress.

The tented reception at the yacht club featured a sit-down dinner of fresh-from-the-coast seafood, as well as the most tender and succulent prime rib, shipped fresh the day of the wedding from Texoma, in the Red River Valley. All evening the well-known-in-local-circles string quartet with the provocative name, Strung Out, accompanied popular jazz singer, Viola Starr, as guests dined, danced, and mingled. Jinx and Charlie wandered from table to table, greeting guests as they accepted hugs and well wishes.

"It was just a matter of time. You two were meant to be together."

"Charlie, your bride is the most beautiful Savannah has ever seen—since her mama, of course."

"Jinx, your gown is gorgeous, and I love your attendants' simple dresses. Perfection!"

Jinx and Charlie smiled till their cheeks ached, answering, "Yes, Miss Parrott, I agree."

"Thank you so much, Miz Mingo. We're so glad you could come. I hope Mr. Mingo's gout soon feels better."

"Well, thank you, Miz Joyner. It's right nice to see you again. Hope you enjoyed your 'round-the-world trip."

As they were chatting with Armistead and Annie Lily Prelioux, two of Savannah's most colorful and eccentric residents, and their equally eccentric daughter, Ravanel, Jinx felt a tap on her shoulder.

"May I have this dance?"

Jinx looked up into her daddy's eyes, eyes that were brimming with tears.

"I'd love to, Daddy."

As Arch twirled his little girl around the dance floor—he'd always been so light on his feet—he said, "I love you, Princess, and I couldn't be happier for you. Or for me. You know I love Charlie like a son."

"I know, Daddy."

"I've already had a man-to-man with him. I know he'll cherish you, Jinx. I expect you to do the same."

"Yes, Daddy, I will."

And with that he led his daughter to her new husband, who was gliding Miss Emma Frances around the dance floor.

"Let's trade," said Arch, taking Jinx's mother in his arms and whisking her away.

As soon as he put his arm around his new bride, Charlie asked, "When can we cut the cake? I'm ready to get you alone."

Charlie hadn't wanted the wedding any more than Jinx had.

Jinx grinned and blushed. "Looks like everyone is almost through eating. Let's do it."

"Yeah, let's do it," Charlie said, raising his eyebrow, making Jinx blush deeper.

Charlie had been waiting a long time—all his life. He was ready to say goodbye to the wedding and get on with the honeymoon. As he watched his bride's cheeks pink, he held her close and kissed her temple before taking her hand and leading her toward the six-tiered cake adorned with yellow, sugared daffodils.

Two

Cyrus Cummings, one of Arch and Virgil's most affluent clients, had offered his mountain cabin in Dawsonville as Jinx and Charlie's honeymoon retreat. They couldn't have been more delighted; neither had been to the mountains since Arch had taken them there when they were just four years old. All they could remember of the trip was that Arch had let them swim in a mountain stream and that the water had been so frigid it made their skin ache and turn blue. But they relished the idea of an out-of-the-way, secluded place where they could consummate their twenty-five-year relationship without the intrusion of Blue and Tweezle. To be on the safe side, they hadn't told a soul where they were going. And they weren't worried about the cold water because they had no intention of swimming.

After feeding each other cake, kissing their parents good-bye, and thanking their guests for joining them on their special day, they streaked for their car and headed to Jinx's house to change into their shorts. No prissy going-away outfits for these two. They had performed their social duties, complete with frills; now they were headed to the mountains. It was after eight o'clock by the time the newlyweds made it out of town, and they had nearly five hours of travel ahead of them.

They were giggling like school children and so excited over what lay ahead when, about an hour outside Savannah, Charlie asked, "You hungry?"

"Heck, yeah! I haven't had a thing to eat since a piece of toast with apple butter for breakfast. I'm starving."

"Me too. My stomach's growling. What do you want to eat?"

"Oh, not much. My tummy is all fluttery, like butterflies. How about some Nabs and a Co-Cola?"

"Sounds perfect. We'll stop at the next filling station we see."

Pulling off and hopping out of their car at a little country store with a single gas pump, they crunched arm-in-arm across the gravel parking lot to the entrance. The screen door screeched as they opened it, and they stepped in onto moaning, creaky floorboards. In search of snacks, they passed a display of Pemican Beef Jerky, large jars of purple pickled eggs, and row on row of chewing tobacco. Right past the comic books they located the peanut-butter Nabs and the big red Coca-Cola cooler.

At the check-out counter, Charlie said to the overweight, wheezing man in overalls, "And add ten dollars worth of regular to that, please."

"Y'all from around here?" he asked, snapping open a small paper bag with a flourish and dropping in their Nabs.

"No, sir, we're from Savannah."

"What brings you out here of a Sar'dy night?"

Smiling at Jinx, Charlie said, "We just got married. Headed for our honeymoon up in Dawsonville.

Grinning broadly, exposing a gap where a front tooth should have been, the clerk bellowed, "Well, congratulations!" And pushing Charlie's money back across the counter, he added, "Treats on me. And top off 'at tank real good, you hear?"

"Oh no, sir, I couldn't accept."

"Sure you can, Son. I couldn't make it to the weddin', so this is my gift to you."

Gathering their gifts, Charlie reached across the counter to shake the generous man's hand and said, "Thank you so much, Sir. I believe this is the most thoughtful wedding gift we got."

"Well, y'all drive safe now, you hear? And have a good life."

Back on the highway, Jinx opened Charlie's Nabs and put them on the console where he could reach them easily. She popped the top on his Coke can, and he nestled it between his legs, leaving his hands free to drive.

"That was mighty nice, wasn't it?" Charlie said, his eyes trained on the dark, winding road.

"Sure was. You just never know when you're going to run across a thoughtful person. I bet we'll never forget him. He'll be part of our wedding story that we'll tell our kids, even our grandkids, don't you think?"

Charlie smiled and reached across the console for his bride's hand.

"Too bad we couldn't bring Daddy's old vintage Ford with the bench seat," Charlie said. "That way you could scoot over real close, and I could put my arm around your shoulder. It'd make the trip lots nicer. Mind you, I appreciate your daddy giving us this Mustang as a wedding gift, but there are just some times I think a bench seat suits better. This is one of those times."

Jinx unhooked her seatbelt and leaned over, kissing Charlie on the cheek. Smiling and settling back in her seat and re-buckling herself in, she reached over and stroked the back of his neck and twiddled his hair with her fingers.

"I love you so much, Jinxie."

"I love you, too, Charlie," she said, leaning back against the seat and yawning.

"Tired?"

"Yeah, it's been a long day."

Turning on the radio, Charlie found a station playing soft ballads.

"Why don't you close your eyes and rest? I'll wake you when we get there."

Jinx woke when she felt the car grind through gravel, come to a halt, and the engine die.

"We made it," Charlie said softly, leaning over and kissing Jinx's cheek.

She stretched and smiled.

"Stay right where you are," Charlie said and jumped out of the car. He ran around to Jinx's side, opened the door, and reached in. Unhooking her seatbelt, he lifted her from the car, and she wrapped her arms around his neck.

"I love you with all my heart, Jinxie," Charlie whispered and leaned in to kiss his wife. As he covered her mouth with his, he tasted her tongue, salty with Nabs and soft from sleep. They both shuddered with anticipation.

Charlie carried Jinx up the three stairs to the porch of the cabin. At the door he said, "Hold on tight," as he propped her on his knee and reached into his pocket for the key. Opening the door, he lifted her across the threshold of their first—if only temporary—home.

Cyrus had made sure that the logs were laid for a fire to ward off the mountain chill and that the fridge was stocked with food and drinks. All they had to do was make themselves at home.

Still holding Jinx in his arms, he said, "Let's find the bedroom. We can explore all this later."

"I agree," Jinx said, resting her head on Charlie's shoulder.

In the bedroom, the couple found their bed turned down, chocolates resting on their pillows, champagne chilling on the dresser.

"Cyrus must have commissioned some elves," Charlie said.

"It was sweet of him to do this for us," Jinx said, though they really weren't thinking about Cyrus.

Charlie laid Jinx on the bed and eased himself down beside her. Resting on his elbow, he cupped her cheek in his hand and kissed her gently, trembling with excitement.

Jinx whispered, "Mama bought me a peignoir for my wedding night."

Charlie smiled and said, "That was nice of Miss Emma Frances. I really want to see it, Jinxie, honest I do. But not right now. Maybe tomorrow," he said, kissing her lightly and reaching for the buttons on her blouse.

His hands shook as he gently unbuttoned Jinx's blouse and pushed it aside, exposing a lacy, white bra against her soft, golden skin. Fingering the front clasp, he popped it open, as if he'd been practicing forever. He had been practicing in his head forever. His breath came out in a ragged gasp when he saw Jinx's breasts. As teenagers they'd necked in the dunes at Tybee and weren't strangers to petting—but only fully clothed. They were tempted, of course, but they'd decided from the beginning that they wanted to save themselves for marriage. Now that the time had come, they were glad they had waited. It had been worth it.

"Oh, Jinxie, you're so beautiful. I just had no idea..." his voice drifting off as he covered her breast with his mouth.

Jinx sighed and arched her back as Charlie tugged at her shorts and panties. As she watched Charlie gently touch her and explore her naked body, she gasped and cried out with delight. When Charlie's excitement reached a fever pitch and he could no longer hold back, he shed his clothes and came to her.

Jinx's mother had told her the night before her wedding, "Darling, please don't be disappointed the first time. Sex takes practice. In time you'll find great pleasure. Just be patient."

But her mother had been wrong. She and Charlie didn't need practice. There was no disappointment. From the moment Charlie entered her, their bodies knew each other's rhythms, and their first encounter was tender yet urgent, full of longing, fueled by their waiting, made perfect by their love.

"Why are you crying?" Charlie asked.

They were exhausted, bathed in perspiration, and Jinx's beautiful auburn hair was damp and clinging to her face. Charlie rested on his elbow, peering into Jinx's face. He smoothed her hair and kissed her eyelids.

"I'm not crying. I don't know what's happening, Charlie. My eyes are just leaking, and I can't seem to stop them. You've touched something in me that I didn't even know was there," she said, smiling, tears streaming from her eyes.

Enfolding her in his arms, Charlie said, "You touched me, too, Jinxie."

And as they drifted into sleep, still clinging to each other, Jinx whispered, "You picked me up, Charlie."

"And you picked me up, Jinxie," Charlie replied.

"It's cold," Jinx said without opening her eyes, pressing herself into Charlie's embrace.

They had fallen asleep, naked, on top of the covers. The chill had crept in during the night.

Charlie whispered, "Here, crawl under the covers. It's still dark out. I'll go build a fire in the fireplace. By the time we get up, the living room should be nice and warm."

Crawling off the bed, he pulled back the covers and helped Jinx under. Once she was settled, he gathered the blankets around her, kissed her cheek, and headed for the fireplace. The wood was just right and ignited immediately before settling down into a gentle, crackling fire. Charlie placed the screen before the hearth and headed back to bed.

"Oh, you're cold," Jinx said and wrapped her arms around him, drawing him close.

Settling into each other's embrace, they fell back to sleep. They awoke two hours later, when the morning sun peeked through their bedroom window. Jinx stretched and nuzzled Charlie, kissing him on his neck.

"I'm starving," he said.

"Well, the only thing we've had since yesterday's breakfast is Nabs and a Co-Cola." Giggling, she added, "And we expended quite a lot of energy last night. We should be hungry."

"You stay right there while I go get our bags from the car," Charlie said. "Then we can forage in the fridge for some breakfast."

Slipping into his shorts, shirt, and shoes, Charlie raced out into the chilly mountain morning to retrieve their bags. Opening them on the bedroom floor, they plundered through until they located robes and slippers.

"Much better," Jinx said, tying her warm pink robe tight and pulling her collar up around her neck, as she headed for the kitchen.

Peering into the refrigerator, she said, "We'll never eat all this food Cyrus has stocked for us. We have bacon and eggs, bagels and cream cheese, a big bowl of fresh fruit, blueberry muffins. What'll it be?"

"Hmmmm, I think I'll have one of those bagels and some fruit," Charlie said.

"Sounds good. I think I'll have one of these muffins. Would you start the coffee while I toast your bagel and fix us a bowl of fruit?"

"Will do."

Jinx arranged their breakfast on a tray, and Charlie carried it to the front porch. The air was still cool, but the sun was warm on their faces. The view was magnificent. Cyrus's cabin was perched on the side of a mountain, and from the porch Jinx and Charlie could see all the way to the valley floor below. Small houses dotted the terrain, while red barns and silos loomed beyond the homes. Squares of green and gold created a patchwork quilt out of the landscape. In the distance, craggy mountains rose from the valley and disappeared into the morning fog.

"I didn't remember how beautiful the mountains were. All I recalled was the frigid stream," said Jinx.

"I know. I'll never forget that time Arch brought us up here. It was fun, but you're right about the cold water. It made my skin hurt."

After they'd cleaned their plates and relaxed a bit in the early-morning sun, Jinx said, "I think I need a shower."

"Me, too. Mind if I join you?"

"I was hoping you'd ask."

"And, maybe, after our shower you'll show me your peignoir."

"I was hoping you'd ask that, too."

They put their dishes in the sink—they'd wash them later—and headed for the shower. There they soaped each other's bodies and found that love making wasn't just for the bedroom.

When, after their four-day honeymoon, they returned to Savannah, Cyrus asked, "Well, what did y'all think of the quaint little town of Dawsonville?"

"What little town?" they asked, giggling and blushing.

Three

They decided that they wanted only one child—one perfectly marvelous child upon whom they and their parents could shower all their attention and adoration. So as Charlie commenced his legal career and Jinx continued to gather praise and a huge clientele with her design genius, they began planning for that one wonderful child. They tried. And they tried. And tried. As their friends celebrated the births of their first, second, even third children, Jinx and Charlie were still in the trying stage. And as much as they enjoyed their attempts to get pregnant, they remained sadly childless.

"What's the matter with us? What are we doing wrong?" Jinx had cried.

"Just relax, you two, and enjoy the ride," good-natured Dr. Wellman had chuckled. "There's not a thing the matter with either of you. And you're not doing anything wrong. Trust me, it'll happen."

And it had. Just eight months, two weeks, and four days later—they were already pregnant—Jinx gave birth to Knox Robinette Collier, nine pounds, four ounces of beautiful strawberry-blond, green-eyed spitting image of his daddy.

He was perfect—or as close to perfect as a child could get. And his parents and grandparents weren't the only ones who recognized what a charming, cunning, close-to-perfect child Knox was. Even the Colliers' friends knew how special their child was and secretly wished their own offspring could be as sweet and polite and, well, yes, as near perfect as Knox Collier.

Even the other children adored Knox, all of them clambering for best-friend status. Their mothers competed for play dates, and Jinx and Charlie's house had a revolving door for daily visits from various friends' little ones. Knox loved all his playmates equally and was delighted with whomever came to be a part of his day. He shared generously and was always the consummate host.

Jinx tried desperately to maintain her design clientele but found it impossible to keep up with Knox and her profession simultaneously. So she chose to put her career on the back burner to raise her only child. Many career women would have resented having to make the choice, but Jinx found that she much preferred being Knox's mother to being decorator to the elite. And it took all her time and energy to keep up with Knox's full social calendar.

But as Knox grew, Jinx was able to keep her creative juices flowing with the help of her friends. None was too shy to ask for Jinx's design advice and thought nothing of enlisting her help for full-blown decorating jobs—pro bono, of course. They were gracious enough, however, to feed her their homemade chicken salad and shrimp and grits as she slaved away at Benson's lavender bedroom or Maitland's twins' playroom. Jinx provided her services good naturedly, happy that she could stay involved in the design industry as she raised her child.

Life was wonderful for Jinx and Charlie. They had parents who cherished them, they loved each other unconditionally and passionately, and they had a perfectly near-perfect child in Knox.

"Mama, I want to ride with you and Daddy."

"But, Knox, you love riding in the plane with Grampy and Pop. And Gran and Big Mommy are going to ride in the plane, too."

"But I want to go with you and Daddy."

Was that a whine? Knox didn't whine—ever—even when he was tired. If he were sleepy, he'd just curl up into a ball, wherever he might be, and fall asleep. When he was hungry, Jinx would hand him a carrot, and he'd nibble contentedly until supper was ready. So this behavior came as a surprise to Jinx. A phase, she thought. All kids go through phases—even the best-behaved children. But why now?

"Darlin', it's going to be a long, boring car ride."

The Cessna could get them from Savannah to Athens in just a little over an hour, while it would take Jinx and Charlie four and a half hours to make the drive. Jinx was counting on their parents to care for Knox while she and Charlie had some adult time together away from children's games and extra pee-pee breaks. As wonderful as Knox was, Jinx and Charlie were due a break from parenting so that they could have some cherished alone time.

"I don't care. I want to ride with you and Daddy," Knox said, sticking out his lip, something Jinx assumed was just part of this new phase that she prayed would be short-lived.

Owning a plane seemed impractical when Arch proposed it to Vernon, but Arch soon had his partner convinced that it was a must. Their client base had spread as far north as the nation's Capital, south to Miami, and west beyond the Mississippi River. Why, one of their largest clients was in New Orleans. Meetings were no longer short automobile rides away.

Vernon couldn't argue with the time they'd save on commutes to and from airports, security checks, waits for flights, baggage claim hold-ups. And what about the lost luggage? That could take days to straighten out.

"And, Vern, the price of business travel is going up by the day."

And then there were the late-night meetings that lasted past the final flight back to Savannah. They'd have to check into a hotel and fly home the following morning, invariably causing them to be late for early-morning appointments.

So they had both earned their pilot's license and shared flying duties on business trips. And pleasure trips.

As practical as their six-seater Cessna was for business, it was great for ski trips in Vermont, deep sea fishing in the Keys, and jaunts to New York for shopping and the theatre. Best of all, it could get them to their beloved University of Georgia for weekend football games in about an hour. They'd arrive at a small airport on the outskirts of Athens, where a large rental van, suitable for pre-game tailgating, would be waiting for them on the tarmac.

And Knox would rather fly with his grandfathers than—as they say in the South—eat when he was hungry. But as much as Knox loved flying with his grandparents to the games, on this day he wanted to be with his parents, and that was that. Jinx was perturbed that she was allowing a four-year old to manipulate her, but she simply didn't have the time or patience to try to reason with him or figure out the cause for his obstinacy. They were packed, ready to lock up the house and leave for Athens, so she caved.

Homecoming weekend. The whole family had season tickets to UGA football games, but homecoming weekend was special. They'd plan homecoming weekends for months: where to stay, whom they'd see, where they'd eat, who would be in charge of tailgate food. It was a huge deal that had to be perfectly choreographed. And this year the grandparents wanted to make it extra special for Jinx and Charlie. Not only had they offered to let Knox fly to the game with them, they had planned to keep him for the entire weekend so that his parents could have some time to themselves.

"Y'all can spend the weekend with your fraternity brothers, even have a lovely meal or two alone," Molly had said.

And Emma Frances had added, "When was the last time you and Charlie had a nice, romantic getaway? Enjoy them while you can, Honey."

They didn't have to argue with Jinx. She'd love a quiet, romantic getaway with Charlie, complete with frat parties and dinners that didn't involve juice boxes, chicken fingers, or Value Meals. But it looked as though Knox had other plans for them. And rather than force a fretful, pouting child on her parents and in-laws, she chose to let him ride with her and Charlie. With luck, they'd pass him to the grandparents once they reached their destination.

"Where do you suppose they are, Charlie?"

Jinx and Charlie had checked into their hotel and gone directly to the stadium, where they expected to find their parents already partying with friends. But their designated spot in the parking lot was empty. No one had seen them.

"Oh, they probably just ran into old acquaintances and lost track of time. No need to worry. Remember, this is Homecoming. You never know what'll happen at Homecoming," a nearby tailgater bellowed as he popped the remainder of his hotdog into his mouth and chased it with a beer.

But Jinx was uneasy. It wasn't like her parents and in-laws to be late for a game.

"Don't worry, Honey," Charlie said, as he smiled and circled her shoulders comfortingly with his arm. Charlie, though, was just as worried as Jinx. But he felt it his job to reassure her, to pick her up.

"Let's get on into the stadium. If they don't show up in a little while, I'll go give the hotel a call."

Wind shear. That's what they called it. Apparently, it had occurred shortly after take-off from the airport in Savannah. Two hunters came upon the downed plane in a wooded area only miles from the pilots' homes. There were no survivors.

"Ma'am, it could have happened to anyone. There was just no evidence of pilot error," the FAA official had said, trying unsuccessfully to calm hysterical Jinx.

But his kind words offered no solace. Only when Charlie, sobbing as well, wrapped Jinx in his arms did she find comfort, knowing that they would pick each other up and, somehow, they'd go up together and survive this tragedy. That's who they were. That's what they did. As long as they had each other, they would pick each other up. And they would gather Knox to them and hold him close, grateful for his one and only tantrum.

Four

How much could the young couple endure? They had lost their parents, and their hearts ached with grief. But they had each other. And they had Knox. Jinx and Charlie avoided talking about the elephant in the room—the fact that Knox would have been with his grandparents on that tragic day had he not thrown a tantrum—and thanked God for their precious child and cherished every moment with him.

They left their small house and relocated to Jinx's childhood home on Tybee Island, the home the Robinettes had owned since before Jinx's birth and had bequeathed to their only child in their wills. As the young family settled into their new home, Jinx experienced fresh grief as she came across memories of her life with her kind, loving parents. The smell of her mother's perfume in Emma Frances's closet brought Jinx to her knees and caused her to weep in pain. Even her mother's sewing box could make her tear up, as could the chess set she shared with her daddy. But as time passed, Jinx came to treasure her parents' possessions and connected each with a beloved childhood memory. And as she and Charlie picked each other up, they were comforted in the knowledge that their parents loved them with their whole hearts, just as they loved Knox.

As Knox entered school, he charmed his teachers, just as he had charmed children and their parents alike. He was curious and studious, just the sort of student all teachers prayed would fill their classes. He was also an athletic and energetic child. To channel his energy Charlie had his son on the football field, the tennis court, and the golf course as soon as he could hold a club, a racket, or a ball. He was well coordinated and excelled at all sports. And he loved the aggression of whacking a ball and tussling on the field.

In high school Knox narrowed his athletic interest to football; apparently he had inherited his affinity for the sport from his father and both of his grandfathers. He was Savannah High's quarterback, a brilliant tactician, diagramming plays and directing his team like a symphony conductor. His brilliance on the football field led his high school to three state championships, just as his grandfathers had.

When Charlie's beloved University of Georgia begged Knox to come play football for them, Charlie was so proud he wept. Knox hadn't considered any school but UGA; he wanted to attend his father and grandfathers' alma mater.

Knox took to UGA just as Charlie hoped he would. He excelled in the classroom and on the football field, as well. He also excelled socially. Guys found him interesting, but not stodgy. They liked his quick wit and his self-effacing humor. Girls found him charming and were rendered breathless by his good looks. In addition to his strawberry blonde hair and green eyes, even in college he had a boyish sprinkling of golden freckles across his nose. And then there was that dimple in his chin, the dimple just like his dad's and his grandmother Molly's.

Just weeks into his freshman year, Knox met pert, petite redhead, Mindy Beth Sloan, who sat across the aisle from him in English 101. They connected as soon as they discovered that they both loved reading contemporary mysteries and laughing at goofy jokes. Their friendship grew beyond the classroom, and soon they were sharing meals and studying in each other's dorm rooms. All the girls who had set their sights on gorgeous Knox Collier soon learned that their efforts to woo him were futile as long as Mindy Beth Sloan was in the picture. They admitted defeat and gave up to look elsewhere.

Mindy Beth's daddy, Everett Sloan, was a renowned Atlanta plastic surgeon while her mama, Mary Davis, was a renowned hostess and socialite. Knox visited the Sloans in Atlanta while Mindy Beth traveled to Tybee to meet Charlie and Jinx. Jinx was taken with this sweet, pretty little girlfriend of Knox's, but she was hoping they weren't rushing things. This was Knox's first real relationship. Sure, he had dated in high school, was quite the catch among all the young girls. And, of course, Jinx's friends, The Girls, all wanted him for their daughters. But Jinx was hoping he'd play the field before settling down. Knox and Mindy Beth, though, kept their relationship exclusive, and Jinx reluctantly accepted their decision.

When party season arrived after their freshman year, Mindy Beth made her debut in Atlanta. Her parents, as was the proper custom, asked Knox's parents if Knox might be Mindy Beth's escort for the debutante ball. Charlie and Jinx would be invited to the dance, as well. Though Jinx was content with her one perfect child, she had often thought what fun it would be to have a daughter to present to society, just as she'd been presented as a young woman. Each year several Savannah girls would travel to Atlanta for party season, and that's all their mamas could talk about for a year before and a year after. The talk made Jinx's eyes cross and her mind wander. Now Jinx would be able to talk about party season, too, even if it weren't her daughter who was being feted.

Jinx went to Atlanta to buy appropriate clothes for the occasion. Needham's Department Store in Savannah just didn't have the right attire. Everything was just so casual and unsophisticated. It was all right for Savannah wear, but a debutante ball called for something special. At a small boutique in Atlanta, Jinx found the perfect ice blue sheath cut up to her knee. It was embellished with crystals, and the color matched her eyes and set off her beautiful, shiny auburn hair. She would be stunning.

Charlie pulled out his old tuxedo, dusted it off, and he was ready. Charlie, Jinx, and Knox drove over to Atlanta and checked into the Westin-Atlanta at Peachtree Plaza before heading out to Buckhead to visit with the Sloans.

Mindy Beth's family lived in an enormous mansion, a hand-me-down from Mary Davis's grandparents. Jinx guessed that it had not been updated since Mary Davis's grandparents had resided there. The furnishings were large and solid and ornate and looked like old money. But there was no personality to the décor; it just sort of sat there, looking old and worn. Jinx so wanted to redecorate it, but she kept her mouth shut and her hands to herself. She was in the Sloan's home to support Mindy Beth's coming out, not to flex her decorating muscles.

Everett and Mary Davis were gracious and welcoming hosts, and

Charlie and Jinx had a wonderful evening in their home. The family had a cook, but the meal was an unpretentious spread of baked ham, cheese grits, okra, home-grown tomatoes, and lemon chess pie. Mindy Beth's parents clearly adored Knox and more than once referred to him as Our Knox. Apparently, they didn't object to the exclusivity of Mindy Beth and Knox's relationship.

Charlie and Jinx preened, so proud of their only child. They could tell that the Sloans were delighted with their daughter's choice of a beau. And though Jinx had once hoped that Knox would play the field when he arrived at college, rather than settling down with his first real girlfriend, that weekend she decided that if Knox wanted a steady girl at his age, Mindy Beth was an excellent choice.

In just five years Knox graduated from UGA with a double major in business and marketing and a MBA. Though the NFL showed interest, Knox rejected professional football for a business career. He so respected his father, and though he had no interest in the law, he hoped to become a successful businessman, just like Charlie. Before he had even finished his degree, Knox had seven job offers from New York to California. He settled on New York, where he accepted a position as a fundraiser for the Museum of Modern Art.

Charlie and Jinx were delighted with Knox's prospects, but they were hoping he'd stay closer to home—at least as close as Atlanta. But they refused to show their disappointment. Knox was everything they ever dreamed he would be: smart, athletic, handsome, charming, a southern gentlemen, wise beyond his years. He had grown up to be a wonderful young man, every parent's dream. So they kept their sadness to themselves, knowing the time had come to let Knox go. He was a man, ready to make his own decisions.

Knox had little time between graduation and his new career. He returned home for a long weekend so that he could gather his belongings and get some help from his mother selecting an appropriate wardrobe for New York. They spent Friday in Ivy's Men Shop being fitted for a brown, a blue, and a gray suit, with a personal guarantee from the owner, Max Schuler, that they would be altered and ready to go by Saturday at closing. Then Knox spent Saturday making the Savannah and Tybee rounds, saying one last good-bye to all those folks who had known him and adored him since the day he was born.

"We're gonna miss you, Son," Mr. Argus at the dry cleaners said, grabbing his hand, palming a ten-dollar bill.

"Thank you so much, Mr. Argus. I'll miss y'all too," Knox said, his voice catching with emotion.

"Oh, Darlin'," Thelma Raines from the lunch counter at the Rexall Drug Store cried, as she stood on tiptoe and flung her flabby arms around Knox's neck, "I can't b'lieve our little Knox is all growed up. Lord, it seems like yesterday your mama brought you in here for your first grilled cheese and Co-Cola. Why, you wudn't hardly big enough to sit up on that stool by yourself. Now, Honey, don't you be going up there to New York and forget about us down here."

"Oh, I won't, Miss Thelma. This will always be home."

Tweezle and Blue sobbed and said their very hearts were being ripped out.

"Darlin', don't you go up there and get all Yankee now, you hear? You're a fine, southern gentlemen, and don't you forget it," said Tweezle, as she hung onto Knox's neck and kissed him, leaving bright red lip prints on his cheek.

"Oh, don't worry, Miss Tweezle. I won't get all Yankee," Knox told her, laughing at his mother's silly friend.

On Sunday morning after he had packed his car for his trip north and made one final sweep of his room to make sure he hadn't forgotten anything, Knox said, "Mom, Dad, let's go sit in the living room. I have something I need to tell you."

Jinx was beside herself with excitement. This was what she'd been waiting for: Knox planned to propose to Mindy Beth Sloan. She was certain that was his news, but she didn't say a word, didn't want to spoil his surprise. Charlie and Jinx had grown to truly love Mindy Beth, and they were ready to welcome her into their family. Since they didn't have a daughter, they tended to spoil Mindy Beth, just as Charlie's parents had spoiled Jinx. Of course, Jinx knew that it would not be her place to plan Knox and Mindy Beth's wedding and reception, but she was already thinking down the road to decorating their baby's nursery.

Had he already proposed? Or did he want to let his parents

know before he asked Mindy Beth's father for her hand in marriage? That was so like Knox—so thoughtful, so caring and considerate. Surely, he hadn't already given her a ring. Knox knew that Jinx had saved her great-grandmother's exquisite marquis diamond set in a platinum filigree band for his fiancée. As she shivered with excitement, Jinx realized that she was getting ahead of herself. First, let Knox tell them his news. There'd be plenty of time later to talk about diamond engagement rings.

As Jinx tried to contain her enthusiasm, Knox said, "Mom, Dad, thank you for all you have done for me. I couldn't have asked for more loving, supportive parents. I'm so proud of you, Dad, and I've worked hard to be just like you. I hope that I can be as honest and have as much integrity as you've had in your practice. I hope I can make you proud."

Of course, Charlie and Jinx just beamed at their child, as Charlie reached over, patted his son's arm and said, "We're very proud of you, Son."

"And, Mom, I've always felt sorry for my friends—sorry that I got to have you for my mom and they didn't. I love you so much. Thanks for taking such good care of me, for giving up your career for me."

Tears sprang to Jinx's eyes as she reached for her precious child's hand.

Then Knox said, "What I have to tell you is so difficult for me to say. I've known for some time, but I've been afraid to tell you."

Confusion furrowed Jinx's brow. How could telling them about his plans to marry Mindy Beth be so hard? Surely Knox knew that his parents loved her and had come to embrace their relationship. Didn't he realize that Jinx and Charlie would accept that marriage was the next step for them?

So Jinx asked, "Why, Darlin', what's the matter?"

Knox took a deep breath, held it briefly, and then let it out in a ragged whoosh. Looking from Jinx to Charlie and back again, he said, "Mom, Dad, I'm gay."

Jinx didn't quite understand what Knox meant. She was still decorating her grandchild's nursery, and her thoughts didn't mesh with what had come out of Knox's mouth. So she just stared blankly at her child.

Finally she croaked, "But Mindy Beth..."

"She knows. She's known for a long time. We've been best friends since the day we met in freshman English. Just best friends. If others wanted to see us as a couple, that was fine. But it was just a friendship, a very strong friendship. It was comfortable. And safe. It worked for us."

"But I don't understand, Knox," Jinx croaked in utter confusion.

"Mom, Mindy Beth has been in love with a guy since she was sixteen, a guy her parents didn't approve of, a guy whom they felt wasn't of their social standing. He graduated from Florida State this year. He's really great and really smart. But regardless of how smart or how great he is, he still isn't from their social circle. But he and Mindy Beth are adults now. They don't have to answer to her parents or anyone else. They're getting married next week."

"But you..."

"Gay, Mom. I'm gay. I've known since I was young. I've struggled with it, tried to deny it. But it's who I am. I can't deny it anymore." When his parents said nothing, Knox croaked, "I hope y'all understand."

But Charlie did not understand. How could this be? His son had never shown any signs of being gay. He dated girls. He was an athlete. He was just like all the other boys, just like all of their friends' sons. He was normal.

The Colliers' silence was uncomfortable and felt interminable.

Finally, Knox said, "Please, Mom, Dad, say something."

Jinx opened her mouth to speak, but no sound came out.

But Charlie, without a shred of malice, looked his son squarely in the eye and said in an even voice, "Knox, I just cannot accept that."

Knox wasn't sure what reaction he was expecting from his father, but, clearly, it wasn't this. Sputtering, he said, "But, Dad, it's really not your choice. This is my life. As I told you, I've struggled with it for some time now, and I've had a difficult time coming to grips with it. I was so hoping I could count on your support."

Charlie responded, "Knox, the Bible says that homosexuality is an abomination. I can't accept it. I certainly can't support it."

"But, Dad," Knox said, his voice breaking. "I'm your son. What choice do you have?"

"Knox, I can't deny my beliefs. If this is the life you have chosen, I cannot accept you."

"But, Dad, I didn't *choose* it, like it was a car or a pair of shoes.

I'm gay. It's who I am," Knox cried, pleading with his dad.

Jinx looked on in stunned silence. *Say something!* she screamed inside her head. But still no more words would come. She was as shocked and taken aback by Knox's revelation as Charlie was. She was equally shocked by Charlie's response to Knox's admission. But still she said nothing.

Since his father, the man he loved above all others, had told him that he could no longer accept him and his mother had sat in stony silence, Knox stood, picked up his car keys from the coffee table, and headed for the door.

His parents did not move from their seats on the sofa.

He opened the door and paused with his hand on the doorknob, hoping his parents would call out to him. When they said nothing, Knox stepped out onto the porch, closed the door to his childhood home behind him, and headed for his car. As he made his way west to Savannah and then north to New York City to begin his new life, tears of pain and anguish coursed his cheeks.

Five

"But, Charlie, Knox is our child."
No matter how many times Jinx pleaded with Charlie, his response was always the same.

Calmly, without rancor, Charlie would say, "I can't accept it, Jinxie."

"But, Charlie…"

"His lifestyle is sinful, Jinxie."

"Be reasonable, Charlie…"

"It's an abomination, Jinxie."

"Please, Charlie…"

"I couldn't accept that lifestyle in our friends' children; accepting it in my own child would be hypocrisy."

As a last resort she had fallen to her knees in front of Charlie and cried, "Charlie, please pick me up."

Charlie knelt with her and lifted her chin, saying, "I love you, Jinxie. I always will. And I will always be here to pick you up. But please don't ask me to change who I am, to turn my back on my beliefs."

Jinx realized she'd never change Charlie's mind about homosexuality, but she felt she could change his mind about wanting to see their child.

But Jinx was wrong.

It had been nearly two years since Jinx had watched silently as her only child backed his car out of the driveway and drove out of her life. She and Charlie had not heard a word from him since that day.

Her heart was broken over the way Charlie had banished Knox

and furious with him over his refusal to accept their child, regardless of his sexual orientation. But, mostly, she was angry with herself for not standing up to Charlie. What Charlie called beliefs Jinx called narrow-mindedness. And what Jinx saw in herself was cowardice.

But it is difficult to take a stand with no support. She had tried but had failed miserably. All of their friends had sided with Charlie and refused to sympathize with her over the loss of her child. They felt that Knox was being foolish, choosing to be gay and wounding his parents with his selfishness. Charlie and Jinx had given Knox everything. How could he treat his parents with such disrespect?

Caroline, the life-long friend who had always told her she would do anything for her, sided with Charlie and sniffed at Jinx's attempts to defend her child.

"You know Charlie is right, Jinx," said Caroline, her nose in the air.

The crowd was gathered at Charlie and Jinx's house for a Saturday night shrimp boil. They could accept her hospitality and eat her food, but they couldn't accept her only child or support her when her heart was breaking. Instead, Caroline ignored her so-called friend's pain and passed judgment on Jinx's only child. Until that moment Jinx had never noticed just how haughty and self-righteous Caroline could be.

"Jinx, I don't know what Bible y'all used over there at that Presbyterian Church when you were growing up."

"Episcopal."

"Huh?"

"Episcopal Church, Caroline. I went to the Episcopal Church. I've never been Presbyterian."

"Well, whatever, same thing," Caroline said, with a dismissive wave of her hand, as if distinguishing between Presbyterian and Episcopalian was just too trivial to bother.

"Anyway," Caroline continued, "as I was saying, I don't know what Bible y'all used over there at that *Episcopal* Church, but we use the real Bible at Mt. Moriah Baptist. And the real Bible says that homosexuality is a sin and an abomination. Just look it up. It's right there somewhere in Leviticus," Caroline spat, stabbing the air with her finger.

Jinx had been going to Mt. Moriah with Charlie since they married, and the Bible they used in the Baptist church seemed to her to be just like the one they used in the Episcopal Church. And she was certain the Bible she read taught love and understanding, not judgment and rejection.

Ignoring her friend's idiotic remark and the fact that her supposed best friend from childhood couldn't remember what church she'd attended, Jinx pleaded, "But, Caroline, he's my child. He's not making a choice. It's who he is."

"Oh, baloney, Jinx. You know you don't believe that nonsense for one minute. You're just making excuses for him. And you know Knox is just testing you. But you mark my words," Caroline said, wagging her finger in Jinx's face, "that boy'll come to his senses and be back home soon with his tail between his legs. He just needs to get that foolishness out of his system."

Jinx was livid. All of her friends behaved as though their children were perfect little angels—squeaky clean, virginal, and obedient. But Jinx knew better. They all knew better. Why, there were elephants all over the room that everyone knew personally but chose to ignore. Jinx was not a vindictive, mean-spirited woman, but this attack on her Knox had gone on long enough. She was about to expose an elephant.

"Oh, let's change the subject, Caroline, and talk about something pleasant. Tell me about Benson. Where's she off to this summer?"

Jinx knew very well where Benson was, and she planned to let Caroline know that she knew.

"Well, she's over in Riegelwood, right outside Atlanta, with Hughie's old-maid aunt, Tilly."

"I don't recall meeting Aunt Tilly," said Jinx, furrowing her brow in mock confusion.

"Oh, you wouldn't have met her. She was considerably older than Daddy Hugh. She was off to Converse by the time Hugh was in elementary school."

"Hmmm...," Jinx began, but Caroline would not allow her friend to interrupt her elaborate tale.

"When she graduated from college, Aunt Tilly went to the Atlanta area to teach and just never came back to Savannah. Never got married, either. She's getting on in years, and Benson thought it would be a good idea to spend some time with her, pick her brain about the olden days, you know, and maybe lend her a hand."

Jinx was impressed with the intricate story Caroline was weaving.

What an actress. What a liar. Benson was about as self-centered a brat as Jinx had ever seen. There wasn't a chance in hell she was in Riegelwood lending a hand to her aging great-aunt.

But to Caroline she said, "What a kind gesture to take her summer to care for an elderly great-aunt. I know you and Hughie must be so proud of her."

"Oh, yes, we couldn't be prouder."

"You say Aunt Tilly lives in Riegelwood?"

"Yes, right outside Atlanta."

"Riegelwood, Riegelwood, gosh that name sure sounds familiar," said Jinx quizzically.

"Well, perhaps you've heard Hughie talk about his aunt," offered Caroline quickly.

"No, no, that's not it," Jinx said, tapping her lips with her finger as if in deep concentration, pausing just long enough to make Caroline squirm. "Oh, I remember. That's where that home for unwed mothers is located. Isn't that right?"

And as Tweezle burst into their conversation with impeccable timing, saying, "What you girls chattin' 'bout over here?", Jinx raised her eyebrow and leveled Caroline with a look that said, *You don't know who you're screwing with, best friend.*

Without taking her eyes off Caroline, Jinx said with honey dripping from her voice, "Why, Tweezle, I was just saying to Caroline how proud she and Hughie must be of their little Benson, going over there to Riegelwood to look after her poor old Great-Aunt Tilly this summer."

"Oh, I know, it's a wonderful thing she's doing, bless her heart. And speaking of being proud of young'uns, I don't believe I've told you that Third" (whose real name was Winston Winstead Sullivan, III) "got re-admitted to Georgia for the fall. Win-Win" (That would be Winston Winstead Sullivan, Jr.) "cried like a baby."

Win-Win cried when his string pulling got his drug-addled, drug-dealing son re-admitted to his alma mater for the third time, but he had stared smugly at the judge when he'd gotten that same child freed from criminal drug possession and trafficking charges.

Third was a spoiled, bratty bad seed. He'd put his sainted grandfather, Winston, Sr., in an early grave with his heinous behavior. His latest foray to the dark side involved selling drugs to minors. Thank the Lord his granddaddy hadn't lived to see the way his own son, Win-Win, had used his daddy's good name and Savannah connections to free his child and send two unsuspecting scapegoats to prison for a lengthy stretch.

Third showed up in court decked out in a white monogrammed oxford shirt with long sleeves to cover white supremacy and Confederate flag tattoos. His khaki pants were so heavily creased they threatened to razor his legs, and his squeaky new wing tips were polished to a blinding hue. He had never owned such preppy finery but, instead, preferred ripped jeans and dirty black tee shirts with pictures of grunge metal bands or vulgar sayings. His shoulder length hair, so greasy and filthy it was of an indeterminate color, had been shorn to a clean and surprisingly blonde, boy-next-door buzz cut.

One by one character witnesses, from preachers to teachers to blue-blood neighbors, paraded in and out of the courtroom to sing Third's praises, while the judge rolled his eyes and clenched his jaw.

In the end there was not enough evidence to implicate Third.

Judge Hunter Allen said, "Third, you don't fool me for one second. I know you, and this get-up you're wearing in my court doesn't change what you are. I want you to clean up your act, you hear, Son? I don't want to see you back here again. Next time I won't be so kind."

The whole time Judge Allen was talking, Third slouched in his chair with a sneer on his face and a bring-it-on attitude.

When the Judge said, "Do you understand, Son?" instead of saying, "Yes, your honor," Third just sucked his teeth and said, "Sure thing."

Judge Allen let it slide. That was one hill he didn't want to die on. He just wanted this delinquent out of his courtroom. He couldn't stand to look at him. Third's grandfather had been Judge Allen's mentor and closest friend. He had stood by, helplessly, as Third killed the heart of his best friend. As he pounded his gavel to dismiss court, he held back the tears at the memory of Judge Sullivan's decline.

The good-old-boy network erupted in cheers, and Win-Win grabbed his son in a bear hug and bellowed, "Ain't nobody gonna mess with my boy!"

Jinx was sitting directly behind Win-Win and Tweezle in the courtroom. She had come in support of Tweezle but regretted that decision. She was repulsed by Win-Win's attitude, by Tweezle's pseudo-cluelessness, and by Third's utter lack of respect for authority. Tweezle and Win-Win had been her and Charlie's friends since kindergarten. She thought she knew them so well. How could they have so abominably screwed up a perfectly good child?

And how could they pass judgment on her kind, loving son who had never taken a drug and had never spoken disrespectfully to a soul?

As Caroline eyed Jinx cautiously, praying she wouldn't blow Benson's cover, and horse-faced Tweezle brayed on about the wonderfulness of her child, Charlie dumped the shrimp boil the length of the butcher-paper-covered plank table on the big porch overlooking the Atlantic and yelled, "Soup's on! Come and get it!"

Everyone clambered for a place at the table, Caroline choosing to sit as far from Jinx as she could. That suited Jinx just fine. And as their guests prattled about nonsense, Jinx watched them shuck shrimp and stuff their faces, juice dripping from their chins and elbows. From time to time, Caroline would glance Jinx's way with a pleading look. Jinx just smiled pleasantly, refusing to show her hand.

Just let her stew, she thought.

Charlie and Jinx continued to see their friends socially, to open their home to the crowd, but Jinx's heart was not in it. How could she enjoy the company of people who were so narrow-minded, mean spirited, and cynical? And two-faced? But Jinx couldn't undo what had been done, couldn't change Knox's life, and couldn't alter her husband's and friends' beliefs; so she just plastered on her best southern-lady smile and went through the motions of living.

And the friends she once cherished now seemed so shallow and insincere. They'd act as though Knox just didn't exist, while filling their gatherings with overblown accounts of their own children's accomplishments and vicious gossip about people they claimed to be their friends.

"What was she thinking when she dyed her hair that color?"

"She has really let herself go. How much weight do you suppose she's put on?"

"Floyd not in the ground two months, and there she is at The Oyster Shucker, batting her eyes and giggling at that old Dub Fulbright."

They were at Blue's house for Wednesday morning Bible study, but they just used Bible study as an excuse to attack anyone who chose not to join them. Had she ever been one of them? Well, she was ashamed to admit, even to herself, that, yes, she had, indeed, been one of them. But it had taken losing her son to realize how vacuous all her acquaintances seemed. Yet, what could she do? Savannah and Tybee were her universe. This was her circle.

In time, however, as she listened to them prattle and gossip, she grew resentful of the lot of them and ceased to consider any of them her friends at all. She bit her tongue. She withdrew. She seethed in silence. But she could bite her tongue and seethe in silence just so long. Jinx was at her boiling point and about to erupt. This had gone on long enough. She and Charlie, the only man she had ever loved, the man who had promised he'd always pick her up, were about to have, as the Mt. Moriah Baptists called it, a come-to-Jesus meetin'.

And then time ran out.

Six

They didn't do funerals at Mt. Moriah Baptist Church the way they did at St. John's Episcopal Church. Jinx had been baptized at St. John's and had attended Sunday school and church every Sunday until she had married Charlie. But since Charlie's great-grandfather had been the first minister and had laid the cornerstone at Mt. Moriah and his parents and grandparents had been married in that little church, going to services at Charlie's Baptist church just seemed the appropriate thing to do. What's more, most of their friends were members of Mt. Moriah, as well. Jinx figured, either way, church was church.

And even though she didn't care for the Baptist funeral traditions, she was pretty sure she didn't have the power to change age-old customs to suit her own sensibilities. At St. John's Episcopal the bereaved family members waited in the preacher's study until all the mourners were seated in the sanctuary. Then they would quietly join the congregation shortly before the service began.

At Mt. Moriah the deceased family stood in front of the church while the mourners arrived for the funeral. One by one they would approach the grieving widow, parent, or child with embraces and words of comfort. It made Jinx most uncomfortable, rather than comforted, but how could she change this long-held tradition? As much as she wanted to, she simply felt that interfering with Mt. Moriah customs would be inappropriate.

So there she stood, alone, in front of Mt. Moriah Baptist Church, waiting to be pitied by all of the citizens of Savannah and Tybee Island.

She had asked Polly Ann, the closest thing to family and her very best friend in the world, to stand with her.

Flaring her nostrils and pursing her lips, Polly Ann said, "Now, you know very well that hoity-toity church wouldn't allow no black woman to stand in front of their sanctuary to greet mourners. It just ain't done."

"Polly Ann, it's bad enough that I have to stand, all exposed, out in front of that church. It just seems so tacky. I'll do it for Charlie, but I just can't face this by myself."

"Oh, yes, you can, Sugah Pie. You've faced lots worst. Now, Nellie and Suzette and Odelle gonna come to Mr. Charlie's funeral, and we'll be sitting in the balcony. You know I'll be there for you, just not standing out front. You understand, right?"

"Yes, I understand, but I don't like it one little bit."

Polly Ann's heart broke for her Sugah Pie, but she wouldn't budge. She couldn't. It just wasn't proper. Jinx was on her own.

One by one the mourners arrived, wringing their hands, knitting their brows, tilting their heads ever so slightly, making sure their eyes and mouths turned down at the corners at the proper angle, whispering their sorrow.

"Oh, my dear, what a sad, sad day it is. How could the Lord take such a nice man from our midst?"

"Thank you, Miz Mamie," Jinx said, as Mamie Bordeaux clung to her and cried onto her shoulder.

"Jinx, my heart breaks for you. We have lost the nicest man this town has ever known."

"You're so kind, Miz Selma," Jinx told her, holding her at arm's length, so as to avoid another weeping spell on her suit.

"Darlin', such a tragedy. Charlie was too nice a man to deserve this."

"Yes, Miz Olene. Thank you so much for coming."

After most of Chatham County, Georgia had told Jinx what a nice man Charlie had been and made an attempt to weep all over her, she saw The Girls emerge from Harper Ann's pretentious gold Cadillac SUV. That gas-guzzling tank of a car even had heated leather seats in the sultry Savannah climate.

They were all appropriately dressed in their finest black dresses and hats. But who in the world told Taylor and Maitland that it was cute for middle-aged twins to dress like twins? There they were in their identical broad-brimmed hats, identical black sheath dresses, identical patent leather pumps, and identical big round sunglasses.

When they approached Jinx, she could see that they had all been crying. Their noses were red, and their eyes were ringed with smudges of black mascara. When they reached Jinx, they all burst into tears. They blubbered and snorted and mopped their eyes with their linen hankies while wailing about how Charlie was the nicest person any of them had ever known. And not one of them would say that Charlie had died. They kept referring to his death as his passing.

Jinx held her tongue until she could stand it no more.

In anger and frustration, she stomped her foot, clenched her teeth, and said, "Charlie did not pass anything; he died. Y'all act as if he passed a test. Or a kidney stone. Or gas. Or maybe you think that he passed by us but will be returning someday to pass by in the other direction. Well, that isn't going to happen. He's gone! He's dead! Just say it, for God's sake."

While The Girls stared at her in shocked horror with their red, puffy eyes stretched wide and their mouths agape, Jinx watched a taxi pull up to the curb. The rest of the mourners watched it, as well, and turned to stare out of curiosity because the residents of Savannah did not take taxis to funerals. Then the door of the yellow anomaly opened, and a striking young man stepped out onto the sidewalk.

He looked so handsome, even more handsome than when he had left Tybee Island for New York two years before. He had cut his shaggy, strawberry blond surfer hair into a very mature, professional style, and he seemed to have put a little weight on his once-lanky frame. The extra pounds looked good on him.

Jinx's eyes filled with tears. Knox had come home.

He spotted his mother and smiled. Jinx parted her friends, all still wide-eyed and shocked speechless, met her son halfway, and walked into his arms. After a long, silent embrace that spoke volumes, Jinx took Knox's arm, and they walked into the church, looking neither left nor right. Knox ushered his mother to the front left pew, the pew his family had occupied all his life, holding her hand tightly as she clung to his arm. As they sat, Revered Troxler nodded slightly at Jinx but did not acknowledge Knox's presence.

Jinx seethed at the overt slight as she waited for the service to commence.

She had wanted a simple, dignified funeral, but this community just didn't know how to do simple. They would not stand for anything less than grand when it came to giving their beloved Charlie Collier a proper send-off.

"Just leave the details to me, Miz Collier," oily Doug Fountain of Fountain Family Funeral Home had said in a near-inaudible whisper, grasping her hand in his fat, pink paws and breathing garlic in her face.

He had tried to mask his lunch with peppermint Life Savers, to no avail. Jinx had ultimately trusted him with the funeral specifics because the way-too-many choices overwhelmed her, Doug's garlic breath repulsed her, and, most importantly, she just didn't give a damn.

But she was repelled by the funeral home's choice of a polished-to-a-blinding-hue walnut casket adorned with an enormous blanket of red, white, and blue flowers that stood at attention at the front of the sanctuary. She'd have preferred cremation, but she'd told Doug, "Whatever..." Enormous wreathes and arrangements of yellow mums and purple orchids and mixed blooms flanked the casket and created a nauseatingly sweet-smelling, ostentatious display.

She held tight to her son as friend after friend waded through the garish arrangements to give testimony to Charlie's goodness and soloists sang somber hymns about gathering at rivers and flying away, their voices cracking with the weight of their sorrow. A harpist played a number she appeared to be making up as she went along, a piece Jinx was certain would go on forever. Those Mt. Moriah Baptists just didn't know when to call it a day.

Then Reverend Troxler stood and spoke ad-infinitum of Charlie's virtues, emphasizing his strict adherence to the word of God and his refusal to be swayed from his convictions by anyone or anything. Jinx could feel the eyes of all in attendance, including Reverend Troxler, trained on Knox, their judgmental tongues eager to cluck. Hot tears of rage stood at the backs of Jinx's eyes and threatened to erupt, but she refused to let the pious Mt. Moriahans see her cry or witness her weakness.

Once the service mercifully ended and the Reverend said his amen, the congregation stood in unison and moved in a herd toward the cemetery adjacent to the church. There they found the green Fountain Family Funeral Home tent hovering over white plastic chairs in neat rows, as well as the newly excavated hole where Charlie's remains would rest for all eternity. The tent was the same tent that Fountain Family Funeral Home rented out between funerals for tailgatin', beach music festivals, pig pickins, and gun shows over at the county fairgrounds.

Jinx and Knox took their seats front row, center, while everyone who claimed to be Charlie and Jinx's dear, dear friends clambered to claim the most righteous seat. As The Girls elbowed one another and hustled to sit next to Jinx, she calmly placed her purse on the vacant seat to her right. Then she turned to locate Polly Ann in the crowd. Jinx needed Polly Ann's strength, needed her support, needed her as a shield against the mourners. Jinx found her standing at the rear of the assemblage of chairs, with no notion of taking a seat. Her back was ramrod straight, her broad hands clutched at her waist. She flared her nostrils and huffed at the tacky behavior of Jinx's shoving, unladylike so-called friends.

When Jinx caught Polly Ann's eye, she motioned for her to join her and Knox in the front row. Polly Ann, though, just raised her chin and gave Jinx a near-imperceptible shake of her head. Jinx knew all along that Polly Ann would never do anything so inappropriate as sit in the front row at a white funeral, but she thought she'd give it a try. Failing at her attempt, Jinx faced forward, leaving her purse in the empty chair. She felt she'd get more comfort from a black patent leather pocketbook than she would from Caroline, Blue, or Tweezle.

Apparently, Reverend Troxler had used all the funeral words he knew inside the sanctuary because his graveside service was surprisingly brief.

"We've gathered to commit Charlie to his final resting place. Ashes to ashes, dust to dust…"

And before Jinx had a chance to truly grasp the reality of Charlie's death, the fact that she had seen her only love for the very last time, the six pall bearers were lowering the burnished walnut casket into the hole in the ground. Just as soon as Reverend Troxler said his final amen and dismissed the mourners, Jinx hissed through her teeth to Knox, "Let's go."

The two stood, and as Jinx clutched her child's arm, mother and son fled the tent, once again looking straight ahead, making a bee-line for the Fountain Family Funeral Home limousine.

The Girls had planned a reception for the whole congregation at Maitland's palatial home on the river. Maitland loved funerals so that she could throw lavish receptions. It provided her an excuse to show off her prosperity. Doug Fountain, who had personally squired Jinx to the church, was waiting at the curb, prepared to take her to Maitland's home.

As Jinx and Knox climbed into the back of the limo, she said to Doug, "Please take me home."

"But Miz Collier…"

"Doug, I said take me home, please."

Without another word, Doug struggled to turn his ample frame forward and stretch his seatbelt across his rotund belly. He started the car, made a U-turn in front of the church, and headed east toward Tybee Island.

Jinx knew for certain that she would never again step foot in Mt. Moriah Baptist Church.

On the ride out to Tybee, Jinx sat close to her son, still clutching his arm. The two of them did not utter a word throughout the ride. Doug was a notorious gossip, and the mother and son did not want anything they said disseminated, dissected, misconstrued, and spewed all over Savannah and surrounding communities. From time to time Jinx would look into her son's eyes, squeeze his arm, and smile. Knox returned her smile.

When Doug brought the big black Fountain Funeral Home limo to a halt in Jinx's crushed-oyster-shell driveway, he groaned as he hauled his portly frame out of the driver's seat and opened the rear door.

"Thank you, Doug, for bringing us home. And thank you for taking care of Charlie's service for me," Jinx said, as Doug offered his puffy hand and helped her from the back seat.

"My pleasure, Miz Collier. If there's anything else we can do to help…"

"Well, Doug, I certainly hope I won't be needing your services again for a good while to come."

"Yes'm, I understand. Well, you take care, Miz Collier," and to Knox he extended his hand and said, "and welcome home, Knox."

Knox reached out and took Doug's doughy hand. Doug, known as Dougie until he joined the family business, had been a pillowy, effeminate teenager, the object of relentless bullying and derision. Knox was one of his few classmates who had treated him kindly.

And Dougie was the only person who had welcomed Knox home.

"Thanks, Doug," Knox said, shaking his hand firmly, "it's good to be home."

Jinx and Knox watched as Doug pulled out of the drive and headed toward Savannah. When his big, black limo was out of sight, Knox put his arm around his mother's shoulders, and Jinx put her arm around her son's waist. Together they climbed the steps to the home where Knox had lived from birth until his relocation to New York, the home he hadn't set foot in for two years.

"I hope you don't mind that I left my things on the porch," Knox said, as he motioned to his duffle bag resting by the front door. "I stopped by on the way to the church. I was hoping you'd let me stay."

Of course he could stay. There was nothing more the mother wanted than to have her only child stay. She had longed for him; her heart had ached for him for two years. So there on the front porch Jinx finally let loose all the emotions she had been holding since the day of Charlie's death. She grabbed Knox, who towered over his mother, wrapped her arms around his waist, and sobbed into his chest. Knox held his mother to him, as he, too, released two years of emotion. If anyone were watching, neither cared. Mother and son were reunited, and that was cause for unleashing their feelings. They made their way into the house, mopping their faces with tissues Jinx pulled from her purse.

"Go put your things away and get into something comfy. I'm going to do the same. Then I'll fix us something to eat," she said, still mopping her face and blowing her nose. "We have a kitchen full of food, all your favorites."

Knox trudged up the stairs to his boyhood bedroom. There he found that his mom hadn't changed a thing. The red and blue plaid bedspreads still covered the twin beds, and his bulletin board, adorned with high school memorabilia, was still affixed to his wall. His bookshelf housed his favorite childhood books, *Tom Sawyer*, *Last of the Mohicans*, *Hardy Boys*; and his football, golf, and tennis trophies were still displayed proudly on a shelf above his bed.

Knox shed his suit jacket and stepped out of his slacks and hung them neatly in his closet. He wasn't the slob he used to be, tossing his clothes on the chair for his mom or Polly Ann to retrieve and hang or wash and iron. He cringed at his thoughtlessness, even though he knew that he was not unique and that all teenagers did the same. But he'd been on his own for two years now with no one to pick up after him. He smiled as he thought how proud his mom would be at how far he'd come in those two years, how self-sufficient he'd become, how successful he'd been in his profession. He would share his journey with her as they became reacquainted.

He dug into his bag for a polo shirt, khaki shorts, and Topsiders. Once he was comfortably dressed, he headed downstairs to the kitchen for some of his favorite foods. He hadn't had a thing to eat since a stale airport bagel at dawn, and he was starving.

He found his mother dressed in a green cotton sundress and sandals, pulling plastic-wrap-covered bowls from the refrigerator.

"Polly Ann's fried chicken," she said, holding up a plate heaping with legs, thighs, breasts, and wings. He loved her wings the most. He said he liked the higher crunch-to-meat ratio.

"You can have all the rest of that stuff. Just give me Polly Ann's chicken wings."

They both laughed, even though Jinx had known he'd say that.

"I'm going to heat us up some butter beans and some of Miz Ida's squash casserole. And Miz Lovell sent us over some of her biscuits. Caroline brought potato salad, of course."

"Is that still the only thing she knows how to make?" Knox said, rolling his eyes.

"Just about. But with Hattie taking care of her, why does she need to learn how to cook?

While Jinx heaped two of her mom's old Blue Danube plates to overflowing, Knox filled glasses with ice and poured them some sweet tea from the cut-glass pitcher in the fridge. They carried their lunch to the round oak table with the blue checked table cloth at the far end of the large, inviting kitchen, the table where Jinx had eaten meals since she was a tiny child.

"Just one thing, Mom."

"What's that, Darlin'?"

"Don't start apologizing and stuff. That's not why I'm here. I came to be with you. I figured you needed me. And I needed to say goodbye to my dad. And, Mom, I know you did what you had to do. I know these people. I know how narrow-minded they are. You didn't have any choice."

The tears welled in Jinx's eyes. She did have a choice. She had just been too cowardly to make it.

"And no crying. I've cried enough. And I know you've cried enough, too. We're going to start fresh. And we don't have time for crying."

Jinx reached over and took her child's hand. She was so proud of him. How could anyone—his father, their friends—not think that he was perfect?

"Tell me what's going on here?" Knox said, picking up a wing and taking a bite of crunch.

"Well, let's see. Benson is spending the summer in Riegelwood, giving birth to a baby out of wedlock. Caroline says she's visiting an old-maid aunt."

"It finally caught up with her, huh?" said Knox, shaking his head.

"Third got arrested for drug trafficking, but Win-Win called in some favors and got him off and then pulled some strings to get him back into Georgia."

"Same old, same old."

"Yep," said Jinx. "The children haven't matured. The parents haven't either."

"Okay, your turn, Knox. Tell me all about New York. About you."

"I have a good life, Mom. I miss Tybee, miss Savannah. And I especially miss you. But New York is so exhilarating, more exciting than I ever dreamed it would be. And I love my job. The people I work with are incredibly creative and enthusiastic about what we're doing. And everyone seems to be in a hurry—like their heads are brimming with ideas and they feel as if they just aren't going to have enough time to get everything done if they don't rush to do it. It's thrilling, Mom—exhausting sometimes, but thrilling."

Jinx really did want to hear all the details of Knox's life, but she already knew how well he was doing. She could read. She knew how to surf the Internet. Every morning, after Charlie left for work, she'd look for the latest Knox Collier news:

The Museum of Modern Art hires Knox Collier of Tybee Island, Georgia to spearhead its fall fund drive.

Knox Collier, recent University of Georgia graduate, wows art world by procuring a $1,000,000 endowment from the Tri-Core Corporation for the Museum of Modern Art.

Knox Collier, second from left, greets Mayor de Blasio at MoMA's holiday

Black-and-White Charity Ball.

Knox Collier of the Museum of Modern Art, left, accepts a $40,000 check from fireman Tony Colletti. Tony serves as fund-raising chairman for the New York Fire Department. This year's donation will provide assistance for local artists.

Yes, Jinx knew how well Knox was doing, how the New York art world had embraced him, how successful he had become. He had been hired to spearhead a fund drive and in two years had been promoted to head of his department.

She reached across the table, took his hand, and, smiling broadly, said, "I know how well you're doing. You're all over the Internet. I read about you all the time. I am so proud of you, Darlin'."

"I had a feeling you were burning up that laptop," Knox said, squeezing his mother's hand.

"What do you mean, laptop? Why, I'll have you know, I own an iPad."

Knox laughed and said, "That doesn't surprise me at all."

"You want some pie? Polly Ann made lemon meringue and pecan."

"No, ma'am, not right now. Maybe later. I'm full," Knox said, leaning back and stretching. "Let's clean up the dishes and sit out on the porch for a while. I just want to look at the ocean. I've missed it."

Side-by-side, mother and son rinsed the plates and stacked them in the dishwasher. Jinx re-covered all the dishes of food and returned them to the refrigerator and gave the countertops one last swipe with the wet dish cloth. Knox refilled their tea glasses, and they retreated to the deep, cozy covered porch and eased themselves into the old Adirondack chairs, where they sat quietly and stared out to sea, listening to the surf rumble to shore and the gulls swoop and squawk overhead.

After their long silence, Knox said, "Mom, move to New York."

Jinx looked over at her son. He was staring out to the horizon, a wistful look on his face. Taken by surprise, she didn't respond, just thought about Knox's invitation.

Turning to her, he said, "What do you have here?"

"It's my home, Honey. This old house and I have history. It's where I belong."

"But why? It's my home, too, but it's not where I belong."

"I just can't, Darlin'."

Knox realized that his invitation had come out of left field when his mother least expected it. And it was poor timing; her husband had just died. It probably wouldn't be a good idea for her to make a major decision just yet.

"Well, then, how about a visit? Just go back with me for a visit. You can stay as long as you'd like. I won't pressure you. Just get a one-way ticket. When you're ready to come back home, we can get you a return ticket, and I'll take you to the airport. Does that sound doable?"

Jinx thought about it. What did she have to stay here for? Well, for one thing, there was Charlie's estate.

"Knox, I have to settle your father's estate."

"Mom, that's what you have Horace for. No one knows Dad's business better than Horace. He'll take care of everything."

"But, Knox, I can't just run off…"

"Mom, you won't be running off. You'll be with me. And if Horace needs a signature or has questions, he'll know how to reach you. He has your cell number, right?"

"Well, yeah…"

"There you go. All settled."

Anxious to be with her child but reluctant to rush things after their lengthy separation, she asked, "Are you certain, Knox? It won't be an imposition? And are you sure we're ready?"

"Mom, I've been ready for two years. Please say you're ready."

Jinx took a deep breath, sighed heavily, reached for Knox's hand, and said, "Well, okay then. I'll give it a try. And, yes, Knox, I am ready."

"Mom, that's great," Knox said, and reached across their chair arms to embrace his mother.

"Well, I guess I'd better order me a ticket," Jinx said, clapping her hands, ready to move forward with a real reunion and reconciliation with her son.

"Just one more thing, Mama."

Knox was calling her Mama. He'd always liked calling his mother Mom, even when he was a little boy, not Mama, the name most southern children give their mothers. But when he had something really serious to say or needed his mother the most, he called her Mama. Jinx braced for seriousness.

"What is it, Darlin'?"

"I have a partner."

"A partner?"

"Yes, Mama, a partner. A man. A man I love. He and I live together."

Jinx did not interrupt, did not change her expression. She just stared lovingly at her son, knowing how hard it must be for him to tell her this. She wasn't sure she was ready to talk about it, but she had to be. She didn't want anything to spoil their reunion.

"His name is Tony. Tony Colletti."

"The fireman," Jinx said and smiled.

"How did you know, Mom?"

"I told you I read the Internet, read everything about you. When I saw the picture of you and Tony Colletti and the way you looked at him, I said to myself, *Knox loves him.* A mother knows, Knox. A mother senses these things about her children. I wanted to believe that I'd seen that look of love when you gazed at Mindy Beth, but I guess I was just fooling myself. It wasn't until I saw the way you looked at Tony, that I was certain that you had never truly loved Mindy Beth."

That's all she could say because she didn't want the tears to come. She accepted her child for the man he was, but hearing him say out loud that he was in love with another man—and saying it herself—was a huge step. It would take time for her to come to grips with it, to feel comfortable with it. But she wanted desperately to try.

Finally, she was able to say, "But I do know that you love Tony."

Knox put his face in his hands and began to cry. Jinx reached over and caressed his head as she had when he was a little boy and needed to feel his mama's touch, needed her loving comfort.

"I love you, Knox," was all she said.

And Knox cried harder.

Jinx just let him cry as she continued to caress his head and sniffed back her own tears.

Seven

After making a one-way airline reservation for Jinx and calling Horace to see if he could meet them the following morning, mother and son fell into bed, exhausted, around midnight.

"On Sunday, Jinx? You know you don't have to rush. This can wait."

"Yes, Horace, I know that. But the sooner I set the wheels in motion, the sooner I can get this behind me and move forward."

"Well, okay, how about three-thirty tomorrow afternoon?"

"That won't work, Horace. I'll need to see you tomorrow morning."

"But church…"

"Oh, baloney, Horace. You've slept through every church service you've ever attended. Missing one nap isn't going to hurt you."

She was acting awfully bold. She surprised herself. And she pleased herself.

"Now, Jinx," began Horace, but didn't know where to go in rebutting Jinx's truth. He had no defense. He did sleep through church, had been known to snore from time to time and get a jab in the ribs from his wife, Enid. "Well, okay, how about ten-thirty?"

"We'll be there. And thanks, Horace," Jinx said, softening.

Their plans in place, Jinx and Knox slept quickly and deeply, spent from their emotionally draining day. Jinx awoke at six, her usual getting-up time, feeling surprisingly well rested. She decided, though, to let Knox sleep as late as he wanted. They didn't have to meet Horace for hours or be at the airport until one o'clock.

She had showered and fixed a pot of coffee and was sitting out on the porch when Polly Ann came trudging up the back steps.

"What you doin' drinking that hot coffee. It's over eighty degrees already this morning. You gonna burn up on the inside, as well as the out."

"Hey, Polly Ann. You didn't need to come out here this morning. It's Sunday. You should be in church."

"You think I'm gonna let you fix my baby his breakfast on his first day home? He needs Polly Ann's grits. You can't make his grits the way he likes 'em."

Jinx pretended that she didn't know that plain old canned evaporated milk was Polly Ann's secret ingredient for making the best grits in the county.

"You're right, Polly Ann. I guess you did need to come out this morning. Thanks."

"Hold that thought while I get me some ice water. You want some ice water?"

"No thanks, but you go right ahead."

Polly Ann opened the screen door, making it screech on its hinges.

"I gotta fix that screechy door," she muttered under her breath. She'd been saying, "I gotta fix that screechy door," for about twenty years. She never would.

She returned with a huge glass filled to the brim with ice and water, as well as her man's cotton handkerchief wet with cool water from the kitchen faucet. She lowered herself into the chair beside Jinx, wiped her dewy face with the handkerchief, and took a long swallow from her glass.

"You sho' did up and bolt after that funeral yesterday. Didn't even hang around for the thank-you-for-comings," Polly Ann said, her eyebrow raised at Jinx's impropriety. Her Sugah Pie knew better than that.

"Didn't see any need to stay."

"Hilda said you was a no-show at Miz Maitland's. Zat right?"

"That's right, Polly Ann."

"Was that good manners?"

Without looking Polly Ann in the eye, Jinx replied, "Don't care if it wasn't good manners. I'm fed up with those judgmental, arrogant people who have the nerve to call themselves my friends. They came to pay their respects to Charlie, but they couldn't find it in their hearts to acknowledge Charlie's and my only child. Did they think I was going to go to their reception without Knox? Or was he supposed to wait outside on the veranda?"

"Guess you're right. But I also guess you know you was the number one topic of gossip since you wasn't present."

Polly Ann was a member of the maid's gossip grapevine, and she'd brought home many a juicy tidbit from her friends who were housekeepers for Tweezle, Maitland, Caroline, and all of Jinx's other acquaintances. The women would talk openly, right in front of their maids, about any personal matter that crossed their minds, as if their hired help was either deaf or didn't understand English. They also figured that even if their maids could hear them, out of loyalty they'd keep the family secrets right at home where they belonged. Of course, they did not.

"I don't know which is tackier," Polly Ann would say, "them white-trash friends of yours or them big-mouth friends of mine."

"I guess that means you don't gossip about me to your friends," Jinx would chide Polly Ann.

"Heck, no. What goes on in this house stays in this house. Ain't nobody's business but ours," Polly Ann would exclaim, including herself as a bona fide member of the Collier household.

"But you're not above carrying gossip," said Jinx.

"And you ain't above listening, Miss Priss," Polly Ann said as they both collapsed in laughter.

But Polly Ann wasn't laughing about the gossip this morning.

"They called you unappreciative," Polly Ann spat indignantly, very protective of her Sugah Pie.

"Oh, don't listen to that nonsense, Polly Ann. Maitland didn't need me at her party. She just needed me as an excuse to throw a shindig and show off her finery. They were perfectly happy to party without me. And if I had shown up, who would they have had to gossip about?"

"I guess you're right about that."

"And, Polly Ann, I'm going to give them something else to chatter about. I'm going to New York with Knox."

"No, you ain't."

"Yep, I'm leaving with him this afternoon, and I don't know when I'll be back."

Polly Ann's eyes grew wide, the white showing all around, and she yelped, "Well, what about me?"

"You can just be gathering gossip while I'm gone."

"No, seriously, Sugah Pie, what am I gonna do without you?"

"I was hoping I could get you to stay out here at the house while I'm gone, sort of look after the place. I know there's lots of stuff that needs to be fixed, like that screechy screen door there, and I'll get out from under your feet and let you fix them. There's also a kitchen full of food that needs to be eaten. You can have all your gossipy old friends over to help you eat it, just as long as you take gossip but don't give any in return. You think you could do that?"

"I believe I could, Smarty Pants. But you say you don't know when you coming back?"

"That's right. But I'll call you and let you know what my plans are."

"Okay, I reckon I can do that for my Sugah Pie," Polly Ann said with her lip stuck out, as if living directly on the ocean at Tybee Island was a punishment she'd just have to endure.

"There's my best girl," bellowed Knox, as he screeched open the screen door, rushed at Polly Ann, and grabbed her in a bear hug. She returned his embrace and planted a big kiss on his cheek.

"Land sakes, look at you. I didn't think my baby could get any prettier, but you 'bout the prettiest thing I ever seen."

Knox sat on the arm of Polly Ann's chair, his arm around her shoulder, and said, "I love you, Polly Ann. Missed you so much."

She patted his leg, saying, "Me too, Baby, me too."

"Now, what you want for breakfast, and don't you tell me no lox and bagels. I drove all the way out here just to fix you a pot of grits. Now what you want to go with them grits?"

"Oh, thank the lord, Polly Ann. I am so sick of bagels and croissants and flax bran. Give me grits, grits, and more grits. And I want two eggs, over easy, four strips of bacon, and two pieces of white toast. And I want some of those peach preserves you and Mom put up. And, Polly Ann, a cup of good old Piggly Wiggly coffee, not some French roast latte mess."

"Well, you're in luck 'cause we don't have no French roast latte mess in this house. But we got all the rest of that stuff. You sit right there and talk to your mama, and I'll bring your breakfast to you on a tray."

"You're gonna spoil me, Polly Ann."

"What you mean, gonna spoil you? If I ain't already spoilt you, you can't be spoilt."

"You're right about that. There's nobody been spoiled the way you spoiled me," he said, as he helped hoist Polly Ann out of her chair so she could spoil him some more.

When Polly Ann went into the kitchen to fix Knox's breakfast, he took her place in the chair next to his mother. He really was pretty, a beautiful man. He wore just his baggy, orange flowered swim trunks and flip flops, standard summer attire for Tybee Island boys. He had fresh comb tracks in his fashionably-styled strawberry blond hair, and the matching hair on his chest glistened in the sun.

"You planning to take a dip?"

"I believe I just might. Can't get this close to that beautiful ocean without going for a little swim. I believe I'll have time before we leave."

"Sure you will. We don't have to be at Horace's for several hours."

Knox could hear Polly Ann through the screen door, humming some Baptist hymn and slamming pots and pans around the kitchen. And he could smell his breakfast long before Polly Ann returned with a tray groaning with eggs, bacon, toast, grits, preserves, Piggly Wiggly coffee, and orange juice. She placed the tray over Knox's chair arms and unfurled a linen napkin, laying it across his lap, as if he were an invalid. Or someone she wanted to spoil.

Before she could start spoon feeding him, Knox picked up his fork and said, "Thanks, Polly Ann, I can take it from here."

With each bite he closed his eyes and moaned in ecstasy.

"Oh, my god, Polly Ann, I haven't tasted anything this delicious in two years, and I've had some of New York's finest cuisine. Scrumptious," he exclaimed between heaping forkfuls.

"Course you ain't," Polly Ann said, preening.

When he had finished his breakfast and cleaned the last of the egg yolk from his plate with a scrap of toast, he leaned back and rubbed his belly. Polly Ann whisked away his tray, leaving him to moan a bit more. Her drive out to Tybee just to fix Knox's breakfast had been worth it.

"Has it been long enough?" Knox asked Jinx.

He and his mother always had this discussion.

"No, Knox. It's been only twenty minutes. You need to wait at least forty-five before you go in the water."

Knox just laughed.

"The rules are never going to change, are they, Mom?"

"Nope, not as long as you're at my house."

Knox drummed his fingers on the arm of his chair until, at the forty-five minute mark, Jinx said, "Okay, you can go now."

With that, Knox jumped up, kicked off his flip flops, sped down the steps, over the dunes, and across the sand to the ocean. He charged right into the surf and dived into the first wave to break. Jinx watched his sleek, young body as it submerged and then leapt and rode the waves to shore. Knox had always loved the sea and had braved the frigid ocean in early spring, long before any of his friends would join him. Now he was back, enjoying the surf, as if he'd never left it. After thirty minutes in the ocean, he dragged himself to shore and ran back toward the house, shaking the water from his hair as he ran. When he reached the porch, Polly Ann stepped through the kitchen door with a warm, fresh-from-the-dryer beach towel and wrapped it around his glistening body.

"You really do spoil me, Polly Ann."

"My boy can't get out of the water without a warm towel waiting for him."

"You're right, Polly Ann. You've always had a warm towel waiting."

As Knox toweled dry, Jinx said, "Well, I guess we'd better get a move on. We'll need to leave for Dad's..." She stopped herself before she could call it Dad's office and corrected herself, saying, "...Horace's office pretty soon."

Horace met Jinx and Knox with condolences and hugs, but Jinx was not in a Horace-hugging mood, even though the two of them went way back. Horace had graduated from law school with Charlie, but after graduation they'd gone their separate ways, Horace to Atlanta and Charlie back to Savannah to join their fathers' law practice. When Arch and Virgil had been killed, Charlie knew he couldn't handle the practice alone. He'd called Horace, who was eager to relocate to Savannah and partner with his former classmate. Jinx had never really warmed to Horace, but he and Charlie, in addition to being law partners, had been close friends. He also had the reputation for being the smartest lawyer in town, even smarter than Charlie. So Jinx trusted him to settle Charlie's affairs for her.

He had been a guest at Maitland's reception the day before, and the grapevine that had traveled all the way to Polly Ann by the end of the evening reported that Horace had been one of the most vocal attendees when it came to discussing Jinx's absence.

"We missed you yesterday at Maitland's."

"So I hear. My ears were burning. Apparently, I'm most unappreciative."

Horace's face reddened with embarrassment, and Knox turned to the window to hide his grin. Jinx just stared at Horace and let him squirm.

"Well, now," he stammered and cleared his throat, "let's take a look at what we have here. Just a few things for you to sign so we can get started settling Charlie's estate."

Jinx sat at the huge table in the conference room, the same table she and Charlie had played under when they were young, the spot where they first said to each other, *I'll pick you up, you'll pick me up, and we'll go up together.* The old table had aged and weathered, become scarred from decades of use, but it still held the nostalgia of Charlie and Jinx's childhood.

"Sign right here," Horace said, shaking Jinx from her memories before she could dissolve into tears. He was pointing to the papers, and she signed by his finger without even reading what she was signing. Then flipping through the sheaf, he said, "And right here at the X. I think that's all, just the two places."

Jinx did as Horace instructed and said, "Do I need to know what I've signed, Horace?"

"Well, they're just documents pertaining to your position as executrix of Charlie's estate and your appointment of me as your legal representative. But if you'd feel more comfortable reading them, that would be just fine."

With a dismissive wave of her hand, Jinx said, "No, Horace, I don't think I need to read all that legal mumbo jumbo. I trust you to do right by Charlie and me."

"I will, Jinx. You know I will. Charlie was my dearest friend. I'd never do anything to hurt his family," Horace said, his voice cracking.

Jinx understood that Horace had loved Charlie like a brother and was grieving over his death, just as everyone else in Savannah. But to avoid having another weeper on her hands, she said abruptly, "Is that all, Horace?"

"For now, it is," Horace told her, pulling a linen handkerchief from his back pocket, sniffing loudly, and rubbing his eyes. "If there's anything else I need, I can just give you a call or run papers out to Tybee for you to sign," he said, careful to avoid eye contact with Jinx.

"That won't work, Horace. You see, I'm leaving town this afternoon."

"Leaving town?"

"Yes, and I'm not sure when I'll be back."

"May I ask where you're going, just in case I need to reach you?"

"Oh, Horace, you know very well you can reach me on my cell at any time, regardless of where I am. You really don't need to know where I'm going."

Horace smiled sheepishly.

"But since you asked and won't be satisfied until I tell you, I'm going to New York."

"Okay, then, let me see, yes, I do have your cell. I'll call. Yes, I'll call if I have any questions or any information I need to pass on to you."

He stood, bowed slightly at the waist, too uncomfortable to hug Jinx good-bye.

"Bye, Jinx. Bye, Knox. I hope you have a safe trip."

Jinx headed for the office door but stopped short, turned to Horace, and said, "Ready, set, go!"

"What does that mean?" asked Horace.

"The timer has started. See how fast you can spread the word around Savannah that Jinx Collier is going to New York."

When Jinx and Knox reached the street, they clung to each other and burst out laughing.

"Oh, Mom, I wish I'd had a picture of Horace's face when you called him out. That was priceless. You've gotten real sassy, gir'frien'," Knox said and snapped his fingers.

His duffle bag slung over one shoulder, Knox rolled Jinx's luggage down the street to Dinah's Café. They had just enough time for a shrimp burger and slaw before hailing a cab to the airport.

NEW YORK, NEW YORK

Eight

Until their plane touched down at LaGuardia Airport, Jinx had forgotten how much she loved New York. She loved the tall buildings; she loved the architecture; she loved the noise; she loved the speeding taxis; she loved the smells from the street vendors' carts; she loved the museums; she loved plays on Broadway; she loved the way New Yorkers moved with such urgency.

And she loved the fashion. It was so sophisticated compared to the clothes she bought at Needham's Department Store back home. Oh, sure, she shopped in Atlanta, but even Atlanta clothes seemed so prissy and almost child-like compared to New York fashion. The clothes she saw in New York seemed so...so edgy. That's what they were to Jinx—edgy. She was already envisioning regular trips to visit Knox in New York, so she planned to buy herself some of those knee-high stiletto boots and a huge fur coat to brave the cold New York winters. She had needed neither boots nor fur in the mild coastal Georgia winters. She welcomed an excuse to need both.

Charlie used to take Jinx to New York once a year—to shop, to visit museums, and to take in a few Broadway plays. They'd stay at the Waldorf Astoria, walking distance from shopping, Central Park, museums, Broadway. It was the highlight of her year. One of the girls, usually Caroline, would keep Knox while Charlie and Jinx flew off for their long weekends. It was hard to drag Charlie away from his clients, but he loved their trips to New York as much as Jinx did. After days of shopping and sightseeing, Jinx would dress in the new clothes Charlie had bought for her on Fifth Avenue, and they'd spend the evening on Broadway. After plays they'd dine at a fine restaurant or head back to the Waldorf for room service in bed. The weekends were carefree, romantic, and sexy.

The two had not been to New York since Knox's move to the City two years before.

Jinx and Knox elbowed their way through the airport, and she smiled as bustling travelers jostled her and screamed, "Move it! I don't have all day!"

It was so much more candid than the southern counterpart.

"'Scuse me."

"Oh, no, 'scuse me."

"My fault."

"No, go ahead."

"You first."

"Oh, no, I think you were here before I was."

New York honesty—how refreshing!

They made their way through the urgent, impatient crowd to the baggage claim.

"There, the black one, right there," Jinx yelled and pointed.

"Mom, they're all black. Which black one is it?"

"The one with the pink and green polka dot luggage tag, Knox."

"Oh, of course, I should have known."

Knox grabbed Jinx's bag as he saw his own whiz by. He watched it travel around the belt till it was, once again, within reach and grabbed it quickly before others could elbow him aside or claim it as their own.

"Got 'em. You okay?" he asked his mother, who was smoothing her dress and tamping down her jostled hair.

"Think so," she answered, gulping for breath. "This is, well...exciting."

"I've got the bags. You just hold on to me. Okay?"

"Okay."

So as Knox prepared to take off through the teeming crowd, Jinx grabbed a handful of her son's shirt and held on tight. Locked together, they made their way to the curb and the long line of cabs. Knox raised his hand and waited patiently as others shoved him and his mother aside and grabbed taxi after taxi.

"I'm still too polite, Mom. One of these days I'll get the hang of it," Knox chuckled as a cab pulled up and he finally grabbed the door handle before anyone else had a chance. "Mine," he bellowed and laughed.

The cabbie hopped out, grabbed their bags, and slung them into the trunk as Knox helped his mother into the rear seat and then followed.

Back in the driver's seat, the cabbie turned to Knox and said, "Where to?"

Knox gave him his Upper West Side address, and, without responding, the driver set the meter and took off like a jet, slamming his passengers against the seat back. Whizzing in and out of traffic, honking his horn, screeching to a halt at lights, he left Jinx wide-eyed and clutching Knox's arm. To divert her attention from the terrifying ride, Jinx tried to take in the sights. New York flew by in a blur, though, as her head whipped side to side. When, thirty-five minutes later, they pulled up in front of Knox's home, Jinx was dry mouthed and rigid with fright.

Knox patted his mother on the arm, chuckled, and said, "Welcome to New York, Mom."

The cab driver jumped out, still without saying a word, hauled the luggage out of the trunk, plopped it onto the sidewalk, and stuck out his hand. Knox paid him and watched him hop back into his cab and disappear into the traffic.

"This is where you live?"

"Yes, ma'am. Right there on the first floor," said Knox, pointing to the windows to the right of the entry.

"Oh, my goodness, Darlin', it's beautiful. I've always wanted to visit an old New York brownstone. I never dreamed my son would be living in one. It looks like it's right out of a movie, you know, one of those cute romantic comedies."

"I was real lucky to find this place. I can't wait for you to see it."

As Knox was gathering their bags, the door to their building opened, and a young woman struggling with a jogging stroller and a small child muscled her way out. Knox abandoned their bags, leaving Jinx alone on the sidewalk, and rushed to the woman's aid.

"Just a sec, Mom. I'll be right back," he said over his shoulder and, to the young woman, he said, "hold on, Rebecca, let me help with that," as he bounded up the stairs.

"Oh, Knox, you're a life saver," said Rebecca, as Knox held the door and grabbed the stroller.

Before he could maneuver the stroller down the stairs, the little girl was hopping up and down, arms stretched upward, chanting, "Knox, Knox, Knox!"

Once Knox had the stroller safe on the sidewalk, he whisked the child up into his arms, kissed her on the cheek, and said, "How's my favorite girl today?"

The little girl just squealed and wrapped her arms around Knox's neck.

"Mom, I want you to meet my neighbors. They live right across the hall. This is Rebecca Eberhard, and this little angel is her daughter, Amelia."

"Hi, Mrs. Collier. I'm so glad to meet you," Rebecca said, extending her hand. "Welcome to New York. I was so sorry to hear about your husband."

"Thank you, Rebecca. It's nice to meet you and nice to be back in New York."

"We're so fortunate to have Knox and Tony as neighbors," Rebecca said, resting her hand on Knox's arm and smiling up at him. "They are godsends. And, as you can see, Amelia is very attached to your son."

Jinx smiled as Amelia eyed her shyly, stuck her thumb in her mouth, and put her head on Knox's shoulder. Knox laid his cheek on her dark curly head and squeezed her close. Jinx's heart hurt to think that Knox would never experience fatherhood. He seemed a natural.

"Amelia, this is my mommy," Knox said, pulling Jinx close and circling her with his free arm.

Amelia took her thumb from her mouth and, with her head still on Knox's shoulder, smiled cunningly and waved her chubby hand at Jinx.

Yes, Knox was a natural.

"Well, Kiddo," said Rebecca, "we'd better be on our way. Hop in your stroller, and we'll be off." And to Jinx she said, "We're jogging to Central Park. It's just at the end of this street. Once you get settled, I hope you'll join us."

"Sounds nice. I'd like that," Jinx said.

"Well, bye. Nice meeting you."

And Jinx watched her first New York acquaintances turn and jog down the tree-lined street toward Central Park.

Grabbing their bags, Knox said, "Ready to meet Tony?"

Without responding, Jinx just smiled, stood on tiptoe, and kissed

Knox on the cheek.

"We're home," Knox called as he unlocked the door and waved his mother into his and Tony's apartment.

"Welcome," Tony bellowed as he approached them, extending his hand toward Jinx, smiling broadly.

He was gorgeous, much more handsome than the picture she had seen on the Internet. She could understand how Knox had been attracted to him. He was tall. Well, Knox was tall—about six-two—but Tony was several inches taller. He was also tan and muscular. He wore his jet-black hair cut short, neatly styled. His smile was warm and inviting, and he showed straight, sparkling white teeth, surely the product of several years of braces. But his true beauty shone from his eyes. They were big and so dark that they appeared as though they didn't have pupils. When he smiled and flashed those perfect snow-white teeth, his eyes smiled, as well.

"Thank you for coming, Mrs. Collier," Tony said, grasping her hand in both of his, making contact with his beautiful black eyes. "I've so wanted to meet you. Knox has told me so much about you. And I'm so, so sorry about Mr. Collier. I wish I could have met him."

"Thank you for your hospitality, Tony," Jinx said, warmed by his gracious, welcoming manner. "But, please, do call me Jinx."

"If you'd like, then Jinx it is," Tony said and smiled broadly.

"Now, you two go put your things away and rest up. You've had a long day. I have dinner under control. Nothing fancy, just spaghetti. I'll call you when it's ready."

"Thanks, Tony," said Knox, reaching over and giving him a brisk, one-armed hug. Then smiling, he said, "It's good to be home."

"Good to have you home," Tony said, returning the hug.

"Come on, Mom, I'll show you to your room," Knox said, as he wheeled her bag down the hall and Tony returned to the kitchen to finish putting together their spaghetti dinner.

Jinx's room, one of two spare bedrooms with a shared bath, was small but comfy. With just enough room for a single bed and a small dresser, it was perfect for Jinx.

"Make yourself at home, Mom."

"Thanks, Knox. It's great."

"I'm so glad you're here. I want you to stay as long as you want."

"I know, Sweetie. But let's just take it a day at a time. Okay?"

"Okay, Mom."

"I'm just going to put my things away and rest until Tony calls us to supper. I mean dinner."

And the two southerners chuckled.

Knox and Tony had no dining table, so the three ate their spaghetti and tossed salad at the bar. Their only other choice was sitting on the futon in the living room, their plates balanced on their knees. The bar seemed more civilized. Jinx sat between the young men and, much to her surprise and delight, soon felt comfortable with Tony. Knox had always been warm and welcoming, but she had never met a more gracious host than Tony. He was quick-witted and told stories so funny he had Knox and Jinx snorting and gasping for breath. After dinner, while Knox washed the dishes, Jinx and Tony remained at the bar and chatted, as if they were old friends catching up.

Knox had told Tony all about his parents, but Jinx knew nothing of Tony, except that he was a fireman and her son loved him.

"I grew up on Long Island. I have two older brothers and two older sisters. That makes me the baby. We had a really close-knit Italian family with lots of aunts and uncles and cousins. Both my mom and dad's parents lived in Brooklyn. In fact, my folks grew up on the same Brooklyn street and were childhood sweethearts. They married the week after they graduated from high school. Two weeks later my dad was in the Army at basic training in Fort Benning, Georgia."

He smiled wistfully, and Jinx detected a sadness as he talked of the young lovers who would become his parents.

"After a tour of duty in Vietnam, Dad came back to Brooklyn to work in a furniture store and go to college at night on the G.I. Bill. When his employers wanted to sell their struggling business, Dad scrimped and saved to buy it. He rebuilt it and became very successful. He now has eleven locations and runs television commercials all over New York and New Jersey. He's known as Furniture Giant."

"Wow, that's quite a success story, Tony."

"Yeah, both my mom and dad are real smart, but they've worked very hard to get where they are."

Mr. Colletti's success had bought his family an enormous faux Tudor mansion on Long Island Sound with high-end, gas-guzzling automobiles lining the driveway. They had a huge swimming pool, and the rolling lawn sloped down to the Sound. Their home was the site of all the weekly Colletti family get-togethers.

"My sisters and brothers all studied business at Columbia so they could join Dad in the company. Dad was hoping I'd do the same, but I wanted to become a New York fire fighter instead."

"Good for you, Tony."

"I was sixteen on 9/11. I'd gotten twelve stitches in my head the day before, when I got sacked and cleated in a football game. Mom, like the protective, worrisome mother that she was, insisted that I stay home from school the next day."

"Why, I certainly understand that, Tony," Jinx said. "Any mother would have done the same."

"Well, I was eating Fruit Loops—for some reason, I'll never forget that I was eating Fruit Loops—and Mom was puttering around the kitchen in her housecoat and slippers. She had turned on the small TV on the kitchen counter, and we were sort of listening to the Today show while we chatted. We saw the first plane fly into the tower. My mom's youngest brother, Anthony—I was named after my Uncle Anthony—was a New York fireman. He reported to the Twin Towers. We were still watching at three o'clock when Mom's other brother, my Uncle Alonzo, called. Uncle Anthony had been in the second tower when it collapsed. He had gotten three groups—forty-three people in all—out of the second tower and was going back for a fourth."

Tony's expression saddened when he said, "That day I decided not to follow my sisters and brothers into the family business. I wanted to be a fireman to honor my Uncle Anthony. If Dad was disappointed, he never let on. Both he and Mom supported my decision to join the New York Fire Department."

Jinx just patted Tony's arm and smiled.

"But they did not support my being gay. They just can't accept that, Jinx. For a long time they pretended that Knox and I were just friends, calling Knox Tony's good buddy. Finally, I insisted they accept the truth. They couldn't take it. They turned their backs on us. It's just the way they were raised. I love them, and I'm sure they love me. They just can't change. I hope you won't hold it against them."

Jinx's face flamed as she recalled how she and Charlie had abandoned Knox altogether. She noticed that her hand was still resting on Tony's arm and yanked it away, as if the truth had blistered her. She would never forgive herself for cleaving to her husband when it meant wounding their only child. The truth did, indeed, burn.

"Oh, I understand. I understand all too well. And, Tony, please believe me when I say that I accept that Knox is gay. But it will take a while for me to get comfortable with the two of you having a relationship."

Jinx could feel the tension between her and Tony build when she said it, but it was true. She was uncomfortable seeing her son and another man living as a couple, and she felt that she had to get her feelings out in the open—let them know exactly where she stood.

"But I accept that you are adults and can make your own decisions. All I ask is that you be patient with me while I come to grips with it."

Tony pursed his lips and nodded and said, "Sure, Jinx, I understand."

Once Knox finished the dishes, he made a pot of coffee. He put the pot and mugs and cream and sugar on a tray, and the three moved their conversation to the living room.

As Jinx doctored her coffee, she glanced around the room. "This place is fabulous, though it's not at all what I'd expected in a brownstone apartment. How in the world did you find it?"

"Well" Knox told her, "it belongs to Ennis Worthy, one of the museum's most generous donors. He was living here when his mother died and left him the family home on Fifth Avenue. So he moved back home, leaving this place empty. I met him at the museum shortly after coming to the city. He was looking for a tenant. I was looking for a reasonably-priced place to live. I think he took pity on the new kid and cut me a really good deal."

"How lucky for you. It's a wonderful place."

"He'd like to sell it. Tony and I are hoping to buy it one day."

"That would be nice, Knox."

"I know it doesn't look like your usual brownstone apartment, but Ennis did a whole lot of work on it. He knocked down a bunch of walls and made this one big room," Knox said, sweeping his arms around the expansive space. "I think it used to be three separate rooms—living room, dining room, and kitchen. In addition to being a benefactor of MoMA, he was also an art collector, so he wanted to create that big wall over there to display his collection."

Jinx set her mug back on the tray, stood, and crossed the room.

Glancing at the wall of paintings, she said, "I see y'all have amassed quite a collection yourselves. It looks as if all of these were painted by the same artist. Right?"

"Yes, the painter is our best friend."

"Well, he is very talented. I love his use of color. It's so bold, so passionate. I can understand why you'd want to own his work."

"Her work. The artist is a she. Her name is Liz Houston. And she is as beautiful and wonderful as her paintings."

And Tony added, "She is wonderful in every way. And funny. And talented. We are blessed to have her in our life."

Jinx could tell that this Liz Houston was a very special woman, indeed, and asked them, "Well, how did you meet this wonderful friend?"

Knox said, "I was leaving the museum one afternoon and passed a group of street artists. This one artist's work caught my eye. I stopped to look, met Liz, and fell in love. I brought her home to meet Tony that very day."

"And she's never left," added Tony.

"Well, I give you props for your taste in art," said Jinx, scanning the room, "but I can't say much for your taste in furnishings. Who in the world is your decorator? John Belushi? This place looks like Animal House."

Knox and Tony's home really was a fabulous space, but they had furnished it with a futon, two University of Georgia bean bag chairs, an enormous flat-screen TV, and tables that looked like orange crates. They were grown men, yet they were living like frat boys.

"Well, Mom, when I came to New York, I was fresh out of grad school. I hadn't gotten my first paycheck and didn't have money for furniture. This was the best I could do. Of course, the expensive flat-screen was a must, even if furniture was not. And once I settled in, I just put decorating on the back burner. I was busy with my career, and then, of course, Tony came along."

With that, Jinx saw Knox glance toward Tony, and both young men smiled warmly.

"And though we're not quite yet in the position to buy the place, we can, at least, spruce it up a bit. But we just don't know where to start."

"Don't know where to start? I thought gay men had good taste. What happened to you?"

Knox laughed and said, "You'd think that between my being gay and having an interior designer for a mother, I'd have gotten the decorating gene. But, as you can see, that gene is broke. So, help, please."

Jinx was already decorating the place in her mind, even though she thought, perhaps, they were just trying to make her feel welcome, give her some busy work to do while she was there. But she didn't care. She'd take the opportunity, no matter how she got it. She relished the idea of getting her hands and her creativity on this wonderful place, but redecorating would have to wait a bit. First she needed to shower and rest—for about a month. She was tired and emotionally spent. She also wanted to rekindle her relationship with her son before she tackled a major project. And Knox and Tony's home was going to be a major project, indeed.

And, of course, there was the issue of coming to grips with and grieving her husband's death. Jinx's head hurt. And her heart hurt. How was she going to get through it?

"I'll be delighted to help," she said, "but not tonight. I'm whipped. Let me sleep on it, and then I'll think about tackling paint chips and fabric swatches."

"No rush," said Knox, "but the job is yours if you want it, whenever you want it."

Jinx hugged Knox good night and then approached Tony. He smiled and opened his arms and broke the ice.

"Thank you, Tony," was all she said, as the two embraced.

"Good night, boys," Jinx said, as she headed for her bedroom, slipped out of her clothes, and pulled her nightgown over her head. So exhausted was she from her harrowing day, she didn't even have the energy to shower. She'd save that until morning. She climbed into bed and pulled the covers up to her chin.

Nine

B ut Jinx couldn't sleep. Once alone in the stillness of the strange room, the events of the past week washed over her, leaving her wracked with pain and grief.

She lay in the unfamiliar bed, clutching her sides for comfort. But the clutching did little to alleviate the gut-wrenching pain. She needed her Charlie, but Charlie was the reason for the pain. She didn't need the Charlie who had just died and left her alone; she hadn't needed that Charlie for some time. She needed the Charlie of years ago. She needed the Charlie who could touch her heart and heal her soul.

She needed the Charlie who had carried her over the threshold into a mountain cabin and had laid her lovingly on the bed. She needed the Charlie who had joined her in the shower and had touched that hidden part in her that made her laugh and cry at the same time. She needed the Charlie who had held her through her grief when their parents were killed, refusing to let her go until he was certain she could survive without his arms around her. She needed the Charlie who promised that he'd always pick her up.

Now her soul heaved with anguish. If only she could spoon with Charlie in that strange bed. That would calm the heaving. She could feel Charlie touching and caressing her and whispering tenderly in her ear as she buried her face in the pillow to muffle her sobs.

In the beginning Charlie and Jinx had been clumsy and playful, but they were never embarrassed or awkward when it came to their sexuality, their intimacy. They were eager to explore each other's bodies, anxious to engage in love making with abandon. They trusted each other completely and were always willing to try new things. Some things made them giggle uncontrollably, but even the giggling added to the fullness of the experience. They had had a wonderful, rich sex life—until Charlie had banished their only child.

But on that night while Jinx lay clutching, she remembered only the good times—the caressing, the tenderness, the longing, the love.

That's when she heard it—those sounds she remembered from so long ago. They were sounds of love, those same sounds she and Charlie had made for most of the years of their life together. But where were the sounds of love coming from? Were they in her head? Was she dreaming? Then she realized they were coming from the other side of the wall, the wall that connected her to Knox and Tony's bedroom. Her son and his partner sounded just like she and Charlie had sounded. Knox and Tony sounded like two people in love.

Jinx buried her face deeper into the pillow and clutched her sides harder as she wept for the loss of her Charlie and for the understanding of her child and the man he loved.

When Jinx awoke the following morning, she smelled coffee. She tried to get out of bed but found that her body ached from the clutching and sobbing and the understanding of the night before. She put one foot gently on the floor and then the other, stood on rubbery legs, and moved slowly to the bathroom. When she looked into the vanity mirror, she saw that she had cried her eyes into puffy slits. She turned on the shower, slid out of her nightgown, and stepped into the steaming stream of water, where she stood motionless while the spray resurrected her. Once she felt human, Jinx stepped out, toweled dry, and wrapped herself in her terrycloth robe. She moisturized her face, brushed her teeth, ran a comb through her hair, and headed for the kitchen.

There she found Knox and Tony, side by side, preparing breakfast, chatting comfortably, smiling at each another. Jinx approached Knox and gave him a big hug and a peck on the cheek. Then she turned, put her arms around Tony's neck, and gave him a gentle hug and a kiss. Both boys smiled and returned to their breakfast preparation.

Over his shoulder Tony said, "Jinx, would you make us a pot of coffee? The bag is in that cupboard over there," he said, pointing his spatula in the direction of the coffee before returning his attention to the scrambled eggs.

They ate their eggs and bacon lined up at the bar, just as they'd eaten their dinner the night before.

As soon as they finished breakfast, Tony said, "This has been fun, but I gotta run. If you don't mind, I'll leave the dishes for you guys to wash."

Tony grabbed his jacket from the hook by the door, gave Knox and Jinx quick hugs, and hurried out the door, calling over his shoulder, "I'll try to be home by six. Let's order Chinese. You guys have a good day."

Though Tony had to return to work that morning, Knox had planned to take a few days to help his mother settle in. His employer was most understanding and accommodating, and mother and son took their time together to get reacquainted and for Jinx to get re-acclimated to New York life. They strolled the streets and stopped in neighborhood shops, so that Knox could introduce his mother to the local business owners. They walked to Central Park where they ate lunches from vendor carts and sat on park benches, watching the tourists take in the sights. And in those few days mother and son shared two years of missed memories.

But when it was time for him to leave, to return to work, Knox reluctantly said, "You sure you're going to be okay?"

"Of course, Knox. I'm a big girl."

"You know how to reach me if you need anything."

"Knox, you've shown me the deli, the grocery, the dry cleaner, the drug store. I can walk to Central Park, as well as the museum, if I'm feeling extra energetic. I know how to hail a cab and locate the subway if I need anything beyond your neighborhood. I'm sure I'll be able to find my way around. You need to get back to work, get back to your real life. Now, shoo."

Knox picked up his briefcase, said, "Are you sure?" one more time, and eased out the door.

Jinx went to the kitchen to wash the few breakfast dishes and pour herself another cup of coffee. She had already showered and made her bed. She had just nine hours to kill before Knox and Tony's return. She padded to the living room in her bare feet, picked up the Architectural Digest she had bought at the corner news stand, and sat on the futon, propping her feet on one of those crates Knox and Tony called a coffee table. Just as she got settled, her cell phone rang. Thinking it was Knox checking on her one last time, she hopped up and crossed to the bar to retrieve her phone.

"Knox?"

"Jinx, this is Horace Gresham."

When Jinx heard Horace's voice, she froze. She dreaded talking with him, but she knew she'd have to, sooner or later. She figured she might as well make it sooner and get it over with.

"Hey, Horace."

"Hey, Jinx, I've been working on Charlie's estate and thought I ought to report in, sort of bring you up to speed."

"So report," she said dismissively.

"Well, you probably knew that Charlie was heavily insured and left you financially secure. You'll never want for a thing for the rest of your life."

"Horace, I was financially secure before Charlie died. And, yes, I knew that he carried several life insurance policies. Is that what you called to tell me?"

"Well, no, Jinx. There's more. Did you know that Charlie had taken out a life insurance policy naming Knox his beneficiary?"

"No, but it doesn't surprise me. Knox was Charlie's child. I'm aware that Charlie purchased life insurance when Knox was a baby."

"Jinx, I'm not talking about the hundred-thousand-dollar policy he bought when Knox was born. I'm talking about the one he bought twenty months ago—shortly after Knox left for New York."

Jinx was confused.

"You mean Charlie took out an insurance policy naming Knox beneficiary after he moved to New York?"

Horace said, "Yes, he did. I just ran across it when I was reviewing some of his files. And, Jinx?"

"What, Horace."

"The policy is worth two million dollars."

Silence.

"Jinx, are you still there? Did you hear me?"

"Yes, Horace, I heard you. Thanks for calling."

And, without another word, Jinx ended the call.

Charlie really had loved their son. He had not been able to

accept Knox's lifestyle, but he had not forgotten him altogether, as Jinx had believed. He had loved Knox and had taken care of him in the only way he thought he could. Only then did Jinx consider the turmoil and anguish Charlie must have felt, torn between his only child and the beliefs he had followed since birth. What a struggle that must have been. Yet he never complained. He just bore his struggle in silence.

While their fickle friends gossiped about her and Charlie's gay son and told Jinx how selfish and cruel Knox was being to his parents, Charlie never responded. He did not criticize Knox or call him selfish. Nor did he say that Knox was making a choice, a choice that he would soon abandon and come to his senses. He just said his beliefs would not allow him to accept homosexuality. He was merely sticking to his convictions. His son suffered; his wife suffered; he suffered. But not once did he abandoned his core beliefs. Charlie Collier was a man of his word, regardless of the consequences.

Jinx crawled onto the futon, curled into a ball, and for the second time in less than a week, cried racking sobs. She spent most of the day crying, purging two years of pain and anger and sorrow. By the time Knox returned home from work, Jinx was exhausted and cried dry.

When Knox came through the door, Jinx met him and said, "I've done it."

Knox said, "Uh oh, Mom, what have you done?"

"I've forgiven your father."

"What happened?"

When Jinx told her child that his father had taken out a large insurance policy naming him the beneficiary after his move to New York, Knox bent forward and began weeping. Jinx put her arms around him and gathered him to her, comforting him as he cried for the father who had banished him but hadn't forgotten him altogether.

"But, Mom, I'd have rather had him than his millions."

"I know that, Honey, but he did what he felt he had to do."

"He did love me, didn't he, Mama?" Knox asked, needing desperately to believe.

"Yes, Darlin', Daddy loved you. He just had a conflict that he couldn't resolve. I know that's no excuse, but he did the best he could. We can't expect more than a person's best."

Ten

After flopping from futon to beanbag chair and exploring the neighborhood for two weeks, Jinx told Knox, "I have to decide what I'm going to do with my life. I can't live in your guest room indefinitely."

Knox told his mother, "There's no rush, Mom."

But Jinx said, "Well, yes, there is, Knox. I have a house that is sitting idle and mail and bills that are piling up and need to be addressed. Also, I'm sure I should be putting in an appearance at Horace's office from time to time. I'd rather kiss a snake on the lips than go back to Georgia, but it's my home. I have to face it."

"Mom, Horace can take care of Dad's business. If he has questions, he can call. If he needs your signature, he can send papers to you. As for the house, Polly Ann is taking care of it, and she can box up all of your mail and send it to you. You can take care of everything from right here."

"Knox, I have to face home at some time. I hate that psycho-babble term closure, but I think that's what I need. I have to go back and see for myself that your father is really gone. The last few years were strained for your dad and me. But, Knox, I loved him dearly, and his death has ripped my heart to pieces. I have to go back and feel our home the way it used to be when we were happy and so in love. You understand that, don't you?"

"Of course, I do, Mom. I want you to stay, but I won't try to persuade you to do something that you're not happy or comfortable doing. But if you don't find what you're looking for when you get back to Tybee, our door will always be open. And, remember, you still need to decorate this place."

"Don't worry, I haven't forgotten. I can't wait to get my hands on it. It'll be fun. I just can't do it right now."

"Oh, by the way," Knox said, "Rebecca just told me this morning that her husband is being transferred to North Carolina, and they'll be leaving in two weeks. Once they move out, the owner plans to sell the place. I thought you might be interested."

"Knox, hold on. I can't just up and move to New York. And I certainly can't move across the hall from you. You and Tony need your privacy. What's more, I'm just not sure where I belong right now. I need some time by myself, to think about it and clear my head. But when I decide what's right for me, you'll be the first to know. I promise."

"Mom, I won't pressure you to become a New Yorker, but I'd love having you across the hall. I've missed you so much. But I'll accept whatever decision you make," he said, taking his mother in his arms and hugging her to him.

"Well, thank you, Darlin', but I have to go home now. I'll be back, though. I promise."

"I understand. Really I do, Mom," Knox said.

Jinx awoke each morning, thinking, This is the day, the day I must go home.

But even though she knew she had to return, she felt as if she were wearing lead boots, boots that kept her planted in New York, unable to face her past.

Then her phone rang.

"Hello?"

"Yoo hoo!"

With only a yoo hoo Jinx knew it was Blue, one of the last people on earth she wanted to hear from. That made Jinx sad because Blue had once been one of her closest friends. She was such a cut-up, so much fun to be around. She could be put up to doing anything crazy the others dared her to do. Race naked down the beach? Blue would do it. Chug a beer in ten seconds? Blue would do it. Steal condoms (out of curiosity, not out of need) from the Rexall drug store? Blue would do it. But she had sided with Charlie against Jinx, and Jinx no longer found her fun-loving and charming. Jinx was no longer in the mood for her ditziness.

Blue and her husband, Roderick, had outgrown the charming cottage their grands had given them as a wedding gift and had bought an old run-down estate on the outskirts of Savannah that Blue swore was once a grand plantation, though there were no records to indicate that it ever had been a plantation of any kind, grand or otherwise. Blue and Roderick were distant cousins, but apparently not distant enough. They had four children with straw-colored hair, pale, close-set eyes, and were all very slow on the uptake. And even though Blue had once been her dear friend, her whole pretentious, inbred family and her phony friendship just made Jinx's skin crawl. And there she was, yoo hooing into Jinx's ear. Jinx was sorry she hadn't let the call go to voicemail.

"When are you comin' home, Jinx? We neeeeeed you!"

The Girls didn't need her. They needed to weep all over her and use her for her decorating expertise.

"I haven't decided, Blue."

And even if Jinx had decided, she wouldn't have told big-mouth Blue. When the time came, she would creep into town under cover of darkness and not alert a soul that she was returning. She just wasn't interested in seeing anyone, especially The Girls.

"But you just can't stay up there too long."

"Any why is that, Blue?"

"Well, we don't want any of that old nasty New York Yankeeness rubbing off on our Jinx," Blue said, all whiney and nasally.

Jinx bit her tongue and took a very deep breath.

"Blue, my son is a New Yorker."

"Oh, fiddle, stop being so silly. You know he's not. Knox is just trying to find himself. He'll come to his senses 'fore too long. He'll realize where his roots are, and he'll come on back home to Georgia and marry himself a nice little southern girl and have a bunch of pretty blond-headed babies."

"Well, Blue, as I told you, I haven't decided what my plans are. But I gotta run. There's someone at the door."

"Oh, Jinx, be careful. You just never know who might be knocking at your door up there in New York. It's a dangerous place, you know."

"Blue, I really appreciate your concern, but I believe I can handle myself."

"Yeah, that's what they all say, but…"

"Okay, Blue, I'll be careful. I promise. Now, bye."

If it were possible to slam down a cell phone, Jinx would have done so. Short of that, she poked END so hard she bruised her fingertip.

So angered was she by Blue's call, she realized that the time had come. Closure time. She crammed the phone into her pocket and headed for her bedroom, where she crouched and dragged her suitcase from beneath her bed. She unzipped and opened it on her bed, turned to her chest, and pulled out the drawers, one at a time. She tossed in clothes, shoes, and cosmetics, not sure what she was packing and not caring at all.

Once her suitcase was full, she called American Airlines and bought a ticket to Georgia on a flight that would leave LaGuardia in just three hours. She needed to hurry, but first she needed to call Knox.

"Knox?"

"Yeah, hey, Mom. You okay?"

"I'm fine, Honey. Listen, I'm going home this afternoon."

"But, Mom…"

"Wait, Knox, let me finish. I promise I'll be back to decorate. I'm just not certain when. But I really need to get on back home and take care of business. And I need for you to understand."

"Sure, Mom, I understand. I just don't want you to leave."

"And I appreciate that, Knox. Really I do. But I have to. And I'll call you when I get home."

"Okay, Mom."

Jinx rolled her suitcase into the hall, locked the apartment door, and headed for the street, where she raised her arm. A yellow cab shot out of the traffic and screeched to a halt directly in front of her. In a flash the driver emerged from the taxi, rushed to Jinx's side, flung her suitcase into the trunk, and was back in the driver's seat before she could settle herself in the back. Time was money.

The cab driver was somewhat attractive, in an Omar Sharif sort of way. His taxi, though, smelled of an overly-pungent meal, full of exotic spices—a dish Jinx was positive she would not like. It certainly didn't smell like fried chicken, okra, and Polly Ann's biscuits—about the only things she missed of Georgia.

Pseudo Omar sped through the traffic at the speed of sound, weaving in and out, out-racing stop lights and dodging pedestrians. Jinx clutched the door handle in abject terror, remembering her careening ride from the airport when she came to New York with Knox, and prayed throughout the journey.

Once they reached the airport, Omar hurled Jinx's suitcase to the curb, collected his hefty fare, and sped off, leaving his passenger to fend for herself. Jinx wrestled her luggage through the throng of travelers, checked in, and headed down the long corridor toward her flight. She stopped by Hudson News to buy a decorating magazine and arrived at her gate with time to spare.

The flight was a breeze: one Diet Coke, one magazine, one brief layover in Atlanta, and a quick cab ride from the Savannah airport to Tybee Island, and she was home shortly after nightfall.

Jinx called Polly Ann from the cab to let her know she was on her way out to Tybee. She didn't want to startle Polly Ann and have her attack her with an iron skillet when she tried to get into her own house.

She also told Polly Ann, "And don't you tell a soul I'm coming," to which Polly Ann replied indignantly, "You think I'm gonna tell them snooty so-called friends of yours a thing? Not on yo' life."

"And not a word to that grapevine, either, okay?"

"Not a word. My lips is zipped."

"Thanks, Polly Ann, I'll see you shortly."

Polly Ann opened the front door wearing her voluminous pink flowered cotton nightgown. Until that moment Jinx had not realized how much she had missed her beloved friend. Polly Ann took Jinx in her arms just as she had done when Jinx was a little girl, and Jinx burst into tears. She also hadn't realized until then how much she had needed Polly Ann's comfort.

As Jinx cried, Polly Ann rubbed her back with her broad pink-palmed hand and crooned, "Let it go, Sugah Pie, let it go."

When she was spent, Jinx looked Polly Ann squarely in the eye and said, "Let's move to New York City."

Thanks to Blue, Jinx had decided somewhere between New York and Georgia that she and Polly Ann should become New

Yorkers, absorbing all the Yankeeness they could. There was nothing to keep her in Georgia.

It hurt her heart to admit she no longer wanted to live in her wonderful house on Tybee, but all of the cherished memories she had created there had died. Her parents had been gone for years, but a lump rose in Jinx's throat each time she pictured them laughing or dancing or lying together in the rope hammock on the porch at Tybee. But, most of all, Charlie was gone, and Jinx knew that she could never again feel his love in that house. And, of course, there was Knox, her New York son who was not going to come home to Georgia and marry a sweet southern girl and have a bunch of pretty blond-headed babies.

What about her friends? Well, they had proven whose friends they really were. What's more, she had decorated all of their homes for lunches, so they probably wouldn't be needing her services anymore. And if they did, they could just find another sucker to use. And Jinx knew, without a doubt, that she didn't want to be a member of Charle's church anymore. Mt. Moriah had seen the very last of her. So what was left? Not a thing except Polly Ann, as far as Jinx could see.

Without a moment's hesitation, Polly Ann lifted Jinx, spun her around, and whooped, "Lawd, Chile, you've lost your mind. Let's start packing."

"I'm sorry, Polly Ann. I didn't even ask if you wanted to move to New York."

"Why not? I got nothin' tying me down here. Ain't got no man to look after, thank the good lord. And my young'uns is gone. They don't give a doodly about their mama anyhow. Why, that Monette too busy living the fancy life up there in Memphis with her doctor husband. Won't even give me no grandbabies—says their lives too full for children. How can a life be too full for children? That's what life is all about—new life! And Marcus, he don't care nothin' about anything but that Army. He ain't never gonna settle down with a woman and give me grands neither. And he ain't never gonna call Savannah home again. So what I got to stay here for? My last baby just told me she moving to New York. I sure can't let her leave me behind."

And, just like that, it was settled: Jinx and Polly Ann were going to become New Yorkers. The two women did have the presence of mind, though, to realize they couldn't just pack a bag that night and take the next plane to LaGuardia.

Jinx ordered a facelift of minor repairs and paint on her beach home, while Polly Ann began plundering, boxing what they wanted to take to New York with them and tossing or donating what they no longer wanted or needed. Once her house was spit shined and perfectly staged, Jinx called Sally Jenrette, the most successful real estate agent from Savannah to Atlanta, leaving a message on her answering machine.

"Sally, this is Jinx Collier. I'm interested in putting my Tybee home on the market. I thought you might be able to help me sell it. Please give me a call when you get this message. I'm in sort of a hurry to get it listed."

Then she called Knox.

"Has that apartment across the hall from you come on the market yet?"

"Does this mean you're coming back for good, Mom?"

"If your offer is still on the table. But I don't want to crowd you, Knox."

"Nothing could make me happier. You're my family, and I want you here. But, Mom, I've found out that apartment has three bedrooms. Will that be too much room for you?"

"Not at all. Polly Ann is coming with me. We'll need to spread out, and three bedrooms will be just perfect."

"Polly Ann!" Knox whooped. "That's fantastic! How did you convince her to leave Savannah?"

Laughing, Jinx said, "Believe me, Knox, it didn't take any convincing at all. She had her bags packed and was sitting on the curb before I could say New York."

Knox said, "Let me make a call, and I'll buzz you right back."

Within minutes Jinx's phone was ringing. "The agent said he'll be listing the apartment next week and has already had about a dozen inquiries. He said he'll hold off any other buyers, though, till you've had a chance to see it. By the way, he said the place needs some work, that it's a little outdated. He did say, though, that the bones were good. I told him it sounded perfect for you. So hurry back."

Sally called Jinx just as soon as she listened to her voicemail.

"I'll take it."

"What?"

"This is Sally Jenrette, and I want your house."

"You already have a buyer?"

"Yes, me. I've coveted that beauty since I was a child and Mama would pack a picnic and take me to Tybee for the day. I'd stroll by your place and dream about how it would be to live in that wonderful home. I will not let it slip through my fingers."

Sally made what seemed to Jinx to be a very generous offer, so she didn't even bother negotiating. Eager to close this chapter of her life, Jinx booked two tickets to New York for the following weekend and left Sally to iron out the details. All that was left to do was sign the closing papers and tell the movers where to take her furniture.

She had managed to hire repairmen and movers and still keep her secret a secret. The Girls did not know that she had returned to Tybee, and they did not know of her plans to relocate to New York.

Jinx had failed, though, to consider The Mouth of the South, Sally Jenrette. She should have told Sally to keep her news quiet, but it probably wouldn't have done any good. The woman was incapable of keeping a confidence.

The following morning while she and Polly Ann were packing the last of the boxes, Blue, Tweezle, Sarah June, and Taylor came charging through her front door without knocking, fists on hips, all of them talking at a fever pitch, trying to yell over one another. Jinx couldn't understand a word from any of them, but she knew instinctively what they were suggesting. She noticed that Maitland was not with her twin sister and their friends. Jinx guessed she was still stinging over her snubbing the soirée after Charlie's funeral.

"Come sit down and stop yelling," Jinx ordered them, shoving boxes and packing supplies off the sofa and chairs.

Polly Ann, not a fan of The Girls, just sniffed, rolled her eyes, and stormed out of the room.

"What in heaven's name are you thinking, Jinx?" screeched Tweezle. "Have you taken leave of your senses?"

Not nearly so dramatic, Taylor took her hand and said, "Jinx, are you sure you want to make such a major decision and such a drastic change this soon after Charlie's passing? Don't you think you should wait a while till you've had time to grieve, time to think straight?"

"Taylor, are you suggesting that I can't think straight?" Jinx snapped.

"Why, no, Darlin', I didn't mean it that way a'tall. But I've read that one should wait a year after major events, like a divorce or a death, to make major decisions. Like a move to New York."

Taylor was the kindest and most level-headed of all her former friends, and Jinx knew she meant well. But Taylor's insinuation that she couldn't make rational decisions really pissed Jinx off.

"Thanks, Taylor, I appreciate your concern, but I really want, no, really have to do this. Knox is my family, and I need to be with him. I'm going to New York."

"But what about your mama's home?" cried Blue. "How can you let that white trash Sally Jenrette just move in? She's not even one of us. Miss Emma Frances would be spinning in her grave."

"Oh, shut up, Blue. And keep my mama out of this. It's my decision, and I can sell my home to whomever I please."

Jinx's sudden outburst made The Girls look as though they'd been slapped.

But recovering, Blue whined and stuck out her lip in a pout and said, "I'd have bought this place in a second, but you didn't even give me a chance."

Dismissing Blue, Sarah June said, "Oh, by the way, Caroline said to tell you she was sorry she couldn't come over this morning. She had her hair appointment with Ramon." Rolling her eyes and waving her hand in the air, she continued, "And you know yourself you have to book with Ramon six months out. She just couldn't cancel. You understand, don't you?"

Sure, Jinx understood. Caroline thought having her roots touched up was more important that saying good-bye to her very best friend since birth. If Jinx had not been certain about her move before, she was certain now.

"Of course, I understand. I understand very well," Jinx said, standing and indicating to The Girls that their visit had come to an end. "Please tell Caroline I understand all too well. Now, if you girls will excuse me, Polly Ann and I have a lot of packing to do," she said, spreading her arms and herding the four out the front door and closing it behind them with a loud bang.

Eleven

By the time Saturday arrived, Jinx and Polly Ann had cleaned out every cupboard, chest, and nook and had all the possessions they planned to take with them to New York packed neatly in clearly-marked boxes.

"Well, I think we've just about covered it, Sugah Pie. We're ready to roll."

Smiling, Jinx said, "I believe you're right, Polly Ann," and then clapping her hand over her mouth, exclaimed, "Polly Ann, the cars! How could we have forgotten? What are we going to do with our cars? We won't need them in New York."

Without hesitation, Polly Ann said, "Let's give 'em away."

"Really? You don't think we should sell them?"

"Nah, we know plenty folks could use 'em."

And Polly Ann was right. Charlie gave Polly Ann a new car about every four years, but all of Polly Ann's friends walked or took the bus. Poor things were exhausted before they could get to work.

"You're right, Polly Ann. Why didn't I think of that?"

"I believe I'm gonna give mine to Hattie," said Polly Ann. "That poor woman's arthritis made her so rickety she gone to walking with a cane. And that snooty Caroline don't care that she has to walk more'n a mile 'fore she gets to her place. And never once she offer to go pick her up in that big old Cadillac, when she ain't got nothin' better to do. Yeah, I'm gonna give my car to Hattie. And I'd love to see Caroline's face when she pulls up to her house in my sporty red Honda. She'll have a spasm."

"Great idea, Polly Ann. What do you think about Hilda? Do you think Hilda would want my car?"

"You kiddin'?" Polly Ann cried and threw her head back, laughing. "Who wouldn't want a new white Mercedes Benz?"

Hilda was the oldest of Polly Ann's friends. She had worked for Taylor and Maitland's mother and had been passed on to Maitland, as if she were a possession. She had loved Maitland's mama but had always thought that her daughter was a spoiled brat—which she was. But Hilda was loyal to the family and needed the work. And at her age it would have been hard for her to find another job.

But Maitland had made selfish demands of Hilda. Each morning she'd hand over her Lexus keys to Hilda, expecting her to do the grocery shopping and run all her errands. She also insisted that her maid tote her rude, disrespectful children to their soccer games and music lessons and cotillion classes. But at day's end Hilda returned the keys to Maitland before walking seven blocks to the bus stop and making three transfers before reaching her home.

"Yes, Hilda it is," smiled Jinx.

Hilda deserved a little luxury in her life, and she was about to own a car that was much finer than her employer's. Jinx, too, would have loved being around to see Hilda pull that big old car up to Maitland's mansion by the river.

The two women wept with joy over their new automobiles. Polly Ann's suggestion had been the perfect solution for the disposal of the cars they knew they couldn't take to New York. Once they'd turned the keys and titles over, Polly Ann and Jinx were really ready to head for their new home.

They picked up their suitcases, handed the keys to the house on Tybee Island to Sally, and said, "It's all yours."

They walked out the front door without looking back. Jinx felt she couldn't, for fear the memories would rip out her heart.

The flight to New York was uneventful for Jinx but was an adventure for Polly Ann, who had never flown. She bought a stale, overpriced blueberry muffin from the snack bar in the airport and vowed it was the most delicious thing she'd ever tasted. In the airport news stand she bought a Frommer's guide to New York City so she'd know something about her new home before she arrived. On the plane she ordered a cocktail, though she'd never had a cocktail in her life. She had to ask Jinx what she should get. Jinx suggested a Shirley Temple.

By the time they reached LaGuardia, Polly Ann was a self-proclaimed expert on New York City and a little tipsy from her Shirley Temple—or, perhaps, from the excitement over her new adventure.

"Did you know that the Empire State Building was built in 1929, and it is 1,454 feet high? And that building has 102 floors. Now, I'd probably be afraid to go up in that thing it's so tall."

"Is that right?" said Jinx, sort of paying attention to Polly Ann's prattling.

"Well, I'll be dang, the Statue of Liberty is made out of copper and wrought iron and the French people gave it to the United States. Lordy, I didn't know that. Guess you learn something new every day."

"You sure do, Polly Ann," said Jinx, smiling and patting her dear friend's arm.

"I want to go see the Apollo Theatre. That's in Harlem. Harlem is in Manhattan, and it was named for Haarlem in the Netherlands. Harlem is predominantly an African American area. The Apollo Theatre is where Stevie Wonder got his start in show business. When he first performed at the Apollo Theatre, he was called Little Stevie Wonder. That part about him being called Little Stevie Wonder ain't in the book. I just knew that myself."

As Polly Ann continued to consult her guide and jabber about her new-found knowledge, the two women pushed their way through the crowd to baggage claim. They had no trouble locating their bags, Jinx's with the pink and green polka dot tag and Polly Ann's red plastic suitcase wrapped with a brown leather belt for extra security. Luggage in tow, they headed to the street where they stepped directly into a cab.

Still frightened by her erratic, torpedo-like rides into the city and back to the airport, Jinx tried to remain calm so that she could soothe Polly Ann as she exclaimed all the way, "Do lawd! Lawd have mercy! Help me, Jesus!" then muttered, "Thank you, Jesus. Thank you, Jesus," when the cab pulled up in front of Knox's building and she dragged herself out and onto the curb.

As Jinx was paying the driver, Knox flew out the door and bounded down the front steps, right into Polly Ann's arms.

"Oh, Polly Ann, you came. I'm so glad. Welcome. Welcome."

"Lemme look at my baby," she said, holding Knox at arm's length. "Mmmm, mmmm, still the prettiest boy I ever saw."

She'd been telling him that since he was a toddler.

"Thanks, Polly Ann. I never tire of hearing that."

Knox gave his mother a hug, saying, "Welcome back, Mom," grabbed the luggage, and hauled it up the steps and into the building.

"Come on in, ladies, and make yourselves at home."

"Mmmmm, something smells yummy," said Jinx as she followed Knox into the apartment.

Tony emerged from the kitchen, an oven mitt on each hand, and said, "Another made-up concoction: chicken and rice with pineapple and apples. Pretty good, if I do say so."

He took Jinx in his arms and said, "So glad you're back, Jinx. We missed you."

Polly Ann stood aside, her back ramrod straight, her hands clasped tightly at her waist. She knew that Knox was living with a man, but she wasn't at all comfortable with the set-up.

"Just ain't natchel," she'd said. She loved Knox unconditionally, but she said, "You'll have to 'scuse me 'cause I'm just old fashioned. In that way."

She didn't have to explain to Knox what *in that way* meant. They'd just silently agree to disagree on the subject and leave it at that.

Then Tony removed his oven mitts and stepped toward Polly Ann, stretched out his hand, and, smiling his disarming smile, said, "Polly Ann, welcome to our home. Knox has told me so much about you. I understand you practically raised him. You did a great job."

Polly Ann felt the blood rise in her cheeks at Tony's flattery.

"He also said you're the best cook ever. Please, I hope you'll make yourself at home. Go put your things in your room, and then come tell me what I can do to make this already delicious dish even more delicious."

And Polly Ann was hooked.

Knox deposited her suitcase in the third bedroom, and once she gave her space a quick once-over and approval, she was in the kitchen barking orders and dispensing her culinary expertise before Jinx could follow Knox to her now-familiar bedroom.

Polly Ann tucked a dish towel in the waist of her slacks, calling over her shoulder, "Knox, you need to take me to the store so I can get me some aprons. I can't work like this."

Then she grabbed one of Tony's oven mitts, flung open the

oven, and yanked out the rack with the casserole. She waved her hand over the top of the dish, closed her eyes, and inhaled.

"Basil, it needs just a hint of basil. And a bay leaf, of course. Everything needs a bay leaf." And waving and inhaling once more, she said, "A little pinch of garlic and a half a onion. You got any of that stuff?"

"Sure, we have all those things. Just check right there in the spice rack and the fridge. Italians can't cook without all that stuff. Help yourself, and doctor it any way you like."

Polly Ann found what she was looking for and started dicing onions and mincing garlic. Then she grabbed spices and began shaking and stirring them into Tony's casserole.

"There, that ought to do it," she said, shoving in the oven rack and slamming the door with her knee.

Then she went rummaging in the refrigerator, pulling out greens and tomatoes and peppers and cucumbers and onions.

"How 'bout I toss up a nice salad? And we can cook that corn on the cob you got in there. That sound okay with you, Tony?"

Tony laughed. He already loved this take-charge woman. He had a good feeling the two of them were going to get along splendidly.

"Sounds fantastic. But are you sure you're up to working in the kitchen after your long trip?"

"Pffft," Polly Ann said, waving her hand, "ain't no trouble a'tall. This is what I do, Chile. Now, you just go on and talk with Knox and Jinx while I take care of this."

"I'd rather talk to you, if you don't mind. I could help you chop up the salad. And I believe I could learn a thing or two from you," he said, smiling and cutting his eyes at her.

Polly Ann gave his arm a swat and said, "You sweet talking thing, get to work on that salad, you hear?"

Tony did as he was told, and as he chopped vegetables, he marveled at the ease with which Polly Ann maneuvered the strange kitchen.

They served their plates right from the stove and took them to the living room. They sat on over-sized pillows on the floor around the large coffee table crate, rather than at the bar, so they could have a comfortable, intimate dinner conversation.

"Mmmmm, mmmm, dee-lish," said Polly Ann. Smacking her lips, she added, "The basil makes all the difference." Then smiling at

Tony she said, "'Course, the fruit along with the chicken makes a mighty tasty dish, Tony, mighty tasty."

Jinx threw back her head and laughed loudly.

"I've been fishing for such a compliment for nearly thirty years, and the best I've gotten out of her has been, 'That's pretty good,' or 'It's okay.'"

"Well," Polly Ann sniffed, "you ain't never made chicken and rice with pineapple and apples."

Tony reached over and patted Polly Ann's arm, smiled, and said, "Thanks, Polly Ann, I'm so glad you like it. But tell me how you made this corn so sweet. It's delicious."

"That's simple. You want your corn sweet, you just put a little sugar in the water."

"Well, that makes sense. Can't believe I didn't think of that."

After dinner, while Tony entertained Jinx and Polly Ann with stories of his work with the New York Fire Department, Knox washed the dishes and tidied the kitchen.

"You have to go inside them tall buildings when they're on fire?" Polly Ann asked. "That sounds dangerous. Back home the firemen just have to go up two floors, three at the most."

"Yep, that's part of the job. It's dangerous, but it's worth it if we can save a life."

"That's so brave," Polly Ann told Tony.

"You know, Polly Ann, my uncle Anthony, I was named after him, was a fireman and was killed when the Twin Towers collapsed on nine-eleven. That's why I wanted to be a fireman," Tony told her, so much sadness in his beautiful dark eyes.

"Oh, Baby, that's so sad. I hope you're careful."

"Yes, I try to be as careful as I can."

By evening's end, Polly Ann was completely taken with Tony.

As she and Jinx dragged their tired bodies down the hall to their bedrooms, she said, "I sure do understand why Knox likes that Tony so much. He's a right likeable fellow."

"Night night, Polly Ann," Jinx said, as she hugged her best friend. "Thank you for upending your life for me."

"My pleasure, Sugah Pie. Yes, it really is my pleasure. Now, you sleep tight, okay?"

"Bob Horton says he can show us the apartment today if you're interested."

Polly Ann and Jinx were eating their breakfast of toast and coffee at the bar. They were still weary from their packing and yesterday's plane trip to New York, but they both had wanted to be up to see Knox off to work. Tony had an early-morning meeting and had already left for the station. Knox was dressed, ready to head to a meeting himself.

"I'm very interested. When can we see it?"

"He said he could be over about three o'clock this afternoon. Does that suit you?"

"Sure, that sounds great."

"Well, then, I have business to tend to at the Museum, but I'll come back home before he gets here so I can take a look with you. I visited occasionally when Rebecca and Josh lived there, but I didn't pay too much attention to the details. And it was also full of their furniture and baby toys. I'm anxious to see it empty, to get the real lay of the land."

"I can't wait to see it either. I really hope it'll work for Polly Ann and me."

After Knox hugged his mother and Polly Ann and headed for the door, the two women finished their breakfast and carried their dishes to the sink. Polly Ann washed, dried, and put them away.

"We have about six hours, Polly Ann. What do you want to do?"

"I just don't know. What do you have in mind?"

"Well, Central Park is just at the end of this street. Why don't we stroll over there and look around. Maybe at lunchtime we can get a hotdog from a street vendor and eat it on a park bench. From there we can just play it by ear. What do you say? Does that sound like a plan?"

"Oh, that sounds like fun. You know, Central Park first opened in 1857. It was designed by a Mr. Olmsted, the same man who designed the 1893 Chicago World's Fair. There's even a zoo in that place," spouted Polly Ann, remembering a few Central Park facts from her Frommer's guide.

"That's interesting. And, you never know, we might just take a horse-drawn carriage ride right through the park."

"Oh, I think I'd like that. I've seen those horse-drawn carriages on TV shows."

"Well, let's go put on our clothes and get going."

Polly Ann donned her slacks, sweatshirt, and comfy walking shoes, strapped her fanny pack around her waist, tucked her Frommer's guide under her arm, and stationed herself by the front door, waiting for Jinx to finish dressing.

"Looks like you're anxious to go, Polly Ann."

"You got that right. I got lots to see. And if this book I bought is accurate, I better get started if I want to see it all before I leave this world."

"Well, let's start seeing."

Central Park did not disappoint Polly Ann. As she approached the park, she spied a soft pretzel vendor.

"Oooo, I gotta have me one of them. You want one, Sugah Pie?" she asked. "My treat."

"No, thanks, Polly Ann. It's only 9:30 in the morning, and I just finished breakfast."

"If you got a hankering for something, it don't matter what time it is. And I got a hankering for one of them pretzels," she said, digging some wadded bills out of her fanny pack and shoving them at the vendor.

"Here you go," he said, and handed Polly Ann a pretzel wrapped in waxed paper.

"Ummmmm, mmmmm, that's about the best thing I ever tasted. I'm gonna get one of these pretzels every time I come to Central Park."

Jinx just smiled, remembering that the dry muffin in the airport had been the best thing Polly Ann had ever tasted.

They did, indeed, take a horse-drawn carriage ride. They also bought hot dogs and ate them on a park bench. They even visited the Central Park Zoo. Polly Ann had never seen exotic animals. She was most impressed with the giraffe.

"Oh, my gosh, Polly Ann, I lost track of time. Mr. Horton will be at the apartment soon. We'd better run."

So the two women hustled out of the park and back to Knox and Tony's apartment. Sure enough, when they arrived, Bob Horton was already there, talking with Knox.

Out of breath from rushing, Jinx extended her hand and, panting, said, "So nice to meet you, Mr. Horton. Sorry we're late. We were playing in the park."

Turning to Polly Ann, she said, "And this is my best friend, Polly Ann Bondurant."

Bob Horton shook Jinx's hand and then Polly Ann's, saying, "It's so nice to meet you. I can't wait to show you the apartment. I just know you're going to love it." Gathering his materials, he said, "Just follow me, and we can take a look."

No chit chat. Just all business. Jinx guessed that's the way it was done up north. Back home, before conducting their business, they'd have had sweet tea and benne wafers on the veranda and would have discovered that their great-grandmothers were third cousins, twice removed. But she figured she'd better get used to this way of communicating. She wasn't a Georgian anymore.

She was a New Yorker, soaking up all that Yankeeness.

Jinx was expecting the apartment across the hall to be similar to Knox and Tony's place. The open floor plan, the high ceilings, the masculine feel just wasn't her style, but she believed she could make it work with some feminine touches and her furniture.

From the moment Jinx walked into the small foyer, its walls decorated with cake molding, ornate wainscoting, and chair rail, she was in love. This home was nothing like Knox and Tony's place. The walls had not been dismantled; the original rooms were intact. The foyer opened into a charming sitting room with more beautiful deep, hand-carved decorative molding around the ceiling and baseboard. On the nine-foot ceiling was an ornately-carved relief surrounding the antique, dropped crystal chandelier. The huge leaded bay window with the old wavy glass panes was in perfect condition. There was a window seat looking out onto the tree-lined street, where Jinx pictured herself reading for hours and waving to her new neighbors and watching the urgency of New York pass by. And the focal point of the sitting room was a fireplace with carved mantle and white marble surround and hearth.

Adjacent to the sitting room was a good-size dining room, just right for her mother's round, antique honey mahogany pedestal table. Off the dining area was the charming, eat-in kitchen. The beautiful, decorative molding from the sitting and dining rooms was repeated in the kitchen, along with the original bead board wainscoting.

Jinx knew that a savvy buyer held her cards close to her vest, but she was certain her enthusiasm was showing. Sure, the place was outdated with its mauve and cream palette and dingy beige wall-to-wall carpet, as well as old kitchen appliances and Formica countertops, but as Mr. Horton had said, the bones were good. But Jinx knew better: the bones were excellent.

"I can see the wheels turning. You're already decorating, aren't you, Mom?" Knox said, smiling at his mother.

"It has potential," was all she'd offer. "May I please see the rest?" she asked, shoving her hands into her pants pockets to keep from clapping in sheer delight.

Three bedrooms, one quite large by New York standards, with an en suite bath, the other two small, sharing a full bath, and, in the hall, a cloak closet, a utility closet, and a small powder room. It was wonderful. Only one thing could lift it from excellent to perfect. Jinx crouched in a corner of the master bedroom, grabbed the edge of the worn and dated carpet, and pulled, exposing eight-inch-wide oak flooring, in great condition. The apartment was now perfect.

Jinx already knew how much the owner wanted. It was a steal.

So before anyone could change his mind or someone else grabbed it out from under her, she said, "Where do I sign?"

"You like it?" said Mr. Horton.

"Yes, I do. Let's sign on the dotted line before anyone else has a chance."

"Mrs. Collier, you're the first person I've shown it to. I was certain if you didn't take it, the next person would. This is a gem. The owner is anxious to sell and is not at all interested in getting involved in a bidding war, so it's all yours."

"Well, it's going to take a lot of work, but I'm up to the task. Like I said, let's sign."

Twelve

"Are you sure it's okay for Polly Ann and me to stay until our place is ready? You know, all those repairs and a major redecorating job can take a pretty long time. I really don't want to cramp you. We'll be glad to find a temporary home."

"Tony and I wouldn't think of letting you stay in some temporary home. This is your home until your place is ready. And it will be so convenient. You can be on site to supervise the workers. Not sure they'll appreciate that, but it will be good for you."

"Well, you're right about that. But only if you're certain…"

"We're certain. Now, get to decorating, 'cause when you finish yours, you have to tackle ours."

"Can't wait," Jinx exclaimed, clapping her hands.

Both places were already coming together in her mind. She had redecorated Maitland's place and had created the designs for Caroline's historic home in the heart of Savannah at the same time without breaking a sweat. These two would be a piece of cake. Her place would require a total overhaul, but Tony and Knox's home already had a good bit of the remodeling completed. The owner had updated the baths and kitchen when he'd lived there, and they were still in perfect shape. It might be a little inconvenient for a while, but Jinx felt that the sooner they could get the remodeling done, the sooner they could settle down to normal.

She had planned to purchase a few pieces of furniture and accessories to give each place a pop, but her home on Tybee housed enough furnishings to fully outfit both New York apartments. She could already see which pieces would fit in the spaces. She grabbed her sketch pad, kicked off her shoes, and curled up on the futon.

Knox and Polly Ann knew to give her her space, to leave her alone while she was creating.

Tony said, "Jinx, could I get you some…"

"Shhh," Knox and Polly Ann whispered simultaneously while Polly Ann added, "you gotta leave her be when her wheels are turning like that. When she comes up for air, she'll let us know she's free for chatting."

Now that he had a very interested buyer, the owner was eager to move forward with the disposal of his property, so Bob Horton had the paperwork assembled within two weeks, ready to make the transfer to Jinx. She had had access to the place during the process and already knew by heart every inch of her new home. She had completed her design sketches and pulled together her paint chips and swatches. She'd hired all the workers she needed, and she was ready to tackle the job.

As soon as she signed the papers and Bob handed over the key, Jinx said, "Let's get a move on."

She put on her blue jeans and sweatshirt, joining the workmen at her new home. She supervised every detail of the operation, sometimes exasperating her crew. But Polly Ann placated the disgruntled men with fried chicken, macaroni and cheese, and pecan pie. The work was done and the two women were settled in their new home in about eight weeks.

When the dust settled, Jinx stood in the center of her living room and surveyed her handiwork. The place was beautiful—one of her best efforts yet. She had chosen yellow as her primary color, and with it she had paired various shades of blue, from robin-egg to navy to turquoise. The effect was stunning. She had brought her furniture from Georgia and had upholstered the overstuffed love seat and side chairs in yellow damask, blue and yellow striped silk, blue floral polished cotton. She had refinished the hardwood floors to a light golden hue and had scattered yellow Persian area rugs about. Stark white molding framed the setting. The effect was stunning.

She could hear The Girls squealing and oohing.

Harper Ann would shriek, just as she had with the unveiling of each of Jinx's designs, "Oh, I want mine just like this."

But The Girls would not see her new home, and Harper Ann could not have her décor. This new home was for Jinx and Polly Ann alone.

And as Jinx mopped her face and blew the hair out of her eyes, she sighed and acknowledged the boxes. Unopened cartons were stacked floor-to-ceiling in corners, lined the hallway from front to back, and were shoved beneath beds and below tables. Her home was beautiful, but the unpacking had to be addressed.

"Polly Ann, we need some help."

"Oh, give it time, Sugah Pie. We'll get it done."

"No, I mean it, Polly Ann, we need help. I'm going to place an ad. I want you to hire a maid."

"A maid? Isn't that what I am?"

"Not anymore. You have cleaned for Mama and me long enough. I know how you hate it, but you've never complained. What do you say we get somebody to help us unpack these boxes and then take over the housekeeping? That'll free you up to do the cooking. That's what you enjoy, right?"

"Why, yeah, but…"

Polly Ann was speechless.

"Then, let's get us a maid."

Polly Ann opened the door to a stick-thin ebony-colored woman wearing an elegantly tailored black wool coat and a small velvet pillbox hat perched at the crown of her head. Her gloved hands were clutched at her bosom, her black leather pocketbook dangling from her left elbow. Her feet bore, incongruously, highly-polished white tennis shoes. Heels together, toes turned out, the woman looked as if she were preparing to plie. Mary Poppins came to Polly Ann's mind.

"I'm here to see the lady of the house. She is expecting me."

"She didn't tell me she was expecting anybody."

"Well, I have an appointment at this address. I've come regarding the advertisement for domestic help."

Polly Ann noticed that the woman had put the accent on the *ver* in advertisement, rather than the *tise*, like normal people do. At least, like normal southern people do.

The woman already had two strikes against her. She pronounced words in a highfalutin way, and she assumed that Polly Ann wasn't the lady of the house. Well, she wasn't theoretically the lady of the house, but Jinx had left the hiring-of-the-domestic duties to her. Oh, there was a third strike: Polly Ann was hiring a maid, not a domestic. Highfalutin, indeed.

But Polly Ann had been taught by her southern mama to be polite and hospitable, so she stepped aside and said, "Please, come on in. I'm Polly Ann Bondurant. Mrs. Collier, the lady of the house, has left me in charge of hiring her, um, domestic."

"Very well, then. I'm pleased to meet you, Mrs. Bondurant. I'm Mrs. Delores Manigault," said the woman, as she removed her gloves, shoved her small hand forward, and briskly shook Polly Ann's hand.

The pleasantries out of the way, Mrs. Manigault slipped out of her coat, revealing a crisp gray uniform with a starched, white collar.

Polly Ann thought to herself, *This woman certainly is sure of herself. She's already dressed for work.*

Miffed by the audacity of this high-fallutin woman, still out of southern habit Polly Ann said, "Can I get you something to drink?"

Mrs. Manigault replied, "Yes, thank you, some tea would be nice. Just lemon. No milk."

Polly Ann was taken aback. Strike four: that Manigault woman was really pushy.

Polly Ann retreated to the kitchen to get the pushy woman her tea. When she returned, she found Mrs. Manigault perched daintily on the edge of a newly-upholstered club chair, eyeing the room.

"It appears you could use a hand getting settled," the pushy woman said, while motioning toward the clutter of unopened moving boxes.

"We just got here. It'll take time, but we'll manage."

Polly Ann certainly didn't want to appear too eager, to let this woman think that she actually needed help of any kind.

As Mrs. Manigault sipped her tea, Polly Ann stared at her, unsure how to conduct an interview to hire a domestic.

After a long silence, the woman placed her teacup and saucer on the coffee table, straightened her back, and said, "I'm prepared for your interview. What would you like to know of my experience?"

Mrs. Manigault may have been prepared, but Polly Ann certainly wasn't. Had she assumed the interview would just conduct itself? Well, she hadn't thought that far ahead. Perhaps she had hoped someone would just walk through the door and start cleaning and unpacking boxes. Instead, this highfalutin string bean of a woman had waltzed in, requesting tea with lemon and an interview, and had thrown Polly Ann off guard.

"Well, let's see. Why don't you just tell me about yourself? Tell me what kind of maid jobs, uh, domestic positions you've had."

"As I have told you, my name is Mrs. Delores Manigault, widow of Mr. Horace Manigault."

"Oh, I'm so sorry for your loss."

"Thank you kindly, Mrs. Bondurant."

"Polly Ann, just Polly Ann. I ain't no Mrs."

But Mrs. Delores Manigault did not return the pleasantry. She did not say, "Oh, please, then, call me Delores."

Strike five.

Polly Ann just wasn't warming to this Mrs. Manigault. In fact, she was quite intimidated by this prissy, straight-laced woman.

Mrs. Manigault continued, "I began domestic service at fifteen, for a fine Park Avenue family. My reputation for exacting work spread, and my services have always been in demand. My last position was with an elderly gentleman who recently passed. I had been in his service for eleven years."

"If you so in demand, why you out looking for work?" said Polly Ann, smugly, in a just-answer-me-that sort of way.

"Well, as I said, I've been working with the same gentleman for eleven years. During that time I was responsible for caring for his needs only. His family provided a chef to prepare all the meals, which was most fortunate since I do not cook."

"Don't cook? How can you not cook?"

"You see, Mr. Manigault's mother, Miss Mama, lived with us and prepared all of our meals. Since she passed, I have had to fend for myself. I manage, but I don't pride myself on my culinary arts."

There she goes again with that fancy talk, Polly Ann scoffed to herself. *She may think she's winning points, but that Mrs. Manigault can just think again.*

"I do hope that cooking is not one of the requirements of the position. Your advertisement did not mention cooking."

"We just need a cleaning maid, not a cooking maid. You see, I'm Mrs. Collier's chef, and I'll be making all of the decisions in the kitchen."

That was the first time Polly Ann had said the word chef. But if that old man Delores Manigault used to work for could have a chef, she and Sugah Pie could have a chef too. And she was it. Chef. Polly Ann kind of liked the sound of that. She felt like saying it again. Maybe even twice.

"Chef. Yes, I'm Mrs. Collier's chef."

"Wonderful. I'd say, then, that you and I will make a splendid team, a perfectly-matched pair."

There she goes again, thought Polly Ann, getting all pushy, already calling us a team, assuming the job is hers.

As Polly Ann fumed, Mrs. Delores Manigault stood and said, "Well, then, I've told you my work history and will gladly provide references at your request. Now, perhaps, you might show me your home so that I can determine what the position entails."

Polly Ann gritted her teeth and pinched her pillowy lips tightly together until they practically disappeared, in order to keep from blurting out just what she thought of pushy Mrs. Manigault. Taking a deep breath to calm her temper, she figured the sooner she showed the domestic around, the sooner she could show her the door.

"Sure," said Polly Ann, standing and motioning toward the hallway to the bedroom area of the apartment.

Mrs. Delores Manigault stood and from her pocketbook extracted glasses, white cotton gloves, a pad, and a pen. She perched her glasses on the bridge of her nose, slipped the gloves onto her hands, and poised her pen over her pad.

Polly Ann was past being surprised by anything this woman said or did. She shook her head and said in exasperation, "Come on."

Mrs. Manigault took notes furiously, stopping from time to time to say, "We'll need a wand to reach cobwebs," or "I have the perfect brush for cleaning grout," or "There's a wonderful, new little device for dusting these plantation shutters. A must have."

Mrs. Manigault touched furniture with her gloved finger, examined it, flared her nostrils and sniffed, and scribbled furiously.

When she had finished her inspection of the apartment, she removed her gloves and said, "Very well, then, when would you like for me to begin? I have a commitment tomorrow, but I will be available the following day. Would that be sufficient?"

And before Polly Ann knew what had hit her, she had hired herself a domestic, and she and Mrs. Manigault had agreed upon an acceptable wage.

Mrs. Delores Manigault replaced her cotton examining gloves, glasses, pad, and pen in her purse, slipped into her coat and dress gloves, re-perched her pillbox on her head, and made her way to the door. When she reached it, she stood with her hands clasped, purse dangling from her elbow, heels together, toes apart. It took a while for Polly Ann to realize that Mrs. Maigault was waiting for her to open the door and dismiss her.

Polly Ann did as she was expected and watched the pushy woman pad silently toward the front door of the building.

"Hey, one more thing," Polly Ann called after her, "if you're gonna call me Polly Ann, I ain't callin' you Mrs. Manigault. I'm gonna call you Delores."

"Very well, then," said Mrs. Manigault without looking back, and disappeared through the front door, onto the street.

Thirteen

True to her word, Delores Manigault appeared at Jinx's door in two days, promptly at nine a.m.

Hands clasped, hat perched on her head, and pocketbook dangling from her elbow, she said, "Until we have a formal arrangement, I assumed I'd be needed at nine a.m. I hope I assumed properly."

Polly Ann was beginning to think she had made a huge mistake hiring this highfalutin woman, but, in all honestly, Delores had sort of made the hiring decision herself. It had just happened before Polly Ann realized it. But here Delores Manigault was, very punctual and ready to work.

"Well, come on in and put your stuff in that hall closet there."

Delores removed her coat, hat, and gloves and opened the cloak closet. She placed her hat, along with her purse, on the upper shelf and folded her gloves neatly and put them in her coat pocket. She hung her coat, buttoned it painstakingly, and neatly smoothed out the wrinkles with her hands.

Good lord, thought Polly Ann, *at this rate this prissy lady won't be getting to cleaning before next week.*

Then Delores produced a canvas bag, removed a feather duster, grout brush, and shutter cleaner and said, "Well, then, let's begin."

"Now, first," said Polly Ann, "we're going to find Mrs. Collier."

"Very well," said Delores with a nod of acknowledgment.

But before they could head for the bedrooms, Jinx appeared in the hallway.

"Well, hey, you must be Delores. Good to meet you," Jinx said and extended her hand cordially.

"I am, and it is a pleasure to make your acquaintance, Mrs. Collier," said Delores, grasping Jinx's hand and giving it one firm, no-nonsense shake. "Thank you so much for this opportunity. Your home is lovely."

Jinx wasn't used to this formality. She and Polly Ann had been close friends for as long as she could remember, and she was accustomed to a familiarity between the two of them. It would take a while for her to warm to this small, rigid woman. But if she could clean, Jinx figured it didn't matter how formal she was.

All morning Delores unpacked boxes, unwrapping items, dusting them, and assembling them in the rooms where they belonged. All Jinx and Polly Ann had to do was put things in drawers, on tables, in cupboards. Once she emptied the last box, Delores collapsed all of them and dragged them to the curb for recycling. Polly Ann marveled that this wiry woman was capable of such brawny work. She admitted, but only to herself, that she was most impressed.

Around noon Polly Ann called, "Yoo hoo, Delores, come on in here."

Delores was not accustomed to people yoo hooing from room to room like uncultured banshees, but she didn't make the rules in the Collier home. She followed Polly Ann's bellowing to the steaming kitchen, where she found Mrs. Collier's chef wearing a yellow, ruffled pinafore apron and mopping her face with a large man's handkerchief.

"Don't just stand there. Come on in. Lunch is about ready."

"Thank you, but I'll just…"

"You'll just come in here and sit your skinny little be-hind down."

Delores was taken aback by Polly Ann's forward behavior, and she was embarrassed by the reference to her skinniness, especially to the skinniness of her be-hind. Delores had always been slight, an anomaly in her family. Her mother and four sisters were all robust women, with ample bosoms and broad derrieres. People were forever attempting to force Delores to eat; and she did eat, just like everyone else. She just couldn't seem to gain an ounce.

Her mama, Nell, had fretted over her behind her back, but, to her face, she had told Delores, "Now, don't you pay attention to that nonsense. You just have a galloping metabolism, is all."

Delores chose to believe in the galloping metabolism theory, but, still, she became uncomfortable when anyone made mention of her small build. Delores ignored Polly Ann's remark but still resisted joining her and Mrs. Collier.

"But it wouldn't be right," Delores said, barely above a whisper.

Polly Ann said, "What you mean it ain't right? I'm frying chicken for you and Sugah Pie, and I expect y'all to eat it. You hear?"

Delores continued to stand. She was accustomed to taking her meals in the kitchen while her employer ate in the dining room. But Mrs. Collier wasn't eating in the dining room; she was sitting at the kitchen table, talking to Polly Ann as she cooked.

Finally, Jinx spoke up: "Delores, Polly Ann and I have always eaten our meals together. We certainly don't want to make you feel uncomfortable, but we hope you will join us."

With that, Delores said quietly, "Well, thank you, ma'am," easing herself into the chair next to Jinx and folding her hands in her lap. It was either eat in the kitchen with her employer or in the dining room alone. Neither was a choice she'd have made, but Delores needed to pick one. The situation caused her great discomfort, but she'd just have to get over that.

"Yeah, me and Sugah Pie been eating together forever, ain't that right?"

Jinx chuckled and said, "We certainly have, Polly Ann," knowing full well where this tale would take them.

"You see, Delores, I was right there when Jinx come into this world. Her mama had the lazy milk. You know, it just wouldn't come in. So I took that precious baby and wet nursed her. If it wasn't for me, that child would have starved to death."

Jinx had heard this story so many times, and each time Polly Ann snatched that poor infant from the jaws of death. Jinx was certain there had been nutrition alternatives—perhaps, canned or bottled milk—but she'd allow Polly Ann her heroism.

Delores was embarrassed and ill at ease with the intimacy of Polly Ann's story. She knew, though, that Polly Ann was just attempting to welcome her into their circle. She would try to accept the invitation in the spirit with which she felt it was intended.

Polly Ann placed a platter of fried chicken and bowls of potato salad and butterbeans on the table. Then she pulled a pan of made-from-scratch biscuits from the oven. She took her place at the table with Jinx and Delores, pulled her large white handkerchief from her bosom, and mopped her face again. Once she had stuffed her handkerchief back where it lived, she and Jinx joined hands and reached across the table toward Delores. It took a moment for Delores to realize that her hosts were preparing to pray—and that they held hands while praying.

As she took their hands, Polly Ann said, "Dear Lord, thank you for this food, our new home, and our new friend, Delores. Amen, Jesus."

Leaning into Delores, Polly Ann elbowed her and whispered, "We pray real fast so our food won't get cold. Jesus understands. He knows my cold fried chicken is good, but he knows it's better when it's piping hot, right out of the drippings. Now, dig in."

But instead of digging in, Delores waited for Jinx and Polly Ann to help themselves and pass the serving dishes her way.

"Thank you," she said, as Polly Ann passed her a bowl of butterbeans. Then she added, "Where in the world did you find butterbeans this time of year?"

"I brought them with me from Georgia. Brought all my canning. Leaving them behind would have been like abandoning a baby. And I shore wudn't gonna give 'em to them snooty, ungrateful so-called friends of Jinx's."

"Polly Ann, please," Jinx chided, but Polly Ann ignored her.

"And, by the way, how does a Yankee know about butterbeans?" asked Polly Ann.

"I know a lot about southern food," Delores said defensively. "I bet you thought you were going to surprise me with your sweet tea, didn't you? I've been drinking sweet tea for a long, long time."

"Like I said, how does a Yankee know about butterbeans? And sweet tea?"

"Well, when Mr. Manigault and I married, I was just a girl of sixteen. My husband had come to New York from Charleston, South Carolina to find work. He took his Civil Servant's exam and went to work at the post office. He was twenty-one at the time and in a janitorial position before he worked his way up to mail carrier. I had been a domestic for about a year, and, as I have told you, I did not know how to cook. So Mr. Manigault sent for his mother to come to New York and teach me my way around the kitchen. Instead, she did all the cooking, didn't teach me a thing, and never returned to her home in Charleston—just stayed on with us till she passed two years ago."

"God rest her soul," interjected Polly Ann.

"Most kind of you," responded Delores and continued. "Most girls would have hated having their mothers-in-law under their roofs, interfering in their kitchens, but not me. I loved Miss Mama from the minute I laid eyes on her, and she loved me, too. She had seven sons and not a single daughter. She took me as her daughter. As I said, I never learned a thing about cooking from her, but I did learn to love southern cooking. Her fried chicken could bring tears to your eyes, and her biscuits melted in your mouth. I loved the way she cooked butterbeans in fatback, but my favorite Miss Mama dish was cheese grits. She left me all her recipes, but I just can't do them justice."

"Well, dig in," Polly said, "before this southern cooking gets cold."

Delores reached for a chicken leg. She took one bite, closed her eyes and chewed slowly. She dabbed her lips daintily with her napkin and said, "Oh, my goodness, Polly Ann, you have channeled Miss Mama. This is positively delicious. It takes me back."

Polly Ann puffed out her chest and preened but said, "Oh, this is just Thursday lunch. You wait till Sunday dinner. I'll fix you some cheese grits."

Delores was touched that Polly Ann was intimating that she was to be included in another family meal and that she was going to prepare a dish especially for her. And on a Sunday, no less.

As soon as Delores finished her lunch, she said, "Well, thank you for sharing your meal with me. Now I'd best be getting back to work. Polly Ann, if you'll just leave the dishes, I'll take care of them right away."

"Naw, the kitchen is mine. Washing the dishes is part of my chef duties. You take care of the rest of the place and leave the kitchen to me."

"Very well, then," said Mrs. Manigault, and headed for that soap scum in Jinx's shower.

What in the world?

Jinx rolled over and squinted at the clock: 6:30. She assumed that meant six-thirty in the morning. But who was laughing in her apartment at six-thirty in the morning? She recognized Polly Ann's booming voice, but who was the owner of the other? Who was Polly Ann entertaining at this god-awful hour? And, better yet, what could they possibly find to laugh about at six-thirty in the morning?

Jinx dragged herself from under the covers and wrapped herself in her robe. She padded down the hall in her bare feet toward the direction of the laughter. When she got to the kitchen, she found Polly Ann sitting at the table in her pink flowered flannel nightgown, nursing a mug of coffee. Across the table sat Delores Manigault, Jinx's housekeeper of one month. Delores was wrapped—actually swimming—in Polly Ann's huge yellow chenille robe, and her small bare feet brushed the kitchen tiles. She was cradling a cup of tea in her hands.

Before Jinx could say a thing, Polly Ann said, "Hey, Sugah Pie. Join us?"

Delores jumped up, sloshing her tea, and gathered the huge robe around her small frame. "Oh, I'm so sorry, Mrs. Collier. Please forgive me," she gasped, grabbing a handful of paper towels and mopping the table and herself.

"Delores? What on earth are you doing here so early? And did you wear your robe and bare feet on the subway?"

These women had a lot of explaining to do.

Delores stood mute, as if Jinx had stunned her speechless.

Polly Ann took over. "Sugah Pie, Delores spent the night here last night."

"Spent the night?" Jinx said, none too welcomingly.

"Well, you see, you been going out gallivanting every night, leaving me here all by myself. I get mighty lonely. You got Knox and Tony. I ain't got nobody."

Jinx said defensively, "Polly Ann, you know very well you are welcome to go with Knox and me anywhere we go. And I do not gallivant."

"Well, maybe gallivanting ain't the right word, but you have been going out to this place and that. Whatever name you put to it, I'm still here alone. And I know you'd let me go if I wanted, but what you do just ain't my style, if you know what I mean. I need friends of my own. And you just haven't given much understanding to my needs."

Jinx gave Polly Ann a confused look, and Polly Ann said, "I been watching Dr. Phil, a lot of Dr. Phil—like all the time you been out gallivanting. Dr. Phil says we all have needs, and we have to understand each other's needs. And I need me some friends. A body gets mighty closed up when she's left all by herself."

Polly Ann was laying it on thick, but still Jinx felt guilty. She had taken Polly Ann from all her life-long friends and from the only place she had ever known, bringing her to this huge, strange city, where she knew no one except Jinx and Knox. Well, in her defense, she hadn't actually dragged the woman away from Savannah. Before Jinx had the words New York out of her mouth, Polly Ann had her bags packed and was headed to the airport. Yet Jinx really had not considered Polly Ann's needs. Certainly, she needed friends and Jinx understood that, but she hadn't expected Polly Ann to invite their new housekeeper into her home for sleepovers.

Before Jinx could respond, though, Polly Ann said, "You were out last night, and I just didn't feel like spending another evening alone. I asked Delores to stay a while and keep me company. Well, we got to talking and laughing, and, before you know it, it's ten-thirty. Delores was planning to go on to the subway, but I just wouldn't hear of it. It ain't safe, and it's just not right for a lady to be walking the streets of New York and riding the subway alone at that hour of the night. So I insisted she stay over."

All the while Polly Ann was explaining the reason why their new housekeeper was standing in the kitchen in a housecoat and bare feet at the crack of dawn, Delores trained her eyes on the wet paper towels she held in her hand.

Then she said quietly, "I'm so sorry, Mrs. Collier."

Jinx felt awful. Delores had absolutely nothing to be sorry about. Polly Ann had invited her to stay, and she had accepted the invitation. Simple as that.

Jinx reached over and touched Delores on the shoulder. Delores flinched and lifted her eyes to meet her employer's.

"Delores, please don't apologize. You've done nothing wrong. I'm glad you didn't try to take the subway at such a late hour. I agree with Polly Ann that it wouldn't be safe. And you did me a favor. While I was out gallivanting, ignoring my friend's needs," Jinx said, raising an eyebrow and giving Polly Ann a sideways glance, "you were considering them."

Relaxing somewhat but still uneasy about being in her employer's kitchen in an oversized bathrobe and bare feet, Delores said, "Well, then, thank you, Mrs. Collier. And thank you for the tea, Polly Ann. Now, if you'll excuse me, I have work to do."

After she deposited her wet paper towels in the trash can, she padded off quietly toward Polly Ann's room.

"Since when do you want to pal around with a highfalutin woman?" Jinx asked Polly Ann when Delores was out of earshot.

"Aw, I misjudged. What I took for highfalutin is really just reserved. Mrs. Delores Manigault is a very fine lady."

Jinx couldn't keep from smirking and shaking her head.

"Hey!" said Polly Ann, "A person can make a misjudgment every once in a while."

It took a lot for Polly Ann to admit she was wrong—or that she had made a misjudgment. Mrs. Manigault must really be a special person. Jinx was grateful she had found her way to their apartment. And she was grateful Mrs. Manigault wanted to be Polly Ann's friend.

"It really ain't safe, you know? And it don't make sense for her to truck on back up to Harlem every night to that empty old apartment when she's just gonna turn right around and come back here the next morning."

"Do you enjoy her company?"

"Daggone right I do. She's a smart lady, and she's seen a whole bunch of stuff. I like hearing about what she has to say."

"Do you mind sharing your room with her?"

"Heck, no. Got that spare bed in there just taking up space."

So Jinx resignedly shook her head and said, "Well, all right then."

And that's how Mrs. Delores Manigault, former highfalutin lady and widow of Horace Manigault, became Jinx's live-in domestic. And Polly Ann's roommate and best friend.

Fourteen

Jinx was hanging the last of the Liz Houston pieces on the massive art wall of Knox and Tony's newly redecorated home. The guys looked on as Jinx pulled her tape measure from her pocket and made sure the small, exquisite painting was positioned just right. Then she placed her level on top of the frame, stepped back, and said, "Perfect." Of all their Houston collection, this one was her favorite. Smaller than all the others, the canvas was a splash of many shades of blue and was aptly named "Water." It didn't even need a title. To see it was to see water.

"Fantastic! When am I going to get to meet the artist? Can't wait to see the person who created this," Jinx cried, sweeping her hands across the massive wall of Houstons.

"Soon, I hope," said Knox. "We've asked her to come over, but she said she wanted to let you and Polly Ann get settled in your new home before she crashed the family reunion. Would you like for me to tell her y'all are settled?"

"By all means."

"How about Friday night? We can christen our new décor with a dinner party," Tony suggested.

Jinx had done an incredible job redecorating Knox and Tony's place. She had raised the ceilings, exposing the pipes and duct work, giving the apartment an industrial look and making it appear more spacious. She had used a palette of earth tones, leaving Liz's art to provide a bold wall of color. The furniture was masculine, in dark woods, neutral tweeds, and simple lines. It was perfect for Tony and Knox, and they both loved it. They did not mind at all giving up the futon, beanbag chairs, and crates. They looked forward to entertaining and having an excuse to use their new dining table and to show off their big-boy home with its big-boy furniture.

After Polly Ann's remark about his mother's gallivanting, Knox had extended an invitation to the dinner party to her and Delores, as well. Polly Ann declined for the both of them, saying that they were getting their needs met at a pot luck dinner at Delores's church.

When Friday night arrived, Jinx let herself into Knox and Tony's apartment. She found that Liz had beaten her there and was already in the kitchen, helping the boys prepare dinner. Their backs to her, the three worked perfectly in sync, like a finely-tuned watch. They laughed and jostled and joked as if they'd been a trio all their lives.

Jinx was taken by Liz's beauty, not an in-your-face beauty, but a classic, subtle, timeless beauty. Her spun gold hair hung straight, well past her shoulders, and she floated, not walked, as she moved, her long, flowing blue print skirt swirling around her legs. The boys talked and laughed loudly. Liz spoke gently and fluidly, as if carrying a tune. Jinx could not believe this was the person who had filled Tony and Knox's home with bold splashes of color, artwork so masculine it looked as if the artist had attacked the canvases with tools, rather than having painted them with brushes.

Then Liz turned to Jinx, flashing her sapphire eyes, making her artwork even more implausible. Her eyes were stunning, yet haunting. They were smiling on the surface, but Jinx was certain they were a front for pain. Jinx was no stranger to that look, that pain. She had seen it in her own eyes.

"Hi," Liz cooed and floated forward. "Oh, Mrs. Collier, I'm so happy to meet you," and, reaching for Jinx's hands, said, "I'm so, so sorry about Mr. Collier."

"Thank you, Liz. I'm so glad to meet Knox and Tony's best friend. And I've been most anxious to see who created this exquisite art," Jinx said with a sweep of her hands toward the wall.

Knox and Tony stepped forward, and each kissed Jinx on the cheek.

"Hungry?" asked Tony.

"I sure am. I've been waiting all day for this."

"Great, it shouldn't take too much longer. Knox, pour your mom a glass of wine, and you guys go on in the living room while I finish up here."

"Sure you don't need some help?" Knox and Liz asked in

unison.

"Nope, I'm doing just fine. I'll let you know when I'm ready."

So the three of them left Tony to the cooking as Jinx inched her way toward Liz's art, eager to talk to the artist about her work. As she asked Liz when she began painting, who inspired her, how she brought her work to New York, she watched Liz laugh and talk animatedly, eager to share her talent with Knox's mom. But as Liz smiled and laughed, Jinx couldn't ignore that look of sadness in those beautiful sapphire eyes. What pain were they hiding?

"Come and get it," Tony called, as he headed toward the dining room table, carrying with huge red checked mitts a large, steaming pan of lasagna.

"Oh, Tony, it smells scrumptious," Jinx cried, as they all took seats at the new dining room table.

"It is, Jinx. And I can say that because I can't take credit. This was my Nonna's recipe. It was my favorite. No matter what was on the menu when we visited, she always made a lasagna just for me. Please, taste. Can't wait to hear what you think."

Filling her plate and taking a bite, Jinx cried, "Oh, my word, Tony, this must be what heaven tastes like."

Knox's salad was delicious, too, made with spinach, mandarin oranges, and avocado, with a citrus dressing. Jinx made it a point to compliment his contribution, just as she had Tony's lasagna. She didn't want her child to feel slighted, ever again.

"Liz, you were telling me about your inspiration. Please go on," Jinx said.

"A lot of my inspiration comes from the city. New York offers everything. Every day brings new ideas. And, of course, life. Life and life lessons give me inspiration."

There it was—the pain. Jinx saw it again, seeping from those exquisite eyes. What had life done to this beautiful girl?

"Do you show your work in a gallery?"

"I wish I did, Mrs. Collier, but it's hard to break into the art world. You have to have connections, and I just haven't found my connection yet. So I'll just keep on showing my art to the world from the New York streets. Someday, someday…" she said, smiling wanly and shrugging her shoulders, her voice trailing off.

"I have no doubt your someday will come soon," said Jinx, leaning toward Liz and patting her hand.

"How about some gelato?" Tony asked, when everyone sighed at their empty plates and pushed themselves away from the table.

"Thanks. Maybe later. I just couldn't right now," they all agreed.

As long as they were eating, the conversation flowed, but once the meal ended, Jinx noticed a change in the air. There was a discomfort, an uneasiness she couldn't quite identify. The three who had, when Jinx arrived, appeared to be joined at the hip, looked anxious and at odds with one another. And they were giving one another shifty-eye signals.

"What's going on? Is something wrong?" Jinx asked.

The three continued to look like spooked animals, their eyes darting back and forth, all appearing to want to speak, but none willing to take the lead.

"What is it? Tell me. You're scaring me."

Finally Knox blurted, "Mom, we're going to have a baby."

Jinx just stared at Knox, dumbfounded.

"Mom, are you okay?"

"I... I... I just don't know what to say. You've caught me off guard, Knox," Jinx said. "That certainly isn't what I was expecting, though I don't know what I was expecting."

The lasagna was merely the appetizer. The baby news was the main course.

"Well, there's more. Let's go to the sofa where we can chat."

"Okay," said Jinx, as she picked up her wine glass and headed for the sofa, her head spinning.

Once she was anchored to the sofa and Liz claimed a nearby chair, she said, "I'm all ears," looking from Knox to Tony and back to Knox again.

"Well, Mom, Tony and I want to be parents."

"Okay, I think I got that much."

She had come to New York to tell her son that she loved him and that she accepted him completely. She thought that's what she had done. But she hadn't thought about this, about Knox's becoming co-parents with another man. Maybe she was more like Tony's mother and father than she wanted to believe. She knew that the two men loved each other, were living together. But perhaps she, too, wanted them to project the illusion that they were just good buddies sharing rent. Keep it in the family, so to speak. If nobody knew, what harm was there? But a baby? Everyone would know if they had a baby. Her cheeks flamed with embarrassment. She was trying to be so understanding, so accepting, so inclusive, so with it. But was she? Apparently not. But she had no choice in the matter. This was her son's life. She wanted to accept him—all of him.

As confused as she was, one thing she knew without a doubt: Knox was not making a choice. He did not become gay to hurt his parents, to test the waters, to find himself. He was not going to come to his senses and go back to Georgia with his tail between his legs, begging his family and friends to forgive him and take him back. And he certainly was not going to marry some sweet little southern girl and have pretty babies with her.

This was Knox. He had a right to love whomever he pleased. He had the right to be loved and nurtured in return. He had a right to have a family just like all of his friends. He loved Tony. He wanted to parent a child with Tony, not some sweet little southern girl.

She looked up from her wine glass. Her voice cracked and tears stood in her eyes as she said, "Congratulations. I'm so happy for both of you."

"Thanks, Mom. I needed to hear that," Knox said as Tony smiled nervously, reached for Knox's hand, and released a sigh of relief.

"Okay," Jinx said cheerily. "Now, next issue, who is giving you a baby?"

Somewhat awkwardly but without hesitation, as if they'd been practicing for this moment, Knox and Tony looked toward Liz. Jinx was so caught up in Knox and Tony's news that she'd practically forgotten Liz was there. She had just faded away during the baby discussion. But she was back, and the boys were looking at her. It took a few beats for Jinx to catch up.

"What? Liz? Liz is giving you a baby?"

Liz smiled, and her beautiful eyes sparkled, not a hint of pain evident as she acknowledged that she was, indeed, going to help her friends become parents.

"She's offered to be our surrogate, Mom. She'll undergo artificial insemination and carry our child."

Dumbfounded, as if someone had thumped her real hard right

between the eyes, Jinx could manage only to stare at Liz, her mouth open in shock.

Liz said, "I can tell this has come as a surprise to you."

Still Jinx just stared, wide-eyes, shaking her head up and down.

Eventually she was able to manage, "Surprise. Yes, that's it. Surprise."

"Mrs. Collier, Knox and Tony are my best friends, the best friends I've ever known. They'd do as much for me."

What could Jinx say? *It ain't natchel?* Where was Polly Ann when she needed her?

But instead she managed, "That's very selfless of you, Liz, a beautiful gift."

Liz batted her now-smiling eyes and said, "In return they've promised to pay my rent for the next millennium and to buy all my unsellable art."

Jinx appreciated Liz's attempt at humor to diffuse the tension, but she, unfortunately, was feeling only dumbfoundedness, apprehension, and anxiety. No humor.

"But, Liz, what will your parents say?"

Jinx had no idea that Liz's parents, Mr. and Mrs. Chester Worthington Houston III, were elitist snobs who lived in Connecticut and summered at their home in Newport, Rhode Island. Mr. Houston had made a name in shipping and had an office on Wall Street. Mrs. Houston had made a name volunteering and entertaining and had a home office and a personal assistant to keep track of all her do-gooder causes. Liz had one sibling, older brother Chester IV, a graduate of Harvard Law and a partner in the largest law firm in their up-scale Connecticut town. He had done exactly as his parents had expected. He had married the girl they'd hand-picked for him, joined the firm they'd suggested, bought the house in the best neighborhood, and quickly had two perfect and perfectly beautiful children.

Liz had graduated with honors and a degree in economics from Vassar, her mother's alma mater, but didn't want the career on Wall Street that her parents had planned for her. She also didn't want the high-powered husband and family. She wanted to be an artist. Her mother and father were horrified. They forced her to choose: family or art. She chose art. She had not heard from them since she'd made her decision.

"Mrs. Collier, my parents won't know. They don't even know where I am. When I refused to follow their respectable lifestyle," she said with air quotes, "they banished me. I embarrass them, and they don't want to have anything to do with me until I come to my senses. So we'll have this baby, Knox and Tony will become parents, you will become a grandmother, and my family will be none the wiser."

Jinx felt so sad for this beautiful, loving young woman. Liz had told her about her parents in a very matter-of-fact manner, but there was that profound pain in her eyes. And now Jinx knew why it was there.

She also knew why these three young people had gravitated to one another. All their parents had turned their backs on them, for one reason or another. But as Jinx listened to these brave, beautiful friends, she vowed that she would never turn her back on them again, that she would be there to support them, regardless of how she felt about their decision to have a child together.

She stood and approached Liz. She sat on the arm of the chair and laid her hand on Liz's back. She didn't need to say anything.

But when the silence became uncomfortable, Tony said, "More wine?"

"Sure, why not," said Jinx.

"Count me in," added Liz. "I need to enjoy it now because I won't be drinking for long."

As Knox poured his mother and Liz another glass of wine, he said, "What do you think Polly Ann is going to say?"

"Well, you know she'll say it ain't natchel. But she'll get over it, Knox, just as she has gotten accustomed to the two of you living together. She loves you unconditionally, just as I do."

"Well, I'll just let you decide when the time is right to break it to her."

Jinx agreed that was for the best. Then she returned her attention to the insemination.

"Okay, when? And where? And how?" asked Jinx. "This is just so foreign to me that I don't even know what questions to ask."

So Liz spoke up. "I've already begun taking drugs to stimulate my cycle and, the doctor hopes, increase egg production. I've been monitoring my ovulation for several months, and the fertilization specialist feels we've pretty well pinpointed when I ovulate. The first insemination procedure will be next month."

"First procedure?"

"Yes, first. We've been told that we may become pregnant on the first try but not to get our hopes up. It could take six or more tries. But I'm committed to this as long as they are or as long as I have eggs to give," Liz said, smiling in Knox and Tony's direction.

"Well, I'm not sure I'm ready for all the details, but what can it hurt?" Jinx said, laughing nervously. "What happens next?"

Knox took over, looking somewhat uncomfortable discussing the subject with his mother but feeling she needed to know and that he was the appropriate one to fill her in.

"Well, instead of deciding who will be the biological father, we've chosen to mix our sperm for the insemination and let nature make the choice."

Jinx could feel her face redden at the mention of her son's sperm. But why? Knox was her child, had been her baby. She had carried him in her womb for nine months and had cared for all his most personal needs for years. Why should discussing his sperm be so difficult? But it was. She'd just breathe deeply and take baby steps.

"Okay, then," she said, self-consciously, "I think that's just about enough information for one night. Perhaps y'all can just fill me in on an as-need-to-know basis."

Fifteen

"Do lawd, I done heard everything. Two men having a baby. And some lady just deciding to carry it for 'em. What next?"

Polly Ann huffed around the kitchen, swatting with her dish towel at something invisible, while Jinx and Delores sat at the table with their tea and listened to her mumble under her breath.

"Not right, just not right," she said to herself, as she threw pots into the cupboard and scrubbed the counter long after it needed scrubbing.

Then Delores, who had become Polly Ann's authority on every subject, said, "Come sit down here, Polly Ann. I want to talk to you."

Still pouting but always eager to hear what Delores had to say on any subject, Polly Ann plopped down in the chair with a thud and said, "Okay, I'm sitting. Now what?"

Delores reached for her friend's hand and said, "Polly Ann, it's a miracle. That's what it is, a miracle. I would have given my right arm had someone been able to carry a baby for me. I so wanted children, but it just didn't happen. And that's not to say Mr. Manigault and I didn't try," Delores said, ducking her head, lowering her lashes, and grinning shyly. "And those beautiful young men deserve to be parents, just like anyone else, just like you deserved to be Marcus and Monette's mother. And if doctors can help Knox and Tony become parents, so be it. And if God hadn't wanted this to happen, he wouldn't have given the doctors the knowledge to make it happen. Praise God."

Polly Ann seemed to soften a bit but was not immediately convinced that Delores was right. Delores, though, was certain that she would soon win Polly Ann over. And, of course, Delores was right, as usual.

As the time for the insemination drew closer, Jinx and Liz spent more and more time together. Jinx needed to get to know the young woman who would be giving birth to her grandchild; and, apparently, Liz, as strong and cool as she appeared, needed some motherly comfort.

Liz, Tony and Knox, Polly Ann and Delores, and Jinx were crowded around Jinx's round oak dining table. Jinx had taken over Polly Ann's kitchen and had made a pork loin and cheese grits to tip off the Insemination Season, as they had all taken to calling it. They had become so comfortable talking about their baby that Liz jokingly said she felt like a science experiment or a lab rat. But it was best that they had all gotten on board and were supportive of the young parents-to-be and Liz, who called herself The Incubator.

"You ladies stay right there," Tony said when they had finished dinner. "Knox and I will clean up and take care of the dessert and coffee."

"I won't argue with that," said Jinx, as she returned to her chatter with the other women while the guys cleared the table.

"Will you go with me tomorrow?" Liz asked, reaching for Jinx's hand.

"Well, sure, I'd be glad to ride along."

"Not just ride along. Will you stay with me during the procedure?"

"Of course, Liz, I will, if that's what you want."

"Yes, that's what I want."

So Liz would not allow the guys to watch the turkey baster thingy, as they were calling the procedure, but she needed Jinx to be with her. Jinx just smiled and squeezed Liz's hand.

Knox and Tony returned with coffee and Polly Ann's pecan pie. No one had room for it but neither could they resist. It was the delicious end to a perfect evening.

Jinx ushered the parents—the three of them—out the door. Yawning, she headed for the kitchen to load the dishwasher with the dessert dishes and coffee cups. She turned off the lights and headed for her bedroom. When she passed Polly Ann and Delores's bedroom, she found them already gowned and perched in their single beds, reading their Bibles, their late-night ritual.

"Night, girls. Thanks for the nice evening, and thanks, too, for all your help getting supper ready."

"It was lovely, Mrs. Collier. Thank you so much for including me," said Delores.

"So glad you liked it, Delores."

"Yeah, Sugah Pie, you outdid yourself. That pork loin was cooked to perfection."

"Well, you're the one who taught me, Polly Ann."

"I know. And you followed my directions to a T."

Jinx chuckled at her friend as she headed for her bedroom. The evening had been wonderful, but she was exhausted. She shed her clothes, and, instead of neatly hanging them in her closet, she dropped them on her bedroom chair. Then she slipped into her gown, brushed her teeth hurriedly, and crawled into bed.

But sleep wouldn't come.

Were Knox and Tony making the right decision? What did they know about being parents? But what did any first-time parents know about being parents? Even if they were perfect parents, were they endangering Liz's life? Was the procedure safe? What would happen if Liz decided she wanted to keep the baby? Even if she didn't decide to keep the child, what part would she play in its life? Would the baby be confused because he—or she—had two fathers and no mother?

She couldn't turn it off. As tired as she was, her mind refused to unwind. No matter how hard she tried to relax, the fears, the anxiety, the unanswered questions wouldn't let her rest. When, at five thirty the following morning, she was still tossing and her mind was still churning, she gave up and got out of bed. She headed straight for the kitchen to start a pot of really strong coffee.

As she sipped her coffee at the kitchen table, her mind still refusing to calm, Polly Ann padded into the kitchen, sat down next to Jinx at the table, and reached for her hand.

"You okay, Sugah Pie?"

"I'm just worried, Polly Ann."

"I know, but there's no need to be. It's out of our hands. What's meant to be will be. Like Delores says, this is a miracle, and if Knox and Tony are meant to witness a miracle, they will. You just have to trust."

"I understand that, Polly Ann, but Knox is my child. I just want what's best for him, want him to make the right decisions."

"It's his life, Sugah Pie. You gotta let him do what he thinks is best, not what you think is best for him," Polly Ann said, patting Jinx's arm with her strong, comforting hand.

Jinx was surprised by Polly Ann's progressive attitude. Apparently, Delores had been doing a lot of talking.

Polly Ann got up to pour herself a cup of coffee just as Delores slipped quietly into the kitchen.

"Good morning, ladies," she said in her usual reserved, respectful manner.

"Hey, Delores, you're just in time. I was just getting ready to make some scrambled eggs. You gals, place your order."

"Thanks, Polly Ann, but I think I'll stick with toast this morning," said Jinx.

"That's generous of you, Polly Ann, but I believe toast is all I'll take, as well. I'm still quite satiated from last evening's meal."

Satiated, ha, thought Polly Ann. She'd come to love Delores, but sometimes her highfalutinness still got to her.

"Well, y'all are gonna be sorry," she said, as she opened the refrigerator and reached for the carton of eggs.

Jinx looked at the kitchen clock: 6:30.

"I'd better hit the shower. We have to leave at seven-thirty. Liz's appointment is at eight-thirty, and the boys and I have to drive up to Harlem to pick her up."

As Polly Ann scrambled her eggs and Delores sipped her coffee, Jinx headed for the shower. Once the water warmed, she stepped in, hoping it would wash her anxiety down the drain and calm her fears. No such luck. She shivered, though the water was warm. She soaped and rinsed quickly, dried, and dressed hurriedly.

Knox knocked on her door shortly before seven-thirty.

"Knox is here, Sugah Pie."

"Tell him I'll be right there, Polly Ann."

Jinx gave her hair one last quick brush and applied a swipe of lipstick before grabbing her purse and sweater—doctor's offices could be quite chilly—and headed to meet her son.

Knox gave his mother a peck on the cheek and said, "Thanks for going with us, Mom."

"I wouldn't miss it."

When they got to the curb, they found Tony behind the wheel of the car, engine running, ready to go.

Knox and Tony had a car, an anomaly for New Yorkers. It was so difficult to find a parking space or it was so expensive to rent one, that most residents chose to walk, take a cab or bus, or ride the subway. But Knox still had his little Honda that his parents had given him when he left home for college, and he rolled the dice every time he looked for a parking space in his Upper West Side neighborhood. He had found one the day before right at their front door. That rarely happened. Sometimes when Knox found a nearby parking place, he'd leave the car there for days, choosing to take a cab or walk to work, rather than lose his spot. But this morning their car sat in a cherished parking spot. Jinx hoped that was a good omen.

"Morning, Jinx," Tony said, as Knox opened the front car door and helped his mother in.

He then jumped into the back.

"Hey, Tony. How are you this morning?"

"Ummm, I'd say nervous just about covers it. Maybe excited, too."

"That's understandable," Jinx said, reaching over and patting his arm.

As they drove, Knox dialed Liz. "We're on our way, about ten minutes out. See you shortly."

Tony weaved in and out of the traffic, and when they pulled up in front of Liz's apartment building, they found her standing on the sidewalk, smiling, her long flaxen hair waving like a flag in the breeze.

"She's an angel," was all Jinx could manage, tears in her eyes as she watched the beautiful young woman who was willing to sacrifice so much for her best friends.

"Hi, guys," she chirped cheerily as she jumped into the back seat with Knox and kissed him on the cheek. She patted Jinx on the back and reached over and squeezed Tony's shoulder. She didn't want to leave anyone out. So kind. So thoughtful. So generous. Jinx hoped her grandchild would get those fine qualities from his—or her—mother.

"Excited?" she asked.

"Yes," they all responded at once.

"I'm excited, too. We're going to make a baby, you guys. Isn't that awesome?"

They were still laughing gleefully, yet nervously, when they pulled into the parking lot adjacent to the medical complex.

"You guys hop out, and I'll go park the car," Tony said. "I'll meet you inside."

The three got out of the car and went inside to wait their turn.

Knox handed Liz the insulated bag with two vials of sperm, saying, "Careful, it's full of babies."

Liz took the bag from Knox and approached the frosted glass and dinged the bell on the counter.

A young woman slid the glass aside and, smiling brightly, said, "Good morning, your name, please."

"Liz Houston," she said, as Knox and Jinx claimed seats and saved two for Tony and Liz.

The receptionist checked her computer and said, "Sure, Ms. Houston, you're scheduled at eight-thirty with Dr. Axelrod. Just give me that and have a seat, and we'll call you when he's ready for you."

"Thanks," Liz said, handing the specimens over to the receptionist and crossing the waiting room to claim a seat with the others.

"Liz Houston," the nurse called.

"Oh, shucks," Liz said and handed the three-year-old People magazine to Knox, saying, "here, finish reading this and tell me how Jessica Simpson plans to lose all that weight."

Knox and Tony laughed as Liz grabbed Jinx's hand and said, "Come on, Jinx, we're going to go make a baby."

"Hi, I'm Betty. I'll be assisting Dr. Axelrod this morning," the nurse said as she reached for Liz's hand.

"Hi, Betty," Liz said. "This is my friend Jinx Collier. I'd like for her to be with me during the insemination. Would that be okay?"

"Sure," said Betty, smiling and placing a hand on Liz's back, "just come on back this way."

Once they were in the treatment room, Betty said, "Just undress from the waist down, drape this sheet over you, and hop up on the table. Dr. Axelrod and I'll be with you shortly."

Once Betty had cleared the room, Jinx asked, "Would you like for me to step outside while you undress, Liz?"

Liz hugged Jinx and said, "No, I want you to stay with me.

Okay?"

"Sure, I'm not going anywhere."

And as Liz undressed and handed her jeans and panties to Jinx, Jinx helped her onto the table and covered her with the sheet.

"Good morning, Liz," bellowed Dr. Axelrod, as he breezed into the room, followed by Betty. And turning to Jinx he said, "I'm Gray Axelrod, and you are?"

"Jinx Collier, a friend of Liz's."

"Welcome, Ms. Collier. If you'll just stand at Liz's head, maybe take her hand, we can get started. Are you ready, Liz?"

"I believe I am."

"You know the procedure. We're going to insert the tom cat to perform the insemination. You may feel a bit of cramping, but it won't be any more severe than menstrual cramps. It won't take long," he said, with a dismissive wave of his hand. "After a little rest, you'll be out of here and back to normal. Sound good?"

"Sounds good to me."

"Well, let's get started."

The procedure went just as planned. It took about fifteen minutes. Jinx held Liz's hand, and only twice did Liz squeeze and wince from the mild cramping.

"We're all through here. Now that wasn't so bad, was it?" said Dr. Axelrod and patted Liz on the shoulder.

"Piece of cake," Liz said, smiling broadly.

"Great," Dr. Axelrod said, and, turning to Jinx, added, "it was nice meeting you, Ms. Collier. Now you two just rest right here for about thirty minutes. Betty will check in on you shortly and will let you know when you can leave."

Much to everyone's surprise, including Dr. Axelrod's, Liz became pregnant with the first insemination. Although she had promised that she was in it for the long haul and would go through as many procedures as it took, she was delighted to find that it would take only the one.

Jinx tried to keep her distance and not smother Liz during the pregnancy, but Knox and Tony drove the poor girl crazy. They insisted upon seeing her every day to quiz her on her vitamin intake and her diet. They brought her bags of groceries and cooked meals she didn't want to eat. They rubbed her belly until she had to tell them, "Hands off, boys!" They invited her to come live with them, but Liz wouldn't hear of it. Since Knox and Tony had paid her rent up to date and beyond, why would she want to leave her apartment? She understood, though, their level of concern and their need to be in charge. They were having a baby. What parents wouldn't behave the way they were behaving?

By seven weeks Liz was showing and had gained an inordinate amount of weight, even though she swore she hadn't changed her eating habits.

At her regular doctor visit her obstetrician said, "Let's do an ultrasound, Liz, to see what's going on," not letting on to what he suspected.

But the ultrasound confirmed his suspicions.

"Twins? No way!" Liz shrieked.

Knox and Tony stared mutely at the doctor.

"Yep, just as I thought. No one gains as much weight as you have, Liz, if she isn't carrying multiples. Look, you can see both babies," Dr. Nelson said, leaning forward, pointing with his pen toward the two small blobs on the screen.

Knox and Tony each took one of Liz's hands and squeezed tight. The three craned forward, their heads together, to get a better look. As they realized what they were seeing, the tears began to stream down their cheeks. Suddenly, they grabbed one another, formed a hugging circle, and sobbed.

"Twins. We're having twins," they all said simultaneously. "Babies, two babies. We're going to have two little babies at one time."

"Wait a minute," cried Liz. "What's this we business? We're not having twins. I'm having twins. Oh, my god, I'm having twins. I have babies, two babies, growing inside me. I signed on for one. How did this happen? There are two. Oh, guys, I hope I can do this for you," Liz cried, by now sobbing in earnest.

Knox and Tony encircled their precious Liz with their arms and assured her she could do it because they'd be with her all the way. And the guys joined her crying—with joy, with excitement, with hope, with uncertainty, and with a great deal of fear.

"Thank you, thank you, Liz," they both blubbered as they

sniffled loudly and wiped their leaking eyes on their shirt sleeves.

And to the doctor Knox said, "When will we know if they are girls or boys or a combo?"

Dr. Nelson told them, "Not quite yet. They'll need to incubate for about ten or eleven more weeks. We can usually determine the sex at around eighteen weeks."

As Liz grew, she stayed close to home. During the day she worked at her easel, resting on her mattress in the corner of her sunny apartment when she became weary. Knox and Tony would stop by after work, bringing her healthy meals and taking her outside for fresh air and short walks. Though she became immense and tired easily, she actually felt wonderful. She didn't experience the first sign of morning sickness, and she was able to eat anything she chose. Her cheeks were rosy and she had that beautiful glow of motherhood. Her doctor was delighted with her progress and assured all the parents that the babies were healthy, robust, and right on schedule.

And Liz had never been happier in her life. She was creating some of her best art and she was creating life for the two most wonderful people she had ever known, two people who loved her unconditionally and encouraged her in every way.

At eighteen weeks the three parents gathered in the examination room to find out if they were having boys or girls or one of each.

As they squinted at the screen, Knox asked, "What are we looking at? What are we seeing?"

"Well, dads, you'd better get out the pink paint, because there's not a penis in sight."

"Girls! Oh, Knox, we're having two little girls!" bellowed Tony.

"Two! Girls! We're going to spoil 'em rotten!"

The fathers-to-be hugged and jumped up and down while Liz's eyes filled with tears.

"Two little girls," she whispered. "Perfect. You'll be wonderful daddies to two little girls."

When Lamaze classes began, Liz had three coaches: Knox,

Tony, and Jinx. And they approached the class as though every expectant mother needed three breathing coaches. The other Lamaze students were a little wary of this odd hodge-podge of people who were having twin girls, but they grew to love this foursome who were learning to become a family.

One night after class Liz said, "Mom," (She had skipped Jinx and had gone straight to Mom.) "when I proposed this baby thing, I thought I'd be doing Knox and Tony a favor—and getting my rent paid and my art bought, of course—but I've gotten so much more out of this than they'll ever know. I feel more loved than I've ever felt in my life. Thank you for loving me."

The two women were sitting side-by-side on the sofa, and, as if she had been doing it all her life, Liz lay down, resting her head in Jinx's lap. The pregnancy had stirred Liz's hormones and made her very sentimental. But Jinx knew that this wasn't just the hormones talking. Liz really loved this new family of hers and was so grateful that they loved her in return.

Then Liz looked up into Jinx's face and said, "You know, we've been so wrapped up in these babies, that we've overlooked something very important."

"What's that, Darlin'?"

"You're going to be a grandmother, Jinx. These girls are going to be so lucky to have you in their lives. But we haven't even talked about what they're going to call you. That's real important, you know."

Jinx smiled and said, "Oh, I haven't overlooked it. In fact, I've been thinking about it a lot, a whole lot. It's not every day a woman gets to be a grandmother for the first time."

Liz laughed and said, "Good Point."

Jix told her, "My grandmother's name was Miriam, and I called her Mimi. Since I'm Jinx, I think I'd like for the girls to call me Jiji. What do you think?"

Liz cried, "Oh, Jinx, I love it. It's perfect."

Appearing from the kitchen with iced tea and scones, Knox and Tony asked, "What's perfect?"

"Jiji," said Liz. "The girls are going to call Jinx Jiji."

"Kind of like Mimi?" Knox said.

"Yeah, kind of like Mimi," Jinx said, smiling at her son.

"Love it," the daddies said in unison.

Sixteen

"Who is this? How did you get my phone number? Stop it this instant!"

Jinx had already hung up on this pervert once. His guttural, grunting noises were unnerving and made the hair stand on her neck.

"Mooooooooooommmmmmmm!"

It wasn't until she heard that "Mooooooooooommmmmmmm" that Jinx realized it was Liz, not some pervert, on the other end of the line.

"I can't find Knox and Tony. They aren't answering their phones. The baaaaaaa-beeeeeez!"

"Hold on, Sweetie. I'm on my way."

Jinx was in Saks when Liz's call came through. Jinx had taken to New York shopping like a fish to water, and Saks was one of her favorite shopping spots. She was decked out in her boot-cut jeans and stiletto-heeled boots—a far cry from her Savannah sundresses and sandals—and each time she passed a mirror, she cut her eyes and took in the new Jinx. In her grief she had shed twenty pounds, and her slimmed-down tush and thighs looked spectacular in denim. She had inherited her mother's short legs, but the long jeans and tall heels made her legs look like they just went on forever. Jinx loved the illusion.

And her hair—she shook her head and watched her edgy chin-length cut slide into place. She could run her fingers through it, and still it slid, effortlessly, right back into place. Liz loved it. It was so different from the shoulder-length sprayed helmet she had worn for years. She had so wanted a change.

Felicity, her favorite Saks clerk, had a hair style that looked like performance art. Snow white, but sometimes pink, yet at other times purple and orange, it was long on the sides, shaved at the back, spiked on top, with bangs that hung past one eye. Jinx did not want shaved and spiked and neon colored, but she did want a stylist who could do something creative with her hair. She wanted someone to make art on her head, to banish the last vestige of Georgia from her being, and make her a bona fide New Yorker. So she asked Felicity for a recommendation.

At first reluctant to pay more for one hair cut than she had paid for a year's worth of cuts in Georgia, Jinx ultimately decided she was worth it and took a taxi to Soho, to the studio of stylist Jesus Weinstein. Every bit as eccentric as his name, Jesus hadn't quite decided his nationality, easily slipping from a British accent to a Scottish brogue to a Slavic tongue. As entertaining as his multiple accents were, his outlandish appearance was startling. Though he couldn't have been more than five feet four, his purple Lady Gaga platform boots put him at about six feet. His purple Mohawk and purple Spandex body suit matched his footwear perfectly. He resembled a tall, thin eggplant.

But as a first-time customer, Jinx had paid up front. It was too late to turn back.

First Jesus sent Jinx to the shampoo station, where the shampoo technician massaged her head into a state of euphoria, something she had never experienced, an experience that was well worth the entire cost of the appointment.

When it ended, she wanted to cry, "Don't stop! Don't stop! Yes! Yes! Yes!"

Then Jesus took over, his artistic hands flying and snipping around her head, flinging chards of hair as if the excess were toxic. And as he sculpted her helmet into submission, his assistant held the unneeded-for-now hair out of the way. Other hairdressers had plastic clips for the job; Jesus had an actual human.

When he finished snipping and blowing her into a perfectly wonderful, wind-blown style, he unfurled her cape dramatically, stepped back, admired his creation, and asked Jinx in his British-Scottish-Slavic accent, "And, my darling, are you pleased?"

Pleased? She was more than pleased. The result was transforming, both inside and out. Jinx shook her head and admired herself in the mirror. A broad smile spread across her face. That was all Jesus needed to know. He bent his spindly, purple frame to hug her and air kiss her near both cheeks.

Jinx left Jesus' shop feeling edgy and trendy and New Yorky. She wasn't ready to return to her home. She wanted to make the moment last—to strut her stuff, to shake her head, to let her edginess mingle with the edginess of other New Yorkers. So she strutted, taking in the sights of Soho, the art, the artistic-looking people, the edgy fashions, the bustlers. Turning a corner from busy Varick Street, she found herself on a quiet side street, all alone in front of a quaint little restaurant called simply Eat. She liked the matter-of-fact no-nonsense name; she liked the smallness of it, the out-of-the-wayness of it. She liked that there were no other diners, just a heavily tattooed and bejeweled young woman sitting behind the small bar, reading a paperback novel. It was strange but somehow appealing. She strolled in and took a seat. She had her choice of tables.

Jinx watched the tattooed woman behind the bar as she continued to read. Finally she sighed, dog-eared her page, and closed her book slowly. Picking up a menu, she made her way around the bar to Jinx's table.

"Been here before?"

"No, this is my first visit. What are your specials today?"

"No specials. Everything's on the menu. Since you're new, though, I recommend the BLT and egg on ciabatta bread. It comes with a side salad with vinaigrette and a drink for $19.95. It's real good."

Jinx had still not gotten accustomed to paying $19.95 for a sandwich, since back home at the Crab Shack for a mere $15.95 she could get a seafood platter with fried shrimp, oysters, and flounder, French fries, cole slaw, all the hush puppies and honey butter she could hold, endless sweet tea, and a dessert of the best 'nana puddin' ever. But the lack of anything cheaper on the menu than a $19.95 sandwich and since she could afford any meal she wanted, she said, "Okay, then, that's what I'll take. Make my drink ice tea," she said.

And the waitress-bar sitter-reader took the menu from Jinx and disappeared without another word.

Jinx had been so focused on her new look that she hadn't noticed her gnawing hunger. But now that she was in the general vicinity of food, her stomach began to growl loudly. She was glad the restaurant was deserted. She figured it wouldn't take the chef long to prepare her simple but pricey sandwich. But she waited. And waited. And waited. She heard no noise coming from the kitchen, and the tattooed woman had returned to the bar to read her book.

And ignore her single customer.

She would never be left alone for twenty minutes in the Crab Shack. Long before now, Vyneeda would have huffed over to her table, as if she'd just run a marathon, and knitting her brow with great concern, would say, "Miz Collier, I'm so sorry it's takin' s' long. Lonnie's out sick t'night, and Cook's back 'ere all by hisself. Now, I've brung you some hushpuppies to tide ya over till your shrimps is done. Careful now, they's right out of the grease and hotter 'n hallelujah."

Jinx smiled at the memory, a little bittersweet, certain Vyneeta would never again fawn over her. But this was a new life, a life she was eagerly embracing. She was in no hurry, though her stomach continued to growl audibly. She'd just watch, with interest, the young tattooed woman behind the counter as she read her paperback and fiddled with her septum ring.

But Liz's call had jolted Jinx from her self-admiration and her memories of edgy haircuts and snail-paced lunches.

She tossed her cell phone into her oversized Fendi bag and headed for the street. All of the store clerks knew Jinx—that southern lady who loved New York clothes and wanted all of them—and each stepped forward to help her as she rushed past.

She waved them off, saying, "No thanks, not now, later."

She left them in her wake, looking bewildered.

Before she cleared the door to the street, she had her arm raised in taxi-hailing mode. Right away a cab pulled up to the curb. As she reached for the door handle, an attractive, gray-haired gentleman with a deep tan did the same.

"Oh, no you don't! This is my cab," Jinx told him in self-assured New York fashion.

"But…"

"No buts. Unless you're having a baby, you'll have to wait for the next cab."

Knox may still be shy about aggressively hailing a cab, but not Jinx.

The man yanked his hand away as if he had touched a hot stove.

Without even a thank you—there was no time for pleasantries—

Jinx hopped into the taxi and slammed the door, leaving the attractive gentleman on the curb, looking as bewildered as the Saks clerks.

Jinx settled herself in the back seat, looked at the driver's ID card, and said, "Ra-heem-ra-jesh-rom-san-ro…"

And the driver said, "Patel. Just call me Patel."

"Mr. Patel…."

"Just Patel, Ma'am. Now, where do you want to go?"

"Babies, we're having babies."

"Patel glanced at Jinx's flat midriff that was obviously not carrying babies and narrowed his eyes at her."

"Oh, no, not me. It's my…"

And for the first time Jinx realized that she wasn't sure what Liz was to her.

"My daughter-in law is having twins. Yes, that's right, my daughter-in-law. We have to go get her."

"All right, it doesn't really matter to me who is having the babies. I just need to know where she is so I can go pick her up."

"Oh, yes, right." And Jinx was surprised that, in her frenetic state, she had the presence of mind to remember Liz's address.

Patel honked and weaved and hand gestured back into the flow of traffic, and they were off to rescue Jinx's daughter-in-law. There must have been more than the usual urgency in Patel's honking and hand gesturing because the traffic and pedestrians parted like the Red Sea. The cabbie floored the accelerator, and Jinx swore that they became airborne on several occasions. For some reason, though, Jinx was not at all frightened. She felt safe in Patel's care. He did everything but drive on the sidewalk, and they made the twenty-five minute trip in less than fifteen.

When the cab pulled up to the curb in front of Liz's apartment building, Jinx and Patel found the expectant mother sitting alone on her small suitcase in the middle of the sidewalk, knees splayed wide, her rotund belly cradled in her arms. Pedestrians passed on either side of her, but not one of them glanced toward the very pregnant woman sitting on a small suitcase in the middle of the sidewalk. New Yorkers had seen stranger.

Jinx leapt from the back of the cab while it was still rolling. Patel slammed on the brakes, left the car idling mid-street, and joined Jinx at Liz's side.

Liz was panting, "E-e-e-e, ah-ah-ah-ah-ah," all by herself.

There were supposed to be two men sitting behind her, cradling her stretched-beyond-belief, out-of-shape body as they comforted her, stroked her, and coached her through her labor.

But where were those two men? They were at Madison Square Garden watching their beloved Knicks, playing in a summer tournament, behaving like overgrown boys, arguing over who shoved whom and whose turn it was to play with the ball. Knox and Tony promised to keep their phones on at all times, but they apparently couldn't hear the ringing over the deafening testosterone that was flying around the arena.

Once Patel and Jinx had settled Liz in the back seat of the cab and Jinx joined her, the cab driver grabbed the little suitcase and threw it in the front seat, no time to fiddle with the trunk.

As Patel pulled back into the flow of traffic and headed in the direction of Presbyterian Hospital, Jinx took her cell phone from her purse and tried Knox's number.

"Darlin', this is Mom. When you and Tony get this message, y'all need to head straight to..."

Liz grabbed the phone from Jinx's hand as she said, "Gimme that thing." Then normally gentle Liz, sounding as if she had all of a sudden been possessed, yelled into the phone, "Listen up, you guys! I am doing you boys a favor—not an I'll-sit-your-cat-while-you-spend-the-weekend-at-the-shore kind of favor. It's more like an I'm-having-your-babies-so-you'd-better-get-your-sorry-asses-to-the-hospital-right-now kind of favor."

That having been said, Liz handed the phone back to Jinx and resumed her *e-e-e-e, ah-ah-ah-ah-ah*.

Jinx caught a glimpse of Patel's raised eyebrows in the rear-view mirror. Had she been wearing her Georgia temperament, she'd have tried to explain the situation to him. But this was New York and Patel really wasn't a part of their inner circle, so Jinx felt no obligation to explain their strange set-up to their cab driver. What's more, Jinx was confident that Patel had seen stranger things in his taxi.

Liz's *e-e-e-e, ah-ah-ah-ah-ah* grew louder and faster as Patel swerved around cars and corners, honking his horn and yelling out the window. Her head thrown back in howl position, Liz cradled her enormous belly as Jinx attempted to make calming-clucking-soothing noises. Liz's audible breathing exercises came to a screaming crescendo just as Patel careened into the hospital parking lot and came to a screeching halt at the emergency room door.

There they found Knox and Tony standing by the entrance with two orderlies, a gurney, and very sheepish looks on their faces. They had made the trip from Madison Square Garden in less time than was humanly possible, but since they were preparing to witness the miracle of birth, they all knew not to question the impossible.

The first of the babies was crowning by the time the orderlies transferred Liz to the gurney, so there was no time for prepping. The attendants wheeled the mom-to-be directly from car to birthing room.

Liz had had the presence of mind to call Dr. Nelson before heading to the sidewalk to sit on her suitcase and await Jinx's arrival. He was already at the hospital, scrubbed and ready to swing into action by the time Liz was lifted to the delivery bed and her legs hoisted into the stirrups. The worst of the labor was over, so with just a few good pushes, Liz delivered Tony and Knox's children.

Both babies weighed in at five pounds, four ounces and were exactly nineteen inches long. But that's where their similarities ended.

Elizabeth Virginia, named for her birth mother, Liz, and grandmother, Jinx, greeted her new world with sweet coos and curiosity, eager to take in the room and all the people with huge sapphire eyes that were months away from focusing. As the nurse lifted her from Dr. Nelson, wrapped her in a blanket, and handed her to Knox, she immediately curled her tiny fist around her daddy's finger, still cooing. With her cap of downy blond hair, a dimple in her chin, and a fair complexion, there was no question who Izzy's father was.

Little sister, Abigail Grace, named for Tony's mother and maternal grandmother, who themselves had been named for Catholic saints, came into the world yelling her opinion, flailing her fists, and pumping her legs as if riding a bicycle. With dark, wavy hair, dark eyes, and a rosy complexion, she was a mini Tony Colletti. No one doubted that Abby Collier-Colletti would forever be in charge.

Jinx wanted desperately to rush to her grandchildren, gather them in her arms, and cradle them. She knew, though, that she would get her turn, just not right now. Instead, she held Liz's hand and smoothed her damp hair away from her steaming forehead. Liz, the selfless young woman who had so lovingly carried Knox and Tony's children, watched as her best friends cuddled their daughters. And as she watched, tears spilled from her eyes.

Jinx reached for a tissue on the bedside table and, gathering Liz in her arms, dabbed at her wet cheeks. So in need of someone to hold her, Liz clung to Jinx and cried onto her shoulder.

"Oh, Liz darlin', are you all right?"

"I'm fine, Mom, honest I'm fine," she said, when, in fact, she really wasn't fine at all. She wanted so badly to be holding onto her own mother, having her mother smooth her hair, rub her back. But she knew that wasn't possible, as long as she refused to bend to her mother's rigid rules. But she still loved her mother and wanted to feel her arms. Emotional moments need a mother's comfort.

"Guess it's just hormones. I understand giving birth produces a lot of those. And I'm just so happy for Knox and Tony. And I'm so relieved that the girls are healthy. I feel so blessed to have been able to help them."

Both Knox and Tony approached, still cradling their daughters.

"Want to hold them?" they offered to Liz.

"Thanks, but I'm awfully tired. I'm afraid I'd drop them. I'll get my chance."

What she was thinking but didn't say was, *I'm afraid I couldn't give them back.* Liz just had no idea she would feel so attached. She had told herself from the beginning that these children were not hers, that she was just carrying these babies for her two best friends who could not carry them for themselves. She wanted desperately to do this for them. She was certain she could handle it.

She had told the boys that she would be whatever the fathers wanted her to be to the girls. She'd be a friend, a favorite aunt, or any title they chose to give her. She also offered to back away altogether, if they felt that would be best for the girls—and for their dads. She meant it when she said it, but now, lying in the hospital bed watching the little girls she had just brought into the world, she prayed that Knox and Tony wouldn't want her to back away. She knew that she wanted—no, needed to be a part of Abby and Izzy's lives.

In two days Liz was ready to leave the hospital. The girls, too, with their healthy birth weights and perfect vital signs, were cleared to leave. When Liz eased herself into the wheelchair, ready for the orderly to escort her to the hospital exit, Knox and Tony, each cradling a daughter, placed the babies in Liz's arms. It felt so natural to her. She felt so maternal toward the girls. She drew them to her and smiled into their tiny, dimpled faces as they headed for home.

Liz would stay with the boys and the babies until her strength returned.

"No arguments," ordered Tony.

And each time Liz began to protest, Knox would say, "Ah, ah, ah, ah," drowning her words.

They were amazed at how normal it felt for the three of them to be sharing baby duty, none of them having a clue what they were doing, all of them learning as they went along. Two o'clock feedings would find them all huddling around the warming bottles in their pajamas, stretching, yawning, and rubbing their weary eyes. Diaper-changing time had them all fumbling and clumsy but, in time, getting the girls covered and protected. They were just like any new parents who were traveling this road for the first time.

In two weeks Knox returned to work, and Liz returned to her studio. Her rent was paid, but she needed to rebuild her stock and get back out on the street with her art. Who knew when a serious collector might happen by?

Tony, on the other hand, would take six weeks paternity leave to care for the girls and find a suitable nanny to take over when he returned to work. By the end of his leave, Tony could change a diaper with one hand and bathe both girls at once. He mixed formula and stored bottles, washed the little girls' tiny clothes, fed and burped the babies, cleaned the apartment, and prepared delicious meals for Knox, Liz, and himself.

But he failed to find a nanny. Day after day the agency sent what they deemed to be suitable applicants, but Tony found none of them acceptable to care for his children.

"She seemed distracted. I don't think she'd pay good attention to the girls."

"She had a nose ring."

"She didn't speak English very well."

"She was too old. I don't think she'd be able to keep up with the girls once they were up, running around."

"She was drinking a soda. God knows what she'd feed our children."

Tony interviewed twenty-three candidates. He rejected all twenty-three. Knox knew that if it were left up to Tony, they'd never find anyone to care for the children. And they had to find someone. Tony couldn't stay home indefinitely.

Then Polly Ann came up with what she felt was the perfect solution. "Who says we need a nanny? What's wrong with us? Why can't we take care of our babies? We can take turns. You got the three of us right across the hall. We can all help out. And what about Liz? We know she's got to take advantage of her light when she paints, but what about when it rains? She can take the baby shift when it rains. Right? And the daddies can take the night and weekend shifts. Sound like a plan?"

Leave it up to Polly Ann to be the voice of reason. Her plan seemed perfect to everyone. There wasn't an old, distracted, soda drinking, nose-ring-wearing, non-English-speaking nanny in the bunch.

"Sounds like a great plan," they all cried in unison and relief.

The girls took cheerfully to their co-op of caretakers and were easy babies to care for from the beginning. As long as they had each other, they were sublimely happy. But separate the two, and there was hell to pay—with lots of screeching and crying. So everyone knew to keep the girls together, and all would be rosy. From the start they slept in the same bed, and soon they were sleeping holding hands. In no time they giggled at each other's antics and invented their own twin language. If ever there had been concerns about parenting skills and the girls' upbringing, no one could remember them.

Knox and Tony had invited Jinx, Polly Ann, and Delores to dinner. When they arrived at the guys' apartment, they found Liz in the kitchen with Knox and Tony, the three of them shoving one another and laughing like siblings. Izzy and Abby sat in their high chairs, taking in the banter of their three parents. Their eyes were wide, their dimpled grins displaying proud, new little teeth. They clapped their chubby hands and shrieked with glee at their Mama and Daddy and Pop Pop. Knox, Tony, Liz, Izzy, and Abby were learning how to be a family. The unusual arrangement might not have worked for most, but it seemed to be a good fit for the five of them.

Although many found this family to be a strange set-up, Polly Ann, with Delores's nudging, had come to accept the situation better than most. She had come from a long line of unwed mothers and had, herself, been single when she'd given birth to her two children, Marcus and Monette. Her mama and granny and an abundance of aunties and cousins had helped raise her children long before Hillary told us that it took a village. Though she'd initially had a difficult time accepting two fathers raising children, she had come around. So two daddies, a surrogate, two babies, a grandmother, and the grandmother's best friend from birth—and Delores, of course—made a perfectly normal family, as far as Polly Ann was concerned.

When Charlie died, Jinx had been devastated and told Polly Ann that her whole family was gone.

Polly Ann had responded, "Family isn't what you're given, Sugah Pie; family is what you make."

As she watched her grandchildren interact with their three parents and Polly Ann and Delores cluck over the whole bunch, Jinx was beginning to understand what her wise friend had meant.

Seventeen

Try as she might, Pandora Featherby could not avoid being rich. Pandora had grown up in a Park Avenue penthouse, obediently attending boarding schools and wearing her Gram's pearls and the twin sets Mummy brought back from her trips abroad.

But when it came time for Pandora to go to college, she rejected Mummy and Gram's beloved alma mater, Hollins College in the beautiful Shenandoah Valley of Virginia, and insisted that only UC-Berkeley would do. Pandora's parents—and Gram—were horrified at the mere suggestion and forbade her to attend that ungodly heathen place on the left coast. When, after three months, Pandora refused to quit pouting until she got her way, her parents relented. They were weary of their high-strung daughter's petulance, and they had more pressing things to attend to: they had booked an around-the-world cruise, and it was too late to cancel.

Pandora came of age in the 60's, and UC-Berkeley was where it was at in the 60's. Pandora wanted to protest. She wasn't sure what she wanted to protest, but she was certain she could find a cause. The War? Poverty? Civil Rights? Migrant workers' rights? Causes were so far removed from Pandora's Park Avenue existence, but she sensed a strong pull to help someone other than herself, for a change.

Pandora felt out of place at Berkeley. There wasn't another twin set on campus. And instead of pearls, her classmates wore puka beads and peace symbols on cords around their necks. On her first Saturday in California, Pandora piled all her cashmere sweaters and plaid wool skirts into her Gucci luggage and headed for the nearest thrift store. There was one on every corner. There, in that patchouli-reeking hole in the wall, she traded her expensive European clothing for torn jeans, used earth sandals, and baggy Guatemalan hemp shirts embroidered with brightly-colored flowers.

She couldn't part with Gram's pearls.

When she returned to her dorm room, Pandora looked at her new self in the mirror. She liked what she saw, but the preppy headband had to go. She yanked it from her head, unleashing her tamed red hair into a massive mane of fiery curls. She was ready to protest...something.

It didn't take Pandora long to find a cause. There was one of those on every corner, too. They were in the classroom, as well. She adored her professors and loved what they had to say. She felt that, for the first time in her life, she was learning something worth learning. She was learning about the world beyond the walls of her Park Avenue penthouse and her boarding schools, and she was learning how to help others. It was a refreshing change for this pampered princess.

By fall break Pandora had been arrested four times—a badge of honor for any Berkeley student of the 60's. Pandora sat in, stood up, and lay down in protest. She burned bras, burned friends' draft cards, and burned the President of Berkeley in effigy. She wore flowers in her hair and sang protest songs about wearing flowers in one's hair. She took a trip to a migrant workers' camp to protest, and on the trip she tripped—for the first time. Pandora lived the Berkeley experience to the fullest, and at the end of four years, she graduated with honors and a degree in sociology and a ticket to the Peace Corps.

It was in Guatemala—she still loved their shirts—that she met Chez. His name was really Eugene, but this was the 60's, and the 60's was no era for a name like Eugene. Chez, too, had attended Berkeley while Pandora was there, but their paths had never crossed. They protested the same outrages and supported the same causes—just at different times and on different street corners. But in the Peace Corps Pandora and Chez were united in their cause—rejecting vulgar consumerism and helping others. They fell deeply in love and performed their own ritual unity ceremony under the stars of Guatemala. They'd do the legal thing back in the States when they could get around to it.

After their stint in the Peace Corps, Pandora and Chez returned to Berkeley, where Chez had been accepted to law school. He wanted to become a Legal Aid attorney, the better to help the down-trodden. They made their union legal and set up housekeeping in a one-bedroom basement apartment that they shared with four other law students. Pandora's parents still didn't agree with their daughter's life choices, but, out of habit, continued sending her a monthly allowance. She and Chez lived on a small portion of it while giving the rest to their causes. Pandora volunteered at a soup kitchen during the day and studied law with Chez by night. They were happy, poor, and making a difference.

Sometime during Eugene's—he thought Chez didn't sound lawyerly—last year of law school, the corporate attorneys came calling.

"Oh, no, Chez. What about Legal Aid?"

"Eugene. It's Eugene now, Pandora. The law firms respect my work with Legal Aid and feel they can use my expertise in their pro bono departments. I will still be helping those who can't help themselves. I'll still be serving our cause, Pandora."

Within three years of joining The Firm, Eugene was making a high six-figure salary, driving a top-of-the-line BMW, and building a house in The Hills. He was helping the helpless, but he was getting rich doing it.

When Pandora's protests fell on deaf ears, she took her causes and walked out on Chez-Eugene, leaving him with the Beemer, the partially-built mansion, and the money. He was too busy indulging in vulgar consumerism to notice.

Pandora met the second love of her life at the soup kitchen. Edouard was a graduate student at Berkeley. Would Pandora ever learn? He was a prince of some small European country, but, like Pandora, felt there was more to life than living in a palace, indulging oneself. Pandora believed she had finally found her kindred spirit. Edouard's parents had been as horrified as Pandora's parents when he'd chosen to attend UC-Berkeley to study phychology, but Edouard must have pouted just as Pandora had because there he was at UC-Berkeley, studying psychology.

After a whirlwind relationship in the soup kitchen and protest line, Pandora and Edouard married at City Hall, returning that same afternoon to their volunteerism.

No sooner had Pandora moved her few earthly belongings into Edward's studio apartment, when Edouard received a call from home. His father had died, and, as heir to the throne, Edouard needed to return home and rule his small European country. Of course, he expected Pandora to accompany him and be his queen.

Pandora said, "No, thanks," and rather than wait for Queen Mother to wire her son air fare, gladly bought Edouard a one-way plane ticket with her allowance and sent him back to his small European country.

Shortly after Edouard's departure, Pandora got a call from Mummy in New York. Daddy had suffered a massive heart attack and died, and Pandora needed to fly home immediately. As much as Pandora had loved her daddy and was heartsick at his passing, she did not relish the idea of leaving her soup kitchen and returning to New York for the funeral. Mummy and her snooty friends would be aghast at Pandora's appearance, as she had let herself go, so to speak. Plus she wore those appalling protest clothes.

But Mummy was so happy to see her daughter that she ignored her appearance and wept copiously into Pandora's colorful, oversized Guatemalan shirt. When it came time for Pandora to return to California and the soup kitchen, Mummy clung to her daughter and begged her to stay.

"I need you, Panny. Now that Daddy is gone, I have no one. I'm begging you, please don't leave me."

"But, Mummy, I'm needed in California."

"Surely you can find a soup kitchen or a protest line or a cause of some sort to complain about right here in New York. Please, Panny, come home."

And that's how Pandora Featherby returned to New York and, in time, became part of this story.

Pandora did, indeed, find causes galore in New York. There was one or more on every corner. So when, in less than a year, Mummy died of a broken heart, Pandora was too firmly entrenched in her New York causes to return to California.

And, of course, Mummy left Pandora the beneficiary to the family fortune—and the owner of a grand Park Avenue penthouse.

So Pandora set to work giving Mummy's money away.

She bought candy from children so they could afford band uniforms. She bought magazines from young men so they could go to college. She sponsored marathon runners. And she loved finding and supporting starving artists. She'd pass a street musician and, recognizing a modicum of talent, would invite him into her home to perform for all of her Park Avenue acquaintances. Someone at the party would know someone who knew someone in the music industry, and before the evening was over, poor street musician would have a music contract and would be on his or her way to Nashville or LA or Motown.

"Pandora, I believe you're about to discover another artist."

Rodney Chastain could sniff out talent better than anyone Pandora knew, and he had brought her some gems. And, with Pandora's help—and her money—those gems had all become wildly successful.

"Last week a friend invited me to have dinner with his family, his family consisting of his mother, his partner, their twin daughters, and the girls' birth mother."

"Run that by me again?"

"You heard me the first time. A woman gave birth to twins for my friend and his partner. Interesting, huh?"

"Yeah, very interesting. But what does this intriguing family have to do with my discovering an artist?"

"The birth mother is the artist. Her work is hanging everywhere in my friend's apartment. She joked that they owe her big time and will keep her in business forever. But I'm sure they'd have bought her work even if she hadn't had babies for them. She's brilliant, Pandora. You have to see her stuff."

So Pandora invited herself to dinner at the Collier-Colletti home and instantly fell in love with their unconventional family—two handsome, charming, witty daddies; two darling little girls; their beautiful, winsome birth mother, Liz; the babies' grandmother, Jinx.

She also fell in love with Liz's art.

"It's stunning, like nothing I've ever seen. I can't believe some gallery owner hasn't snatched your work right up."

Indignant, incredulous Pandora, if she had her way—and she usually did—would have the talented, young artist's work snatched right up before the month was out.

Over dinner with the Collier-Collettis, Pandora peered around Knox and Tony's tastefully decorated home and said, "Who decorated this place? It's beautiful."

Tony said, "You need a decorator?"

Pandora said, "Hell, no! I don't give a fiddly fart about

decorating, but I do know a thousand women who do. I'm sure they'd all love a fresh, new look. And this is a fresh, new look, if ever I've seen one. Now, who's your decorator?"

Without a word Knox, Tony, and Liz all pointed at Jinx. She had been a congenial guest at the dinner party but had, for the most part, taken a back seat to Liz, the purpose for Pandora's visit. But when the guest praised Jinx's talent, she admitted that she was, indeed, Tony and Knox's decorator.

"No! You did this?"

"Well, yes, I did. I have a degree in interior design, but I gave up my profession long ago, when Knox came along," Jinx said, looking lovingly at her son, assuring him, as she always did, that she preferred being his mother to being a professional interior designer. "After that I just decorated for friends. My motto was *will decorate for lunch*. And, believe me, I ate a whole lot of lunches-for-trade."

"Well, I recognize talent when I see it, and you've definitely got talent. And if you want business," Pandora said with a shrug, "I'll get you business. And I promise you'll earn more than lunches. Interested?"

Jinx told Pandora, "Well, as I said, I haven't thought about decorating professionally in a long time, a very long time."

"But, Mom, you still have what it takes," Knox said, waving his arms around to display his mother's talent. "And you'll never have to decorate Benson's bedroom again or eat Miss Caroline's bland potato salad," said Knox. And the two of them chuckled at their private joke.

There was nothing to prevent Jinx from resurrecting her once-in-demand career. Charlie was gone; Knox was grown; The Girls had surely found someone else to fulfill their decorating demands. She had loved transforming Knox and Tony's apartment and her new home. And she was confident she had done a fantastic job on both. Why not transform others' spaces—and get paid for it? 'Cause, yep, she still had it.

Pausing a moment to ponder the daunting but exciting prospect of owning her own design business, Jinx finally said, "Sounds interesting, Pandora. Maybe I will give it some thought."

"All right, then," said Pandora, "we can have a dinner party at my place and invite everyone who knows everyone. But first you'll need to get all your samples and whatnot and whatever licenses it takes to run a business, right? Oh, and don't forget business cards. You'll need lots of business cards. We'll just give them to everyone."

Pandora's enthusiasm was infectious, and she had the whole table buzzing and ready to pitch in to help Jinx start her decorating business.

"Mom, why don't you turn that extra bedroom into your office?"

"Great idea, Knox. I have all that furniture in storage. I couldn't let go of your dad's desk, you know, and I saved my old work table. I'm sure they'll fit into that room."

"Well, I'd better head on out so you guys can get to work," Pandora said. "This has been the most fun. I'm so glad I invited myself to dinner." And, turning to Tony, she said, "I thought I was the best cook in New York, but I believe I've met my match. Superb. I need to get that veal parmesan recipe, if it's not a family secret."

"It's family, but it's not a secret. It's all yours, Pandora," Tony said, giving their new friend a hug. "Thanks so much for coming. I insist we see lots more of you. We need to make up for all that wasted time we haven't known you."

"You're a charmer," Pandora laughed and patted his cheek. "I can see why Knox snagged you."

And turning to Liz, she said, "Now, Liz, you call me tomorrow. We have work to do. I already know a bunch of galleries that would kill for your art."

And, hugging Jinx, she said, "Just call me when you're ready for me to announce that you're in business."

"I will, Pandora," said Jinx, "and thanks so much for offering to help."

"It's what I do. I can't stand to see talent go to waste. God gave it. It's a sin not to use it. And once you've made it big, I'll return with my hand out, expecting you to support my many causes," Pandora said with a belly laugh.

"It's a deal," Jinx and Liz told their new friend who was confident that they were both going to make it big, thanks to Pandora.

Turning to Knox she said, "Put me on your calendar, will you? If you were hiding talent like this, I'm sure you have lots more I don't know about. Let's get together and talk about it."

Knox just smiled and took Pandora's hand. He was in the

business of raising funds for MoMA. He was certain he'd hit the mother lode, but, more than that, he'd made a new friend. He loved her already. But, then, everybody loved Pandora Featherby.

Eighteen

Once they'd said their goodbyes to the whirlwind that was Pandora, they all started talking at once.

"Oh, my gosh, that was incredible!"

"Where do I start?" asked Jinx.

"Don't worry, we're all here to help."

"My art is going to be in a gallery!" screamed Liz.

"Oh, Liz, it's about time."

"I gotta go," said Jinx. "Hope you don't mind if I don't help clean up, but I have a hundred things to do and my mind is spinning out of control. Bye, Sweeties, it's been amazing."

"Night, Mom," Knox said, hugging his mother and seeing her to the door. "This is what you were born to do. You put it on hold for me. Yeah, yeah, I know it's what you wanted. But I'm a grown-up now. It's your turn. No one deserves this more."

"Love you."

"Love you, too. Now, get to work," Knox said, as he watched his mother skip across the hall to her new life.

Polly Ann and Delores were asleep when Jinx let herself into her apartment. She hadn't realized that she had partied so late. She so wanted to share her news with Polly Ann. She'd be delighted. She'd always thought that her Sugah Pie was wasting her talents on those thankless friends of hers.

"They're just taking advantage of you. You deserve better," she'd say over and over.

"But, Polly Ann, I love decorating for them. They're my best friends, and they keep my creativity alive."

"But you're an artist. Artists charge good money for their art.

They don't give it away."

"They're my friends, Polly Ann," she'd say, over and over, defending Caroline and Maitland and Tweezle and the rest.

"Pfffttt, some friends," Polly Ann would huff. "They pay you in food. What kind of payment is that? You can buy your own food. You ain't destitute. And most of that stuff they serve you ain't fittin' for human consumption. That Harper Ann thinks we don't know her secret ingredient in her chicken salad? Phooey! Ain't nothing but Texas Pete. Texas Pete don't belong in no chicken salad. She say it give it a kick. No, it don't. It just make it taste bad. You put capers in chicken salad. You put Texas Pete in cheese grits."

Jinx had ignored Polly Ann's rant, but she had been right—not necessarily about the Texas Pete but about Jinx deserving better. Polly Ann would be delighted when she learned that her Sugah Pie was finally going to get paid for her creativity, thanks to Pandora Featherby.

Jinx cleared her throat and made a bit of a racket as she passed Polly Ann's bedroom, hoping to rouse her so she could share the news with her best friend. But Polly Ann snoozed on. Jinx gave up and reconciled herself to waiting until morning. So she brushed her teeth, slipped into her nightgown, and crawled into bed.

But she was wired and couldn't sleep. Her brain was alive with ideas for her new venture, and she just couldn't seem to turn it off and relax. Decorating her new home and Knox and Tony's place had gotten her juices flowing, and she found it hard to stifle her creativity once she'd reawakened it. But she had run out of outlets, until Pandora Featherby showed up for dinner. After an hour of tossing, Jinx turned on her lamp and reached for the pad and pencil in the drawer of her bedside table.

Then she started making a to-do list:

1. Take guest room furniture to storage.
2. Bring desk and work table from storage.
3. Locate portfolio in storage unit.
4. Purchase small sleeper sofa for office. (Can double as bed for possible guests.)
5. Clear large wall to display PMS colors. (Order PMS color chips and display rack.)
6. Order carpet, fabric, wallpaper samples.
7. Order fixture catalogues.

8. Purchase paint palettes.
9. Research legal requirements for starting business.
10. Purchase office supplies.
11. Order business cards.

Number eleven stopped Jinx in her tracks. How could she order business cards? What would the cards say? Her business didn't even have a name. So before Jinx could order her first sample or rearrange the furniture in her office, she needed to decide what she was going to call her business. It seemed like the perfect place to start. So with her feminine script Jinx began trying out names:

Jinx Collier Interior Design
Jinx Collier Interiors
Jinx Collier Designs
Jinx Designs
Collier Designs
Collier Interiors
Jinx Interiors
Designs by Jinx
Interior Design by Jinx
Interiors by Jinx

Nothing seemed to work. None of the names appeared original or catchy. Jinx wouldn't feel compelled to enlist the services of any one of those companies. Would anyone else?

Her brain was tired, her body exhausted. She needed to call it quits, for now. What's more, she didn't have to do everything in one night. Did she? Jinx dropped her pad and pencil on the bedside table and turned out the light. This time sleep came easily.

The following morning Jinx cracked an eye and looked at the clock. It was past nine o'clock. She couldn't remember the last time she'd slept so late. She sat up and stretched.

Smiling, she said out loud, "I'm going to be an interior designer." It had been a long time since she had called herself an interior designer. It felt good. It felt right.

Then it hit her. She reached for her pad and wrote with a flourish:

Jinx

Simple. Uncluttered. To the point.

"I'd do business with that company," she said, as she held her pad at arm's length, cocked her head, and smiled at the name of her new design business.

Then she slipped from bed and padded barefoot to the kitchen to tell Polly Ann her news.

"No! Absolutely not!"

"But, Pandora, it's gorgeous. I could have so much fun, and it would be stunning when I finished with it."

"It's stunning enough for me, just as it is."

"I bet you haven't changed a thing since you inherited it."

"You got that right. In fact, it looks just like it did when I was a kid."

Jinx ran through Pandora Featherby's Park Avenue apartment, poking her head into rooms and mentally decorating as she went. But Pandora refused to let Jinx touch one thing. Jinx had not been invited to Pandora's to decorate; she'd been invited to eat—and meet. Pandora had invited the eighteen people who knew absolutely everyone in New York City. If these eighteen didn't want Jinx to decorate their houses, they could find plenty who would.

"I don't want my place redecorated, but these people you'll meet tonight will introduce you to more beautiful apartments in need of your touch than you ever imagined. Now, come on in here and taste test for me."

Jinx stepped into the kitchen to find Pandora leaning over a hot stove, vintage 1950, stirring pots furiously. Pandora said she cooked for closet eaters.

"None of that watercress crap in my kitchen. They're all vegetarians until they step through my door. Here, anything goes. They love my brisket, my fried chicken, my stuffed pork chops. Their secrets are safe with me."

Tonight Pandora was serving pot roast, mashed potatoes, corn on the cob, and chocolate meringue pie. She called it good old soup-kitchen food.

"Sticks to your ribs."

Jinx took one look at the overflowing pots and said, "More like stick to my thighs."

But it was just one meal; surely one out-of-control meal couldn't hurt. And it really did look and smell delicious.

Pandora was twirling around her kitchen, her orange flowered caftan flowing about, when the first guest arrived. Former New York mayor Michael Bloomberg went straight to Pandora's stove and began lifting lids and peering into pots, smacking his lips.

"You've outdone yourself this time, Panny," he said, scooping up gravy from the pot roast, blowing on it, and spooning it into his mouth.

Pandora crossed the kitchen, threw an arm around the mayor's shoulder, and planted a kiss on his cheek. "Better than that rubber chicken shit you have to eat at all those banquets, right?"

Mayor Bloomberg roared and said, "Oh, Pandora, your dear sainted mother would roll over in her grave if she could hear you cussing like a sailor."

Pandora winked and said, "But you won't tattle on me, will you, Mike?"

One by one they came, New York's most influential—from playwrights to power brokers—and Jinx met them all.

"How is your baby?"

"Excuse me?"

The man was incredibly handsome, and he looked somewhat familiar, but she had absolutely no idea who he was or what he was talking about.

"Your baby. Did everything turn out all right for you and your baby?"

"I'm sorry, I think you must have me mixed up with someone else. My baby is nearly thirty years old."

"Then you lied to me."

"I what?"

"You stole my cab because you were having a baby. At least, that's what you told me."

Jinx furrowed her brow in confusion. Then it hit her.

The handsome gray-haired gentleman reached out, took Jinx's hand, and said, "Sam Bradley. I'm so pleased to finally meet you. I'd really like to hear the whole story."

Jinx felt her face flush. She so wanted to make a good first impression with Pandora's guests. What a way to start. But she could tell by the glimmer in Sam Bradley's eye that all was not lost.

"Grandchild. Well, actually grandchildren. They're twins. I stole your cab because my grandchildren were on the way and I needed to get to the hospital."

"Grandchildren? Can't be."

Jinx lowered her lids and, in true southern-belle fashion, blushed. "Well, yes, it can be. Two little girls."

"Soups on. Get it while it's hot. Find your places, and we'll get on with this show," bellowed Pandora from the kitchen door.

Jinx left Sam, reluctantly, to find her place and her dinner partner. She was so hoping it would be Sam so she could continue to talk about her granddaughters, but it was not to be. Her dinner partner was Jeremy Niemeyer, the diminutive, eccentric Broadway producer. Jeremy was chatting before he was even seated. He pulled his chair closer to Jinx, the better to monopolize her attention. And as he chatted non-stop, his ill-fitting dentures clacked up and down.

She was thinking, "Why, Pandora?" when Pandora leaned over to refill her wine glass and whispered in her ear, "He knows everyone. Now, smile and act interested."

And as Jeremy chatted on and on, Jinx looked beyond him to find Sam staring at her. He had been cornered by his dinner partner, Serena Belmont, the former Las Vegas dancer who had married well and been widowed young. She spent her money lavishly and spent her time entertaining and being entertained.

And as their dinner partners prattled, Sam made eyes at Jinx. He winked and made faces and flirted. He did everything to entertain Jinx short of hanging a spoon off his nose. It was all Jinx could do to keep from giggling, but she wasn't here to flirt with a man. She was here to make contacts for her new business venture. And as entertaining as Mr. Bradley was, she had to be polite and act as though she were paying attention to Jeremy—because Jeremy knew everyone.

Before the evening was over, Jinx had a pocket full of business and calling cards and appointments to take a look at four Manhattan apartments. And everyone had a pocket full of Jinx's business cards to scatter about New York.

As Pandora handed Jinx her coat and reached to hug her good-night, Jinx felt a tap on her shoulder.

"Care to share a taxi? That way you can't steal mine from me."

Jinx blushed and then laughed at the man who had been flirting shamelessly with her all evening.

"Are you going to the Upper West Side?" asked Jinx.

"I could be."

"Do you live on the Upper West Side?"

"No, I live two blocks that way," he said, pointing toward his home, which was in the opposite direction and far from the Upper West Side.

"Then, why would you want to share a taxi to the Upper West Side?"

Then it hit Jinx: Sam Bradley was hitting on her, trying to pick her up. Her naïveté made her blush crimson.

Sam just smiled.

He was handsome. And charming. But Jinx was not interested. Sam's flirtation had been fun, but that's all it was. She wasn't here to find a date.

Truth be told, Jinx didn't know how to flirt or to date. She had dated only one man in her life: Charlie. And as she stood there awkwardly, face to face with handsome Sam Bradley, she knew that she wasn't brave enough to escape her coupledom that she had shared with only her husband. What's more, her coupledom had betrayed her. The only man she had ever loved had promised that he'd always pick her up, and look where that had gotten her. Charlie had abandoned her when she had needed him the most. She wasn't willing to risk that again. Flirting and dating were out of the question. Jinx was in New York for Knox and her grandchildren. And now her business.

"Thanks, but I think I'll take my own cab." And holding out her hand to him, she said, "It was nice to meet you, Sam."

His brilliant smile faded a bit as he shook his head resignedly and said, "Nice meeting you too, Jinx."

He was polite enough to hang back so as not to share an awkward, silent elevator ride with her. She reached the street, still shaken by the uncomfortable encounter, and was grateful when a cab pulled to the curb and quickly drove her away from Park Avenue and Sam Bradley.

Nineteen

"Wake up, Trilby, darling. I have news, big news."

"Jeremy, this had better be good. What time is it anyway?" Trilby said, stretching and yawning.

"It's ten-thirty, well past the time normal people are up and at 'em. I realize, my precious, that you ain't normal people. But, still, get that pert little tushy out of the sack and listen to me. I have someone you need to meet. She's divine, and she talks with that charming southern accent we adore. You are just going to love her."

"And why do I need to meet this person, Jeremy?"

"To get rid of that sorry-as-shit decorating job that vulgar Ethan What's-his-name pawned off on you as retro. Seventies isn't retro, Honey. It's just god-awful tacky. But all that's about to change. Wake up, wake up, sleepy head. There's a new decorator in town."

"How do you know she's good?" Trilby asked, slipping from bed and sliding her feet into her slippers. "Whose home has she designed? I don't want to get burned again."

"Darling, I have no idea whose place she's done. But Pandora Featherby threw a party for her last night. What else do you need to know?"

"Oh, okay, if Pandora says she's good, she's bound to be good. Give me her number."

After fumbling for a pen and pad and jotting down the name and number Jeremy recited, Trilby hung up and stumbled to the bathroom to get her day underway. Solly had left for his office hours before, so she had their apartment all to herself. She loved her Sol—the only man she'd ever loved—but she needed some time alone, away from his adoration.

Trilby Bettencourt and Sol Ciccone had met at the University of Pennsylvania thirty-five years earlier where Trilby had been admitted only because her daddy had single-handedly funded several departments and where Sol had been highly recruited and offered full scholarships. They were a mismatch if ever there was one, but their attraction was instantaneous and passionate.

Trilby's parents, the Bettencourts of Grosse Point, were horrified by Trilby's choice of suitor. They were expecting their daughter to return to Grosse Point after college and settle down with the son of one of their acquaintances, marry in their Presbyterian church, brunch at their Club, volunteer just enough to appear beneficent, and play bridge on Wednesday afternoons. Why, that's what all Presbyterian Grosse Point girls did. Instead, Trilby had chosen a scholarship student, no less—a boy who had grown up in an Italian Catholic family in Pittsburgh, the son of a postal worker father and a secretary mother. A secretary, for god's sake!

But there was no dissuading Trilby. She loved Sol. Those Grosse Point boys seemed so vanilla compared to sexy, Italian Sol. Mr. and Mrs. Bettencourt threatened; Trilby stood firm. Mr. and Mrs. Bettencourt humored; Trilby rolled her eyes. Mr. and Mrs. Bettencourt promised trips; Trilby took a trip of her own—to Las Vegas to marry her darling Sol. After a passionate honeymoon weekend at Caesar's Palace, Sol and Trilby returned to Pennsylvania where Sol began classes at the University's Wharton School of Business. While Sol excelled at Wharton, Trilby supported them by working as a secretary. Yes, a secretary. Karma is not only a bitch, it has a terrific sense of humor.

After Wharton Sol and Trilby moved to Pittsburgh, where Sol took a job with a floundering steel company. Moving quickly up the company ranks—and turning the sagging company around—Sol eventually bought the steel company and relocated its executive headquarters to New York City. After twenty years in the city, Sol and Trilby were preeminent movers and shakers, one of the most sought-after couples in New York. If you wanted to be seen, you'd hang out with the Bettencourt-Ciccones. If you had a cause you wanted to promote, you'd court the Bettencourt-Ciccones. If you wanted to become successful, you'd want the Bettencourt-Ciccones in your corner.

So Trilby Bettencourt-Ciccone invited herself into Jinx's corner.

Jinx read everything she could find about the power couple. She'd learned that Sol was a successful steel magnate and that Trilby was a successful socialite. But she had no idea what to expect when she showed up at Trilby's apartment. The building's exterior was unadorned gray granite, giving no hint of what lay inside. She presented her card to the doorman who studied his list and ushered her into the lobby. The interior walls were as simple as the exterior—plain gray marble with glass and pewter wall sconces. Jinx found the elevator and told the operator that she was going to the eighteenth floor.

The operator, a hefty man with a shiny black face, flashed a toothy grin and said, "Nice choice, ma'am."

Jinx would soon understand what he meant.

When Trilby opened the door, Jinx was astounded by her beauty. She had to be in her mid-fifties, but she was a stunning woman. She wore her prematurely white hair in a shoulder-length bob, a stark contrast to her golden tan and pale green eyes. Her cashmere pants and sweater were the same green as her eyes, and her toenails shone bright coral on bare feet.

In the entry hall Jinx asked, "Shall I remove my shoes?"

Trilby was taken immediately by Jinx's southern accent and her cordial manner.

"Oh my, no. There's not a thing in here you can hurt. I just hate shoes and refuse to wear them unless I absolutely have to."

Jinx followed Trilby from the entry into the living room where she stopped, in shocked horror.

"I know, I know," said Trilby, waving her arm in disgust. "Don't ask me how it happened. It just did. I trusted an idiot, and this is what I got. I went off to the Mediterranean, and when I returned, I found that someone had thrown up in my apartment. Now, my dear, I need your help."

It was hideous. Olive greens and oranges and golds. Danish Modern furniture and plush carpeting. The kitchen appliances were almond, that color that always looked dingy.

"He called it Retro. I was thinking 30's, maybe 50's. But the 70's? Could there have been an uglier era? Who wants to be reminded of sideburns, polyester, and disco?"

And while Trilby was prattling about her abhorrent decor, Jinx saw it—the most beautiful building in all the world. The Bettencourt-

Ciccones' living room had a huge wall of windows overlooking the Manhattan skyline, and framed in that glass wall was the Chrysler Building. Jinx felt a chill run up her spine and tears spring to her eyes. It happened whenever she saw her very favorite building. And she had never had as spectacular a view of it as she was experiencing from the Bettencourt-Ciccones' penthouse apartment.

Jinx's parents had taken her to New York for the first time when she was seven years old. They took her to see the Rockettes perform at Radio City Music Hall. They ice skated at Lincoln Center. They ate at the finest restaurants. They attended Broadway plays. They traveled to the top of the Empire State Building. They shopped on Fifth Avenue. All Jinx remembered about the trip was the Chrysler Building. She loved it. She wanted to live in it. She wanted to decorate it.

Instantly, the Bettencourt-Ciccones' ghastly décor disappeared before Jinx's eyes, to be replaced by her own vision. She would combine the Art Deco influence and the lines of the Chrysler building with Sol's steel business. It would be stark and high tech and sleek. She smiled as Trilby talked, but Jinx was aware only of her own thoughts. Her creative juices were flowing once again. They'd lain dormant far too long.

She began making mental notes. Grey, lots of gray to emulate the steel. Others combined black with gray, but she would not. She would go with chocolate brown, giving the space warmth. She'd use lots of stark white trim for contrast. She would rip up the vulgar plush carpeting and install light maple floors. Maple made a space look larger, cleaner, and brighter. For color she'd use splashes of red and yellow. That Danish Modern dining table would have to go. She'd replace it with a sleek table for sixteen, one stained the darkest brown. The chairs, though, would be softer—upholstered in reds and yellows. The kitchen would be industrial—stainless steel and concrete with red and yellow pendant lights. She'd decorate Sol's den with lots of red while she would go with the softer yellow for the bedrooms. The place was practically decorating itself.

Jinx was beside herself with excitement, but she didn't want to appear overly anxious—like country come to town.

After her walk-through, she said to Trilby, "Let me prepare my sketches and pull together some samples and swatches, and I'll get back with you so we can make some decisions."

She pulled out her date book and began leafing through. She held it close, so that Trilby could not see that all the pages were blank.

She furrowed her brow and studied the pages, finally saying, "How does a week from Thursday at eleven sound?"

Trilby said excitedly, "Oh, Jinx, that sounds great. I know how busy you must be. I do so appreciate your working me in."

Jinx suppressed a smile as she left the apartment, shaking Trilby's hand and thanking her for the opportunity. By the time she got to the elevator, she was grinning broadly. She was still smiling when the elevator doors opened and she stepped inside.

She turned forward and said, "Lobby, please."

Without looking her way, the elevator operator said, "Nice, right?"

Still staring ahead, Jinx thought, *But not nearly as nice as it's going to be.*

Jinx wasted no time pulling together swatches, samples, and paint chips to prepare a presentation for Trilby. She was invigorated, energized. It felt so good to be flexing her creative muscles after such a long, dry spell. And what a way to christen her new business. Trilby's apartment was spectacular. And it was going to be even more spectacular when she finished with it. Jinx stood, stretched, and kneaded her stiff back. She rubbed her eyes and looked at her watch. Eleven-thirty. She had been at it for ten hours. When she got on a roll, though, she just couldn't seem to stop. But she needed some rest. She turned off her office light and headed for her bedroom.

As she passed Polly Ann and Delores's room, she noticed that their light was still on. She peeked in to find Polly Ann sitting up in bed, reading her Bible, and Delores, her glasses perched on the end of her nose, was working on some sort of needlework.

"I didn't realize y'all were still awake," Jinx said, yawning and stretching. Then to Delores she said, "What are you making, Delores?"

"I'm working on a piece of needlepoint."

It was beautiful, with geometric shapes in shades of teal, brown and coral.

"Delores, that's so lovely," Jinx said, approaching the bedside. Reaching out to touch it, she said, "It's a hand-painted canvas, isn't it?"

"Why, yes, it is. It sounds like you know something about needlepoint, Mrs. Collier."

"Well, some of my friends back in Georgia liked to needlepoint, but I never took up the hobby myself. I do know, though, that hand-painted canvases can be quite pricey."

"Yes, they can be if you don't paint them yourself."

"Do you mean you painted that canvas?"

Resting her canvas in her lap and removing her glasses, Delores said, "My grandmother told me that I couldn't call it mine unless I created it from beginning to end. She insisted I either paint the canvas or draw a graph from which to work. I had to choose my own color palette; and once I had finished stitching and blocking my work, I had to mount it, frame it, or make it into a pillow or rug. Grandmother began teaching me to needlepoint when I was only three years old."

"Did she teach all of her grandchildren to needlepoint?"

"Just me. Her grandmother passed her talent to her, and she chose me to receive the gift."

"You must have been very close to your grandmother."

"Oh, I was. I was blessed to be her chosen. She was quite an interesting woman."

"Interesting?"

"Well, I guess interesting would actually be an understatement. First of all, she insisted we call her Grandmother, saying, 'Granny and Meemaw and such just sound so frivolous, and I am not a frivolous woman.'" Delores's eyes twinkled and she grinned at the memory of her staid, non-frivolous grandmother. "Grandmother's family migrated from Jamaica during the Renaissance Period in Harlem. She immediately became immersed in the culture. She counted among her friends Langston Hughes and W.E.B. Dubois and entertained the likes of Ella Fitzgerald and Billie Holliday in her home. She wasn't able to attend college, but she had a thirst for knowledge and read voraciously."

"She does sound interesting," Jinx said.

"She felt that everyone should be creative, and she showed her creativity through her needlepoint. She even spun and dyed her own yarn and, of course, painted all of her canvases. Her pieces were truly works of art, and she gave it all away to her friends. Lord knows where all of her beautiful pieces are."

"So she wanted you to carry on her legacy," Jinx added.

Chuckling, Delores said, "And she wanted to keep me at home where she could keep an eye on me. She'd say, 'No need for Delores to be out on the street, flitting around. She's a lady, and ladies belong at home.'"

"Well, it sounds like your grandmother was a smart woman."

"That she was. I'm glad she shared her talent with me. It has given me so much joy."

Examining the needlepoint closely, Jinx asked, "Have you ever thought of selling your work, Delores?"

Delores said, "Mrs. Collier, if I sold my work, it would no longer be a joy. It would be a job. And, what's more, I could never charge what my work is worth. It takes lots of paint and canvas and wool and hours to create a piece of needlepoint. And then it has to be blocked and either framed or made into a wall hanging or pillow or rug. No, I wouldn't sell my work. I just create for myself and my friends. It's a labor of love, not a labor for money."

"Are you sure?"

"Absolutely."

"And there's nothing I could say to make you change your mind?"

"Like I said, Mrs. Collier, needlepoint is my joy. If I were to sell my canvases, it would become a chore. And I'd hate for that to happen."

"But, Delores, my vision for the design job I'm working on is stunning. With your needlepoint it would be spectacular."

"I don't want to disappoint you, Mrs. Collier, but I just can't."

"Delores," Jinx said, "what if I told you that my client would pay one-thousand dollars for one of your pillows? And I believe she needs three."

Jinx had no idea that Trilby would be willing to pay one-thousand dollars each for three pillows, but if Delores would agree to making them, Jinx would include them in her proposal.

Delores mentally calculated one-thousand dollars times three and was stunned speechless. Her eyes stretched wide, and her jaw went slack.

Jinx continued, "Actually, Delores, you could probably get more than one-thousand dollars per pillow, but I figure it would be best to start low and work your way up."

Still Delores said nothing.

"Delores, is there anything I could say to make you change your mind?"

In a shaky voice Delores finally spoke: "Mrs. Collier, that's three-thousand dollars."

"Yes, I know that, Delores."

"But I've never had that much money at one time."

"You can now, Delores, if you'll reconsider."

"I still don't know, Mrs. Collier. What if I don't enjoy needlepointing anymore?"

"Simple. You just stop doing it for profit and go back to doing it for sheer pleasure."

"But I've always made my own designs. I don't know if I can create a canvas to someone else's specifications."

"You won't have to, Delores. Tomorrow I'll take you to the home I'm decorating. I'll show you the space, give you the color palette and describe the theme of the décor. The rest is up to you."

"Well," said Delores, "I'll give it a try, as long as you promise I'll have creative control and can quit any time I want."

Jinx stifled a laugh. Only Delores Manigault would demand creative control on her first paying job.

"I promise, Delores. You will have creative control."

Polly Ann had been uncharacteristically quiet. Normally she'd toss in her two cents, whether anyone wanted it or not. But she hadn't uttered a word, had just sat quietly and pretended to be reading.

Jinx noted her silence and realized that Polly Ann Bondurant's nose was out of joint. She was jealous of Delores. And she was probably thinking, "And I done saved that ungrateful Sugah Pie's life."

So Jinx turned to Polly Ann and said, "And you'd best be studying all those fancy New York cookbooks you've been collecting."

"Why's that?" Polly Ann said, with a half-interested air, refusing to look Jinx's way.

"Because, Ms. Bondurant, after I decorate and Delores needlepoints, my clients are going to want to have a shindig to show off their home to all their New York friends. And they are going to need the very best caterer for the affair. Do you think you'd be interested?"

Polly Ann sniffed and said, "I might," never taking her eyes from her Bible.

"Well, think about it, okay?"

Shrugging, Polly Ann said, "Sure, I'll give it some thought."

Shaking her head and stifling a laugh, Jinx said, "Well, goodnight, girls. Sleep tight," and headed for her bedroom. She had only enough energy to brush her teeth and slip into her nightgown.

Crawling into bed, she slept quickly and soundly, but somewhere around three in the morning she was awakened with a start by a thud coming from somewhere in the apartment. Her heart raced as she noticed a soft light glowing in the hallway. She slipped noiselessly from her bed and tiptoed to the bedroom door. Peeking around the corner, she glanced down the hall. Empty. She listened for more thuds but heard nothing. She crept quietly toward the light, which she found coming from Polly Ann and Delores's bedroom. Peering around the doorway, she saw Delores sound asleep. Polly Ann's reading light was on, but she, too, was sleeping. Sitting upright in bed, she was still wearing her reading glasses. Her bed was strewn with cookbooks. One lay open on the floor, where it had slid from the bed and landed with a thud.

Twenty

"I know, Delores, it's horrible, but it won't be after we work our magic."

"But who on earth would have made such a mess of this beautiful place?"

"Someone who loved the disco era, I'm guessing. I know we have our work cut out for us, but I think we're up to the task."

"Okay, Mrs. Collier, where do we start?"

"Delores, do you see that building right there?"

"You mean the Chrysler Building?"

"That's the one."

"Prettiest building in all of New York City."

"Exactly! That building and Mr. Bettencourt-Ciccone's steel business will be the inspiration for our work. And this will be our color palette," Jinx said, as she spread paint chips and fabric samples across the hideous Danish modern coffee table. "Gray will be our predominant color—soft gray walls with lots of white trim. We'll strip down to the sub-flooring and install maple wood floors. Our accent colors will be red and yellow. And as she slid a picture across the table, she said, "And this will be the focal point of this room—a ninety-inch curved charcoal gray leather sofa. It has very clean, simple lines with no arms and stainless steel legs. It'll need three thirty-inch wide and twenty-inch tall needlepoint pillows along the back. Think you can handle that?"

Delores squinted at the picture, studying its planes and shape and color and design. Her eyes darted from the picture to the windows to the Chrysler Building to the ceiling and back to the picture again. Jinx knew that look. Delores was studying and painting and measuring and choosing canvas and pulling wool and changing her mind and tossing that out and pulling that back and rearranging. Delores was creating. Jinx sat silently and watched Delores study. She knew the process couldn't be rushed and that the artist needed complete silence as she created.

After about ten minutes the glazed look disappeared from Delores's eyes, and she exclaimed, "Got it!"

"Great, Delores. I know that feeling, when your vision comes together. How long will it take you to complete your vision?"

"Well, it'll take about a week to design and paint my canvases and gather my wool. I think I can finish the needlepoint and make the pillows in about ten weeks. To be on the safe side, can you give me three months?"

"I believe that will be fine. It will probably take me about that long to supervise the work and arrange for the purchase and delivery of all the furniture, appliances, and art objects."

Polly Ann stared out the window while Jinx and Delores discussed their projects. Even though she was going to be included, she was still quite jealous of the friendship that was developing between her Sugah Pie and her new best friend, Delores.

"Now, Polly Ann, let's move on to the kitchen."

Polly Ann turned without saying a word and dutifully followed Jinx into the kitchen.

"Ooo-eee this is one ugly place. Even I couldn't cook in here, and I can cook just about anywhere. Look at them dingy appliances."

"Well, that's about to change." Sweeping her arms across the space, Jinx told Polly Ann, "All the new appliances are going to be stainless, and the countertops will be dark gray, glazed concrete. There will be a sub-zero side-by-side refrigerator right there and double wall ovens over here. No more crouching; everything will be at eye level. There will be a deep, double sink, a wine cooler, and a separate ice machine. The six-burner gas counter-top range will have a pot faucet. Over here will be a large prep island with a separate vegetable sink and disposal. There will be pendant lights over the island to illuminate the prep space. Now, do you think you can cook in that kitchen?"

"Well, maybe so."

Jinx was confident that Polly Ann would turn out a feast fit for royalty, but she also knew that her dear life saver just wasn't going to give an inch as long as that nose was out of joint because of Delores and Jinx's new working relationship. But Jinx knew how to be patient.

They were much more than she had expected, yet Delores's needlepoint creations captured Jinx's design vision to perfection. The women had had only the one meeting to discuss Jinx's decorating plans, yet Delores had understood perfectly Jinx's vision for the Bettencourt-Ciccone home. The woman was genius. Jinx had shown Delores her color palette and fabric swatches and had described her plan. Then she had, reluctantly, given Delores the creative control she demanded for her part in the project. Jinx had been wrong to doubt Delores's ability. Her work was museum-quality art.

They were more than pillows. They were bolsters, curved to fit the lines of the huge gray leather sofa. And, instead of backing her designs in silk or velvet, Delores had needlepointed the backing and deep boxed edges to match the gray of the sofa. And the designs... What had Jinx expected? Well, certainly nothing as spectacular as Delores's creations. She had incorporated the red and yellow accents of Jinx's palette, creating the illusion of yellow sun and red sunset. And Delores had captured Jinx's vision of urban meets industrial design to perfection, with geometric, metallic shapes in varying shades of gray. But the focal point of each design was the abstract rendering of the three most famous structures in New York City: the Chrysler Building, the Empire State Building, and the Statue of Liberty.

As Jinx stared in disbelief, her lips moving but no sounds coming out, Delores said, "You don't like them."

Delores's remark shook Jinx from her adoration. "Don't like them? Oh, Delores, I love them. I more than love them. I worship them."

"Oh, Mrs. Collier, I was so worried. I didn't think I was going to like creating needlepoint as a job, but I really enjoyed the challenge. I so hoped you would approve and would ask me to make more for your clients."

Jinx laughed and said, "Oh, Delores, you'll have no shortage of work once Trilby's friends get a look at these. They'll all want a

Delores Manigault design. And, Delores, you'll never have to settle for one-thousand dollars per piece again. You'll be able to name your price."

And reserved Mrs. Manigault clapped her hands to her mouth, but not before she let out an unladylike yelp.

Polly Ann had been puttering around the room, acting as if she weren't at all interested in Jinx and Delores's conversation or Delores's needlepoint pillows. But when the praise reached the name-your-price level, Polly Ann clucked her tongue and let out a huff.

Jinx ignored her.

"Now, Delores, we'll have to find you a dress of understated elegance. We'll want you to look stunning at the party, but not so stunning that you'll draw the attention from your work.

"Me, at the party? Oh, no ma'am, I can't do that."

"But, Delores, as much as I hate to admit it—considering my genius at interior design—your designs are going to be the star of the night. You'll have to be there to show them off to Trilby's guests."

"I just can't, Mrs. Collier."

"Well, it's now or later. As soon as those people see your work, they're going to be scrambling to get to you first. Delores, I know where to find you, and you can rest assured that I will out you."

Jinx could hear Polly Ann still huffing and pouting, so she turned to her and said, "And just when are you planning to have samples of your menu ready for me to approve for the party?"

Polly Ann felt like grinning with delight, but she refused to give Jinx the satisfaction of knowing how happy she had made her by including her in this meeting. Instead, she said, "I'm not certain; I'll have to check my book. But I think I can be ready by the third."

And with that she lifted her chin, sniffed, and strolled out of the room.

True to her word, Polly Ann was ready for Jinx and Delores to sample her menu on the third.

She banished them both from the apartment and told them to return at precisely three in the afternoon. She set to work, peeling and chopping and tossing, flinging cookie sheets into the oven, furiously stirring pots on the stove. She worked frantically until two-thirty, when she backed away from the dining table, smiled with satisfaction, and headed to her bedroom to freshen up.

When Jinx and Delores returned at precisely the appointed hour, they found Polly Ann primped, polished, and dressed in a simple but fashionable black sheath, a colorful, flowered scarf at her neck. She stood beside her work of art, a dining table laden with beautifully displayed, delicious-looking heavy hors d'oeuvres.

"Now, before you say a word, this kinda food just ain't my cup 'o tea. If it had been left up to me, we'd been having southern cooking, stuff that tastes like heaven. But I done my best with the instructions I been given. This here's New York food. Now, dig in."

But Polly Ann could make New York food taste like heaven. She had prepared mini lamb chops with mint jelly. When Jinx asked where she had gotten such tiny lamb chops, Polly Ann just said, "I got my sources." They were melt-in-your mouth, just as the chicken liver crostinis with capers and crab wontons with sweet chili garlic sauce were.

"You see, you got to have your meat, your poultry, and your seafood so you can please all your palates. And, course, you got to cater to them vegetarians, too. So you got your crudités over here with your pickled asparagus, grilled zucchini, and marinated broccoli and cauliflower with herb dip. This here's stuffed shiitake mushrooms with chestnut and apple chutney. And, if I do say so myself, they're mighty tasty."

Jinx said, "Oh, my, Polly Ann, everything looks so beautiful, it's a shame to eat it. I just want to admire it. But, if you don't mind, I'm going to give it all a taste."

"Course you gonna taste it. That's what we here for. So, like I said, 'Dig in.'"

Between bites Jinx and Delores praised and gasped and slurped and licked their fingers.

"Polly Ann, where did you find these beautiful ripe berries this time of year? And chestnuts. Who can find chestnuts?"

"Well, if you gonna be in the catering business—and I am in the catering business—you gotta know where to shop. I found Grace's Marketplace up on third and seventy-first, and me and Grace have got real tight. I told her she does me right and I'll give her all my business. I think we got a good thing going. Look at all this pretty food.

"Now, looky over here at this brie—soft as a baby's behind. Give it a try with these homemade peach preserves. Here, let me spread a little on this herb crostini for you."

Polly Ann was in her element. She was lapping up the compliments, doling out delights, knowing her art was just as beautiful and appreciated as Delores's.

Jinx had planned to give each of the hors d'oeuvres just a taste, to make sure she approved of Polly Ann's menu. But once she and Delores began sampling, they couldn't stop. The two of them sampled and tasted and munched and gobbled until the table was practically bare and they could hardly waddle to the sofa. The three women leaned back, propping their feet up on the coffee table, and discussed the finishing touches they needed to apply to their near-perfect party plans.

As they chatted and laughed, Jinx realized just what a great team they made. She had been smart to enlist Delores and Polly Ann's help. Yes, she was certain their little business venture was going to be quite successful.

Polly Ann's hors d'oeuvres and Delores's soft sculptures nearly stole the show—but not quite. Jinx's industrial-meets-urban design brought gasps from Trilby's guests. It was like nothing these New Yorkers had ever seen. They were accustomed to swag and damask and plush. Jinx's clean lines and minimalist vision were met with applauses of delight. It was stunning, and, of course, all of Trilby's guests had been forced to endure her retro-disco motif. Anything would have been an improvement. But Jinx's design was more than an improvement. It was magnificent.

"Oh, Jinx, it's pure genius!" Trilby trilled, as she hugged her close and kissed her cheek, leaving pink lip prints. "Oh, darling, look what I've done to you in my excitement," she said, dabbing at Jinx's cheek with her hanky.

"Trilby, I am delighted that you like it. And thank you so much for trusting me. I'll never be able to thank you enough."

"Hello," said a voice over Jinx's shoulder.

"Oh, Sam," said Trilby, "I want you to meet Jinx, the genius who transformed this place. Jinx, this is our good friend, Sam

Bradley."

Sam took Jinx's hand and said, "Trilby, Miss Jinx and I have met, but thank you for introducing us once again."

"It's nice to see you, Mr. Bradley."

"Sam, just Sam," he said, still holding Jinx's hand, mesmerized by her beautiful ice blue eyes.

"Well, I have other guests to greet, and I can see you two don't need me. I'll just leave you alone," said Trilby, smiling, patting Sam's arm, and turning to the gathering crowd.

"Pandora said you were good. That was an understatement. This place is incredible."

"Thank you," said Jinx.

Jinx's Savannah friends and clients had loved her work. They acted completely helpless when it came to decorating and had begged for her help for something as simple as choosing place mats. But New York was the big league. These people didn't want just place mats. They wanted it all. She had been nervous, not knowing if New Yorkers would embrace her vision. But the reception was greater than she had imagined.

"It was a delight working with Trilby's space. I'm so glad it turned out well."

Then Sam said, "How are your granddaughters?"

Jinx felt her hands go clammy and her shoulders begin to tense. She was here at Trilby's home on business. She wanted to keep it that way. But Sam—Sam who had asked to share a taxi with her the last time she had seen him—was back and asking about her family. But she did not want to share a taxi with a man. She didn't want to share her family with a man. She didn't want to share herself with a man.

So she responded to Sam with a curt, "They're fine. Thank you for asking." Then she added as she slowly backed away, "The crowd is growing. I'd better start working the room."

"Sure. I didn't mean to monopolize you. You have cards to pass out, clients to meet. I hope we'll have a chance to talk later."

"Of course," said Jinx, turning and approaching the crowd, uncomfortable with Sam's eyes on her back.

But despite the slight Sam distraction, the evening was a dream come true. This was why Jinx had studied design—not so she could decorate Benson's room lavender and pink as a sixteenth birthday surprise. Trilby's guests were all so complimentary, and many of them begged to get onto Jinx's calendar, a calendar Trilby had assured her would be full before the night was out.

When the party ended, Jinx once again had a pocket full of cards, Polly Ann had a scavenged buffet table and a half dozen catering requests, and Delores was already designing her next soft sculptures.

"May I offer you ladies a ride home?" Sam asked.

After the other guests left, he had hung back to help them clean up the buffet table and gather their gear.

"Thank you, Sam. I appreciate your help and your offer of a ride, but my son is on his way to pick us up."

"Well, perhaps we could get together this weekend. Dinner, maybe?"

Sam Bradley was persistent, but Jinx had not changed her mind. As charming and gentlemanly as Sam was, she just wasn't interested in going out with him—or any man.

"Thank you, but I have plans."

"Well, some other time, then?"

"Thanks, Sam, but I'm just not in the market for a relationship. Now, if you'll excuse me," Jinx said and turned to finish helping Polly Ann gather her trays—but not before she caught the look of disappointment on Sam's face.

She was sorry to have offended Sam Bradley—again—but she was just protecting herself. She had tried to be polite, to let him down easily, but Sam just didn't get the message—or refused to accept Jinx's message. She had been wounded by Charlie and The Girls, and she just couldn't allow herself to be put in the position of being hurt so deeply again. Charlie said that he would always pick her up, and she had trusted that he always would. The Girls had promised to help her in any way they could, and they even told her that they loved her. But actions speak louder than words. What they called love certainly didn't sound like love to Jinx.

That old saying, *fool me once, shame on you; fool me twice, shame on me,* came to mind. Jinx refused to be fooled again. If she didn't have relationships, then no one could hurt her. She would just love her son and his family and Polly Ann and Delores and immerse herself in her work. It would be quite enough to sustain her.

Twenty-one

"Jinx?"

Jinx didn't recognize the voice, but she recognized the accent. Only a southerner could make two syllables out of the name Jinx. She couldn't quite place the dialect—it was too twangy to be deep south, like Georgia—but it was southern, nonetheless.

"This is she."

"Jinx, the designer?"

"Yes, this is Jinx, the designer. What can I do for you?"

"Oh, Darlin', you can come to my rescue. I have a blank slate of an apartment, and I've been told you're the only person who can help me out of this predicament."

"Well, I may not be your only salvation, but I'd be willing to take a stab at it."

"Oh, Honey, that's music to my ears. And excuse me for being so rude. I'm Delta McMillan. My husband, Helms, and I just moved to New York City from Albuquerque. We've bought this big ole empty place, and, I swan, I have no idea what to do with it. So, please help!"

"Well, let me check my schedule," and this time Jinx wasn't blowing smoke. Her appointment book was bulging. "Looks like I have next Tuesday afternoon free. Would that work?"

"Oh, Honey, I don't think I can hold on that long. Like I said, I'm just standin' here lookin' at this big ole empty apartment, and I need some help *raht* now. You sure you don't have a few minutes for me before Tuesday?"

"Well, I'm free this morning, but that may be pushing you a bit."

"Oh, no, please come rescue me this instant."

"Well, okay, Mrs. McMillan, just give me your address, and I'll be there just as soon as I can grab my purse and hail a cab."

"Terrific! And none of this Mrs. McMillan stuff. I'm just plain old Texas Delta."

Jinx had known that was no New Mexico accent.

Delta McMillan gave Jinx her Upper East Side address, adding, "We're just across from Central Park. Just come on up to the penthouse. I'll tell the doorman I'm expecting you. Oh, I'm so excited! I can't wait. This is going to be so much fun. Bye now," drawled plain old Texas Delta and hung up the phone.

How in the world did a woman from New Mexico hear about me? thought Jinx. Delta had just gotten into town. Surely she hadn't yet met Pandora. Well, she guessed she'd find out just as soon as she grabbed her purse and iPad and hailed a cab.

While she gathered her things and ran to her powder room to check her make-up, she called to Polly Ann, "Gotta run out. Looks like we have a new client. Don't know any details, though."

Polly Ann stuck her head out of the kitchen and said, "Okay, Sugah Pie, me and Delores will hold down the fort till you get back. Now you take lots of notes, and make sure this new client needs some catering and needlepointing."

"I'll make sure," said Jinx as she rushed from her apartment and onto the street. She threw up her arm, and a cab screeched to the curb. She was getting pretty good at being a New Yorker.

She gave the cabbie the McMillans' address and settled back for the ride from her apartment building to Delta McMillan's blank slate.

The traffic was maddening, the horns deafening. Pedestrians and motorists alike screamed at one another. When she had first arrived in New York, Jinx had been both energized and terrified by the city's mayhem. Though she would never be a screamer, she had learned to take the attitudes of New Yorkers in stride. She smiled and watched her chaotic city whiz by.

The McMillans' building was no different from most New York apartment buildings Jinx frequented these days: gray limestone, fancy address, liveried doorman, pricey apartments. The cab pulled up to the curb, and the doorman stepped forward to open the car door for her.

"Morning, ma'am," he said, as he extended his white-gloved

hand to help Jinx from the cab. She paid the cabbie, tipping him generously, and accepted the hand for help.

"You must be Ms. Jinx. Mrs. McMillan is expecting you," said the doorman, heaving open the heavy brass door to the building. "Just follow this corridor to the elevators on your left. My name is Christopher. If I can be of further assistance, please let me know."

"Thanks so much," said Jinx, as her heels clicked down the marble corridor toward the bank of elevators.

Another man in uniform, including white gloves, greeted her and pushed the button to summon the elevator. When it arrived, he held the door open and escorted her inside. There another man in uniform greeted her. Two people to man one elevator seemed excessive, but this whole building seemed excessive to Jinx.

"Floor, ma'am?"

"Penthouse, please."

The elevator whizzed so fast to the McMillan's floor that Jinx's ears popped.

"Oh, my, you're a darling," cried Delta McMillan, as she flung the door wide. "I'll never be able to thank you enough," she exclaimed, grabbing Jinx's hand, pumping and squealing with joy.

Delta McMillan was Texas in every way. At least five-foot-nine, she was an aging beauty queen. Her black hair was big, as were her shockingly aquamarine eyes, her perfect white teeth, her perky bosom, and her personality. She wore a simple black silk tunic over black leggings, paired with ballet flats of some animal print. Her only adornments were a pair of enormous, dangling turquoise earrings and a large silver and turquoise bracelet. Jinx guessed her to be a youthful fifty.

"Thank you, Delta. I'm pleased to meet you. I'm so delighted someone felt my work was good enough to recommend to you. By the way, who did suggest my services? I'd like to thank her. Or him."

"Oh, law, I couldn't even begin to tell you," Delta said, waving her perfectly-manicured hand in the air. "I've met so many people since we got to New York City, it could have been just about anyone. I'm gonna have to get me a secretary to keep up with all these goings-on. All I do know is that whoever told me about you said you were the very best."

"Well, I'm flattered, whoever it was. So let's take a look at what we've got here."

It was, indeed, a blank slate: white walls, concrete floors, unfurnished kitchen, one gigantic room of indistinct space with two huge walls of floor-to-ceiling windows overlooking Central Park. A quick spin of the rest of the apartment revealed three bare bedrooms, all with en-suite baths, a small powder room, and a good-size office for Helms McMillan. Where to start?

"Delta, we've got our work cut out for us. First, tell me a little about your decorating style. What colors do you like? Do you have pieces you'd like for me to incorporate into my design? Furniture? Art work?"

"Southwestern. I love southwestern decor. And Helms and I have amassed quite a collection of original southwestern art. We'll definitely be bringing all of that with us to New York."

Oh, brother, thought Jinx, as she tried to continue smiling, the forced effort making her cheeks ache. *What have I gotten myself into? I know absolutely nothing about southwestern décor, and what I've seen, I find gaudy and repulsive. And southwestern art? Cow skulls and horses and cowboy boots and Native Americans with flowing headdresses?*

"Well, Delta, I don't have any experience with southwestern design. I'll have to do some research. If you'd prefer to get a professional with experience in your style, I'll understand," said Jinx, so hoping that Delta would find another designer.

"Oh, no, I'm sure you'll do a fabulous job. And I'll give you all the research you need."

"Research?" Jinx asked. "What kind of research?"

"Well, the guy who owned the company my husband bought here in New York has a private jet he says we can use any time we want. How 'bout you fly out to our ranch in Albuquerque and check it out. That way you can see our style, understand what you have to work with."

"That sounds like a great suggestion. I like getting an idea about my clients' tastes before I begin. It gives me a vantage point, and there are no shocks or surprises when I present my completed design," said Jinx, laughing nervously.

"Are you free this weekend?"

"Excuse me?"

"Could you fly to New Mexico this weekend? You could take a look at the house and then do a little sightseeing and shopping in Santa Fe. Feel free to pick up anything you think the apartment needs while you're there. I'll just give you my credit card. And, Honey, don't worry about the limit. The card doesn't have one," Delta said with a wink. "Helmsy is a very generous man. What's more, he's uprooted me from the home I love. He'll do anything to keep me happy."

The two women laughed at Delta's oh-so-honest admission.

Jinx had never visited the southwest, but a trip to New Mexico had always been on her to-do list. But she hadn't planned to toss some things in an overnight bag and just take off at a moment's notice. Could she manage it? She had to meet clients the following week, but she didn't have any firm plans for the weekend. What's more, she'd been offered a credit card with no limit and an order to shop. How could she turn that down?

So to Delta Jinx said, "I believe this weekend will work, but my two partners will have to accompany me. I'll need their input."

"Why, sure, that would be great. And y'all can stay right at the ranch. There's plenty of room for all of you. Our cook and housekeeper and gardener live out back in our guest house, so y'all can rattle around in the house all by yourselves. Does that sound okay?"

"Delta, that sounds more than okay. It sounds very, very generous."

"Well, great, Jinx," Delta said and showed deep dimples when she smiled. "Now, I'll have my driver, nice young man named Ronald Ramirez, pick y'all up at the airport and take you out to the ranch. He'll be around all weekend, ready to take you and your partners anywhere you need to go. Oh, this is just going to be so much fun. I just can't thank you enough," Delta gushed, as she wrapped Jinx in a warm hug.

Jinx's head was spinning. Since her arrival in New York, she'd learned to rush, to live with that New York sense of urgency, but this was a level of urgency she'd never experienced. The rich and powerful didn't get rich and powerful by sitting around waiting for something to happen. If Jinx wanted to run with the big dogs, she was going to have to kick it into high gear.

"While I'm here, Delta, let me take some measurements, make some notes, and then I'll be on my way. To New Mexico."

"Oh, sure, I'll just get out of your way so you can work your magic," said Delta as she stepped aside for Jinx to get started.

She pulled her iPad from her bag and went to work. Not only did she have a program that would measure room dimensions, she also had a sketch program that would allow her to make a quick layout of the space she'd be designing. So much had changed since she'd decorated Benson's bedroom, but she'd quickly learned to adapt to the times. She opened a new document, titled it DELTA AND HELMS MCMILLAN, and began making notes, taking measurements, and sketching the blank space onto her screen. Within thirty minutes she had all the information she'd need to get the job started.

"Well, that'll do it, Delta. Thank you so much for this opportunity. Now, if you'll just give me your cell number and email address, I'll be on my way."

"Oh, sure, here's my card," said Delta, as she rummaged in her huge Gucci satchel and pulled out a monogrammed sterling card holder. "And, of course, that limitless credit card," she said, smirking.

"Thanks, Delta, and here's my business card for you," said Jinx, making the exchange.

The elevator whizzed Jinx to the ground floor as the operator and greeter ushered her toward the doorman. Christopher had, somehow, sensed her leaving and had a cab hailed and waiting when she stepped from the building.

"Good day, ma'am," he said and tipped his cap as Jinx slid into the cab.

She gave the driver her address and didn't even flinch as the taxi flew from the Upper East Side to the Upper West Side. She was getting the hang of this time-is-money attitude.

"Pack your bags, girls, we're going to New Mexico," Jinx called out as she unlocked her door and barged in.

"Huh?" said Polly Ann, peeking from the kitchen.

"Pardon?" said refined Delores, as she paused, dusting wand in mid-swipe.

"We have a new client, a new, very wealthy client."

"Is there any other kind?" Polly Ann quipped.

Jinx laughed and said, "I hold here in my hand a credit card with no limit that we will take to New Mexico. While there we will sightsee and shop for Helms and Delta McMillan's penthouse apartment that overlooks Central Park. Are y'all in?"

"When do we leave?" asked Polly Ann.

"Tomorrow morning."

"What time?"

"Whenever we're ready."

"What a wonderful adventure," said Delores, clapping her hands.

Twenty-two

The private plane was waiting at a small airport near LaGuardia. It was, indeed, very private with twelve butter-soft, tan leather seats that could convert to beds clustered around low tables. There was also a roomy bathroom with a shower and a bidet. The aircraft was staffed with a pilot, a co-pilot, and two flight attendants. The crew welcomed them all by name and assured them the plane was theirs, all theirs, for the weekend and that they would do everything in their power to make the three ladies comfortable. Throughout the seven-hour flight, the crew doted on Jinx, Polly Ann, and Delores, feeding them, offering them moist, warm towels, making them giggly with champagne, providing pillows and cashmere throws when they became drowsy.

But not a single crew member seemed to know who owned the plane. Delta had said it belonged to the guy who sold the business to Helms, but she just couldn't seem to remember his name. Perhaps it was a secret. Maybe the owner preferred to remain anonymous for some reason. Warren Buffet? Bill Gates? Jinx didn't care, just as long as that flight attendant kept bringing those jumbo shrimp.

The hours of eating, napping, and being coddled flew, and soon the three women were stepping into the warm, dry climate of New Mexico. Ronald, their limo driver, was waiting on the tarmac with a sign that read WELCOME, JINX. He'd already retrieved their bags from the cargo hold of the plane and had them carted and ready to ferry to the waiting limo.

Ronald escorted the women into the roomy back seat, poured them tea, and took his place up front. Chatty and personable, he gave the three a running commentary of passing sights as he drove them to the McMillans' ranch, only a short distance from Albuquerque.

Helms and Delta McMillan's imposing spread was called McRanch. Well, one thing Jinx knew for sure: the McMillans had a sense of humor. She clicked on her iPad, opened the document that read DELTA AND HELMS MCMILLAN, and under her notes typed *McRanch* and *ha ha*.

Ronald used his remote to open the large, wrought iron gates to the avenue that would lead them to the main house. *Things may appear closer than they are* came to mind as Ronald drove and drove and drove toward the rambling ranch house, seemingly without making much progress. When, finally, he wheeled the limousine into the circular drive in front of the towering double doors to the home, Jinx was dumbstruck. It was enormous. Delta and Helms's Albuquerque house made their spacious New York apartment look miniscule. She couldn't wait to peer inside. This place could hold a whole lot of cow skulls and cowboy boots.

All of Jinx's pre-conceived notions about southwestern art and décor vanished as Ronald escorted her and her partners through the massive hand-carved wooden doors and into the McMillan's home. From the towering sand-colored marble entry foyer, they stepped down into an enormous, high-ceilinged great room that ran to the back of the house. The rear wall of the home was glass, floor to ceiling, and it framed a majestic mountain range against a cloudless, azure sky. The vista took Jinx's breath. When, at last, she could pull herself away, she discovered on the left wall the massive stacked-stone fireplace, it's opening large enough for an average-size adult to walk right through. The huge room was furnished with oversized, overstuffed sofas and chairs, all simple, all tasteful, all in basic earth tones. On the floor was an enormous, irregular-shaped brown and white spotted rug. Cow? Jinx had no idea what it was, but, somehow, it worked in the vast area. Then she spied the remaining wall and gasped. It was adorned with original art, but there were no cow skulls or horses or Native Americans in headdresses. It was covered in Georgia O'Keefes—well, perhaps there was an O'Keefe skull or two—and Albert Bierstadts, as well as works by local artists Jinx couldn't identify but adored instantly. Exquisite tapestries, pottery, and hand-woven baskets, some substantial, some delicate, all intricate and ornate, all sporting a southwestern flair, sat on tables, credenzas, shelves, and in étagères.

Jinx eased herself into one of the huge chairs. She had never seen anything quite so spectacular. Why did Delta need her help? She, clearly, had impeccable taste. But Jinx wouldn't question. She'd wrap her arms around this job and and love every minute of it.

That's when she noticed Delores taking in the Georgia O'Keefe paintings. Her eyes darted from one to the next, her small hands clasped tightly at her chest. She was studying. She was already creating.

"Planning your canvases, huh?"

"Oh, yes, ma'am. Aren't they exquisite? Look at those colors, Mrs. Collier. And the depth. My goodness, I've never seen anything quite like them. They're so, so…"

"Sensual?" offered Jinx.

Delores looked at her and, shaking her head slowly, said, "Yes, sensual. That's what they are. Sensual."

"Whoo-ee. This is some place, Sugah Pie. Ain't them mountains some'pm else? I haven't ever seen mountains. I just didn't know they'd look like that."

"Excuse me, Miss Jinx," Ronald said, "I've put your bags in your rooms. If you'll follow me, I'll show you the way so you ladies can get settled."

The three women followed Ronald down a wide, well-lit hallway, its walls adorned with yet more southwestern art and artifacts. Jinx's head whipped left to right, trying to take it all in, as she made her way to her room.

"Will this suit, Miss Jinx?" Ronald asked as he ushered her into her splendidly appointed bedroom with a tall four-poster bed of light birch wood made up with a beautiful hand-made quilt of blues and purples. The walls were painted a soft lavender and were adorned with yet more exquisite paintings. Polly Ann and Delores's rooms, too, were beautifully appointed, one a sunny yellow, the other a luscious peach, both displaying yet more art.

"This place just gets better and better," Jinx gasped, her eyes darting.

"Yes, ma'am," Ronald said. "Just get settled and make yourselves at home. Maria will serve dinner at seven o'clock."

"Thank you, Ronald," Jinx said, delighted they had their own private chef and hoping that Polly Ann would not be offended and, more than that, would not offend.

Turning to Polly Ann and Delores, Jinx said, "Now, y'all just look around while I make some notes and take some pictures. I shouldn't be too long."

Polly Ann and Delores knew to leave Jinx alone to study the space well, so they excused themselves and went outside to get a better look at the beautiful mountain range.

Ronald met Polly Ann and Delores as they strolled out of the house and across the polished-stone walkway and said, "You ladies watch your step. We're known for our rattlesnakes around here, and I wouldn't want either of you to get a nasty bite."

With that, both women squealed, did a little dance, and rushed back into the house. There they sat quietly, careful not to disturb Jinx, and eyed the floor to make sure a rattler hadn't followed them back inside.

Jinx's fingers flew furiously over her iPad, as she took copious notes. Then she traveled around the house, taking picture after picture, discovering more art, making notes about the pieces she'd use in the McMillan's New York apartment.

Just as Jinx was finishing, a short, dark woman stepped from the kitchen and said, "Good evening, ladies, I am Maria. Your dinner is served."

And the three of them followed Maria into the dining room where their chef had set three places at a table for sixteen.

Jinx was not a fan of Mexican food, but, then, the only Mexican cuisine she'd ever tasted was in a chain restaurant in the South. What Maria had prepared for the three of them was like nothing Jinx had ever tasted. She served them a chicken dish with a delicious sauce, the chicken so tender it melted in the ladies' mouths. Along with the chicken they ate a black bean and salsa relish, as well as a rice dish. Maria served a basket of tortillas, as one would serve a basket of biscuits back home. Even Polly Ann rolled her eyes, smacked her lips, and praised the cook.

"Ummmmm ummmmm, this is some kind of good. I think I'm just gonna have to do some recipe swapping with Maria."

Delores chuckled, and Jinx laughed out loud.

"Well, Polly Ann, I can't believe what I'm hearing. You're

actually admitting that someone other than you can cook."

Polly Ann smiled sheepishly and said, "Yeah, hard to admit, but that Maria knows her way around a kitchen."

"Well, you'd better take real good notes, Polly Ann, 'cause we're going to need some delicious, authentic southwestern food at the McMillans' grand reveal of their new home."

"I'm already on it, Sugah Pie. Taking notes real good."

And as the three friends dined, Jinx gazed beyond the wall of windows to the expansive New Mexico landscape, which was like none she'd ever seen. She found it interesting, but she wasn't sure she liked it. It's hard to take an immediate liking to something so foreign, so other worldly. She was accustomed to trees, green canopies of trees, trees that enfolded her and made her feel safe and grounded. Even in her Concrete Jungle, trees lined her street of brownstones. She could sit on the window seat of her front room and feel as if she were perched in a tree house. But this landscape extended flat and treeless to the base of the majestic mountains, which were also treeless.

And as Jinx took in the vista, the sun began to set against the looming mountain range. She had seen sunsets back in Georgia. They had been beautiful. *Red sky at night, sailor's delight.* She had loved the red skies because she knew that she'd be able to sit on her back porch overlooking the Atlantic Ocean the following morning and watch the fishermen ferry their skiffs toward the horizon.

But this was like no sunset that she had ever seen. As it slid to the horizon, it created undulating ribbons of alternating purple, red, fuchsia, and orange on the mountain range. The colors were vivid, majestic, breathtaking. She thought about taking a picture with her iPad but changed her mind. It would be a sacrilege to try to capture those colors in a photo; a picture just wouldn't do it justice. What's more, she didn't need a picture; she would never forget this sight. And, right there, as she dined on authentic Mexican food with her friends, Jinx's vision for the McMillan's confusing, blank slate in New York City overlooking Central Park began making sense. Until that moment she'd had no idea where she was headed with this job, what she could do to transform the McMillans' New York apartment to please them. Jinx stood from the dining table and approached the bank of windows where she knew beyond a doubt that she was staring into the palette that would transform the McMillans' colorless apartment: royal purple, vivid red, shocking fuchsia, bright orange. Armed with the anchor piece of the decorating puzzle, Jinx's vision for the the McMillans new home began taking shape.

The following morning the three visitors were dining on Maria's huevos rancheros with green chili when Ronald came rushing through the front door and said, "Ladies, I have a great surprise for you today. We're going for a train ride."

"Train ride? Why would we ride a train when we have a perfectly good limousine?" asked Polly Ann in her abrupt, tell-it-like-it-is manner, as if she'd been riding in limousines all her life.

"We're going to take the train from Albuquerque to Santa Fe. It's the only way to go. We'll see the countryside and experience it like the locals."

"Well, if you say so. And I guess you should know since you are a local," said Jinx, about as excited over riding a train as Polly Ann appeared to be.

As soon as they finished their breakfast, Ronald hustled them out to the limo, and he whisked them away from McRanch toward the Albuquerque train station. When they arrived, he bought four tickets, and they stood in line with the other sight-seers, as well as locals and commuters preparing to make the eighty-minute rail trip to Santa Fe.

Much to Jinx's surprise, it was, indeed, a great adventure. Once on the train, they found two bench seats facing each other and settled in for the commute. Throughout the trip Ronald served as the New Yorkers' tour guide, relaying to them the history of the area and entertaining them with amusing local anecdotes. Though his family was from Mexico, three generations of Ramirezes had lived in Albuquerque. So the New Yorkers didn't get just the tourists' overview; they were schooled by an expert. Polly Ann hadn't even needed a Frommer's Guide. The well-informed visitors arrived at the Santa Fe train station by late morning.

"What next?" Jinx said to Ronald, as he helped each lady down from the train.

"This is where I turn you loose for the day. You're free to shop, sightsee, visit the museums, enjoy the park in the center of town.

There are many restaurants—you can't go wrong with any of them—or you can join the regulars for lunch at a food truck in the park. I'll meet you in the park at five-thirty, in time to catch the train back to Albuquerque." Waving and backing away from the ladies, Ronald called, "Adios," and disappeared into the crowd.

Their first stop was The Georgia O'Keefe Museum with room after room of exquisite pieces. Delores clasped her hands in excitement because she had already decided that O'Keefe's art would serve as the inspiration for her needlepoint creations that she planned to design for the McMillans' New York home. She was not allowed to take pictures inside the museum, but she did pull out her tablet and sketch some rudimentary designs as a guide. Jinx had commissioned Delores to produce four soft sculptures—they were no longer pillows—and would give her twelve weeks to complete the work.

"You think you can finish four pieces in just twelve weeks?" Jinx had asked.

"It'll be a full-time job, but I can give it a try. I might have to let the dusting slide a bit."

"Delores, forget about the dusting for now. Our business comes first."

Delores just smiled. She'd rather needlepoint than dust any day.

When they left the museum, Jinx said to Polly Ann and Delores, "Y'all go have fun. I have work to do. Just remember we have to meet Ronald in the park at five-thirty."

Going their separate ways, Jinx strolled into a furniture store and immediately spotted a piece she needed to anchor the McMillans' dining space—a dark walnut table, large enough to seat twelve, with upholstered high-back chairs. The lines were clean and wouldn't take the focus off the exquisite chandelier she planned to remove from the great room at McRanch and relocate to the New York apartment. Made from what appeared to be a bleached-white wood, it was constructed of many branches that curved in all directions, giving the illusion of antlers. It was stunning and unique and would be the perfect focal point and conversation piece for the dining area in the McMillans' new home. Jinx just prayed the New York conversation about her choice would be positive.

For the living area of the penthouse apartment, Jinx found sofas and chairs with simple lines. The furniture would be functional, not ornate. They would not attract attention. That would be the job of the art—the O'Keefes and Bierstadts, the pottery and tapestries, as well as Delores's soft sculptures.

After placing her order and brandishing Delta's bottomless credit card, Jinx moved on to fabrics. She found a shop with beautiful, hand-woven pieces in the palette of New Mexico mountain ranges at sunset: purples, reds, fuchsias, oranges. There were stripes and prints and tweeds—everything she would need to drape and cover her newest blank canvas.

At five-thirty, tired but exhilarated, armed with a well-used credit card, Jinx found Delores and Polly Ann back in the park, resting on a bench. Polly Ann was perusing one of several southwest cuisine cookbooks she had purchased. Jinx had just joined the two and slipped off her shoes to rest her shop-weary feet when they saw Ronald striding toward them.

"Hello, Ladies. Have a good day?"

"Great," they all agreed.

"Well, we'd better be off before the last train leaves without us."

So they all fell into step beside Ronald and trudged on leaden legs toward the train station.

Their return trip needed no tour guide, and Ronald let the women relax after their day of Santa Fe overload. Jinx kicked off her shoes and folded her legs beneath her. As the train rumbled and swayed toward Albuquerque, she peered out the window at the extraordinary scenery and, once again, experienced the purple-red-fuchsia-orange New Mexico sunset against the stark, southwest mountains. She marveled that there could be more than one so exquisite.

When Polly Ann told Jinx that she and Delores had stopped for lunch at a food truck in the park and had eaten something delicious that neither of them could pronounce, Jinx realized that she had forgotten all about lunch. At the mention of food, her stomach began to growl, and she was so hoping that Maria was preparing a meal as scrumptious as their last. When they arrived back at the ranch, she was overjoyed to find Maria bustling in the kitchen and the dining table, once again, set for three.

"Maria, you suppose you could share some of those recipes with me? Or are they family secrets?" Polly Ann asked sheepishly.

"They are family recipes, but they are not a secret. I would be happy to share them with you."

"Maybe you could give me Mrs. McMillan's favorites so I could make them for her coming-out party," Polly said.

"Of course, that would be fine. I know all of Mrs. McMillan's favorites. Mr. McMillan's, too," Maria said, as she smiled proudly.

After the women finished their dinner, Jinx and Delores dragged their exhausted bodies to their rooms to shower and collapse into bed. Polly Ann stayed behind to help Maria tidy the kitchen. Afterward, the two women sat at the kitchen table, where Maria recited recipes from memory and Polly Ann scribbled furiously on a scratch pad.

The following morning when the women emerged from their bedrooms, packed and ready to head back to New York, Ronald was waiting to take them to the airport. After they enjoyed Maria's scrumptious send-off breakfast, they made their way to the waiting limo, Polly Ann and Delores stepping gingerly, on the lookout for lurking rattlesnakes.

Twenty-three

Delores was tying off the final stitch on her last soft sculpture when Jinx yelled, "Last call. Gotta get a move on."

The three partners had pulled off a coup: they had completed their renovation in only twelve weeks—quite an accomplishment for a job the size of the McMillans'. But their clients had been living out of suitcases—albeit designer suitcases at the plush Crowne Plaza—and were anxious to unpack and settle into their own place. And Delta had played upon Jinx's soft southern nature to pull it off.

Knox had eased his car to the front of their brownstone and was double parked, holding up irate, honking motorists. He didn't flinch. Double-parked vehicles held up New York traffic all the time. It was just part of city living. Those being held up felt obliged to honk and swear and shake fists, knowing full well that they'd soon be on the receiving end of the honking and swearing and fist flailing.

Tony was helping Polly Ann load the food into the trunk of the car, as Jinx and Delores rushed from the building and hopped into the idling vehicle.

"Got everything?" asked Knox, as he put the car into drive.

"I hope so," said Jinx, exhausted and nervous about tonight's unveiling.

She had never tackled anything quite as challenging as the McMillans' large apartment, and she wasn't sure how New York was going to react to it. It could be a real hit. It could just as easily be a miss. Once Jinx had found her color palette, the apartment just fell into place for her. For her. She loved the finished product, and so did Delta. But was New York ready for her sleek, urban take on southwestern chic?

The focal point of the grand living space overlooking Central Park was a free-standing, double-sided fireplace that separated the sitting and dining spaces. The dining table and chairs, which Jinx had upholstered in a muted purple, fuchsia, orange, and red southwestern print, were the subtle addition for the antler-inspired majestic chandelier that hung low over the grouping.

For the sitting area Jinx had chosen a long, sleek tuxedo couch of deep red suede and overstuffed chairs covered in stripes of her palette. The two walls of windows Jinx left unadorned, while the remaining two walls she painted a vivid grape-purple. She covered the grape walls, floor to ceiling, with the McMillans' exquisite art. Occasional tables and free-standing shelves held southwestern pottery and sculptures. In the center of the sitting area stood a large, low glass table, its base bleached, curved wood branches, mimicking the lines and texture of the spectacular dining chandelier.

The space was stunning. Jinx just hoped the McMillans' guests would think it was a good stunning.

When the four arrived at the McMillans' building, Christopher, the doorman, greeted them warmly. They had become well acquainted with him over the past twelve weeks. He was waiting with a rolling cart and graciously helped them unload Polly Ann's food from the car.

"We'll call you when we're ready," Jinx said to Knox and added, "thanks for your help."

"My pleasure, Mom. Now, go break a leg," he said, smiling sweetly at his mother and pulling away into traffic.

The two elevator operators met the ladies and helped them with their cart. Delta was there to greet them at the other end of their flight.

"Oh, my goodness, it smells delicious. I've so missed real Mexican cooking. May I?" she asked Polly Ann, pointing toward the stuffed jalapenos.

"Oh, please," said Polly Ann, "sample everything."

Biting into a jalapeno, Delta cried, "Oh, Polly Ann, it's marvelous. I feel like I'm back home."

While Delores helped Polly Ann set up her buffet, Jinx made one last sweep of the apartment, to make sure that everything was in place and ready for inspection. While she was at the back of the apartment, she slipped into the small powder room to check her make-up. She applied fresh lipstick, then ran her fingers through her hair and let it slither back into place. Turning to leave, she caught sight of herself in the long mirror attached to the back of the powder room door.

Her last two years with Charlie and then his sudden death had taken its toll, and she'd felt her life would never be the same. True, it wouldn't ever be the same, but Jinx was proving, much to her own surprise, that life, even if different, could be good again. She was recovering well and was thriving in her role as mother, grandmother, designer, and New Yorker.

Her recovery showed in her appearance, as well. Her auburn hair, thanks to Jesus, no longer had that set, helmet-hair look. She loved her free, edgy, razor-cut style. Also, her complexion looked luminous, thanks to bi-weekly facials, and her slimmed-down figure was svelte in her new purple-and-red silk print above-the-knee dress and purple platform Jimmy Choos. She smiled. She was confident that she was ready to face New York's critical eye.

In the three months since Delta McMillan had moved to New York, she had managed to meet every socialite and was already serving on three charity boards. She had that charming, Texas come-hither personality, and everyone flocked to her. And, fortunately for Jinx, they all showed up to her unveiling.

"Oh, Jinx, me next!" they cried when they saw what her magic could do. They all wanted to be next in line, to have what their new friend, Delta, had.

Pandora Featherby came charging in, caftan flowing, arms spread wide, bellowing hearty welcomes to all.

"Darling, you've done it again. Genius, pure genius," and, leaning in, whispered, "only you, my dear, could make antlers look chic."

"Oh, Panny, I love you," said Jinx, wrapping her arms around Pandora's neck. "If it weren't for you…"

"Oh, hell, I didn't have a damn thing to do with this. It's your talent. If I hadn't recognized it, the next person to come along would have," said Pandora as she floated off to greet Mayor de Blasio.

"Jinx, everyone loves it," drawled Delta. "It's so beautiful. I'd heard you were good, but I just had no idea how good."

"Delta, I'm so glad you like it," Jinx said, basking in her client's delight.

Then Jinx spied one of her first clients, Trilby Bettencourt-Ciccone, chatting with Delores. She was certain they were discussing Delores's latest sculptures. Trilby insisted she had the most beautiful Manigaults and that Delores would never again be able to create anything so magnificent. She'd come close with Delta's O'Keefe-inspired creations, though. Even Trilby would have to admit that.

When Trilby saw Jinx approach, she opened her arms, hugged her warmly, and said, "Oh, Jinx, you have done it again. It is spectacular. No one can do it the way you do, my darling. Congratulations! And now, if you'll excuse me, I'm going to go sample some of Polly Ann's delicacies before they're all gone."

And as Trilby turned her attention to the buffet table, a young man, about the age of Knox, sidled toward Jinx, a seductive grin on his face.

"Sexy stuff."

"Beg your pardon?"

"Your design. Sexy. Suggestive. Alluring. The Georgia O'Keefe alone is enough to turn a guy on."

He reminded Jinx of her philosophy professor at Marywoods. Since she was a design student, she took classes in philosophy, sociology, and psychology, rather than chemistry, physics, and anatomy. However, if it didn't have an element of design, she merely tolerated the class.

But she more than tolerated her philosophy class, solely because of her professor. Though she was madly in love with Charlie, she wasn't blind or devoid of hormones. She knew sexy when she saw it.

Jeaux—it sounded so pretentious thirty some years later but so clever and mature to her nineteen-year-old self—entered a room hips first, all jutting pelvis and tight, torn blue jeans. He wore his dishwater blonde hair tied at the nape of his neck with a string, not a rubber band, and several wavy tendrils broke free to frame his square jaw, long before unruly tendrils were in vogue.

His form-fitting jeans were tucked into heavy boots that jangled with large silver buckles as he slunk, rather than walked. His shirts were patterned in muted paisley or a geometric print and were made of some synthetic material that clung to his androgynous frame. The sleeves were always pushed above his elbows to expose sinewy forearms. He sported a tattoo on his inner left wrist, some vague symbol known only to him and his inner circle. On his right wrist hung several tribal-looking colorful, braided bracelets.

Curiously, he wore a large silver chain attached to a belt loop, the other end disappearing into his right jeans pocket. Jinx always wondered what was attached to the hidden end. His hooded green eyes hinted that it was worth knowing. Jinx never would.

Jinx hid a smirk as this faux Jeaux stood before her, hands in hip pockets, bedroom eyes beckoning, pelvis jutted forward. What seemed so authentic and appealing on the Marywoods campus all those years ago looked only ironic and foolish in Delta McMillan's newly-transformed home high atop New York City. She had no idea who he was, nor did she have any desire to find out—even if he had a Park Avenue apartment to decorate and knew every New Yorker. But how could she escape this poseur?

Then she saw him.

He was standing at the windowed wall, Central Park at his back, a drink in one hand, one foot crossed over the other. He was dressed casually in camel slacks, a blue wool blazer, and highly-polished loafers. He looked attired for Sunday brunch at the Club, not an Upper East Side cocktail party. Convention, though, didn't seem important to him. When he was sure he'd caught her attention, he smiled and sauntered toward her.

"Pardon me," he said, rescuing her as he stepped between her and the faux Jeaux.

"Do you know everyone?" she asked, relieved to see him.

"Well, not everyone, but lots."

"How in the world do you know Delta McMillan? She just got into town."

"Her husband introduced us."

"Her husband? You know Helms?"

"I do."

"Well, he just got into town, too. How did you meet?"

Pausing for effect, Sam Bradley said, "He bought a company from me."

"He bought…?" Jinx began but stopped as the scene unfolded in slow motion and she felt the puzzle pieces falling into place.

Sam smiled slyly when he was certain Jinx had finally put two and two together.

"You're the one who recommended my services to Delta. You're the one whose name she just, somehow, couldn't remember."

"Guilty," he said, with a shrug.

"The plane! The private jet to New Mexico. That belongs to you?"

Not Bill Gates. Not Warren Buffet. But Sam Bradley.

"Well, it belongs to one of my companies."

"But you arranged the trip."

"I can't take all of the credit. I just offered the plane. Delta did the rest. But I hope you found your flight comfortable and my crew attentive."

"Why, yes, the flight, the crew, everything was wonderful. But I had no idea," Jinx stammered, her voice trailing, nowhere else to go.

"Would you have accepted had you known?"

"Well, I, I…"

She probably wouldn't have, but she hadn't been given that choice.

"My staff said you were utterly charming and rather cute when you got tipsy."

Blushing crimson, Jinx sputtered, "Shame on your staff for plying me with champagne and then tattling on me. I call that entrapment."

"Well, entrapment aside, I hope you and your partners enjoyed your trip."

"Yes, the entire visit was fantastic. I'd never visited New Mexico. It was quite a treat. And, really, thanks for the loan of the jet."

"Now that I've shared my jet with you, will you share dinner with me?"

"Wow, you just don't give up, do you, Sam Bradley?"

"No, and, as you can see, I'll go to great lengths to plead my case."

But Jinx was still not interested in a relationship. Her son, her granddaughters, her design business: that was still her life, her very full life.

Twenty-four

"Pardon me."

The young man wrestled his load into the elevator. He carried a brief case and a canvas lunch bag in one hand, his heavy winter jacket under his arm. With the other he attempted to maneuver his free arm into his suit jacket. His tasteful regimental striped tie was draped casually around his neck.

"Here, let me help you with that," Knox said, as he reached to share the guy's load.

"Thanks, I owe you," the flustered young man said, gladly relinquishing his brief case, jacket, and lunch bag, trusting this New Yorker not to bolt with his belongings.

Knox would have stuck out his hand in greeting, but now they were both full, and the fellow was using both of his to finish dressing in the elevator.

"Hi, I'm Knox Collier. You new?"

"Yeah, first day. Didn't gauge my commute very well. Looks like I won't be making a very good first impression."

"Oh, you'll get it together in time. Where to?"

"Accounting," said the newcomer, finally dressed and reaching for his brief case and lunch bag. "Robert, Robert Singletary," he said, taking Knox's hand and giving it a firm shake. "Thanks for the help. And the welcome. I needed a friendly face this mornin'."

"Glad I could help," Knox said, and when the elevator stopped, added, "Follow me. I'm next to accounting." When they reached Knox's office, he said, "Here we are. Good luck, Robert," and, once again, stuck out his hand.

Robert grasped it, breathed deeply, squared his shoulders, and said, "Thanks, Knox, see you around," and headed for his first day in the accounting department at the Museum of Modern Art.

"Hey," Knox called, just as Robert pushed open the door to Accounting, "how about lunch?"

"Brought mine," Robert said, lifting the canvas bag.

"Save it. I'll stop by at noon."

Pausing to consider the invitation, Robert said, "Sure, thanks. Noon it is."

Then he disappeared into the first day of his new job.

Knox remembered what it had been like his first day on the job. He hadn't known a soul, and he'd been living in a temporary cheap-by-New York-standards hotel room until he could find a permanent home. He'd felt so vulnerable and out of place.

He was all decked out in his new, big-boy suit that his mama had bought him when he'd graduated from the University of Georgia, and he was eager to begin his grown-up career. But his world, his perfect world, had just imploded. He had come out to his parents, and his father had banished him. He had expected pain and disappointment, of course, perhaps disbelief and disapproval, even denial; but he had certainly not expected his father to disown him.

But that's exactly what had happened.

He was hoping that Robert's transition hadn't been so traumatic, but he was sure that the relocation from the South hadn't been easy. Major moves never were. And Knox was certain Robert was from the South. He'd detected that familiar southern drawl when Robert said, "I needed a friendly face this mornin'," dropping his *g* from morning. He felt an immediate kinship with this new transplant and so wanted to make him feel welcome. And he'd felt that a casual lunch was just about as welcoming as it could get.

When the time came, he found Robert waiting for him in the hall.

"Good morning?" Knox asked, as the two fell into step and headed for the elevator.

Stepping in and pressing One, Robert answered, "Well, you know, I had to get all the formalities out of the way. I met everyone in the office but can't remember most of their names. Also had to fill out all those unavoidable employment forms. I thought I'd never get through. I think this afternoon will be better, though. I just might be able to get down to some work. But I'm starved. What's for lunch?"

"There's a little sandwich shop right down the street that serves cheap, filling food. And it's pretty tasty, too. Hard to mess up a sandwich."

"Sounds perfect, especially the cheap part."

Stepping from the elevator and into the sunlight, Knox and Robert joined the sea of New Yorkers, making their way to lunches and meetings.

"Here we are," said Knox, pushing open the glass door and motioning Robert in.

They joined the crowd of patrons, waiting to give their soup and sandwich and salad orders. The line moved fast as the counter staff quickly jotted orders and handed them off to the kitchen staff.

"Ham and Swiss on rye, please. And give me the red-skin potato salad as my side. Hold the pickle. And water," Knox ordered.

"That'll be nine ninety-five," the order taker said as Knox handed over his credit card.

Robert stepped to the counter, eyed the overhead menu, and said, "Turkey with lettuce and mayo on white. And I'll take the macaroni salad. And the pickle, too, please. And a Coke."

"Eleven sixty-five, please."

Robert counted out the correct change and handed it over.

"Number 198. We'll call you when it's ready," said the already-lunch-crowd-weary order taker, as she handed Knox and Robert their number and their drinks. They turned to find a table and, spying a two-topper at the back of the restaurant, bolted to claim it.

"So what's your story?" said Knox.

"Just graduated from Chapel Hill in December."

"Ah, a Tarheel, huh?"

"Yeah, didn't have much choice. My dad is an art professor at Carolina. I grew up in Chapel Hill."

"But you didn't study art?"

"Nope. Love art. No talent. Both my parents are artists. Dad paints. Mom's a sculptor. She does it just for fun, though. Sells a piece occasionally, but she makes stuff mostly for friends. My twin sister is an artist, too."

"You have a twin sister?" Knox said. "My partner and I have

twin daughters."

"Really? Moira's my sister's name. She's a ceramicist. She lives in Asheville. Lots of artists there. Don't know what happened to me. I got a head for numbers, not colors."

"But you got a job at MoMA. Why?"

"Like I said, I love art. I just can't produce it. I figured I'd get a job that could take me anywhere. Everyone needs an accountant. I applied at MoMA so I could be an accountant and still be around art."

"Good planning. Glad it worked out for you."

"And I knew I wanted to be in New York City. I've wanted to live here since I was nine and my folks brought me here for the first time. There's just nothing like it."

"I agree. Wouldn't want to live anywhere else either, even though I sometimes miss the South."

"One-nine-eight," called the woman at the counter.

"Hold the table. I'll run get our orders."

Knox rushed to the counter and grabbed their sandwiches.

"Where you living?" Knox asked, as he doled out their order.

"I'm crashing on the sofa with some fraternity brothers. They have a place in Brooklyn. They're both web designers and work at a company not far from their apartment. Real convenient for them. It's not very convenient for me, though, but it's the best I can do right now. I hope to find something a little closer to work. Well, actually, a lot closer."

"I can probably help with that. I know a great agent who knows everything that's available. He'll hook you up." And pulling out his phone and scrolling through his contacts, Knox said, "Here's his number," and handed the phone to Robert. "Just tell him I told you to call."

Robert transferred the information to his own phone and said, "Thanks, I'll give him a buzz. I'm ready for a place of my own."

"How 'bout you? Been in New York long?"

"It'll be six years this summer. Came here right out of University of Georgia. I grew up on Tybee Island, outside Savannah."

Robert said, "Love Savannah. The architecture is incredible. And I once drank a little too much and skinny dipped at Tybee with a girl I didn't know. Not my proudest moment. She was real pretty, though."

Knox laughed and said, "Yeah, Savannah is beautiful—the architecture and the girls. And I know a few girls who would skinny dip with you for a beer. I probably even know yours."

"Sorry, I didn't get her name," Robert said and blushed. "And, by the way, I don't do that anymore."

Again, they both laughed.

"And I'm like you. I like art but am better at business. My mom is an interior designer. But I took after my dad. He was an attorney."

"Was?"

"Yeah, he died over three years ago," Knox said. It still made him so sad to say it out loud. "I'm an only child, so my mom moved to New York after he died."

"Sorry about your dad. But that's great that your Mom moved up here. Do you get to see her often?"

"All the time. She has a place in our building, right across the hall from me and my family. It works out real well. She gets to be with her grandchildren, and I get to have my mom nearby."

"Sounds nice. I miss my folks already."

"Well, hang around. My mom would love to mother you."

"I might take her up on that."

"How about Saturday?" Knox said. "We're having some folks over for dinner. Mom will be there. I'd love for you to join us."

"Thanks, I'd like that."

"And you'll get to meet my partner and our little girls."

"Count me in."

Twenty-five

"Thanks so much," Knox said, as Tony stirred the clam sauce. "What would I do if you didn't bring home your strays? I'd be miserable. I need your friends to keep me in practice. And, remember, they're my friends, too," said Tony, smiling broadly.

Knox was so blessed. Tony was the kindest, most patient and giving person he'd ever met. And together they had the most adorable little munchkins on earth. Just as he was thinking about their little girls, Abby and Izzy came squealing into the kitchen, clean and naked from their bath, Jinx panting after them with a towel.

"Come back here, you scamps."

But still they squealed—Abby, the leader, doing the major squealing—and trotted around like little ponies, their mini pink feet making wet prints on the kitchen tile.

Knox grabbed them as they flew past and swung them in the air, making them giggle and squirm.

"Okay, kiddos, you heard Jiji. Gotta get dried off. And y'all know better than to run around in the kitchen when Pop Pop is cooking. You might get burned. And I would cry real hard if my little girls got burned."

Together they grabbed Knox's face and said, "Don't cry, Daddy. Peeze don't cry. We promise we not burn."

"Okay, that's good to know. Now, go on with Jiji and get ready for bed. Then you can come out and speak to Miss Pandora."

"Pan Pan? Pan Pan coming to see us? Yeah, Pan Pan, Pan Pan, Pan Pan," they chanted as they wiggled free and streaked back down the hall, Jinx trailing after them.

"How did we get so lucky?" Tony said, draping his arm around

Knox's neck and giving him a hug.

Before Knox could answer, there was a knock at the door. He left Tony to the cooking to greet their guests.

Robert was first to arrive. He showed up with a bottle of wine and a bouquet of yellow roses for Jinx.

Exhausted from her energetic granddaughters' bath time, Jinx joined Knox to greet their first guest.

"Oh, Robert, how sweet of you," Jinx cried and hugged the young stranger's neck.

As he returned her hug, he smelled her fragrance: White Shoulders. It was the same perfume his mother wore. He thought he might cry. All of a sudden, he was so homesick.

"Make yourself at home, Robert. I'm going to find a vase for these." And sniffing her bouquet, Jinx said, "Oh, they're beautiful. Yellow is my favorite color."

"Great apartment," Robert said to Knox, scanning the space.

"Thanks, Mom is our decorator. We love what she's done to the place."

Wandering around the large living-dining area, Robert spied Tony and Knox's huge wall of art and said, "Wow, love your art," and approaching said, "these look like Houstons." When he got closer, he cried, "Oh, my god, oh, my god, they are Houstons!" And racing up and down the wall, cried again, "They're all Houstons! Where did you get these? How did you get so many Houstons? Oh, my god!"

Breathing hard, he grabbed a chair and sat, still facing the art wall. He couldn't believe his eyes. Liz Houston was his favorite artist. He knew very little about her because she didn't have much of an Internet presence: no LinkedIn, no Facebook, no Twitter, no Instagram. She had only a simple website to display her work. She seemed to be a very private person. Robert had learned, though, that she had been a street artist until someone had seen her work and recognized her extraordinary talent. Robert had no idea that someone was Knox.

His parents had bought two of her small pieces during their last trip to New York, and had coveted them. They had promised to will them to him. As soon as he arrived in the city, he began looking for her work. He found a small gallery in Soho that was displaying her art exclusively. In the ten days since he'd been a New Yorker, he'd gone to the gallery each day to study her paintings. He also hoped he might meet her. The proprietor said Miss Houston came in from time to time, but much to Robert's disappointment, she had not shown up while he was there.

"Are you okay, Robert?" asked Knox, concerned.

"Yes, yes! I just love her work. Where did you get so many pieces?"

"We got them from Liz. She's our best friend." He didn't add, though, that she had given birth to their daughters.

"Your best friend?" Robert yelped and jumped from the chair. "You mean to tell me that Liz Houston, my favorite artist, is your best friend? I don't believe it! I just don't believe it! What are the odds?"

"Well, we asked her to join us tonight, but she had another engagement. She's appearing at the gallery in Soho where her work is on display."

The gallery in Soho. The same gallery Robert had been stalking for ten days, in hopes of seeing Liz. And the one night he chose not to go, she was making an appearance. Robert just shook his head in dismay and disbelief. He told Knox about his daily trips to that very studio in hopes of meeting Liz, and they both burst out laughing.

They were still laughing when Tony and Jinx emerged from the kitchen and said, "You guys all right?"

Catching their breath, they were just beginning to tell Robert's story when there came a knock at the door.

"Yoo hoo, it's party time," called Pandora, as she bore a plate of her famous seven-layer chocolate-lemon-coconut-caramel squares.

"I know they sound disgusting," she'd tell wary tasters, "but I just threw in everything I love, and I'll be damn if they're not divine."

When Abby and Izzy heard their beloved Pan Pan's bellow, they came racing from their bedroom. They twirled and pranced in their pink pajamas and bunny slippers, so excited to see Pandora and so happy to be part of the adult celebration.

Pandora fell to her knees and gathered the little girls to her, kissing their sweet heads, enveloping them in her voluminous flowered caftan.

"My precious angel babies, I have missed you till my heart has broken. I have wept puddles of tears."

Playing along with Pandora's drama, Abby and Izzy threw their arms in the air and cried, "My heart is broken, my heart is broken."

Then Pandora grabbed them closer to her, and the three friends giggled in a pile on the floor. It was their game, the game they played each time they met.

Struggling to her feet, Pandora pushed her hair band back into place and greeted everyone with hugs.

Shaking Robert's hand vigorously, Pandora said, "Welcome, my new friend, to New York. We're so happy you decided to join our group. I promise you won't regret your choice."

Turning to Tony, she wrapped her arm around his shoulders and said, "How's my favorite I-talian? Let's get this culinary show on the road," and the two of them retreated, arm in arm, to the kitchen, leaving the rest to chat until dinner.

The adults passed the girls from one to another. Abby, her curly brown ponytails bouncing, her dark eyes animated, chattered confidently, her hands making pictures in the air. Izzy, her silky, flaxen hair in ponytails as well, batted her beautiful sapphire eyes as she spoke quietly, barely above a whisper. Reserved and shy, she smiled sweetly, her dainty little hands clasped beneath her chin.

When Knox said, "Okay, girls, bedtime," they didn't protest. Instead, they circled the room, giving everyone a kiss, took Knox's hands, and skipped down the hall to their bedroom.

Tony and Knox's dinner party was a success, just as they all were. The two always made their guests feel comfortable and loved, welcoming new friends into their circle. The lively conversation was heated, animated, and always stimulating and thought provoking. The group didn't even shy away from politics and religion. But no matter the topic of conversation, Robert managed to steer the dinner guests back to Liz. He was like a kid in a candy store, and he was on a sugar high.

By the end of the evening, his infatuation was the running joke of the party.

"Oh, the crisis in the Middle East is beyond comprehension, and Liz painted all those pictures over there."

"This linguini is delicious, but Liz painted all those pictures over there."

"Jinx, I have two new clients for you, but Liz painted all those pictures over there."

Robert blushed but waved all their joshing aside.

"I don't care, y'all. I came all the way from North Carolina for this, and here it is. Now, if you'll just introduce me to her…" he said, a pleading look on his face.

"Hold tight," Tony said. "You will meet Liz. I promise."

"When?"

Everyone laughed at his impatience, but they realized that the boy was mightily smitten.

Twenty-six

"Let us clean up, Jinx. You did the cooking."

"No, you kids go sit down and talk. I have this under control. Also, the kitchen is just way too small for three people. Now, scoot."

Before they could protest, Jinx shoved them away gently and began clearing the table. Liz shrugged, took Robert's hand, and guided him toward Jinx's sitting room and her comfy, down-filled sofa. Kicking off her shoes and gathering her feet under her soft, flowing pastel skirt, she relaxed and looked up at Robert, inviting him to join her. He didn't shed his shoes, but he sat close, close enough to smell the squeaky-clean fragrance of her beautiful long, flaxen hair. He'd only seen hair that fair, that silken once before. Her hair looked just like Izzy's, Tony and Knox's little girl. He was from a family of brunettes and had been mesmerized by Izzy's fairy-like ponytails. He'd thought she looked like a dainty woodland nymph.

When he had visited their home, the little girls had climbed onto the laps of friend and stranger alike, charming all the guests with their cunning. Izzy, the quiet one, had lifted her arms to Robert and smiled sweetly.

He was a young man and had not yet thought about being a parent. But as he placed the angelic child on his knee, he thought, *If I'm ever a father, I want a little girl just like this.*

As Robert talked with her, she answered his questions in a nearly inaudible whisper, batting her huge blue eyes and clutching her tiny, dainty hands beneath her chin.

When Tony called bedtime, she kissed Robert on the cheek and said, "Night, night, Waboo." Both little girls were cute, but Izzy stole his heart.

They must grow blondes up here in New York, he thought to himself, as he admired Liz's beautiful, silken hair.

Liz and Robert turned sideways, face to face, so close as to feel each other's heat, and continued their dinner conversation.

The week before Tony and Knox had promised to get Liz and Robert together. So with Jinx's helped, they'd planned dinner at her house and had invited the two of them.

The attraction had been instantaneous. The other dinner guests sensed it and almost felt as if they were intruding on an intimate, personal experience. But Liz and Robert had been gracious, not selfish, and had welcomed the rest into their circle of intimacy. It had been fun, not awkward, for the rest of them to watch the two get acquainted and connect so completely.

But now dinner was over. Tony and Knox had retreated across the hall to their apartment to relieve Polly Ann and Delores of their baby-sitting duties. Jinx was in the kitchen, promising she didn't need their help. It was just the two of them, Liz and Robert, happy for the privacy and eager to know more about each other.

"Seriously, you've been to the gallery every day since you got to New York?"

"Well, every day except last Saturday when I had dinner with Knox and Tony, the one time you went to the gallery," Robert exclaimed, throwing up his arms in frustration.

Liz threw back her head and let out a tinkly laugh that sent chills up Robert's spine and made him want to jump up and yell from the sheer exhilaration of being in his favorite artist's presence.

As soon as he had left Knox and Tony's house after the dinner party where he'd discovered the wall of Houstons and his new friends' connection to Liz, he'd stopped on the street, pulled out his phone, and called his parents.

"Hello, Darlin', how is New York?"

"Oh, Mom, New York is wonderful. Is Dad there?"

"Why, yes, he is. What's the matter?"

"Nothing, Mom, just get him on the phone. I have something incredible to tell y'all."

"Rob, pick up the phone in your office. Robert's on the line," he could hear his mom calling, her hand semi-muffling her voice.

"Hey, Son. This is a nice surprise. How's New York?"

"Mom, Dad, do y'all remember what I said was the first thing I was going to do after I got a job?"

"I believe you said you were going to get a decent place to live."

"Okay, after that."

"Well, you said you were going to save your money to buy your own Houston because we refused to give ours to you," said Robert's father, belly laughing into the phone.

"Yep, that's what I said. And y'all are not going to believe this. I haven't bought a Houston, but I work right across the hall from Liz Houston's best friend."

"Well, what a coincidence," said Robert's mother.

"I've found a gallery full of her work. I go there every day, hoping I'll meet her. I never dreamed I'd be working with her best friend. But I had dinner at his place tonight, and he's promised to introduce me to her."

"Well, Son, all I can say is I'm happy for you and so very jealous."

"Gotta run. I see the bus. I'll keep you posted."

And here he was, sitting side-by-side with his favorite artist, who just happened to be the most beautiful, charming woman he'd ever met. He'd been acquainted with his share of sorority sisters at Carolina and was very popular with all the art students since his father was an art professor at the University. But none of them compared to Liz Houston. She was captivating.

He knew her website by heart, had memorized the one small photo of her. He was expecting pretty, but that picture hadn't done her justice. She wasn't pretty; she was gorgeous, in a fresh, wholesome, girl-next-door sort of way. And her infectious laugh and welcoming personality didn't shine through the picture on her website.

And Liz was just as taken with Robert as he was with her. In her dating years, before art consumed her, she had leaned toward the Nordic blonde tennis types she met at her parents' club. They were all tall, lean, and square-jawed. They were also arrogant and aloof, guarded and hard to get to know. But Robert, Robert with his jet black hair and milk chocolate eyes ringed with thick, curly black lashes was different from the club snobs in every way. He wasn't tall, perhaps just a couple of inches taller than she. She was five-eight, so that would put him at about five-ten. Nice height. She wouldn't have to talk up to him; he wouldn't talk down to her. Eye-to-eye, face-to-face. So comfortable.

When Knox and Tony had suggested their meeting and Jinx had offered to host the get-together, Liz was reticent. She wasn't sure she wanted to date, or even make a casual male friend, for that matter. She felt her plate was full.

And she came with baggage—lots of baggage. It was baggage she was comfortable with, but was she ready to share that load with another? She didn't think so. But the three persisted, made her feel as if they were ganging up on her. To shut them up, she had caved. But when the evening arrived, she was all jitters and clammy hands.

But there'd been no need for jitters or clammy hands.

When Knox answered Jinx's door and welcomed Robert, he was cordial to everyone: Jinx, Knox, and Tony. But he had eyes only for Liz. He approached her, grinning like a smitten schoolboy, and handed her a single sunflower.

"For you," was all he'd said.

Why a sunflower? Did he know that she thought roses were trite, that mixed arrangements were so ordinary, so overdone? How did he know that her favorite flower was a sunflower? And that the perfect number of sunflowers was one? Well, she hadn't known until he'd handed her the single sunflower that her favorite number was one, but she was certain as soon as she took it from his hand. Somehow, he'd known before she had.

"Thank you, it's perfect," Liz said before disappearing into Jinx's kitchen and returning with her one sunflower in a cobalt blue glass bud vase. She placed it in the center of the dining table. It was the perfect centerpiece.

As they sat side-by-side after dinner, Liz said, "Thank you, again, for the beautiful sunflower. It's my favorite."

"I thought about roses, but, all of a sudden, they seemed all wrong. I saw a small florist shop. There were sunflowers in the window in the middle of winter, and I knew that nothing else would do. The shop owner tried selling me a handful, but only one seemed right."

She smiled, feeling as if Robert had read her mind.

"Tell me about life in North Carolina," she said.

"Humid."

"Is that all?"

"Well, no, it's really quite nice. I grew up in Chapel Hill, a university town. It's all about the University. My dad is an art professor there. My mom is an artist, too, but she's an artist just for fun, not by profession. She is a sculptor. My twin sister, Moira…"

"You have a twin sister?"

"Yes, I do. You'll just love her. She's terrific. And she's a ceramicist, an incredibly talented ceramicist. She didn't go to Carolina, though. She studied at Penland, in the mountains of North Carolina."

"Oh, I've heard of Penland. It's very well known."

"And it was perfect for her. She's now a visiting artist at Penland and teaches classes there. She lives in Asheville where there is a huge artist community. She also teaches several classes at the University of North Carolina at Asheville. I can't wait for you to meet her."

"Am I going to meet her?"

"I hope so," Robert said seriously, "if you want."

"I'd like that. Yes, I would love to meet Moira. And your parents."

"Kids, it's after midnight," Jinx said from the kitchen door. "I'm turning in."

Both Liz and Robert jumped up and began apologizing over each other.

"I'm so sorry. I didn't realize how late it was. We lost track of time. We'll be leaving…," stammered Robert.

"Nonsense," snapped Jinx, "I wouldn't hear of you two leaving here at this hour of the night. Robert, you wouldn't make it back to Brooklyn for hours. You'll both stay right here. Liz, I've made up the sleeper sofa in my office for you. Robert, I'll get you some bed clothes so you can sleep right here on the sofa."

"Are you certain, Mrs. Collier?" asked Robert.

"Robert, I couldn't be more certain, and, remember, I'm Jinx," and she disappeared to get Robert's bedding.

"I'm so embarrassed," said Robert, his face reddening.

"Don't be," said Liz. "She's used to my crashing here. She never likes for me to go home alone at night. She's great, just like a mom. You'll see."

Jinx returned, arms laden with sheet and blanket and pillow.

"And here's a toothbrush and toothpaste and a fresh towel and wash cloth. You can use the powder room right down the hall."

"Thanks so much Mrs….Jinx."

"Y'all just take your time. Sit here all night long if you want. But I need to call it a day."

Jinx approached Liz, leaned over, hugged her, and kissed her on the top of her head.

"Love you."

"Love you, too, Mom."

And to Robert she said, "Thanks for coming, Hon. See you in the morning."

When Jinx was out of earshot, Robert said, "Did you call her Mom?"

"Yeah."

"But, why? Don't you have a mom?"

"Well, I did. Until she and my dad disowned me."

"Should I ask?"

"Sure. It's not a secret. I didn't do what they wanted me to do."

"What is it they wanted you to do that you wouldn't do?"

"Be respectable. They sent me to Vassar to get this art nonsense out of my system. They insisted I major in business. I did, with a minor in economics. I graduated first in my class. They thought I'd land on Wall Street. But Vassar hadn't beaten the art nonsense out of me. They made me choose. I chose art. I embarrassed them. They chose to disown me."

He reached for her hand. She didn't stop him. But he didn't take advantage of her vulnerability. He only held her hand.

She was touched.

"I'm so sorry, but I'm glad you chose art," was all he said.

She smiled.

"Me, too."

"Where's your studio?" he asked.

"Harlem. I have the most amazing space right in the heart of the area where the Renaissance movement was born. I can feel the inspiration of all the writers and artists and musicians as I work. It's a wonderful place, and it has the most fabulous light in the city. Trouble is it's drafty and frigid in the winter and stifling in the summer."

"And where do you live?" he asked.

"In the corner of my studio," Liz said. "It drives Tony and Knox mad. I have a mattress and a mini kitchen with a hot plate in the corner. It's all I want. If I need a home-cooked meal, I drop by

Tony's kitchen. There was a time my Harlem home-studio was all I could afford. Now I'm pretty sure I could buy an apartment and keep my studio, but I just can't let go of the light. I never know when it's going to be perfect. But I want to make sure I'm there when it is. I don't want to waste a moment of it."

"I'd love to see it."

"Stop by. I'll heat you up a can of beans on my hot plate."

As the evening progressed, the conversation became more intimate, if one can get more intimate than divulging the details of parents disowning their child. But they talked of their dreams, Liz's dream of being an artist and embracing the dream with passion, of Robert's dream of being an artist like everyone else in his family, only to discover he had no talent for art.

"I know my mom and dad were disappointed. How could they not have been?"

"How could they have been disappointed in you? I'm sure you're a wonderful son."

"Oh, no, not disappointed *in* me—disappointed *for* me. They knew how desperately I wanted to be able to do the things they did, to share my sister's talent. It just wasn't there. But, Liz, they adore me and have praised every little milestone in my life, no matter how miniscule."

"They sound wonderful."

"Oh, Liz, they are. They've always made my sister and me feel so special. We're really blessed."

"How so?" Liz asked, wanting to know how parents make their children feel special about who they are.

"Well, let's see..." Robert said, searching his memory for a perfect example that would explain to Liz just how precious his parents were. "When I was just a kid and was tapped for the Order of the Arrow in Boy Scouts, Mom and Dad treated it as such a huge deal. Both of them attended the ceremony and sobbed unashamedly. You'd have thought I'd won the Nobel Peace Prize. My sister had just received a scholarship to a summer study program for young artists up at Penland, yet they gave my Boy Scout medal equal weight, acted as if it were just as important. No, that's not quite right. They really believed my Order of the Arrow was just as important as Moira's art scholarship."

By now Liz and Robert's knees were touching; they were holding hands. Liz could feel Robert's warm breath on her face as he told her about his wonderful parents, his blessed life in North Carolina.

So moved was she by his description of his loving family that without thinking, without planning, without permission, Liz leaned forward and touched her lips to Robert's.

He lingered for a moment before he pulled away, smiled, and said, "Thank you. I've wanted to feel your lips since I handed you that sunflower."

Then he cupped her cheek with his hand, leaned in and kissed her, really kissed her. It was a kiss that made them both sigh and shudder.

"My god, Liz, it's four o'clock," said Robert, when they finally came up for air. "We probably should be getting some sleep. And I know we must be disturbing Jinx."

"No, her room is way down the hall. We're not bothering her at all." And in a whisper she added, "But Polly Ann and Delores are probably holding a glass up to the wall. Those two don't miss a trick."

They both stifled giggles.

But Liz wasn't ready to go to sleep just yet. She had baggage to unload, and she so hoped Robert was strong enough to help her carry it. If not, she needed to know right away. This evening had been so much more than she had expected, more than she could have imagined. She wanted to know more of him, see more of him, be more to him. And if there was something between them, and she believed there was, he deserved to know the truth about her before they moved further. Any less wouldn't be fair.

"But it's late, very late. Maybe we need to get to bed."

"Not just yet. I need to tell you something."

"Oh, okay," Robert said. "What is it?"

Breathing deeply to steel her nerves, Liz said, "You know that Knox and Tony are my best friends, right?"

"Yeah, otherwise I wouldn't be sitting here with you," he said, grinning and squeezing her hand.

"They have been so good to me. That wall of art in their apartment kept me in my studio for a very long time. When I was struggling, they bought my paintings, pretending they just couldn't live without them. In the beginning, they really couldn't afford the expense of art, but they couldn't stand to see me do without. Their generosity, their support kept me in rent and Beanie Weenies. They're the best, the kindest people I know."

"I could tell tonight how close the three of you are. Y'all are lucky to have one another."

"And not just the three of us. There's also Jinx and Polly Ann and Delores. And, of course, Izzy and Abby."

"Of course, Izzy and Abby. They are so cute."

"Knox and Tony have wanted children ever since I've known them," Liz said. "They tried adoption, but agencies were still reluctant to give children to gay couples."

"Seems unfair when there are so many children who need loving homes. And they clearly have a loving home."

"Yes, but that's just the way it was. They tried but just kept butting up against brick walls. It was so frustrating for them."

Liz was shaking by now.

She took a deep breath and said, "So I offered to be their surrogate, to have a child for them. There's nothing Knox and Tony wouldn't do for me. I wanted to do that for them."

Robert just stared. Then he saw it: the hair, the beautiful flaxen hair.

"But the child I promised turned into two children. I gave birth to Abby and Izzy."

Still Robert just stared, his eyes turning glassy with tears.

"I'm sorry if I'm chasing you away," said Liz, still holding onto Robert's hand, "but it wouldn't have been fair not to tell you. The girls are Tony and Knox's biological children. I just carried them for them because they couldn't."

Robert wiped his sleeve across his eyes and sniffed.

"Liz, I've never heard of anyone doing anything so selfless, so giving. I just don't see how you could do that."

"It was easy, Robert. They love me unconditionally, encourage my passion, and never expect me to be anything I can't or don't want to be. They would cry unashamedly if I were tapped into the Order of the Arrow. I'm certain of that. And I love them the same. I offered to back off after the girls were born so they wouldn't be confused, but Knox and Tony said they wanted me to be a part of their lives. Izzy and Abby call me Mama. Their dads will tell them the whole story when they are old enough to understand."

Robert moved closer and held tight to Liz's hands.

"I'll understand if you want to part ways right now. It's a lot to handle," said Liz, so hoping Robert still wanted to stay. "But it would have been unfair to keep this from you."

Without hesitation Robert smiled, squeezed Liz's hand, and said, "I'm not going anywhere."

Then Robert moved closer and put his arm around Liz's shoulder, drawing her closer. She sighed with relief and rested her head on Robert's chest.

They didn't make it to bed. They were still holding on when Jinx padded down the hall to the kitchen to make coffee at seven in the morning.

Twenty-seven

Polly Ann fried Liz and Robert bacon and eggs before sending the two on their way. She felt that twelve hours was long enough to have dinner guests stick around before they started getting in the way. Jinx, on the other hand, didn't care how long they stayed. She loved seeing Liz so happy. She had shown no interest in men since Jinx had known her; she deserved someone to love her the way Tony and Knox loved each other, the way she and Charlie had once loved each other. Perhaps Robert was the one.

Once out on the bustling, Saturday-morning street, Liz and Robert kissed chastely and went their separate ways. Robert had an appointment to meet the real estate agent Knox had recommended, and he had only thirty minutes to find the address. Now, more than ever, he was anxious to get off of his buddies' couch in Brooklyn and closer to his new friends. Especially one friend.

Liz, on the other hand, needed to hurry home to her easel. The weatherman had predicted a sunny day, and she was working on a piece for one of Pandora's Park Avenue acquaintances. Liz also had to get home to straighten her studio, make up her mattress in the corner, and wipe down her hot plate. Robert was coming over at six for Beanie Weenies—or, perhaps, Chinese take-out.

Robert watched as Liz skipped down the street toward the bus stop. As soon as she rounded the corner, he pulled his phone from his pocket. He couldn't wait another minute to tell his parents about his evening. They already knew he was meeting Liz. He was certain they'd be standing by the phone, waiting for a report.

"Mom, she's wonderful."

"Rob, pick up," Robert's mother called to his father, not even bothering to muffle the phone with her hand.

When she was sure he was on the line, she said to Robert, "And how was it?"

"She's more incredible than I'd imagined. She's beautiful and warm and funny and kind."

"You got all of that from a dinner party?"

"Well, after the others went to bed, Liz and I talked all night. I just told her goodbye. And I'm seeing her again tonight—going to her place for dinner."

"Terrific. Sounds exciting. And how is the apartment hunt going?" asked Dr. Singletary, anxious for his son to get off his friends' sofa and into a place of his own.

"Well, Dad, I have an appointment not far from here, I think, to look at a place. I have less than thirty minutes to find it, so I'd better run. I'll call y'all tomorrow and let you know if it works out—with the apartment and Liz."

"We'll be waiting," said Robert's mom.

It was small, but the first place Brandon showed Robert seemed ideal. It was only a one-room studio, but it was an easy bus commute to work and not too far from Knox and Tony's apartment. Best of all, it came furnished. It had a small sitting area with a sofa, a three-drawer chest, and a desk/dining table on one wall, a Murphy bed on the opposite. In one corner was a miniature kitchenette with a two-burner range, sink, and an under-the-counter fridge. The opposite corner was dedicated to a very small bathroom with shower, which would not have worked for Robert had he been any taller or wider. A miniscule closet would hold his one dress suit, a couple of shirts, his dress shoes, and his tennis shoes. The small unit was on the fourth floor of a four-story walk-up, and from his one-chair balcony Robert would have a pleasing, if not spectacular, view of the bustling street below. Best of all, the rent was within his meager budget.

"Let me work up the papers. I'm pretty sure I can have you in by next weekend," said Brandon.

"Perfect, thanks so much," Robert said, reaching to shake Brandon's hand. "You have my number if you need anything from me, right?"

"Right, and here's my card," Brandon said, pulling his business card from his pocket and handing it over.

When the two parted, Robert realized just how weary he was. He had barely slept Thursday night, so excited about meeting Liz the following evening. Then he had gone to work Friday, and as much as he was enjoying his new job, the learning curve was arduous. And, of course, he had not slept the night before but, instead, had sat up till dawn, talking with Liz. He needed to get back to Brooklyn and catch a nap and shower before heading back to Harlem for dinner. New York living was exhausting.

Two bus transfers, a subway ride, and a three-block trek later, Robert dragged himself up the stairs, let himself into the apartment, and collapsed, face down, on the sofa. He was snoring before he could kick off his shoes. Luckily, his roommates were out of town, and he had the place to himself.

At three o'clock he awoke, refreshed. He smiled to himself. *Did that really happen? Did I just spend the night with Liz Houston?* Certain that he had, he jumped to his feet and screamed, "Woot! Woot!" where only he could hear.

He sprinted to the kitchen, opened the fridge, and found a single can of Coke. He needed a jolt of caffeine. He popped the top, took a huge gulp, and headed for the shower.

"This is one thing I won't miss," he said out loud, as he kicked his roommates' dirty clothes and towels into the corner of the bathroom to clear a path.

He turned on the water, and as he waited for it to warm, he shed his clothes and hung them on the hook at the back of the door. He downed the remainder of his Coke, crushed the can and set it aside for the recycle bin, and stepped into the warm water.

As Robert showered, he couldn't wash the contented grin from his face. But he really didn't want to. He knew it was premature, too soon to be feeling the L-word, but he was so taken with Liz. He felt he had known, had loved her forever through her art, but she had just met him the night before. What's more, her life was very complicated. He needed to go slowly, tread lightly, so as not to further complicate her life, to scare her away.

But there was no denying—Robert wanted Liz.

After shaving and drying his hair, he pulled on clean jeans and a long-sleeve tee shirt.

"Liz, it's Robert."

"Oh, hi. Did you get some rest?"

"Yeah, felt good. How about you?"

"A little. I had some work to do, though. And I wanted to get the place presentable before you came over."

"Well, I'm on my way. Don't know how long it'll take, though."

"I'll be waiting. How about we order Chinese? There's a great place nearby that'll deliver."

"Perfect. I love Chinese."

"And, Robert…"

"What?"

"I can't wait. I had such a good time last night."

"Me, too. See you soon."

Robert pulled on his heavy jacket, the one he'd bought just for New York winters, tugged his cap over his ears and wrapped a scarf around his neck, locked the door, and ran from the apartment building. He wasn't quite sure how he was going to get there, but he grinned through subway rides and bus transfers and sprints and was there before he even knew he was near. He spied a small florist's shop on his way and stopped in for another sunflower. New York florists were geniuses. He still wondered where they found sunflowers in winter.

"Hi," she said, greeting him at the door, wearing a pale blue sweater and jeans, fuzzy white slippers on her feet. "Come on in."

"What a great place," he said, as he caught sight of her studio.

"It's a bit on the chilly side this time of year, but we can huddle by the space heater," she said, pointing toward the heater by her mattress in the corner. Come on, sit down. It's not fancy, but it's comfy."

Robert kicked off his shoes and was glad he'd worn his warm, woolen socks.

"I hope you like sunflowers."

"Yes, I do. Very much."

"The florist had lots. I thought only one would do."

"One is perfect," she said and, smiling, kissed him on the cheek.

The light must really be incredible in this place. Why else would Liz choose to live in a room as cold as a meat locker? Robert thought to himself, as he pulled his jacket around himself and wandered across the room, looking at Liz's completed work and work in progress.

"Each piece is more beautiful than the next. But I love them all."

"Thanks. The piece on that easel is for a friend of Pandora's."

"It's wonderful. That's part of your Urban series, right? I recognize the lines and the stark colors."

"Good eye. It's going in a Park Avenue apartment. The client insisted on Urban."

"Well, your client is going to be pleased."

"I hope."

"Urban is my dad's favorite. The pieces he and Mom own, though, are from your Seasons series. Mom likes Seasons best. Dad bought two autumn pieces for her October birthday."

Liz hoped people liked her work, and they did, but still she became shy talking about it.

"Here, make yourself at home," she said, as she piled decorative pillows against the wall behind the mattress, the only furniture in the room, save four easels and one antique chest. She then unfurled a beautiful, handmade, brightly-colored quilt to drape over the two of them.

"I have wine. It's white. Would you like some?"

"Sure, that sounds great."

Everything sounded great coming out of Liz's mouth. She could have said, "I have arsenic. It's poisonous. Would you like some?" and he'd have said, "Sure, that sounds great."

Robert was like a tongue-tied child in the throes of his first crush.

Liz returned from her kitchenette in the corner with two mismatched wine glasses and the bottle of grocery-store wine. She poured some for both of them, placed the bottle on the floor, and joined Robert in his nest of pillows and quilt.

"I found an apartment," he said.

"So soon? That's great. Where is it?"

"It's on East 97th, not too far from Knox and Tony's place. It's really small, though, really small. It's just a studio, but it'll work fine for me. Best of all, it's furnished. I'll just have to get dishes and towels and sheets. My agent thinks I can move in next weekend."

"Really? That's fantastic."

"All I need to do is pack my bags, and I'm good to go—away from Brooklyn. Can't wait. My buddies have been so gracious, but it's time to give their space back to them."

The two huddled close, sipping their wine, as the conversation swayed from Liz's artistic inspiration to Robert's childhood in North Carolina to Liz's privileged life in Connecticut to their friends Knox and Tony.

"Oh, my gosh, Robert, it's after ten o'clock. I bet you're starving," Liz cried, flushing with embarrassment. "You must think I'm a terrible hostess."

"No, I don't think you're a terrible hostess," Robert said, smiling and squeezing Liz's hand. "I've enjoyed every minute with you. But I am a bit hungry," he added, as his stomach growled. "All I've had since Polly Ann's breakfast is a Coke.

"Well, then, we need to get you fed," she said, and jumped up from their mattress nest and headed for the antique chest.

She opened the top drawer and pulled out a handful of menus, saying, "I don't cook, but I sure know how to order in." She plopped back down on the mattress and began shuffling through the stack. "Oh, here it is. Hunan Palace. Isn't every Chinese restaurant named Hunan Palace?" She handed the menu to Robert, saying, "Everything is delicious, but I especially like the chicken cashew and beef with broccoli. The spring rolls are great, too. I like them better than the egg rolls."

He handed the menu back to her and said, "Well, then, I don't think I'll need this. I believe it's settled. Let's get a chicken cashew and a beef with broccoli and share. And maybe some rice. And some of those spring rolls. And make sure they put in lots of hot mustard. Can't have Chinese without hot mustard."

"I knew I was going to like you," Liz said, grinning impishly. "I love hot mustard. I could suck it right out of the packet."

Liz reached for her phone and tapped the pre-programmed number for Hunan Palace. Within thirty minute their food was at the door. Robert paid the delivery boy, and Liz spread a blanket in the middle of the studio so they could have a Chinese-food picnic on the floor. She brought plates, silverware, and the half-spent bottle of wine, and the two settled down side-by-side for the best Chinese food Robert had ever eaten. By one in the morning, they had polished off every grain of rice and were working on their second bottle of wine.

"Wow, I really was hungry," said Robert.

"Me, too," said Liz. "Told you it was good."

"It's so late, Liz. Hope I haven't overstayed my welcome. I'd better be going."

"Why don't you just stay? It's way too late to head back to Brooklyn."

"Really?"

Liz smiled and said, "I'm just offering you shelter for the rest of the night. Nothing more."

Robert could feel his face redden. He returned Liz's smile and said, "Nice offer. I accept."

Once they'd rounded up their picnic leavings and washed their few soiled dishes, the two bedded down, fully clothed, for the night. Lying side by side, Liz reached for Robert's hand.

"I've had such a good time tonight, Robert. And last night, too."

"Me, too, Liz."

He so wanted to add, I came to New York just to meet you. I've been looking for you since I arrived.

And even though he believed it to be true, he didn't want to scare her with his admission, to chase her away. One day, maybe, he'd be able to let her know. Now, though, he'd be content just to hold her hand and share body heat as they drifted off, happily, into sleep.

From the start they wanted to spend every waking moment together. Young love is like that. But they were practical. They had jobs. So they pledged to tend to their jobs during the week, seeing each other only on weekends. But the weekends were theirs, theirs to enjoy in each other's company, theirs to milk every second until they had to drag themselves apart and return to Monday.

Though there were a million things they could do in wonderful New York City, Robert's favorite activity was watching Liz paint. He would sit on the mattress in her studio, wrapped in Liz's quilt, and watch her for hours. She said she wasn't used to having someone look over her shoulder while she worked and felt somewhat self-conscious at first, but she soon warmed to his presence. He loved it best when she left him, that moment when she forgot that he was there and was transported to a world of her own, a world where she almost floated and her being just seemed to glow. A look of serenity would come over her face, and she could live alone in her private world for hours. He was content to watch her create in her private space until she touched back down in his world and returned to him.

They spent nights at his place in his hide-and-seek bed that lived its days in the wall, waiting for the lovers to find it and set it free. They clung to each other on the thin, lumpy mattress, tangled in Robert's green-striped sheets, one of his few possessions. After love making, he'd smooth her spun-gold hair from her face and pull her close. He would spoon her tall, thin frame, her skin so fair it appeared translucent, and she'd drift into sleep as he kissed her shoulder and breathed his warm breath on her neck.

And as he listened to her purr in sleep, he knew that he loved her and regretted that it had taken him twenty-four years to find her. They should have been childhood friends, romping and playing in the creek out behind his parents' home. They should have been high school sweethearts, attending football games and proms at Chapel Hill High. They were perfect together. Everything about them fit: their sensibilities, their senses of humor, their bodies. She stirred, and he pulled her ever closer. And as she purred him into sleep, he knew that he couldn't alter the past. But he could plan his future. He was certain this was forever.

Twenty-eight

"They'll do no such thing, Robert. We have a perfectly good guest room. It's not huge, but it's private. They'll stay with us."

"That's awfully generous of you, Knox, but they can stay at my place. They can have my bed. I can sleep on the sofa."

"Robert, you wouldn't have room to turn around in your place. Admit it, it's not a three-person apartment."

It was true. Robert knew it. But they could make do. Knox, however, insisted that Robert's parents stay with him, Tony, and the girls.

Robert had been in his new, miniature, Upper West Side studio apartment about three months. The bitter winter had passed, the last of the snow had melted, and there was a hint of spring in the air. He felt his southern parents, so accustomed to mild North Carolina winters, would be comfortable in New York now. They just couldn't wait to visit to make sure their only son was all right. They wanted to see his apartment, wanted to see where he worked, wanted to meet his new friends. But mostly, they wanted to see Liz, the woman who had stolen their son's heart.

"Mom, Dad, the snow has melted. Time for you to come for a visit."

Knox owned the only car among all the friends, so he offered it to Robert on the day his parents were to arrive. He'd pick them up from the airport; he hated for them to have to rely on a taxi.

"Want me to go with you to the airport?" offered Knox.

"Nah, I can manage. But thanks."

"No problem. Will Liz be going with you?"

"No, she has to make an appearance at the gallery. She's going to meet my folks and me at Angelo's for dinner. I thought a casual, comfortable setting would be a great first-meeting place, a perfect place to drop several bombs."

"Good idea," said Knox, smiling, fully aware of the bombs to which Robert referred.

Robert saw them first, each with a backpack perched ergonomically correctly on their backs. They were both craning their necks—to locate Robert and to locate their suitcases on the conveyor belt. They found Robert first and left their baggage to go round and round until they were through greeting their son and were ready to stake their claim to the two 25-year-old mauve tapestry bags. They felt no compunction to keep an eye on their luggage. Who else would want 25-year-old mauve tapestry bags?

"Oh, Darling, you look wonderful," said his petite mother, standing on tip-toe to hug her son's neck."

"Good to see you, Son," said Professor Singletary, much more formal than his wife.

"I'm so glad y'all could come. Let's grab your bags."

There they were, twirling around, all mauvey and gaudy. Robert recognized them and grabbed them as they rumbled by. His parents were the only people on the planet who didn't have wheels on their luggage.

Robert had found a parking space in the nearest lot—had whizzed in just as another motorist had pulled out. He'd angered a lot of other drivers, as evidenced by their scowls and curses and extended middle fingers. But first come, first served, and he'd gotten to it first. He just prayed he wouldn't return to find that Knox's car had been keyed.

Robert's mother, Jocelyn, scurrying along on her tiny feet in an effort to keep up with the men, chatted as they made their way to the parking deck. Robert hoisted the cumbersome suitcases into the trunk, helped his parents into their seats, and inspected the car for key scratches. There were none.

"I hope we're not imposing on your friends, Robert. We can certainly stay in a hotel."

"Mom, they wouldn't hear of it. They wouldn't even stand for your staying with me. They say my place is too small. They have a guest room that they rarely use, and they're dying for y'all to stay with them. And you're just going to love them. Tony and Knox are the nicest guys ever. And they have the cutest little girls."

Robert could tell that he was prattling. He always prattled when he was hiding something from his parents. They knew that. He was hoping they were too busy taking in the sights to recognize his jabbering. But they would know everything soon enough. Liz insisted they know right away about the girls and her surrogacy. She wanted to give them the option of bolting, just as she had Robert. She hoped they'd be as understanding as Robert had been, but she was not so confident about that. Robert was their child, their only son. Would they want him involved with a woman who had had twins for a gay couple?

Robert found a parking space just one-half block from Knox and Tony's place. It was his lucky day. He grabbed the bags from the trunk and ushered his mom and dad down the street and up the steps to their new, temporary home.

"Come in, Robert. And welcome, Dr. and Mrs. Singletary," Tony said, as he grabbed one of the mauve bags.

"Hi, Tony, you are Tony, right?" said Jocelyn, reaching out her small hand to her host.

Tony laughed and said, "Yes, I'm Tony, the Italian one. Knox is the WASP. He's back in the girls' room putting ponytails in their hair. I do the cooking. Knox does the ponytails."

"Hi, Tony, I'm Rob Singletary. Thanks so much for opening your home to us. That's most hospitable of you."

"It's our pleasure, Rob. Most of Robert's friends live right in this building. Seemed only natural that you should stay here. We've all been so anxious to meet you. Come on back, and we'll get you settled."

Tony took the Singletarys' luggage to their room, and the couple followed. When they passed Izzy and Abby's room, they found Knox on his knees, putting the finishing touches on Izzy's wispy hair. Robert just smiled at little mini Liz. And, of course, there was precious Abby who had also stolen his heart with her sassy self.

"Waboo," they both squealed when they saw him and ran to hug his legs.

He crouched down and scooped them up, kissing each on the cheek, and said, "Abby, Izzy, I want you to meet my mom and dad. This is Jocelyn, and this is Rob."

Abby threw up her hand and yipped, "Hi!"

Izzy smiled at their guests and put her little butterfly hands beneath her chin. She got Robert every time she did that—made that lump rise in his throat. It was such a simple thing, a sweet thing, but still it touched him.

"Jocelyn, Rob, this is Knox, the WASP," said Tony.

Jocelyn blushed while the rest of them laughed.

"Hi, Jocelyn, Rob, so nice to meet you," Knox said, reaching to shake their hands. "Please make yourselves at home. Here is your bathroom. There are clean towels for you. Unpack, kick off your shoes, and get comfortable."

And the Collier-Collettis left Robert to help his parents get settled.

"Juice, peeze," said Abby.

"Me, too," said Izzy.

"Okay, girls, juice it is. Orange or apple?"

"Apple," they crowed, in unison.

By the time Tony had filled their sippy cups, the Singletarys had settled in and joined the family.

"Look, Mom, Dad," Robert said, pointing to the wall of Houstons.

"Oh, my," gasped Jocelyn, as she approached the wall with a sense of reverence.

"Spectacular!" exclaimed Rob, joining his wife at the wall and pushing his glasses up on his nose to get a better look.

"Aren't they amazing?" said Robert.

"Indeed, indeed," was all Dr. Singletary said, standing close, admiring Liz's work.

"I am so excited about meeting Liz. I feel like a little girl on Christmas eve," said Jocelyn, clasping her hands.

The others laughed, and Knox said, "Liz is very special, sort of like Christmas eve."

"Yoo-hoo," called Jinx as she let herself in and joined the group. "Jocelyn, Rob," she cried, arms outstretched, "it's about time we met. Welcome to New York, my fellow southerners."

"Hi, Jinx, we've heard so much about you. We just couldn't wait to meet you," said Jocelyn, returning Jinx's hug.

"Oh, my, listen to that southern accent. Love it. Jocelyn, when I miss the South, I call Robert just to hear him speak southern."

The others laughed, and Knox said, "Well, what about me? I'm southern."

"Oh, fiddle," said Jinx, with a wave of her hand. "You don't even say *y'all* anymore." And turning to Robert, she said, "Honey, please don't ever stop saying *y'all*."

"I promise, Jinx," Robert said, and came forward to give her a kiss on her cheek.

"Jinx," said Jocelyn, "thanks so much for being so kind to my child. He says you've made him feel so welcome."

"Well, it has been our pleasure. I don't know how we managed before him. He's just such a big part of our family," Jinx said, patting Robert on the back.

As the group was getting acquainted, Polly Ann and Delores burst through the door.

"I'm sorry we're late. Lawd, I thought that church bazaar would never end. And, you know, Miss Delores here got to speak to everybody and his brother 'fore we could get out of there."

"Well, Polly Ann, we couldn't be rude, now could we? Those people were there to support a fine cause."

"Yeah, you right, as usual. But we made it."

"This gotta be Dr. and Mrs. Singletary. Glad to meet you," Polly Ann said, thrusting her hand at the two. "That's a mighty fine boy you got there. We like him a lot," she added, winking at Robert. "Oh, 'scuse me, I'm Polly Ann Bondurant, and this is Delores Manigault. We're Jinx's business partners."

"Nice to meet you both," said Dr. Singletary, standing to greet Polly Ann and Delores.

"It's a pleasure," added Jocelyn.

"Well, this has been fun and I hate to break away, but we have to meet Liz at Angelo's in thirty minutes," said Robert, examining his watch. "We'd better get a move on."

"But we just got here," protested Polly Ann.

Robert put his arm around her shoulder and said, "Polly Ann, I'll bring them back. You'll be right across the hall. You can visit all you want."

"Good. Then y'all run along, and tell Liz hey for me."

"I'm so sorry I'm late," panted Liz, as she greeted Robert and his parents at the door of Angelo's. "When you have an interested collector, though, you just can't walk away." Smiling, she reached with both hands outstretched and said, "I've been so excited to meet you. Thank you for including me tonight."

Liz was relieved by the Singletarys casual appearance. She had been expecting Robert's parents to be like her own: ramrod straight, clothing pressed and creased, every hair in place, and both of them looking down their snooty, patrician noses. But Dr. and Mrs. Singletary bore no resemblance to her mother and father, whatsoever.

Dr. Singletary wore blue jeans, a button-down blue oxford shirt, and Doc Martens. His white hair was unkempt and shaggy and hung to his collar, and he wore round tortoise-shell glasses. Mrs. Singletary was a small woman, about four-eleven and slight. She wore plain, black slacks with a white blouse and an oversized blue cardigan dwarfing her petite frame. She wore no make-up, and her salt-and-pepper hair was pulled back into a loose ponytail. Several wisps had sprung free and framed her face.

Liz was delighted to see that Mrs. Singletary was not bothered by errant wisps of hair. The disarray would have sent her mother to bed with a migraine.

Liz's heart was thrumming as the hostess guided them to a booth toward the back of the restaurant. She was hoping for a seat near the exit, in case she needed to make a quick get-away. She was just so nervous about meeting Robert's parents. Well, it wasn't so much the meeting that had turned her knees to jelly; it was the news that she and Robert had to share with them. And if the revelation that she had carried twin girls for a gay couple weren't enough, she and Robert had another announcement to spring on his parents: Robert had proposed to Liz.

The two had known each other only three months. Robert was aware that he was rushing things, but he had been certain from the moment he handed Liz that sunflower in Jinx's apartment that he wanted her, wanted to take her in his arms and kiss her and tell her that he would love her forever. He realized that would have been impetuous, but, when after three months his feelings had only grown, he felt he couldn't wait another minute to profess his feelings.

He wanted his proposal to be special, but since he was only months into his career, he was too poor for diamonds and fancy restaurants. What's more, Liz, despite her privileged upbringing, was no longer a diamonds-and-fancy-dinners sort of girl. She had left that all behind when she had walked away from the Connecticut country club life. She had become a sunflower-and-picnic sort of girl.

One afternoon as Robert walked from work to his bus stop, he passed an antique shop. There in the window he spied a beautiful, antique emerald-cut sapphire ring in a filigreed platinum setting. The sapphire was Liz's birthstone and matched the color of her eyes. And Izzy's eyes. He knew immediately that the beautiful sapphire ring in the window was meant to be Liz's. He felt that this was the sign that it was time to ask Liz to be his wife. He entered the shop and announced that he'd take the sapphire ring in the window.

"What size do you need? That ring is a size six." said the proprietor, with a haughty, superior air.

"It's perfect," said Robert, not knowing Liz's ring size but certain that the ring would be an exact fit.

"Let's eat at my place Saturday night," he'd said to Liz casually.
"Sounds fine."

She'd gotten accustomed to his cramped quarters and take-out dinners on his small desk/dining table. She'd also learned to maneuver his mini bathroom. She even liked his not-so-comfy Murphy bed that they'd hide in the wall after nights of love making and spooning.

When Saturday arrived, Robert spread a yellow tablecloth— purchased just for the occasion—on the small living room floor and placed yellow votive candles across the floor, on tables, on the mini kitchen counter, on the window sill. By the time Liz showed up, the candles were lit, a lone sunflower stood in a bud vase in the center of the tablecloth, the grocery-store wine was chilled, and the Chinese food was waiting. They would share chicken cashew and beef and broccoli and spring rolls with lots of hot mustard.

"Oh, Robert, I can't believe this is your place. It's beautiful! We ought to burn candles and eat Chinese food on the floor all the time," Liz said, wrapping her arms around his neck and kissing him tenderly. "What's the occasion?"

"I love you. That's all the occasion I need," he said, smoothing Liz's hair from her cheek and leaning in to softly kiss her neck.

"I love you, too, Robert."

He had planned the evening to perfection: they'd drink wine and eat Chinese food by candlelight. When their meal was over, he'd turn to her, slip the emerald-cut sapphire ring onto her perfect size-six finger, and ask her to marry him. But as soon as they'd proclaimed their love for each other, all the plans vanished into thin air. He couldn't wait another minute. He knew that the moment was right. He sank to his knees amid the burning votives, coaxing Liz to join him. The lights flickered in her sapphire eyes; her hair looked like spun gold. Robert thought he might cry with joy.

"Liz, I love you so much. I realize I've known you just a short time, but I feel as if I've loved you forever. I want to be with you forever." Taking the ring from his pocket, he said, "Liz, please be my wife."

Tears sprang to her eyes—and Robert's, too—as she said without a moment's hesitation, "Yes, yes, Robert, I want to be your wife."

And Robert slipped the beautiful antique sapphire ring onto Liz's perfect, size-six finger. But what would Robert's parents say? Would they think the two had lost their minds? And what about Abby and Izzy?

"I'm Sean. I'll be serving you tonight. What can I get you to drink?"

Sean, the waiter, shook Robert from his reverie. He was going to enjoy Angelo's pizza and a beer. Then he and Liz would tackle the tough stuff.

He looked at Liz, took her hand, and smiled, saying, "We'll have Sam Adams all around and one large veggie-lovers pizza." And addressing his parents, he said, "Is that okay with y'all?"

"Sounds perfect, dear," said Jocelyn.

When Sean left to get their beers, Liz reached into an oversized shopping bag she'd placed on the floor beside her and pulled out a package wrapped in purple felt and tied with a green silk ribbon.

"I brought you something," she said, and handed the gift to Rob and Jocelyn.

"Oh, my, you shouldn't have, Liz," they said in unison, but took it from her, just the same.

When the two pulled at the ribbon, the purple wrapping fell away, exposing a sixteen-by-sixteen framed Houston. They both gasped.

"Oh, Liz, it's breathtaking," Jocelyn said in an almost-inaudible whisper.

"It's from your Urban series," said Rob, sounding as if he were having trouble breathing. "It's my favorite series. We have two Seasons, but I've so wanted an Urban."

"I know, Dr. Singletary. Robert told me. I do hope you like it."

"Like it? Oh, Liz, I'm speechless. It's stunning."

"Thank you," said Liz, just as Sean returned with their beers.

"Here," said Jocelyn, "let's wrap this back up so we don't spill beer on it. It'd hate that, wouldn't you, Rob?"

"Oh, Jocelyn, it would break my heart," he said, clutching his chest as they all laughed.

Shortly after they had re-secured Liz's painting, the pizza arrived.

"Told you it was the best," said Robert.

"It's delicious," both of his parents cried.

When they had polished off the pizza, they pushed away from the table, declining dessert but agreeing to just one more beer.

When he was sure they were free of Sean and would have this time alone, Robert said, "Mom, Dad, Liz and I have something to tell you." And taking a deep breath and smiling at Liz, he said, "I've asked Liz to marry me, and she has said 'yes.'"

"Oh, that is wonderful news!" Jocelyn cried, ignoring the fact that her son and his fiancée had known each other for only a few months.

"Congratulations, Son," Rob said, as he reached across the table to grab Robert's hand in both of his.

Jocelyn stood and wrapped her arms around Liz's neck, hugging her and kissing her on the cheek.

Rob said, "I thought we were getting just a Liz Houston. We're getting *the* Liz Houston. Welcome to our family, Liz. We couldn't be happier."

Robert's parents began bombarding the young couple with questions about the wedding, when were they planning to get married, where would the ceremony be held, what about a reception.

"We just don't know any details yet," Robert said. "She said 'yes' just last weekend."

"And Dr. and Mrs. Singletary, I really don't want a huge to-do. I'd like to keep it simple, with just family," added Liz.

"I understand, Liz," said Jocelyn, "and, please, we're Rob and Jocelyn."

Liz smiled, knowing they still had to deal with the tough stuff, and said, "Thanks, Jocelyn."

When the euphoria settled to a hum, Robert said, "Now Liz has something else she'd like to share with you."

She took a deep, ragged breath and tried to calm her thrumming heart. She looked over at Rob and Jocelyn, both still grinning from the upcoming-nuptials news.

"I'm sure Robert has told you that Tony and Knox introduced the two of us."

"Yes, he did," said Jocelyn. "What wonderful young men. And how generous of them to open their home to us."

"They are generous, Jocelyn. They are the kindest people I know. They're my very dearest friends. They love me and have seen me through some very tough times. But they've had tough times, too." Taking a deep breath, Liz continued, "They wanted children so badly, but adoption agencies just wouldn't place children with a gay couple."

"How sad. And how narrow-minded," scoffed Jocelyn. "But how wonderful that they didn't give up. They persevered and proved to those adoption agencies that they would be terrific parents," Jocelyn said, shaking her fist in the air, as if in defiance of those obstinate adoption agencies.

"Well, they were never able to convince the adoption agencies to give them a child." Clearing her throat and clutching her clammy hands in her lap, Liz continued, "So I agreed to be their surrogate, to carry a baby for them. Except, I ended up carrying two. You see, I gave birth to Abby and Izzy."

Liz waited for the response, having no idea what that might be.

Dr. Singletary didn't say a word, but Jocelyn's hands flew to her mouth.

"Oh, Liz, how could you? What love. What selflessness," she said as she came to Liz's side and gathered her in her arms. Her future mother-in-law's reaction caused Liz to cry silent tears of relief into Jocelyn's oversized sweater, as the two woman clung to each other.

Dr. Singletary reached across the table, grabbed Robert's hands, and said, "Son, you treat this wonderful woman with respect and reverence, you hear?"

"Yes, sir, I hear. I promise I will."

By this time all four of them were laughing and crying and holding hands in the middle of the table.

Rob lifted one hand and hailed Sean, "Sean, my man, what kind of cake do you have back there?"

Sean approached the table and said, "Well, we have coconut, chocolate, lemon, carrot."

"What do you have that's still a whole cake?"

"I think there's a lemon in the kitchen that hasn't been cut."

"Well, then bring us a lemon cake with four forks. We won't be needing a knife or plates. We'll eat it right off the cake. And put a candle on that thing."

"And what is the occasion, sir?"

"It's our birthday," said Rob, looking from Jocelyn to the young couple.

"Whose birthday?" asked Sean.

"Everyone's. All four of us. It's our first birthday."

"Yes, sir! One whole lemon cake with four forks and one candle coming up."

Twenty-nine

"You say they love me, Pandora."

"That's right, Jinx. And they want to know you personally, not just on a business level. But you won't let them in."

"Pandora, I've heard 'I love you' all my life, but look where it's gotten me."

"But Jinx…"

"Let me finish, Pandora. My friends, my dear and precious friends that I've known since birth, promised to love me and have my back forever. I promised the same to them, and I meant every word of it. Sadly, they did not. When I needed them the most, they all turned their backs on my son and me, hiding behind their beliefs," Jinx said, spitting out the word beliefs as if it were caustic. "You use the word love, but if that's love, I want no part of it. I know that Knox and the girls love me, but it's been so long since I've felt loved, really loved by Charlie and my friends, that I just don't know what romantic love or love of friends feels like or looks like or sounds like."

By now tears were streaming down Jinx's face, tears of sadness for her past, tears of loneliness for her future. But Jinx had decided that she'd rather be lonely than hurt by two-faced, back-stabbing so-called friends.

"Oh, Jinx," Pandora said as she wrapped her arms around her and patted her back. "I don't promise you'll never be hurt again, but I do promise that my friends would never wound you intentionally. Most of all, they would be very open-minded and would never harshly judge you or your child."

"I just can't, Pandora," Jinx said, reaching into her pocket for a tissue to wipe her tears. "Even after all this time, the pain is still so raw. I can't open myself up to that kind of hurt again. I just have to keep it professional. I hope you understand, Pandora. Please, please understand."

Patting Jinx's hand and smiling understandingly, Pandora said, "Of course, I understand, Jinx. I'm just so glad that you have let me in. And if, at some point, you're ready to let others in as well, you just let me know. Okay?"

"Okay, Panny, I promise I will." But Jinx didn't add, *Don't hold your breath.*

"Hello?"

"Is this Miss Jinx speaking?"

"Yes, this is Jinx. May I help you?"

"Why, yes, you may. This is Mrs. Rutledge Tarkington Rogers speaking. You, perhaps, have heard of my late husband, Rut Rogers, former U.S. ambassador to the Baltic states."

Having never heard of Ambassador Rut Rogers, Jinx skipped right over her caller's assumption and said, "Well, good morning, Mrs. Rogers, to what do I owe the honor of your call?"

Is that what one said to an ambassador's widow? Jinx hoped so. She'd never been schooled.

"Well, my dear friend Pandora Featherby…"

But, of course, Pandora Featherby had something to do with it. Most of her calls started with, "Well, my dear friend Pandora Featherby…"

Since Pandora had discovered Jinx's decorating talents, she had taken it upon herself to fling Jinx's business cards to her friends, hundreds of them, singing Jinx's praises with each fling.

And, apparently, Mrs. Rutledge Tarkington Rogers had been caught in the card fall-out.

"…says that you are the finest decorator in all of New York City."

"Well, I don't know about finest…" said Jinx, her voice trailing, never knowing where to go from there.

Pandora told everyone that Jinx was the best decorator in New York. Jinx was just waiting for someone to scoff, "Well, I thought

Pandora said…" It hadn't happened yet, so she'd just ride the wave of hype until such occasion arose.

"I am so in need of your services, my dear. Perhaps you could come right over."

"Right over?"

"Yes, do you have an immediate opening on your calendar?"

"It's Sunday, Mrs. Rogers. I don't work on Sundays."

"Then that's perfect. Your calendar will be free."

Jinx couldn't argue with that. Her calendar was, indeed, free. She had helped Knox and Tony get the girls ready for Sunday school and had seen Polly Ann and Delores off to church. Her plan, now that she was alone, was to drink her coffee, finish reading the paper, and take a nice, long shower. But it looked as if that was about to change. Pandora had been so helpful jump-starting her business; she just couldn't blow off one of her influential friends.

And as Pandora would say, "You never know who knows whom."

"Well, all right, Mrs. Rogers, let me get myself together, and I'll grab a cab. Please give me your address and phone number," Jinx said, grabbing her iPad to add Mrs. Rogers to her fast-growing data base of business contacts.

She recognized the address. Not too far from Pandora and Trilby, it was a little off the beaten path and not so tony as their spectacular addresses. It was in an aged, shop-worn, old-money area, where apartments needed lots of work. Lots of work. Jinx smelled a nice, extensive job for Delores, Polly Ann, and herself. This Sunday appointment might be worth her while, after all.

"Please do come in, Miz Jinx. Miz Rogers is expecting you," said the aged, watery-eyed African American woman, as she ushered Jinx into the cramped entrance hall. The woman wore a starched, gray uniform and white ruffled apron. On her head, perched askew, was a jet-black curly wig. Her feet sported black tennis shoes, slits cut along the insides to free her bunions.

"Right this way," the woman said, as she shuffled at a snail's pace toward the main part of the apartment.

When, finally, the two arrived at the sitting room, Jinx found whom she believed to be the widow of Rutledge Tarkington Rogers.

"Bernadette, that will be all, thank you. You are free to go," the woman said to her domestic.

Bernadette, without responding, turned and inched, still snail-like, from the room.

"Welcome, Jinx. I am Mrs. Rutledge Tarkington Rogers. So good of you to come."

Jinx had never seen such a person. Very tall, at least six feet, and ramrod straight, she had to be close to one hundred years old. She balanced on black, lace-up orthopedic oxfords and a three-pronged cane. Mrs. Rogers was dressed in a faded green double-knit pantsuit that had to be thirty years old. It was washed and worn and stretched out of shape, and the bottoms of the pant legs barely grazed the tops of her white ankle socks. At her neck she wore a large, flowered scarf that she had looped dramatically around and around. Her few wisps of dyed red hair formed a halo around her theatrically made-up face. Her cheeks were rouged pink, and her very short lashes were mascaraed into tiny black spikes. And she had painted her non-existent lips into a crimson gash. But the most striking thing about her appearance—if all that weren't striking enough—was her ear lobes. Weighted down by heavy, pendulous gold chandelier-like earrings, they were long and flat and resembled stretched and melting clocks in a Salvador Dali painting.

Jinx found the woman's appearance quite unsettling.

"Well," Jinx said, looking around at the worn and cluttered sitting room, "what can I do to help you? You have a lovely space here. So much light, beautiful hardwood floors. Are you just interested in freshening up your décor or are you planning a major renovation?"

Jinx was hoping she didn't want a major renovation. Where would she put the woman while her crew was working? And would Mrs. Rogers live long enough to see a major renovation to fruition?

"Oh, no, my dear, this isn't the room I want redecorated. It's my bathroom. It's just gotten so drab. I'd like for you to spruce it up a bit." And shuffling at the same snail's pace as Bernadette, she said, "Please follow me."

They passed the dining table, set for a dinner party of eight. Jinx noticed, though, that the place settings were covered in a fine coat of dust, the linens yellowed with age. Jinx guessed that Mrs. Rogers' dining table had once seen elegant dinner parties with interesting jet-setters, politicians, and ambassadors. She was certain, though, that Mrs. Rogers had not entertained in years, perhaps decades. But she would forever be prepared, should the occasion arise.

"Here, my dear, right through this room," said Mrs. Rogers, as she led Jinx through her magazine-book-and-newspaper strewn bedroom into the bathroom that she wanted to spruce up a bit.

The room was white. There was nothing more to say about it. Just white. The sink, toilet, and bathtub were white. The floor was laid with small white hexagonal tiles. The walls, too, were tiled white. There was a worn, white cotton curtain at the single small window and a white cloth shower curtain hanging on the rod over the tub. The wooden door was painted white, as well. The towels were even white.

"Well, Mrs. Rogers, we have a lot to work with. What did you have in mind? A walk-in shower with travertine tile? A slate floor would be nice. And vessel sinks are all the rage. Just tell me what you think?"

"Oh, no, my dear, I don't want to change anything. I just thought maybe we could add a touch of color. You know, new towels, a frilly curtain at that window, a new shower curtain. I like pink. Don't you think pink would look good in here? Wouldn't that work?"

This woman, this hundred-year-old woman, had called Jinx on a Sunday to take a cab all the way across the city to buy her some towels? And not just any towels—pink towels. Jinx was fuming. She was not a personal shopper. She was an experienced interior designer. And did she think pink would work in the bathroom? For god's sake, the bathroom was white. Any color would work.

But Pandora's words came to her: you never know who knows whom.

And as old as Mrs. Rogers was, she probably knew everyone.

"Mrs. Rogers, do you have a computer?"

"Why, no, my dear."

Mrs. Rogers kept calling her my dear. She probably called everyone my dear because she couldn't remember names.

"Well, we're in luck because I do have a computer, and we're going to solve your decorating problem right now."

The two women returned to the sitting room, where Jinx pulled her iPad from her bag.

"Here, Mrs. Rogers," Jinx said, sitting on the worn, pink-flowered sofa and patting the cushion for the old woman to sit.

Leaning on her pronged cane, Mrs. Rogers eased herself onto the sofa next to Jinx.

Jinx booted up her iPad and typed in Bed Bath & Beyond. Entering towels in the search line, page after page of towels appeared.

"Oh, look at that," exclaimed Mrs. Rogers, as if she'd never seen a computer or known that she could order towels on line.

"Here, Mrs. Rogers, take a look at all your choices. You can get every one of these towels in pink. Pick the ones you like, and we'll order some for you."

Mrs. Rogers picked out unadorned pink towels, and the two of them ordered a half-dozen in bath size, a half-dozen hand towels, and a half-dozen wash clothes. They also ordered a plain, pink shower curtain and bath mat. They even found a frilly pink curtain for the small bathroom window.

When it came time to pay for Mrs. Rogers's order, Jinx said, "Now, if you'll just give me your credit card."

"Oh, I don't have a credit card. I pay by check," said the old woman.

No credit card? How could she not have a credit card? Once again, Jinx shook her head in disbelief.

"Well, I'll tell you what, I'll put the order on my credit card, and you can write me a check. Would that work?"

"Oh, yes, that would be wonderful. Here, I'll go get my checkbook now," Mrs. Rogers said, as she hoisted herself from the sofa with her cane and shuffled off toward her bedroom.

Jinx pulled her American Express card from her bag and completed the order quickly. The sooner she could get away from here, the better. This time Pandora had not done her a favor. This time she was doing Pandora a favor.

When Mrs. Rogers returned and Jinx told her how much the order total was, she painstakingly made out the check with her tremulous hand.

She tore it from her book slowly, folded it, handed it to Jinx, and said, "Here, my dear, I've added a little something extra for your time."

"Thank you, Mrs. Rogers, but that wasn't necessary," Jinx said, certain the old woman had given her a couple of dollars, perhaps minimum wage, for the hours she was wasting on her free Sunday.

But it was over. She would not have to step foot into this dusty mausoleum again. Jinx returned her iPad to her bag and dropped in Mrs. Rogers's check.

Turning to leave, she said, "Mrs. Rogers, Bed, Bath & Beyond will ship your towels here to your home. I'm sure Bernadette will be able to help you hang your shower curtain and towels in your bathroom. Thank you for trusting me to help you with your decorating. It's been a pleasure meeting you."

Then she ran from the building before Mrs. Rogers could ask for blue towels in her powder room.

In the cab back to the Upper West Side, Jinx was still furious. She had worked so hard to be taken seriously, but that old woman had made her feel trivialized. She reached into her bag for a tissue, and when she did, Mrs. Rogers's check popped out and fell onto the cab floor. She picked it up to cram back into her bag. That's when she saw, for the first time, the amount of the check. In addition to the cost of the towels, Mrs. Rogers had paid Jinx one-thousand dollars for her wasted time on her free Sunday.

Jinx was shamed. Poor Mrs. Rogers was just a lonely old woman who had to pay people to help her buy towels. She had once been a socialite jet-setter who had traveled the world, hob-nobbing with powerful people. Now she waited to host elegant dinner parties that would never happen and paid for the briefest company.

Jinx reached into her bag and pulled out her phone. She scrolled through her contacts and pressed the number of her newest entry.

"Hello?" said the frail voice at the other end.

"Mrs. Rogers, this is Jinx. I've been thinking, I believe I need to come back and hang your curtains and towels myself. I wouldn't feel right if we didn't get them just right. Would that be okay with you?"

"Oh, my dear, that would be wonderful. I agree that Bernadette and I would probably just bungle the job, and I'd hate for that to happen after the time you've put into it."

"Well, you just call me as soon as our order arrives, and I'll clear my calendar for you."

"Oh, okay, my dear, I'll do that. And thank you."

"And one more thing, Mrs. Rogers, would it be okay if I brought my granddaughters with me? I keep them for their parents sometimes, and I just might not be able to get anyone to stay with them at a moment's notice."

"Most certainly, my dear. It wouldn't be an inconvenience at all."

"Thank you so much, Mrs. Rogers. Now, you do still have my number, don't you?"

"Why, yes, I do. Your card is right here by my phone."

"Good, just give me a call when the towels arrive."

Telling Mrs. Rogers good-bye, Jinx leaned back and watched her city fly by, feeling a profound sadness for her lonely, reclusive new client.

Thirty

"Jinx, our purchase has arrived. I'm just so excited! I want to open the package so badly, but I promise, my dear, I'll wait till you arrive. How soon can you come?"

"Well, let's see, it's eight a.m. I'm just having my coffee. It will probably be several hours before I can shower, dress, and get a cab to your place. And, of course, I have to dress the girls. It's still all right for me to bring them, isn't it?"

"Oh, yes, you must. I've so looked forward to meeting them."

"Then how about eleven?"

"Sounds just perfect," said Mrs. Rogers. "And, by the way, do you own a car?"

"My son does. Why do you ask?"

"I own a parking space below my building, but I don't own a car. Haven't for about fifteen years. Seems when your eyesight fades, they just won't let you drive a car anymore. Imagine that," she chuckled. "I hate for that expensive space to go to waste, though. So if you have access to a car, please feel free to park in my place."

"That would be just splendid, Mrs. Rogers. The girls' car seats are in their fathers' car. It would be so much more convenient than hailing a cab."

"Very well, then. Just take the parking entrance at the west side of the building. I'm space 2D, just like my apartment. I'll see you and the girls at eleven."

Jinx finished her coffee and walked across the hall in her robe to Knox and Tony's apartment. Using her key, she let herself in. The guys were drinking coffee and reading the paper, their Saturday morning ritual. The girls were sitting on booster seats, eating

Cheerios and strawberries.

"I need to borrow the girls."

Knox and Tony just stared at her.

"Just borrow. I promise I'll bring them back. Is that okay with y'all?"

"Sure," they both said, still not sure how to respond to a grandmother's request to borrow her own granddaughters.

"They need to put on their pink, smocked Sunday school dresses, pink tights, and patent leather Mary Janes."

"What's going on?"

"I'm going to a client's house this morning. She's a lonely, old woman who loves pink. So I'm taking her the cure for loneliness— Abby and Izzy, dressed in pink."

Tony was the first to respond. He smiled, put down his paper, and said, "Come on girls. Let's get all pretty. You're going visiting with Jiji."

"Thanks, guys, I'll be back to get them at ten-thirty."

Turning to leave, she said over her shoulder, "Oh, and I'm going to need the car," and rushed out the door to shower and put on her pink sweater.

Jinx returned at ten thirty to find the girls pink and glowing, their hair neatly pulled back into ponytails and tied with big pink grosgrain ribbons. It was chilly out, so Tony had buttoned them into their pink fluffy coats. They looked like precious little cherubs.

Knox pulled the car to the curb from a spot two blocks away, and the two dads helped buckle the little girls into their car seats.

"Now, you girls be sweet and mind Jiji, okay?"

"We promise," they said, in unison.

Pulling into the traffic, Jinx said, "Girls, we're going to visit a really nice lady. Her name is Mrs. Rogers."

"Wahjuh?" Izzy said.

"That's right. Mrs. Rogers."

Jinx recalled how startled she had been at Mrs. Rogers' garish appearance. She hoped that the girls wouldn't be frightened by her or say anything hurtful about her hair or make-up or, worse, her melting earlobes. But Jinx would just have to take her chances. If they said anything embarrassing, she'd somehow figure out how to handle it.

She pulled right into the underground parking lot and into space 2D. She helped the girls out of their seats, smoothed their clothes, fluffed their ponytails, and took their hands. They skipped to the elevator, and Jinx lifted Abby to punch the button. When the elevator arrived and the doors opened, they walked in and Jinx lifted Izzy to punch the button for Mrs. Rogers' floor. The girls were learning to take turns.

"Please come in, Miz Jinx. Miz Rogers is expecting you," Bernadette said, just as she had the first time Jinx visited.

"Hi, Bernadette. These are my granddaughters, Abby and Izzy. Girls, say hi to Miss Bernadette."

Both girls smiled sweetly and waved their chubby little hands.

Bernadette smiled, patted their heads, and said, "Hello, Abby. Hello, Izzy. Give me your coats, and I'll hang them up for you."

Helping the girls out of their coats, Jinx handed them to Bernadette and herded her granddaughters into the sitting room to meet Mrs. Rogers. She was standing by her chair, balancing on her cane, just as she had been the first time Jinx had met her. She wore her faded green pantsuit with the brightly-printed scarf around her neck. Nothing had changed. She was still a lonely old woman excitedly anticipating the slightest attention. When she saw Abby and Izzy, one arthritic hand flew to her mouth, the other still firmly clutching the cane handle.

"Oh, my, what angels."

"Mrs. Rogers, I want you to meet Abby and Izzy."

"I'm so glad you came to see me, Abby and Izzy," she said, easing herself into her chair. "Can you come give me a hug?"

Jinx had no idea what they would do. Would they cling to their grandmother out of fear? Would they cry? Would they say something hurtful? Without hesitation, though, both girls stepped forward and held up their arms to their hostess. Mrs. Rogers opened her arms and gathered the little girls to her. They let the old lady cradle them and pat their backs. Then Jinx watched as Abby spied the old woman's sagging earlobe. She held her breath. What would her granddaughter say? Or do? A grin broke across the little girl's face as she reached her hand toward the long, dangling flap.

Jinx could feel her pulse beating in her ears.

Gently cupping Mrs. Rogers's large, gold chandelier earring in her tiny hand, Abby said, "Bootiful."

Jinx let out her breath in a whoosh. She needn't have worried. Children are so innocent and see nothing but the beautiful. They have to be taught imperfection. Jinx had told the girls that they were going to visit a nice lady. What Abby saw was a nice lady who happened to be wearing bootiful earrings.

Jinx swallowed hard and said, "Well, Mrs. Rogers, I can't wait any longer. I'm so anxious to see our new towels and curtains."

"Right there," she said, nodding toward the package, still holding tight to the little girls.

Jinx found the package and slid it across the floor till it rested beside Mrs. Rogers's chair. Bernadette had placed a pair of scissors on top, ready for Jinx to free their treasure.

"You open it, Jinx," said Mrs. Rogers, calling her by her name, instead of calling her my dear. "The girls and I will watch." Then to the girls she said, "Isn't this exciting? It's just like Christmas."

Jinx fell to her knees in front of Mrs. Rogers and brandished the scissors. Towels, towels, and more towels spilled out of the wrapper. There was pink everywhere. Abby and Izzy's eyes widened, and they oohed. They left Mrs. Rogers's side just long enough to gather armfuls of pink and deposit them in their hostess's lap.

"Pretty!" they both cried and clapped their hands.

"Oh, yes, they are so pretty," agreed Mrs. Rogers.

"Mrs. Rogers, could you please watch the girls while I hang the curtains and arrange the towels?"

"Oh, Jinx, I would be delighted," she said, smiling for the first time and patting the little girls once more, her lap still piled high with a mountain of pink.

Jinx worked fast and had the bathroom as pretty-in-pink as she could before returning to invite Mrs. Rogers to view her handiwork. She found the three of them, Mrs. Rogers, Abby, and Izzy, all sitting at a small round table by the window, each girl perched high atop a stack of books. They were eating Lorna Doones from fancy dessert plates and drinking apple juice from delicate tea cups.

"Tea party, Jiji," Izzy said when she saw her grandmother.

"We all decided we needed to have a tea party. I hope you allow them to have sweets."

"Of course, we love tea parties, don't we, girls?"

Mrs. Rogers must have been planning this tea party since she had learned the girls would be coming with their grandmother to decorate the bathroom in pink.

"Would you care to join us?" asked Mrs. Rogers.

"Thank you, but I think I'll just rest over here on the sofa until your party is over. Then I'll show you your new bathroom. I think you're going to love it."

Jinx decided to make a visit to Mrs. Rogers' house a regular event. Sure, her calendar was filling up with other clients, but she wanted to take time from her work schedule to visit this sweet, lonely old woman. She had seen just how much Mrs. Rogers enjoyed visiting with the girls. She'd, somehow, conjure an excuse to stop by each week.

"I need to run an errand. Could you please watch the girls for about an hour?"

"Don't you think we need to spruce up your guest bath next?"

"We were in the neighborhood and thought you'd like some of this delicious pumpkin bread I found at the market around the corner."

And Mrs. Rogers always agreed to her visits and seemed happy to see her and the girls.

One Wednesday Jinx feigned an emergency and asked Mrs. Rogers to babysit for Abby and Izzy. She dropped them off and left the building to walk around the neighborhood for about an hour. When she returned, she found the three sitting at their table, once again having a tea party. But this wasn't just any ordinary tea party. All three were draped in fur stoles, the little girls' stoles reaching to their ankles. They also had elaborate hats on their heads: Abby wore an emerald green pillbox with a jeweled brooch and peek-a-boo veil. Izzy sported a purple cloche that sprouted a spray of iridescent green and purple feathers. Mrs. Rogers wore a large-brimmed red felt hat with a huge, black grosgrain bow.

"We went to see the Keen, Jiji," Izzy crowed when she saw her grandmother.

"And we curty to her," squealed Abby.

"That's right," said Mrs. Rogers, "we've been to visit the Queen today, and she served us tea and crumpets."

"Cumpet," the girls chirped and showed Jinx their Lorne Doone crumpets.

"And show Jiji what you did when you met the Queen."

"Down, please," they both said to Jinx.

Jinx lifted them down from their towers of books, and they stood side-by-side, eyeing Mrs. Rogers.

Mrs. Rogers coached them by slowly sliding one foot behind the other. Then both girls put their right toes behind their left heels and spread their arms, fanning their fur stoles out from their sides. Then they bent their knees and curtsied.

"Very lovely," Mrs. Rogers said, clasping her hands and smiling broadly. "The Queen was most impressed with them, Jinx. They were such polite young ladies."

"The keen likes polite ladies," said Abby.

"Well, I am so glad that you were polite. I'm very proud of you. I'm glad you've returned, though, because it's time to go home. Now, thank Mrs. Rogers for taking you to see the Queen."

Both girls ran to their hostess and leaned into her, their hugging arms still trapped in their fur. As Mrs. Rogers released them from their mink cages and reclaimed their hats, both girls hugged her and said, "Thank you, Mrs. Wahjuh." And precious Izzy whispered, "I love you."

Mrs. Rogers patted her pudgy, little cheek with her craggy hand and said, "And I love you, Izzy."

"Me, too?" asked Abby.

"Yes, Abby, I love you, too," said Mrs. Rogers.

Before leaving, Jinx said, "Don't you think it's about time we tackled that powder room?"

"Why, yes, Jinx, I was hoping you'd say that. I know you're so busy, but I think we really need to do something to it. Since you've spruced up my bath, the powder room just looks so dismal."

"Well," said, Jinx, "do you have anything special in mind?"

"Yes, as a matter of fact, I do. Purple. I think I'd like purple. What do you think?"

"Oh, yes, that would be the perfect pop of color right off the entry foyer. Just leave it to me. I'll place another order and have our things delivered here. Just give me a buzz when you get them."

"I'll do that, Jinx."

Mrs. Rogers gave the girls a final pat and said, "Now, you must come back to visit when Jiji returns to decorate the powder room. Will you do that?"

"Yes, we will come back," they both told her and gave her a

farewell hug.

The purple towels arrived within three days. Jinx dressed the girls in their best tea-party dresses and rushed right over to Mrs. Rogers' apartment.

The towels were rich and royal and really did perk up the tiny foyer powder room. When she finished her decorating, Jinx went to the sitting room to find Mrs. Rogers and the girls having their tea party. While the girls ate their Lorna Doones and drank their juice, Mrs. Rogers joined Jinx on the worn, flowered sofa.

Easing herself down beside Jinx, she said, "Thank you for bringing those angels to visit. They are just darling little girls. They have given me a new lease on life. Now, is their father your son or their mother your daughter?"

This conversation was still hard for Jinx. She was so protective. She had come to accept her family completely, but would everyone? There was only one way to find out.

"Well, Mrs. Rogers, they have two fathers, my son, Knox, and his partner, Tony, who is a New York fireman."

Mrs. Rogers reached forward, and, taking Jinx's hand, she said very matter of factly, "How brave of them. You must be so proud. And they must be excellent parents. Just look at those perfectly adorable little darlings," she said, sweeping a shaking hand in Abby and Izzy's direction.

"Thank you, Mrs. Rogers," was all Jinx needed to say.

Still holding Jinx's hand, Mrs. Rogers said, "You know, Jinx, I've always loved children. Rut and I discussed having children of our own but decided it would not be fair. We felt that children should be raised by their parents, not governesses and nannies. And, with our many commitments, we just felt we wouldn't be able to give children the attention they deserved and needed. We were both raised by governesses and nannies, you see. Please don't misunderstand, we had wonderful parents, but we'd have preferred being raised by our parents, rather than nannies."

How sad, thought Jinx. The poor woman has no one—no husband, no siblings, no children—no family at all.

But Jinx vowed that she and the girls would do all they could to insure that Mrs. Rogers would not be lonely and alone.

Thirty-one

Jinx had, once more, helped Knox and Tony get Abby and Izzy ready for Sunday school and watched Polly Ann and Delores, dressed to the nines, head off to church. Jinx had not yet committed to a church in New York. Mt. Moriah had left a bitter taste in her mouth. She still wasn't willing to put herself out there again, to open herself up to the kind of pain she had suffered at the hands of the congregants at Mt. Moriah.

"Mom, you'll meet new people," Knox said, refusing to give up.

But Jinx had not given in to Pandora's coaxing, and she wasn't about to give in to Knox's either. Jinx still wasn't convinced that New York Tweezle would be at all different from Georgia Tweezle. Or Caroline. Or Blue. She had decided to limit her relationships to those she met through business, and she was sticking to that decision. She attended dinner parties at Knox and Tony's apartment and met all their acquaintances. She was cordial, but at evening's end, she said her good-byes and returned home, friendless. Her choice made Knox sad. He hoped she'd someday come around.

But not on this Sunday morning. Alone with her coffee, she settled at the kitchen table to read the paper.

Then the phone rang.

"Hello?"

"Jinx?"

"Yes?"

"Pandora here. Have you read the paper?"

"I'm reading it right now."

"Gotten to the obituaries yet?"

"No. I don't read the obituaries. I don't know any New

Yorkers."

"Yes, you do. Find them. I'll wait."

Jinx flipped through until she came upon the obituary section. There it was, the full length of the page and three columns wide. Across the top of the obituary was:

MRS. RUTLEDGE TARKINGTON
(ANNALESE KATHERINE COLERIDGE) ROGERS
1917 – 2017

Jinx's first thought was, I didn't even know her name was Annalese Katherine. Why, with a beautiful name like Annalese Katherine, would she call herself Mrs. Rogers.

Only then did Jinx realize that her friend, who had, indeed, been one hundred years old, was dead.

"Are you there?"

"Yeah, I'm here. Oh, Pandora, how sad."

"It's not sad, Sweetie. She had a full life. It was just her time."

"I guess," Jinx sighed.

"Listen, the funeral is at St. Patrick's, Tuesday at eleven in the morning. Can you meet me?"

"I think I have an appointment, but I'll reschedule."

"Good. I'll be on the front steps at about ten-thirty."

"Okay, thanks for calling, Pandora."

After she hung up, she began reading Mrs. Rogers' obituary. She was the only child of a wealthy industrialist father and socialite mother. She'd grown up in New York society and then studied as a young girl in Europe. Upon graduation she'd returned home and enrolled in Sarah Lawrence College, where she earned degrees in French and Art History. From there she went to Columbia University, gaining a master's in business and a doctorate in economics. She married Rutledge Tarkington Rogers at St. Patrick's Cathedral, after which they embarked on a lifetime of diplomatic service and charitable works.

The woman must have been brilliant. Why, then, did she take a back seat to her husband, even shedding her name for his? Why didn't she do something with her degrees? All that work for nothing. Mrs. Rogers' death saddened Jinx. Mrs. Rogers' life baffled her.

Then Jinx heard Knox, Tony, and the girls coming in from

church, the girls chatting, their Mary Janes clattering on the hardwoods in the hallway. She was still in her robe and slippers, but she needed to talk with Knox and Tony. Mrs. Rogers had promised Izzy and Abby another visit with the Queen. How could she tell them that they wouldn't be going? How could she explain Mrs. Rogers' death? Better to tackle it head-on, though, get it behind her.

Shuffling across the hall, she let herself into her son's apartment. There she found Tony and Knox helping their little girls out of their Sunday coats.

"Jiji," they both cried and flew into her arms.

Over their heads Jinx mouthed to Knox, "I need to talk with you."

Taking the cue and winking at Tony, Knox said, "Girls, run on in the kitchen, and Pop Pop will fix you some apple juice."

When they were out of earshot, Jinx said, "Sad news. Mrs. Rogers died last night."

"Oh, Mom, I'm so sorry. I know how much you've come to care for her," Knox said, taking his mother in his arms.

Straightening, Jinx said, "Yes, I'm very sad. I really had become quite fond of her. So had the girls. I just don't know how to tell them. They loved their tea parties with her." And, smiling wistfully, Jinx said, "They were planning to visit the Queen again this week."

"It's okay, Mom," Knox said, patting his mother comfortingly on the back. Then he called, "Izzy, Abby, come here a minute."

The little girls came running to the living room, their juice boxes in hand.

"Girls, Jiji just came to tell me that Mrs. Rogers has gone to live with Jesus, and she won't be able take you to see the Queen."

And they both cried, "We want to go live with Jesus, too. Peeze."

"Well, one day, when you're older, like Mrs. Rogers, you can go live with Jesus. But for now you need to stay with Daddy and Pop Pop. Okay?"

And they both answered, "Okay," and Abby grabbed her sister's hand and screamed, "Come on, Izzy!" And off they clattered down the hall to play in their bedroom.

"Mom," said Knox, "adults just make life way too complicated. Kids get it right. Hold hands. Run. Squeal. Wait till it's your turn."

When the cab pulled up in front of St. Patrick's, Jinx saw Pandora standing on the church steps among a crowd of people, caftan flowing, talking and gesturing with her hands. Jinx was delighted to see that others had come to pay their respects. She stepped from the cab, paid the driver, and joined Pandora and her acquaintances.

"Hi, we'd better go on inside. We want to get a seat," Pandora said, grasping her arm.

Why would they worry about getting a seat? There were 2,200 of them in St. Patrick's. How many of those seats could a lonely old woman's funeral fill?

Pandora rushed her up the stairs and through the massive doors. There they found a sanctuary full of people come to celebrate the life of Mrs. Rutledge Tarkington Rogers. Stymied by the huge crowd, Jinx trailed down the aisle after Pandora. Near the front of the sanctuary, Pandora ordered a pew of folks to please scrunch up so they could wedge in beside them. Seeing that the request was coming from Pandora Featherby, the grievers gladly obliged.

"I'm stunned," Jinx whispered to Pandora when they were settled in the pew.

"About what?"

"All these people. I thought she was a lonely old woman. I had no idea this many people would turn out."

"Jinx, there was absolutely nothing lonely about her. Yes, she was alone, but she was never lonely. She chose to be alone for the past few years. Said she was just worn out with entertaining and with people in general."

"I just thought nobody cared," said Jinx.

"Oh, heavens, no. Her home used to be wall-to-wall people when she and Rut were younger. They were the most popular couple in all of New York City."

"But what happened?"

"She got old, Jinx. She got tired. She just wasn't up to receiving guests anymore. I'm sure she got weary of my popping in, but she tolerated me. I've loved her all of my life. And she loved me. She wouldn't deny me my visits."

"Pandora, I read her obituary. She was really smart, wasn't she?"

"Oh, my, the smartest. And she stayed sharp and informed right up to the last minute. She was a voracious reader and kept herself abreast of world politics her whole life."

"Her education was very impressive. Why didn't she do anything with her degrees? Why did she take a back seat to her husband, even giving up her name?"

"Oh, Jinx, she did lots with her degrees. She was her husband's greatest advisor, on every subject. He adored her and called her his brilliant partner. He said she was the brains of the operation and that he was simply the PR guy. They were a great team, a perfect match. And, as for the name, I guess that was just a sign of the times. She didn't feel that she was taking a back seat by taking Rut's name. She was very proud to be his partner."

"One more thing, you say she got tired of people visiting her. But she called me. She asked me to her home. Why?"

"Because I asked her to."

"But why, Pandora?"

"I wanted you to see true friendship, Jinx. I understand that it's hard for you to trust again after what you've been through. But I wanted you to see that there are honest, sincere friends out there— people who want nothing from you but the joy of knowing you. I couldn't think of a better way of showing you how wonderful friendship can be than with Anna Kate."

"Anna Kate?"

"Yes. That's what her friends called her. I was lucky to call myself her friend."

Jinx shook her head in disbelief and said, "Did you know that Mrs. Rogers gave me a thousand dollars for ordering towels for her?"

Pandora chuckled and said, "No, but I'm not at all surprised. She sent the kid who delivered her Chinese food to med school."

Pandora reached for Jinx's hand and said, "She was a kind, generous soul. You needed to know her."

Jinx said, "Thanks, Panny," just as the Archbishop stepped to the pulpit and, smiling, said, "We have come here today to celebrate the extraordinarily selfless life of our dear friend, Anna Kate Coleridge Rogers."

One by one governors and mayors and senators stepped into the pulpit and told what Mrs. Rogers had meant to all of them. About a dozen young people came forward to say that without Mrs. Rogers' help they'd have never made it through college. Dr. Chin, the former Chinese food deliverer, was one of them. There were no tears, just laughter, and, in some cases, applause.

After an hour of Mrs. Rogers anecdotes, the final speaker, a slight, bent gray-haired gentleman, rose from the front pew and made his way slowly to the pulpit. When he turned to the congregation, Jinx recognized him as former President Jimmy Carter, the beloved statesman from her home state of Georgia. He spoke eloquently of Ambassador and Mrs. Rogers' service to the United States in that soft, southern drawl that Jinx had missed so much. He also talked of Mrs. Rogers' selfless devotion to her beloved husband and to his career.

President Carter concluded by saying, "Anna Kate was my friend. I knew that she was always there for me. If ever I felt down or despondent, I knew all I need do was give her a call." Smiling his toothsome grin, he continued, punctuating the air with his fist, "She refused to allow me to be down. She would give me a pep talk that would always pick me up. Yes, that is what Anna Kate did for me. She picked me up."

I'll pick you up, you'll pick me up...

Jinx reached into her purse for a tissue to dab her eyes.

Two mayors, an ambassador, the Police Chief of New York City, and two United States Senators stood and lifted the simple cherry casket. As they bore their friend up the aisle of St. Patrick's Cathedral for the last time, a young man stepped forward, one of the young men Mrs. Rogers had sent to college, and began singing *Softly and Tenderly Jesus is Calling*. The song brought a lump to Jinx's throat. She had first heard it at Mt. Moriah Church, back when she was young and in love with Charlie, surrounded by her lifelong friends.

Pandora reached for Jinx's hand and gave it a good squeeze.

Thirty-two

"All right, my friend, first order of business: you're going to have a party—a blow-out, no-holds-barred soiree."

"Wait just a minute," Jinx said, holding up her hands in defense. "I said I'd give it a try, but from recluse to no-holds-barred soiree in one fell swoop?"

"That's right. You, with my help, of course, are going to have a party for Liz."

"And why are we having a party for Liz?"

"Well, as you know, since I introduced her to my friends, her work has been on display in the Airmont Gallery. Nice place, but it doesn't set the world on fire. A little bit of foot traffic. Some fellow artists who want to barter. It's just time for Liz to move on. And up."

"So…"

"So she has just gotten an invitation to show at the Gillespie."

"The Gillespie? Isn't that…?"

"Yes, where all the best start."

"Oh, my gosh, Pandora, that's fantastic."

"Now, don't tell her I told you. I'm sure she'll want to break the news to you herself."

"Not a word," Jinx said, pretending to lock her lips.

"So, the party… The Gillespie always draws a huge crowd, but we want to make sure that everyone knows about Liz's opening and that the crowd is spilling out into the street and around the block. So the week before Liz's grand showing, we'll open your home to all the art lovers of New York. We'll eat—Polly Ann's scrumptious food, of course—and socialize at your place, and, with Knox and Tony's permission, we'll conclude the festivities at their apartment, where the guests will see, first hand, Liz's art on display. When those people get an up-close-and-personal look at her work, they'll be lining up at the Gillespie before her exhibit opens."

"Sounds great. I'd love hosting a party for Liz."

"And for you, Jinx."

"What?"

"It'll be your coming out. We'll show New York that you're ready to be its friend."

"Try to be its friend."

"It's a start. And I'll be right here, Jinxie."

Once again the tears filled Jinx's eyes. Though she had never let anyone but Charlie call her Jinxie, somehow it just sounded right when Pandora said it.

"Thanks, my dear friend," Jinx said and hugged Pandora tightly.

Now that she had Jinx on board, Pandora untangled herself and reached into her huge multi-colored canvas satchel for a pad and pen.

"So let's say we have a guest list of about two hundred."

"How many?"

"About two hundred."

"I thought that's what you said, but Pandora, we'll never get two hundred people in this place."

"Oh, not to worry, Jinx. First of all, you know as well as I do that not everyone who is invited is going to show up. Some will be sick, some will be out of town, and, sadly, some will just choose not to come. Their loss," Pandora sniffed with a toss of her unruly, red mane. "But we'll still draw a sizeable crowd. You have lots of room here, and, of course, everyone will want to see your place. And who wouldn't? It's gorgeous. I guarantee you'll get some design jobs from this party. But back to the issue at hand. They'll wander from room to room, so there won't be congestion in any one space. We can also set up the bar in the hall, between your place and Knox and Tony's. We'll leave both front doors open, and the guests can wander as they please. Food in your place, art in the guys', and drinks in the middle. Perfect set-up."

Jinx just shook her head and said, "Pandora, you're a genius. Nobody can throw a party like Panny."

"You got that right. Now let's get together with Polly Ann and start getting all the details worked out."

"Now that you've had a chance to look over the guest list, what do you think?"

"Well, Pandora, I don't know ninety percent of the people, never heard of them."

"That's the whole point, Jinx. They are all art lovers—and potential friends. There's not a mean-spirited, judgmental one in the bunch."

Jinx just smiled at Pandora's devotion to bringing her out of her shell, to making her trust again. But was she ready? Was she prepared to start afresh? Did she need to put herself through this, just to have friends she wasn't sure she wanted?

"I can see the wheels turning, Jinx. I know this is overwhelming. But, I promise, you're not going to do this alone. And if, after the dust settles, you decide you're not ready for this, then you can go right back to your reclusive, friendless life."

Jinx laughed out loud at Pandora's honesty. "Well, how can I say no to such a proposal?"

"You can't," Pandora said with a self-satisfied smile.

"I noticed that Sam Bradley is on the list," Jinx said through pursed lips. "I had no idea he was such an art lover."

"Oh, of course," Pandora said, averting Jinx's gaze.

"Did Sam put you up to this?" she asked.

"Now, Jinx, you know very well that nobody puts me up to anything."

Jinx had to admit that Pandora was no pushover, and no one could convince her to do anything that she didn't want to do.

"Okay, everybody, find your places," Pandora yelled, clapping her hands and waving her flowing, flowery sleeves back and forth, as if directing the New York Philharmonic. And floating from room to room she called out, "Food looks scrumptious, Polly Ann. You've outdone yourself. Delores, plump your pillows over there. We want them standing out. You're going to get lots of business today." Scurrying across the hall, she cried, "Oh, Abby, Izzy, you girls look beautiful. So glad you could join us for the party." The little girls giggled and ran to their beloved Pan Pan and gave her a big hug around her waist. Reaching down to kiss the girls on the top of their heads, Pandora called out, "Knox, check that piece of art over there, the one right in the middle, it needs straightening. Right. Got it."

Liz appeared somewhat nervous, rubbing her hands together and smiling self-consciously. Robert took her hand, leaned in, and kissed her sweetly on her cheek. His touch, his love calmed her.

"Ready for this?" Pandora asked.

"I think so, Pandora," Liz said. "You know, I'll never be able to thank you enough. Without you I'd still be sitting on a lawn chair on the sidewalk in front of the museum."

Squeezing Liz's hands, Pandora said, "It was only a matter of time. You really didn't need me. You're brilliant, so talented. You deserve all this. Now enjoy the attention." And patting Liz's cheek, Pandora was off to coordinate something—she wasn't sure what, but she was certain something needed her attention.

No one was sick, no one was out of town, and very few guests just chose not to show up. They were elbow to elbow, spilling out onto the sidewalk in front of the brownstone. Folks were perched on Jinx's bed, as well as the desk in her office, drinking and chatting. They surrounded Polly Ann in her kitchen as she made her way between them with platters of hors d'oeuvres. They crowded around the bar in the hall until it ran dry, at which time Knox emptied his and his mother's private wine stash to serve to their guests. They wedged their way into Knox and Tony's home, vying for a spot in front of Liz's wall of art, gasping with excitement when they finally got a glimpse of it for the first time.

"The party is wonderful, Pandora," Jinx whispered when she could finally make her way through the crowd to her friend.

"Yes, it is. Everyone loves Liz's art, Polly's food, Delores's needlework. And, Jinx, they love you. You're the consummate hostess. And, by the way, I've never seen you look more stunning." Smiling and patting Jinx, Pandora sailed off to greet and charm.

Jinx did look stunning. She wore a turquoise sheath that played off the blues in her décor and made her ice-blue eyes sparkle. She had spent the morning in Jesus's salon, having him work his magic on her beautiful, auburn hair. She shook her head with confidence and let her hair slither back into place.

"Great party."

She turned to face Sam Bradley.

"Glad you could come. Pandora says you're quite the art lover," Jinx said, trying to keep a straight face.

"Oh, yes, I love art, any kind of art. Modern, Old Masters, Abstract. You name it, I just love it all."

Jinx knew BS when she heard it.

"Well, the art, the stuff you love so much, is across the hall," she said with a grin.

"Oh, I love interior design, too. I was just admiring your place. You've done a great job. Perhaps you could help me with my place."

"Does your place need redecorating?" Jinx asked.

"Um, well, no," he answered, and they both laughed.

"Sam Bradley, you are absolutely shameless."

"Yes, I am, Miss Jinx," he said, as he turned and headed across the hall to look at Liz's art. Before he was out of ear shot, he called over his shoulder, "But I'm not giving up. Ever."

Jinx blushed, tried to shake it off, and returned to her guests. She discovered that they were all warm and inviting, and she found herself relaxing in their friendship. She realized, too, how grateful she was that Pandora had insisted on this coming-out party.

And she was relieved to discover that there was not a Blue or a Tweezle in the bunch.

There was, indeed, a crowd spilling out of the Gillespie and snaking around the corner. Liz was there to greet them all, looking stunning in a chic, sheer black halter dress, her shimmery blonde hair hanging loose beyond her shoulders, sparkling in the overhead lights. Everyone crowded around her, all of them eager to establish a relationship with the artist so that they could say, "Well, I knew Liz Houston when…" Jinx was so happy for her and watched with the eye of a proud parent as Liz laughed and accepted the accolades she so deserved.

Jinx extricated herself from the throng of Liz's adoring fans to stroll the museum and check out the show. She stopped in front of a piece that she had never seen, one that simply took her breath away. It was an abstract entitled New York Street, a study in blue—every blue in the spectrum. She loved Liz's work, but this piece was like no other she had ever seen. She knew she must own it. It would be the perfect anchor for her lovely blue living room. It would hang above the fireplace, a perfect complement to her design.

She was already hanging it in her home when a voice behind her said, "Sorry, that one's taken."

Crestfallen, she turned to find Sam Bradley.

"Beautiful, isn't it? I loved it the moment I saw it. I knew that I just had to have it."

"Because you are such a lover of art."

"Exactly," he said, "because I am a lover of art."

The following day, around mid-morning, Jinx was padding around in her slippers and housecoat, still exhausted from the gallery extravaganza, when she heard the buzzer at the front door of the building. Engaging her intercom, she called, "Who is it?"

"Delivery for Ms. Jinx Collier."

A delivery? Jinx wasn't expecting a delivery. She'd received all of her samples, and her client orders had already arrived.

"Can you tell me who sent the delivery?" she asked.

"Yes, ma'am. It came from the Gillespie Gallery."

The Gillespie? Jinx hadn't ordered anything from the Gillespie. Gathering her robe around her, she stepped into the foyer, where she saw the deliveryman holding a large package in front of the glass door.

When she opened the door, the man wrestled the package inside and said, "Sign here, please," handing her his clipboard and pen.

Once Jinx had signed, he was on his way, leaving her alone with her large mystery package. She dragged it inside her apartment and placed it on the living room floor, where she proceeded to tear away the wrapping. There she found Liz's piece, New York Street, the work that Sam Bradley had said he couldn't live without.

She reached for her phone.

"Sam, I just can't accept this."

"But you wanted it, didn't you?"

"Yes, but I can't take such an extravagant gift from you."

"Why not, Jinx? I haven't given you a housewarming gift yet. So we'll just call it your housewarming gift."

"You don't owe me a housewarming gift, Sam."

"Nobody owes anyone a housewarming gift. People give housewarming gifts because they want to, not because they have to. I want to, Jinx."

"But, Sam, it's just that…"

"Don't you like it?"

"Of course I like it. I love it."

"Then it should be yours, Jinx."

"Sam, I just don't know what to say."

"Ummm, how about thank you."

Jinx felt herself smile. Yes, the gift was extravagant, but it was a lovely, thoughtful gesture—a gesture from a man who just refused to give up.

Taking a deep breath, Jinx said, "Thank you, Sam."

Thirty-three

"Who was that?"

"Liz."

"What's up?"

"I don't know. She just says she's coming over. Needs to talk."

"Sounds mysterious. Wonder what it's all about?"

"I have no idea, but we'll know soon. She's over at Robert's. She should be here in a few minutes," Tony said, settling back on the sofa to finish their bedtime story with the girls.

"Right here, Pop Pop," Abby said, her tiny finger marking the spot where they'd stopped reading when the phone rang.

"And Little Ghost said, 'But I didn't come to scare you, Tillie. I just came to ask you to be my friend and to invite you to the park to play.' So the two new friends joined hands and headed for the park. The end."

"Oh, I love Little Ghost, don't you, Abby?"

"Yes, Izzy, I want Little Ghost to go the park with us. We'd just play and play, and we wouldn't be scared at all."

"Okay, girlies," Tony said, as he stood and swooped the twins into his arms, "time to hit the old sack."

"Hey, everybody," Liz said, ringing the bell but letting herself in before the guys could answer.

"Mama, Mama, Mama," the girls squealed and wiggled from Tony's arms. "We want Mama to take us to bed." And they ran to their mother, each grabbing a hand as she leaned to kiss them both.

"Hi, my preciouses," Liz said with her sweeter-than-honey voice. "Looks like Daddy and Pop Pop have let you stay up past your bedtime. Let's run say your prayers and get you tucked in."

Tony and Knox watched as their beautiful friend skipped down the hall holding hands with their little girls.

"How did we get so lucky, Tony?"

Smiling and wrapping Knox in a hug, he said, "I don't know, but I am so grateful. We have been so blessed."

"Okay, they're settled," Liz said when she returned from bedtime duty and eased herself into a chair.

"What's up?" Knox asked. "Tony said you needed to talk. Is something wrong with you and Robert?"

"Oh, heavens no," she said with a wave of her hand. "We're fine. Perfect, in fact."

"Then what?"

"Sit and I'll tell you."

Eyeing Liz suspiciously, Tony and Knox eased themselves down to the sofa.

"You. You guys are what's wrong."

"What did we do?"

"It's not what you did. It's what you won't do."

"And what is it we won't do?"

"Get married. You guys won't get married."

"So?"

"You have to get married."

"But…"

"Nope. You don't get to talk. I'm going to do the talking tonight."

So Knox and Tony looked wide-eyed at each other and settled back to hear what Liz had come to say.

"I know you consider your relationship private, and you don't want to make a statement or be held up as some sort of example. Why, I can't imagine, but that's your call. I also know you don't want the girls exploited and that you feel you can avoid that by keeping a low profile. But Knox, Tony, you need to get married for Izzy and Abby. Our children deserve to have parents who are married, not just going through the motions of being a family."

"Now, wait a minute, Liz. Tony and I are doing no such thing. We are not just going through the motions. We are just as committed as any couple, just as committed as you and Robert. We just don't feel we need a piece of paper to prove it."

"Oh, blah, blah, I've heard all that," Liz said. "That's old. And, yes, you do need that piece of paper. For Izzy. For Abby. If it weren't for them, I'd say, 'Do whatever you want.' But it's not just the two of you anymore. You have to consider our children. No one is asking you two to ride on a parade float or picket the Legislature. You won't even be expected to canvass for signatures on a petition. You just need, no, must make your union legal, for our girls. Now, I'm doing my part. I expect you to do yours."

"Well…," Tony began.

"Nope, there's no well, no but. This is non-negotiable. I haven't asked for much from you guys. I have never even played the but-I-carried-those-babies-for-you card, and you know I could. It's just simple, you must become a real family for our children."

"Don't say we're not a real family," Tony said, his eyes narrowing, his cheeks flaming.

Liz had a ready answer. "The girls think of you as a family now. But there'll come a time, a time when they go to school, a time when they are with other children, children whose parents are married. Don't you think they'll understand? Don't you think they deserve to feel like those other children, with parents who are married? Also, think of the legal ramifications. You owe the girls the security of a legal marriage."

Knox looked at Tony and back to Liz.

"Can we think about it? Talk about it?"

"Nope. There's nothing to talk about. Get married. Simple as that."

And, without another word, Liz got up, hugged both Tony and Knox, and walked out the door.

Thirty-four

"No, Mama, tutus!"

The crowd—fifteen total—would gather at Knox and Tony's apartment. From there they would proceed, en masse, the two blocks to Central Park. Once there, they would find a quiet, unoccupied spot—a perfect place for a wedding.

Father Patrick had arrived. He rocked back and forth from the balls of his feet to his heels, impatiently waiting for the crowd to gather. Why couldn't people be ready when they said they would be?

Polly Ann and Delores bustled around the apartment, plumping pillows and arranging hors d'oeuvres for the small reception that would follow the ceremony. The men—Robert, Rob, Knox, and Tony—looked like spit-shined school boys on their way to Sunday school. Missing were Trilby, Delta, and Pandora, but they would burst in at the last moment, as they always did, making excuses for their tardiness and pointing fingers at one other.

Liz, Jinx, Izzy, and Abby were in the girls' bedroom, along with Robert's mother and sister, Jocelyn and Moira. Liz and her friends had just met Moira, but they were already taken with her. Slight as her mother, she looked so much like her twin brother, Robert, with dark hair and large chocolate brown eyes. Abby and Izzy took to her immediately and were already calling her Aunt Moira. They begged her to help them get dressed for the party, which is what they were calling the wedding.

Liz was wearing the dainty white cotton sundress with yellow-ribbon trim that Jinx had made for her, and she had woven yellow and white wild flowers throughout her flaxen hair. She had done the same for Izzy and Abby's hair, and the three of them looked like lovely woodland fairies.

All was going as planned until the little girls began whining, "Peeze, peeze, we want to wear our tutus!"

Jinx had made dresses for the girls identical to their mama's simple wedding dress. They were to be flower girls. But they didn't want to wear their new white sundresses; they wanted to wear their tutus, tutus that Liz had given them for their birthday, because mamas know that their little girls love nothing more than twirling in tutus.

They stood on their tiptoes with arms over their heads, twirling in their white eyelet panties and ballet slippers, chanting, "Tutus, tutus!"

"Let them wear their tutus, Mom. What does it matter?"

"It matters a lot, Liz. It's a wedding, not a free-for-all."

"But it's their wedding, too. Their dresses are darling, but they'll be able to wear them to Sunday school and tea parties."

Jinx shook her head in resignation, shrugged, and said, "Okay, girls, Mama says tutus, so tutus it is."

With that, Izzy and Abby flew around their room, squealing with delight. They pulled on white tee shirts and squirmed into their pink tulle tutus. And, of course, they began twirling because that's what tutus are for.

At least they had sweet ballet slippers and flower-bedecked hair. They also had small white baskets filled with sunflower petals to fulfill their duty as flower girls. Jinx would just have to be satisfied with that. As much as she wanted to coordinate the whole affair, she had to remind herself that this wasn't her wedding.

And while the girls were twirling, entertaining their guests with their antics, Liz whispered, "Jinx, may I speak with you alone for a minute?"

Jinx knew that it was serious. Liz usually called her Mom, not Jinx.

"Sure, Honey, let's go into Knox and Tony's room where we can have a little privacy."

Leaving the girls twirling and giggling, Jinx and Liz went into the guys' bedroom, closed the door, and sat on the edge of the bed.

"What is it, Darlin'?" Jinx said, when she noticed the tears in Liz's eyes.

"I wrote my parents. I told them everything. Everything. About

Knox and Tony. About Abby and Izzy. About my art. And I told them about Robert. I told them we were getting married today." And putting her face in her hands and weeping, she said, "I asked them to come. I so hoped they'd show up."

Jinx reached for Liz and wrapped her arms around her, drawing her close. And instead of telling Liz that everything would be all right—because everything would not be all right as long as her parents refused to see her—Jinx said, "Oh, Liz, we all love you so much, but I know we're not your parents. And I know you need your parents. I'm so, so sorry."

And Jinx just let Liz weep.

"Thanks, Mom. I needed that," Liz said, wiping her eyes with the back of her hand. "I just needed for you to know that I'd gotten in touch with them. But now I need to get myself together. I'm going to splash some cold water in my face. Thanks, again," Liz said, giving Jinx a quick hug before disappearing into the bathroom.

Jinx waited for Liz to return and said, "You ready?"

"Yep, all ready. I'm getting married today," she said, the smile back on her face, if not in her eyes.

When Jinx, Liz, Jocelyn, Moira, and the girls appeared in the living room, everyone stared quizzically at Abby and Izzy's attire. Just as Liz began explaining the tutus, Pandora, Delta, and Trilby burst through the door, apologizing for their tardiness.

"Well, if Trilby hadn't had to change her shoes a dozen times."

"Pandora, you know how I hate shoes. But I couldn't very well go barefoot to a wedding. I had to find something that didn't kill my feet. And I didn't change them a dozen times."

"And, Pandora, if you hadn't had to stop for those special petit fours…"

"Trilby, you know a wedding reception isn't complete without Hugo's petit fours."

"Now, calm down, girls," drawled Delta, the others' mediator, "we're all here now, and we're goin' to a weddin'."

Father Patrick tapped his watch. He had promised his mother Chinese take-out for lunch, and the Bennetts were bringing their baby by for his christening at two.

"Well, now that we're all here," he said, "let's go to the park and find us a chapel."

Then there came a tap on the door.

269

"Who's missing?" they all asked, taking a head count.

And Father Patrick, once again, looked impatiently at his watch.

"Oh, excuse me, we must have the wrong apartment," said the elegant-looking couple, when Knox answered the door.

"Well, that's okay," laughed Knox. "The more the merrier. Would you care to join us? We're having a wedding."

"Mommy? Daddy?" cried Liz.

Why had they come? And why hadn't they let her know they were coming? Did they just decide at the last minute? Had they forgiven her? Did they accept that their daughter was an artist and not a financier? But it really didn't matter why Liz's parents had shown up for her wedding. All that mattered was that they were there.

Liz ran to them, and mother and daughter sobbed as Liz's father wrapped the two in his arms and joined in their crying.

"Everybody?" Liz cried, turning from her parents to the crowded room.

Everyone rushed the couple before Liz could introduce them, pumping their hands, patting their backs, letting them know that this is where they belonged on the day that their only daughter was to marry the love of her life.

Out on the street they paraded the two blocks to Central Park, Father Patrick leading what looked like a circus troupe. Abby and Izzy continued to twirl, while Liz skipped behind, holding her parents' hands. Polly Ann and Delores marched proudly in their Sunday hats; Delores wore her yellow pillbox with netting while Polly Ann had chosen a large, natural straw hat with spring flowers marching around the broad brim. The others followed behind while Pandora brought up the rear in one of her many flowing, flowered caftans. New Yorkers have seen it all and rarely noticed or reacted to passersby. Father Patrick's troupe, however, attracted attention. Folks stopped and stared, smiling as if they were watching a parade march by.

Just as the group entered Central Park, Izzy and Abby spotted a large white furry dog relaxing on a blanket while its owners shared a picnic. They screamed with delight and ran toward the dog. The girls loved puppies and had cried and pled for one of their own. Knox and Tony had told them that an apartment was no place for a puppy, but, still, the girls adored dogs and wanted to pet every one they saw. As they raced toward the huge dog, all the adults in their party screamed for them to stop. The girls ignored the demands and continued to run, their parents chasing after them.

The dog's owners called out to the group, "She won't hurt them. She adores little girls. Not so much little boys, but she just loves girls. We think it's because they're pink and smell sweet. Actually, she thinks she's a little girl. And please don't tell her she's not because it would hurt her feelings."

By the time Knox and Tony reached the twins, they were climbing on the big dog, hugging its neck. The dog reacted by smiling a great big doggie smile, flapping its tail, and nuzzling Izzy and Abby.

"Her name? What her name?" commanded Abby.

A little less demanding, Izzy said, "Say her name, peeze."

"Miss Kitty," said the young woman. "Her name is Miss Kitty."

"Oh, Miss Kitty," crooned Abby. "I love Miss Kitty." And she planted a kiss between the gentle, smiling dog's ears.

"Come on, girls," said Knox, "we have to go. Say goodbye to Miss Kitty."

Abby said, "Bye, Miss Kitty," and upended her flower-girl basket, showering the big white dog with yellow sunflower petals. Izzy chose to do the same. Then both girls made hats out of their baskets, the handles serving as chin straps. Modeling their new headgear, they took their daddies' hands and sashayed off to find a wedding chapel.

They discovered a secluded little spot with an arbor of flowers, the perfect spot for a wedding. Liz and Robert, along with best friends Tony and Knox, took their places in front of Father Patrick, while Abby and Izzy stood between their parents, twirling in their tutus, sporting their new basket hats. The wedding guests formed a semi-circle in front of the wedding party. As Father Patrick began to speak, Miss Kitty trotted in front of the guests, sat on the grass, and watched the wedding quietly, yellow sunflower petals still adorning her fluffy, white coat.

As Father Patrick began to speak, curious onlookers inched forward. First standing at a distance, they came closer and joined the invited guests as the smiling priest spread his arms wide and said, "Friends, loved ones, and all of you who have come to witness this blessed event, yes, yes, all of you, please join us, won't you?"

And the crowd grew: bikers, skaters, mothers with strollers, joggers, passers-by, nannies with toddlers, street performers, businessmen breaking for lunch.

Father Patrick forgot the time, knowing his mother would forgive his tardiness, because this occasion was so very special, it could not be rushed.

"We are all gathered here today to witness the bond of love as we join in marriage Liz and Robert and Tony and Knox. And I won't even ask if anyone objects, because how could anyone object to these joyful unions?" Father Patrick beamed as his voice boomed out over the park.

Jinx pulled a tissue from her pocket and dabbed at her eyes. She so wished that Charlie were with her to celebrate their child's love, to know their beautiful granddaughters. She recalled that a very wise woman had once told her that family is not what you're given; family is what you make. Charlie and Knox had been Jinx Collier's family, the only family she'd ever dreamed of having, the only family she had ever wanted. But she had lost her family. When she arrived in New York, she had no one and nothing but a hope of rekindling her relationship with her son.

In the years since Jinx had made New York her home, she had created a family—an unconventional family, but a wonderful, loving family, just the same. And she was certain that each one of them would pick her up. And she would gladly pick up each and every one of them. And she didn't doubt for a minute that they could all go up together.

"Lovely wedding, don't you think?"

Jinx turned to see Sam Bradley standing at her side. She just smiled, no longer surprised at seeing him.

"I think this would be a perfect spot for our wedding."

"Our wedding?" she whisper-gasped.

"Yep, Jinx. Never giving up."

Then Sam Bradley reached for Jinx Collier's hand. And instead of pulling away, Jinx laced her fingers through Sam's, because she was certain he was never giving up.

As Jinx held tight and watched her family and her new friends surrounding Liz and Robert and Knox and Tony fill the air with their laughter and chatter, her eyes, once again, filled with tears. This time, though, she didn't reach for her hanky to dry them but let the joy spill down her cheeks as she thought to herself, *Now, this is family.*

And this is what love sounds like.

ABOUT THE AUTHOR

Padgett Gerler was born on the coast of South Carolina but grew up in the Shenandoah Valley of Virginia. In the 1980's she relocated to Raleigh, North Carolina to attend North Carolina State University. Upon graduating with a BA in accounting, she passed the CPA exam and began her career as a certified public accountant, first in public accounting and then as a CFO in corporate accounting. In 2010 she left accounting to pursue a career in writing. Prior to *What Does Love Sound Like?*, Padgett published her novels, *Getting the Important Things Right*, *Lessons I Learned from Nick Nack*, and *The Gifts of Pelican Isle*. *Lessons I Learned from Nick Nack* was awarded the indieBRAG Medallion, as well as honorable mention in the 2014 Writer's Digest Self-Published Book Awards competition. She also authored the short story "I know This Happened 'Cause Somebody Seen It," which was published in the anthology *Self-Rising Flowers*. She is the first-place recipient of the Southwest Manuscripters Short Story Award for her short story "The Art of Dying." Padgett and her husband, Ed, reside on pastoral and inspirational Winchester Lake in Raleigh, North Carolina.